Blanche Willis Howard

The Open Door

Blanche Willis Howard

The Open Door

ISBN/EAN: 9783743422957

Manufactured in Europe, USA, Canada, Australia, Japa

Cover: Foto ©Andreas Hilbeck / pixelio.de

Manufactured and distributed by brebook publishing software (www.brebook.com)

Blanche Willis Howard

The Open Door

THE OPEN DOOR

BY

BLANCHE WILLIS HOWARD

AUTHOR OF "ONE SUMMER," "GUENN," "ONE YEAR ABROAD," ETC.

BOSTON AND NEW YORK

HOUGHTON, MIFFLIN AND COMPANY

The Riverside Press, Cambridge

1889

The Riverside Press, Cambridge:
Electrotyped and Printed by H. O. Houghton & Co.

" Laissez-moi faire à loisir le tissu ne notre roman, et n'en pressez pas tant la conclusion."

MOLIÈRE.

THE OPEN DOOR.

CHAPTER I.

"WHAT are you going to be when you are a man?" the Countess von Kronfels' guests would ask handsome little Hugo, as he pranced about the cheerful samovar, begging for nine lumps of sugar in his infinitesimally diluted tea.

"King!" the child would reply with superb conviction, straightening his four-year-old back, and regarding them an instant with bold, unconscious eyes, before resuming his quest. Why the ladies always made this inquiry, and why they always laughed at his reply, he did not deign to consider. Indeed, he scarcely noticed them. He was too busy, too serious, too intent upon pleasantly personal matters. Sweets for the moment, royalty later; such was his clearly defined sketch of existence. But Fate drew other lines.

More than a score of swift years passed. The child became a man. His throne was an invalid's chair; his sceptre, a crutch; his crown, pain.

He had had, indeed, his bright, brief reign, his goodly share of the purple state which by the grace of this obsequious world encompasses the heir to an old name and large wealth; and he had revelled in that more glorious sovereignty which nature may deny a prince and lovingly bestow upon a vagabond, — the absolute monarchy of youth, beauty, and strength, the kingship of a fearless spirit.

His golden days were dead and gone. One September evening four men, with blanched faces and slow and heavy tread, bore his unconscious body through the long hall, past a group of frightened servants, to his own rooms. His young strength fought hard for life. His soul balanced many weeks between this world and the next. At length the suave doctors pronounced him "saved," which meant, being interpreted, that his broken machinery had been cleverly repaired, that the ugly wound on his head was healing, and that everything, indeed, was highly gratifying, except the recalcitrant spine, which, refusing to respond to the skill of world-renowned specialists, threatened to make him a cripple for life.

After six months' seclusion, the invalid felt a strong and sudden longing for the coming spring, and expressed a wish to be taken out into the garden. "Put me out there, anywhere," he said in the scornful tone with which he always now alluded to himself, and the servants carried him with clumsy kindness across the threshold. Although nearly as helpless as the dull dead weight brought in a half-year before, he was now painfully sentient and tortured by a hot and rebellious soul.

Wrapped in furs, pale, motionless, his eyes closed, he lay back in his wheel chair, where the noon sunshine fell warmest on the lawn, and no straight-legged peasant-boy, tramping by lustily to Leslach, but was more "king" than Count Hugo.

"You can go, Lipps," he said to his servant.

Lipps adjusted a rug, moved the chair a half-inch to the right and waited, his eyes fixed like a dog's upon his master's face.

"You can go, I say," repeated the invalid wearily.

Lipps readjusted the rug, and moved the chair a half-inch to the left.

"Good heavens, man," began the count vehemently, his dark eyes looking unnaturally large and brilliant in the pale, thin face, "can't you leave me alone? Have n't I had you pottering about all winter? Can't you obey orders? Can't you let me" — he hesitated, then added bitterly — "enjoy myself?"

Lipps's stolid face brightened at the familiar outbreak.

"The count was so pale and his eyes were shut," he explained apologetically.

"You thought I was going to shrivel up like one of those frost-bitten snow-drops?"

Lipps grinned.

"You — donkey!" remarked the count, in a low, pleasant voice, and with a kindly glance at the man.

"Yes, sir," returned Lipps cheerfully.

"No such luck for me," muttered the count. "There, there, don't stand and stare like a Chinese idol! Go off, now. You will find my sacred person all here an hour later, — every fragment of it. Nobody wants to steal me. Lipps, if you don't want me to swear, take your stupid eyes off me! Oh, I know very well what is the matter with you."

Lipps looked abjectly conscious of guilt.

"Come, come, Lipps, out with it. Speak up like a man, and confess that you suspect me of having arsenic or a dagger concealed in the tragic folds of my dressing-gown. Or, perhaps, I'm going to swallow my crutch?" the count went on languidly. "Lipps, there are things one does n't talk about, you know, but really you weary me with your anxious watchdog ways. You are uneasy. What is more, you have removed my pistols from their old place on my wall."

"I only thought that the count would n't be likely to be wanting them for anything just now," stammered the man, shamefaced and conscience-stricken; "that is, not till he 's well and strong again."

"Precisely. And the pistols took up room on the wall where you wanted to hang medicine-bottles, or bandages, or books, or something. All very reasonable. That mask of hopeless idiocy does not help you, my poor fellow. And I have to speak at last, because you bore me unmercifully, you make me nervous, Lipps. If you don't treat me better, the doctor will send you about your business."

Lipps grinned with delight at this pleasantry. He knew that no mortal power could send him away from Count Hugo.

"But seriously, Lipps, the next time you see me examining any object, don't feel called upon to secrete it, the moment you think I am asleep," the count resumed with great sweetness of manner, "and you go into the house now and put those pistols where they belong. And be perfectly easy in your mind about me."

"The count is getting well as fast as ever he can," Lipps declared stoutly.

"Undoubtedly," Count Hugo returned with a curious smile. "But you see, Lipps, if you are fool enough to be attached to a man who abuses you systematically, and swears at you when his pain is bad, and has even been known to fling his crutch after you; if you tend him like a baby, and sit up nights with him, and refuse your legitimate Sunday out, and forget your beer, — some fine day you will find yourself in a retreat for aged imbeciles."

" The count never swears at me except when I deserve it," Lipps protested.

" There, go in peace, you great soft-hearted phenomenon, and no more nonsense, you understand, — no more foolish fancies. Go now. You tire me. You make me talk. The noises out here are too much for me. I never knew the world was so loud. I must be born again; yes, here is the whistle. If I have the ghost of a wish I will summon you."

He closed his eyes. Lipps, having basked again in the invalid's affectionate smile, and reassured by his bantering tone, withdrew reluctantly, looking back over his shoulder at the outstretched, motionless figure, and walking cautiously, on tiptoe, across the turf.

It was a mild day toward the last of February. The chill of winter lingered in the shade, and the west wind, sweeping up at intervals from the Cold Valley, sent an occasional sharp gust across the invalid's face. But the sunshine was strong and full of promise, the stir and thrill of spring were in the air, in every swelling bud in the villa-garden, in every slender, yearning twig of the bare shrubbery near him. Men were working in the vineyards on the broad hill behind the house, and in the market-gardens skirting the slope below it. Hungry crows were cawing and circling heavily over freshly up-turned fields. It was a land of hills. Irregular lines of them intersected one another abruptly, never rising to the sublimity of mountains, yet presenting an ever-varying landscape of plain, valley, and height; and of long, fair reaches, overhung with fleeting, bluish mists. Down in the valley lay the city with its large vague murmur, and dense smoke columns rising from many factory-chimneys, black and tall in the hazy atmosphere, like huge guardian spirits of toil and traffic watching over their own.

"It is like the ocean — far away — at night," thought Hugo, used to the extreme quiet of his rooms. "It is the distant roar, not of waves, but of life; and I — I am worse than dead."

The ·villa stood on a broad, handsomely curving street at the west end of the city, and in the late count's days seemed fairly out of town in its semi-rural solitude. But the city had stretched grasping arms up to it and beyond, toward the village of Leslach, and with a rapid growth of cottages and stately houses was steadily pushing the country-element farther west. A huge sandstone structure was building directly beyond the villa garden, and the scaffolding of another high house was already up. Hugo heard the incessant click of scores of chisels on blocks of stone, the irregular fall of mallets, the harsh rhythm of saws and planes, the tread of slow hoofs as carts were backed up, the unloading of bricks, the rattle of spades against pebbly earth, and the voices of vigorous, hard-working men; and to all these common sounds he listened as if for the first time, and to his painfully acute senses, each separate tone in this powerful symphony of work taunted him with his helplessness.

"Oh, my lost strength," he sighed, "my good lost strength!"

High on the stone house, an inconsequent oriel-window leaped out to surprise the passer-by, and had the air of being a merry caprice on the part of the architect. Here, under a rude canvas shelter, a young stone-carver was working on the massive head of a broad-eyed deity with ringlets, — a Pomona,

possibly, since a horticultural exhibition of amazing
variety flanked the goddess on either side. Chiselling
his solid fruits, the man on his high perch sang in
a high, fresh tenor, and every one who listened was
glad at heart for the glad song, except Count Hugo.

"It hurts to hear the fellow sing like that," he
groaned.

The clock on St. Mary's church tower struck twelve.
Hugo could see the spire from where he lay. The
factories responded with their long shrieking whistles,
and the bells proclaimed the noon rest. From the
great gymnasium, whose roof was visible from the
villa garden, a thousand schoolboys came tumbling
out, and the hum of their riotous voices, the scuffling
of their turbulent feet on the pavements, the shrill
laughter and shouts of the happy young mob sent up
new and painful waves of sound to the still listener.
The men ceased work, except the carver, who tapped
busily with his mallet and sang on. Some of the masons, with blue blouses and brawny arms, passed by,
singly, and in groups. Wives and sisters and sweethearts brought bread and beer in little baskets. Hugo
could hear the careless laughter following some rough
joke. A squad of infantry marched, singing, down an
adjacent street. He listened to their measured tramp
and the loud swinging folk-song. Some red-capped
schoolboys had climbed the hill, and were making
prodigious leaps, with poles snatched from the building materials.

It seemed to the cripple that the whole wide world
was teeming with movement, color, contrast, and
happy unrest; that out of the silent earth pulsating
life was reaching up about him; that new, mysterious strength stirred in the cool and sunny air that

touched his cheek; that everywhere was force — for all the world, but not for him — force that in cruel irony mocked his weakness.

"If my spirit were but crippled too! If I need not hear or see or feel! If I did not long with every atom of my being for life, — strong, glad life!"

Hoofs came clattering up the street. A young horse plunged by in a clumsy hard gallop, the blue and white and silver of his rider's uniform brilliant in the sunlight.

Hugo shuddered and shrank under his furs, as if he would conceal himself from every eye.

"My God," he groaned, "I was like that! I, even I! And now I am an old man. Old, at twenty-seven. Worse than an old man, for my heart is hot within me. Worse than dead, infinitely worse."

Bitter rebellion shook his soul, fierce protest against the laws that held him in the bondage of joyless life.

"They shot my poor Comet, when they found he was done for. Why were they less merciful to me?"

The noisy, leaping boys had run home. The street was stiller. Some of the workmen were lying outstretched in the sunshine on the sandstone blocks, and some were smoking their pipes against the wall, and ruminating in dull content. A little bare-armed baby, with a red blanket pinned over its head, cooed and crowed in the arms of the singer, who was neglecting his dinner to play with it. The young mother stood awkwardly swinging her empty basket, and smiling on the child.

"Wait till you've got a half dozen of your own, Dietz," called out baby's recumbent papa from his sunny sandstone couch, "and you won't be leaving your grub to fool with devil a one of them."

"Not much," some of the others joined in, with a laugh.

Dietz had slow ways and the baby's hands were clutching his beard, but at length he turned his head toward the men, and, smiling at them an instant before he spoke, "Why not?" he said tranquilly, then resumed his attentions to the little red bundle.

Hugo's face was weary and drawn as if from bodily pain.

"And why should they not laugh?" he asked himself. "I am a weak fool. Have I not exhausted the subject of me and my future? Have I not chosen my course? I am the meanest kind of philosopher. Not one of those old fellows would own me. Patience, Seneca! Give me a little time. Fling an empty-headed dragoon into a ditch, and does he arise a full-fledged Stoic?"

He smiled faintly with satirical recognition of his shortcomings. "It would be easy enough," he reflected. "There are a dozen ways. I have had time to reduce the thing to a science this winter, while poor old Lipps thinks that he has removed the danger with the pistols. A pity he took alarm. Though I think I have pacified him now. Unaccountable, this thing we call affection; the man is dull, yet he read me like an open book. No, no, he must not be made uncomfortable. That is, not beforehand. I must see to that."

"I should never, indeed, choose an explosive exit, when a quiet one was attainable. Now here's the sharp point of a penknife, and there's an artery. Two and two are four — and all is well. My mother would wear Paris mourning, and Lipps for some months would be more stupid than ever. Countess

Mercedes would burn some relics. So would little Laura at the Variétés. Then each would act her part, one in the world, the other on the stage, as before. Not one soul would really mourn, except, perhaps, Lipps. It may be a delusion born of my weak state, but I believe the man loves me better than his pipe, and sometimes, when I meditate crossing the border, the thought of his heavy perplexity and dull regret, should he seek and not find his querulous, exacting master, holds me back like a rough, honest hand.

"And my father ! Why does he restrain me? My father, with his wise, satirical face, and his overweening pride in his good-for-nothing son. Pride ! Well, when a brilliant old bachelor marries at fifty, his only son is necessarily a marvel, and even an old diplomate may have one weakness. It is a sick fancy, easily explained by the hole in my head and the fever, but when I am near — quite near the end of all this weariness, I see him, his positive self, not tragic, no pose, no theatre-ghost — he could not be ill-bred and melodramatic in any phase of being ; but all the same I see him, his quiet, smiling presence, and I hear his mocking yet tender voice, as of old when I flew into a great passion: 'Seize the advantage, Hugo. The mills of the gods grind slowly. All things have their ebb and flow. Seize the advantage, my son.' He would have seized the advantage of his own mistakes, of a friend's treachery, of famine, flood, and pestilence ; no doubt of an injured spine and helplessness. But he was wise, and I am a hot-hearted fool, fighting fate, then passive from sheer weariness, until a trifle, a breath of air, a sweet sound, rouses old longings, and the struggle begins anew.

" Now what if there were an advantage? It would be a vastly clever thing to find it, upon my word ! "

He smiled drearily, and taking a note-book from an inner pocket, began to turn the leaves listlessly.

" Who would ever suspect me of making friends with these worthies? One man in a dungeon occupied himself with a flower, and another with a mouse, and I in mine with my wise father's books.

" Here you are, old Seneca ! Now what have you to say about it?

" ' Do you seek the way to freedom? You may find it in every vein of your body. The eternal law has decreed nothing better than this, that life should have but one entrance and many exits. Why should I endure the agonies of disease when I can emancipate myself from all my torments and shake off every bond? For this reason, and for this alone, life is not an evil; that no one is obliged to live. The lot of man is happy because no one continues wretched but by his fault. If life pleases you, live. If not, you have a right to return whence you came.' "

He shook his head sadly.

" Old Seneca, old Seneca, there are some glowing embers in your ashes. There is a throb of passion somewhere here ! There 's a protest against pain. You plead too much, old Seneca. You had not trampled upon yourself enough when you wrote that, my friend. I, an ex-dragoon, accuse you of feeling. No, no, your sentiments are not lofty enough for me. If I 'm going in for philosophy, I want the unadulterated article."

Again he turned the leaves of the little black book, closely and faintly written in pencil, the companion of many hours of pain and loneliness.

" Something cold and temperate suits me. And there 's one of those estimable old heathen — I forget which — whose talk is as passionless as a peak of the High Engadine. Ah, here he is : —

" ' Above all things remember that the door is open. Be not more timid than boys at play. As they, when they cease to take pleasure in their games, declare that they will no longer play, so do you when all things begin to pall upon you, retire. But if you stay, do not complain.'

" With that, all is said," thought Hugo, re-reading the passage slowly. " Epictetus, you 're my man ! The door is open. If you wish, retire — I like that ' retire,' — if you stay, do not complain. Stay or go, but don't whine. That 's sense. It appeals to me. It is curt and — military."

Horse's hoofs sounded again. The lieutenant of dragoons had mastered his strong and awkward young animal, and was walking him panting down the street, now and then giving him a condescending stroke of approval which told him he was a good fellow to let himself be conquered by the weaker party.

A bugle-call echoed along the opposite hills. A young girl's laugh sounded fresh and free.

Hugo's face set slightly, then relaxed into a derisive smile.

" Oh, rawest recruit among the philosophers ! I must learn to hear hoofs and bugles and woman's laughter unmoved, if I stay ; and I will stay, for a while at least, since, thank God, ' the door is open.' "

The rider was passing the gates.

" Good fellow ! Good Ajax ! " he said to the powerful, panting brute.

" Why, it 's Raven ! " and Hugo instantly blew a

long shrill note on a silver whistle attached to his chair.

The horseman involuntarily halted, and peered with good-humored inquiry into the garden, while Lipps precipitated himself out of a conservatory window and hastened breathless to his idol.

"Open the gates for Lieutenant von Raven, and beg him to come in," said Hugo, surprised at his own animation.

Lipps ran down the drive, swung open the gate, and Lorenz von Raven rode in. Seeing Hugo, he dismounted, but before he spoke to the invalid, he said:

"He's wet, Lipps. Lead him up and down the court-yard, will you?" His attention divided between his retreating horse and Hugo, he advanced with a broad smile on his ruddy face.

"Upon my word! — my dear fellow — really now!" he ejaculated with friendly incoherence, and a queer disjointed manner, laughing a little, aimlessly, stretching and straightening his handsomely booted and spurred cavalry-legs, and switching a sumach bush with his whip.

"How are you, Lorenz?" Hugo began quietly, extending his hand in welcome. "I hope you didn't mind my whistling. It's a novel way to call a comrade. 'Is thy servant a dog?' you might retort, but I'm glad that you don't feel inclined to."

"Oh dear, no! Of course I didn't mind that. I didn't see you at first."

"I suppose not. Lipps seems to have deposited me in a very good place for seeing and not being seen."

"Indeed," muttered Lorenz, absently. The airy preliminaries over, he felt ill at ease before this helpless bundle of furs and rugs, with a white face and extremely big, alert eyes. "It does not seem in the least like Hugo," he decided. "I wonder if I'd better speak of the accident. I wonder what he would like me to talk about."

"How insolently well he looks," thought Hugo. "How strong and straight he stands."

"Ages since I saw you," Lorenz began abruptly. "Landstein ball, was n't it?"

"Now that is deuced awkward," he reflected with growing discomfort. "His dancing days are over."

"No, I have seen no one," Hugo returned, languidly. "I have been in an unbearable humor all winter. Only experienced bear-tamers have dared venture into my den."

"We all came," Lorenz hazarded, hesitatingly, "at first, you know, to inquire. Of course the countess told you."

"Yes, she told me. You were very kind."

Lorenz made a valiant effort to put the heavily dragging conversation into a proper pace.

"You gave my Ajax a look, did n't you?"

"Yes. Good back, I thought, and neat little head."

"He's going to make a racer, you know," Lorenz began, brightening visibly — then stopped with an unintelligible stammer, and stared helplessly down upon his friend's pale face.

"Great powers," he thought, "and there is no more racing for him!"

Hugo stirred uneasily, then broke out with —

"Oh, come now, Raven, don't go on like that. Don't be afraid of me. Don't handle me with gloves. It's no crime, so far as I know, to lose the use of one's legs. You need n't mince matters with me, you know. Speak out, if you like. It makes me savage to be stared at in compassionate silence. As if words could hurt after — this!"

He uttered his impatient appeal with nervous rapidity, and accompanied the final contemptuous word with a sweeping gesture embracing his whole person. His hand, falling back abruptly upon his breast, felt the little black book in the inner pocket.

"Now I'm glad to hear that," returned Lorenz, greatly cheered. "People are different. One can't tell. Had an uncle. Great uncle, you know. Hurt in the same way. Ages ago. Before my time. Awfully mashed, you know. Horse fell on him. Never allowed anybody to mention it. Cripple all his life. Remember we children were deucedly afraid of him. But he lived any amount. Eighty," — he added, nodding convincingly at Hugo. " Eighty-five at least, when he died."

"That is encouraging," Hugo returned dryly.

"Oh, yes. Is n't it?" said Lorenz, exhilarated by his success. "I don't know but that he was eighty-six."

"Come now, Lorenz," Hugo interrupted, "can't you let the old gentleman sleep with his fathers? You 'll trot him up to a hundred if you keep on."

His voice was quiet, but his smile was flashing and queer. Lorenz was not sure that it did not look rather bad-tempered, and hastened to say, —

" Sorry I could not be at the races. Last September, you know. My cousin's wedding. Had to go to Berlin. Three days. Inconvenient season. Famous work you did on Comet," he added, heartily. " Nothing like it, they all said."

"I 've proved that, before gods and men," Hugo rejoined with bitterness.

"Oh, an accident," deprecated Lorenz. "Nobody 's to blame. Devil's own luck. Nothing to do with riding. I say so. Whole Casino says so. Only yesterday von Paalzow said, 'Thinks he can ride, does he? Ought to have seen Kronfels on Comet.' Poor Comet!" he exclaimed, with warmth.

The frown between Hugo's eyes deepened, and after a moment he asked abruptly, —

"What 's the news, Lorenz? Is there no scandal? Has the Wynburg world grown pious since I disappeared from it?"

"No, but they say you have," rejoined the other, laughing.

"I? Who says so?"

"The countess herself."

"She ought to know," Hugo remarked, with a curious intonation.

"She 's glad you are so serious. Says it 's a comfort to her. Proper for you to be religious now. Appropriate." Raven went on. "Says you have a little holy book always with you. Priest and breviary, you know. I did n't know. Thought it might be true."

Hugo's amazement resolved itself into laughter.

"Proper and appropriate," he repeated. "Lorenz, I 'm obliged to you. I have not laughed like this in six months. I did not know that I should ever laugh again. But this would make a corpse laugh."

Lorenz looked at him doubtfully.

"Odd to imagine you goody. Made us fellows smile. But what 's your joke?"

"Why should it be more incumbent upon a crippled

man to be religious than upon a well man?" demanded
Hugo.

"Don't know," replied Lorenz, with candid indifference. "Cripple's got more time," he suggested,
with admirable simplicity.

"Precisely. That's my joke."

"I don't seem to understand it," Lorenz admitted,
good humoredly.

"It might not interest you. It's only a queer association of ideas. There used to be an old woman who
came to us now and then. She was a pauper. At
least she lived in a Home with other old parties. She
wandered in here one day, and as she demanded books
instead of food or money, the servants naturally concluded she was a suspicious character. They were
trying to eject her when I, luckily for her, rode into
the court-yard. I let her tell her tale. She made an
impression upon me at once. She was the only logical woman I ever knew, 'I like to read,' she confided
to me. 'It's the only joy I have left, and I can't get
anything but tracts and pious things. Why don't
they send tracts to rich people, who have pleasures
enough to compensate for dull reading? Isn't it
enough to be poor without also having to read tracts?'
she demanded indignantly. 'I may be a sinner, but
nobody can deny I'm getting a good part of my punishment in this world, and the rich sinners are not,
and it's an impertinence for them to dictate to me
what I shall read.' My mother was horrified, and
said the old woman was impious if not crazy. But I
admired her sense. I gave her on the spot all the
yellow-covered novels I could find, and I subscribed
to a circulating library for her, which kept her supplied with light literature until she died. And this

much I must say for the plucky old soul, — I never heard a complaint from her lips except the protest against tracts. 'Tracts are all very well,' she used to say, 'but it's hatefulness to thrust them at you just because you are unfortunate. There is enough in my life to make me serious. When I read, I want to forget. Let the rich people read the tracts and get ready for heaven. The Bible says they will have a tight squeeze to get in.' Then she would chuckle and smile knowingly at me. She was sure of my sympathy, but neither she nor I suspected that it was a kind of prescience."

Von Raven stared. "Hugo always was odd," he thought.

"Dull story, eh?" said Hugo. "You still don't find my joke? It must be a poor one."

"Don't know much about old women," Lorenz observed with a self-satisfied smile.

"Then tell me something about young women," Hugo returned quickly.

"There's not much new, except Countess Mercedes, you know."

"What about her?" Hugo asked brusquely.

Lorenz eyed him inquisitively and hesitated.

"Had n't you heard? They say it's a sure thing this time. The French Embassador. She's uncertain as the wind. Would n't bet much money on it."

Hugo gave no sign of surprise. "Old Vallion!" he was saying to himself in a whirl of pain, incredulity, and reminiscence, "Old Vallion." He held himself rigid upon his cushions. "Epictetus, you old *poseur*," he thought, "what have you to say to this? Epictetus, you never waltzed with Mercedes!" and his smile grew more mocking and his eyes more bril-

liant, until Lorenz decided it could n't have amounted
to much after all, the affair between Kronfels and the
Countess Mercedes, — but he related to a comrade the
same day, " Hugo does get a look on him, you know !
Why he looks like anything, — you know ! Looks
like the very devil, you know ! "

" The marquis must be sixty-five or so," Hugo said
politely.

Von Raven shrugged his shoulders.

" Oh, well ; what can she do ? She can't marry
a nobody. And she must have money. We lieutenants are mostly too poor for her. She 's getting on
too." Hugo's queer smile continued. Lorenz's single
sentences were like amputated members of his whole
harangue. " Beautiful, but six and twenty. And awfully sharp, you know." The young man's remarks
assumed a faint tinge of reminiscence, if not personal
grievance. " A man does n't enjoy being made uncomfortable. Don't know whether a girl is laughing
at him or not. Feels like a fool. When I conclude
to settle down, shall take a pretty little thing. Not
too much to say for herself, you know ; most of us have
made up our minds to that." It was a long speech for
Lorenz. The cavalry-boots stepped about in a brisk
and convincing manner, and the florid lieutenant
pushed up his stiff cap and wiped his retreating, narrow forehead as if the proclamation of his views had
cost him some effort.

" I never found her sharp," said Hugo quietly.

" Oh, you ! " rejoined Lorenz significantly. " I suppose not. Everybody thought " — he began, but
Hugo's expression was not inviting. " That is," floun-
dered Lorenz, " everybody thinks it 's a good thing."

" Admirable, I should say."

" She wants family and money. Old Vallion has no end of both. Her mother pushes it like mad, you know."

" I can imagine it," said Hugo.

" Then there is Elsa — jolly little thing — kept back in the school-room. Kicking her bars. And Olga, pretty as girls go. No show beside Mercedes. Deuced row all round."

" Of course," was the quiet response.

" Upon my word," and Lorenz gave a loud laugh, " I'm glad I have no sisters. No end of work to establish them. Poor things !"

" Oh, they seem to enjoy the man-hunt," Hugo returned with an ugly sneer. " I notice they don't have to learn much from their mammas. They are armed and equipped from the start, nowadays. Particularly the naive ones. But give me some more delicacies of the season, Lorenz. Mamma has scrupulously refrained from bringing any world noises in to me lately. I understand now. She does not wish to startle my pious ears."

" You have a way of looking precisely like your father, you know. Odd ! Never noticed it before. Reminded me of him a dozen times this morning. If you had glasses and shaggy eyebrows, now ! "

" There would have to be radical changes inside of my cranium, before I could hope to look like him. But go on, Lorenz."

The sunshine fell upon Lorenz's high-colored, good-humored, vapid face. Seated on a garden-bench, one tall boot crossed over the other, he spoke with the drawl affected by his set, and in the dislocated manner peculiar to himself. Without malice, but in the easy slighting tone with which people like to discuss

the absent, breaking out, now and then, into an empty
laugh, he related the good thing Hubert had said to
the pushing Jew banker; the duel they had hushed
up about R.'s pretty wife; how the duchess had deliberately turned her back upon the Baroness Marie,
upon which Count Dings — what could one expect
of a fellow who had bought his title! — had deliberately left her standing in the middle of the hall,
like the cad that he was, — when up rushed that shy
little secretary of the Austrian Legation who never
dares say his soul is his own and offered her his
arm, his face as red as a turkey-cock; how Hans'
black mare was lame and he had bought a full-blood;
how little Laura was making a famous fool of Richard, whose papa had found it out, and was furious when he was n't maudlin; how the court-theatre
was growing worse and worse with ugly soubrettes,
worn-out tenors, and Juliets painfully suggestive of the
allotted threescore years and ten; how Kurt's gambling debts were mountains high, and there was really
no help for him unless he married the little American girl and done with it; her mother was hanging
diamonds on the child, and throwing her at Kurt's
head; the little thing herself was a good little thing,
but it was rather rough on Kurt, since all the world
knew that he was madly in love with his cousin Me-
lanie and she, not a penny to her name, and he only
his pay — and his debts, etc., etc.

So the endless stream ran on.

At first, Hugo listened with a semblance of interest. But the chronicle began to grow remote as a six-
teenth-century tale, and his thoughts wandered.

"Have I not heard it all before? This was my
world," he reflected with dull surprise. "I cared for

it. It seemed to care for me. I was important in it. If the spirit hovers over the scenes it frequented in the body, it must be greatly astonished to discover, in spite of some honest tears, how unimportant it was in the world, and I am experiencing this, while still on earth."

Again he smiled like his father, and Lorenz was encouraged to believe himself entertaining.

"I wonder," thought Hugo, his eyes fixed on Lorenz's complacent face, "what Mercedes thought she loved in me. Except for my powers of locomotion I am the same man. I can't ask her to take a stroll in the garden, but I could have loved her still. What if she had come to me, and knelt down by this chair, and looked at me with her beautiful eyes, and said low, — she can speak low and soft though Lorenz never heard her — suppose she had come and said : Hugo, I love you, more than any other soul on earth — and more, all the more, now that you have this sorrow — and I will come to you and love you and help you bear it. What would I have said ? What would I have done ? God knows ! I might have been a coward and taken her at her word. I might have been a man and sent her away. But to hear such words from such a woman's lips would be so glorious, a man's heart would leap with joy, in spite of his crippled legs. It seems to me I could bear it all and be glad, if Mercedes had come, with pity and faithfulness and love in her eyes. But the woman does not live who is loving enough for that! Yet why I am even now a greater horror than that old *roué*, Vallion, I can't make out. Well I am. I am a horror for all time." He looked intently at Lorenz's muscular well-proportioned form and laughed, to the latter's surprise, as he was not aware that he was saying anything amusing at the moment.

"Ought to be going," he said at length. "Don't whistle. I'll go round and mount. Good by, Hugo."

"Good-by, Lorenz. Thanks for your visit."

They shook hands. Lorenz could think of nothing more to say. He strode off a few steps, turned, hesitated, and came back. He had a vague sense that there was something else incumbent upon him, and he was what is called good-hearted, — for instance, always kind to his dogs.

He looked down once more upon Hugo's pallid face, and the rugs and shawls and furs, and said kindly enough, —

"If I can do anything in the world for you, send for me, will you? And I'll come in now and then, if you like, and cheer you up."

"Thanks," returned Hugo, extending his thin hand. "If you happen to meet Countess Mercedes, give her my congratulations."

"Rather premature," laughed Lorenz, "and you will get her announcement."

"Of course," Hugo assented, "but perhaps you could mention to her sometime that we discussed it, and that I thought well of it. She might be pleased to receive such a message from an old friend, before the formal congratulations begin to pour in. Tell her I said I thought it was an admirable arrangement for all parties. And wish her happiness for me, — much happiness."

"All right. Good-by again, Hugo," and off he went to find Ajax, satisfied that he had remedied his incompleteness. In a few moments he rode down the drive, calling out his cheerful banalities as he passed.

A red-cheeked maid, coming out of the house with a snarling little yellow dog, met the rider face to face, and stopped and stared in open-mouthed admiration. The dog's bell tinkled incessantly, and he snapped at everything and nothing, with a never-dying grudge against all nature.

Lipps was again hovering anxiously near the invalid.

"Take your mummy into the house," said Count Hugo. "Put it on its sofa. I have had enough — gayety, for one day."

CHAPTER II.

ADELHEID, Countess of Kronfels, was in the habit of rising between ten and eleven A. M. This event was accompanied by the vehement pealing of electric bells, and by the breathless hurrying up and down stairs and through long corridors of her own maid, the second maid, the first housemaid, and the corpulent butler. Although from one year's end to another, there was slight variation in the ceremonies of the Countess of Kronfels' morning toilette, although her slaves and vassals had never failed to produce the requisite bath-tubs, the hot and cold water, the toast and tea, the morning post, and to regulate heat and ventilation, and consult thermometers, all in the desired sequence, she invariably presupposed something was about to be wrong in the matutinal rites, and began each day with a jealous suspicion that her fellow-creatures might underrate her importance.

Her methods, however open to criticism, had the advantage of securing praiseworthy speed and punctuality in her service, for none knew when her habitually cold and imperious manner would resolve itself into violence. Until her attendants were aware that she had advanced from her exclusively personal observances to the toilet of her little yellow dog Mousey, their vigilance was unremitting, and they dared breathe freely only when she was enveloped in a voluminous wrapper, surrounded by Mousey's ivory brushes and tortoise-shell combs; Mousey's towels,

embroidered with his own monogram; Mousey's
sponges, flannels, and rugs; Mousey's bath of warm,
scented water, and the object of her adoration snarling on his blanket stretched across her knees.

For if the countess tyrannized over her quaking
household, Mousey enacted the rôle of god of ven-
geance, and for every affront which she offered harmless human beings in her power, the insolent, bad-
tempered little cur exacted retribution. Let philosophers determine the nature of the attachment between
the old lady and her mongrel pet, whose every snap
and snarl were her laws. Indeed a tradition existed
to the effect that the first and only time that the countess attempted to chastise Mousey for some breach of
canine etiquette, he turned fiercely and bit her. Happily his teeth were poor. But the countess grew pale
with fright and remorse, and tearfully entreated the
sulky little brute, who was far too clever not to recognize his crime and was guiltily backing under a
chair, expectant, no doubt, of capital punishment, to
"come to his mamma," which, after a long period of
coaxing, and extravagant endearment, he finally consented to do. The reconciliation was complete, but
who ruled the villa after that was no secret. The
second maid, who ventured to say, "Why, I thought
they always killed 'em when they was nasty enough to
bite their masters," was discharged on the spot for
impertinence.

Mousey was tiny, flaxen-blonde, shaggy and silky,
with the cleverness of a fiend peering out of his
wicked black eyes. He had a pampered body, an
undeniable malformation of the hind legs, and no
tail. He was ugly, vicious, unfaithful, hypocritical,
and of nameless race. Men were apt to raise their

eyebrows with an amused expression, when the countess descanted volubly upon his "points," but if a guest was so reckless as to imply a doubt of Mousey's pedigree, never again did he have the honor of dining at the villa. Better discover a blot on the Kronfels' scutcheon, than on Mousey's. He slept in the countess's bed. He feasted at her table. She did not love animals. To her there was but one dog, and she was his prophet.

The moment of the countess's descent to her son's rooms was nearly as absorbing to her retainers, as were her first bells and commands. Large, corpulent, pale, with cold light eyes, a thin and severe mouth, a small straight nose with flat nostrils, and the conspicuous whiteness which, according to the erudite interpreters of this feature, denotes "cruelty," yet altogether what is called a handsome presence, she came slowly down the marble stairway, panting slightly with a suggestion of asthma, and holding her treasure under her left arm, above which Mousey's sagacious, diabolical eyes gleamed through his silky, overhanging yellow locks. The procession was headed by the portly butler to fling open the doors, while behind the majestic, slowly advancing figure, the countess's own maid followed with a breakfast shawl, and a second maid with Mousey's ball, doll, and white lamb's wool rug brought up the rear.

Such was the train which, heralded by occasional irrelevant yelps, approached the wing occupied by Count Hugo, and happily remote from the countess's precincts. He was lying on his sofa, weary from his unwonted exertion, and wearier from his painful thoughts, which seemed to revolve continually in a fatal circle. The unutterable melancholy of his eyes filled Lipps's heart with discomfort, and the poor fellow whose strength lay not in book-lore, was blindly groping in the recesses of his memory for the name of the volume over which he had seen the count smile some days previous, when the butler's knock announced the approach of the countess and her suite.

Bidding her son good-morning, she extended her large, well-shaped hand, which he mechanically raised to his lips, rejoining : —

"Good-morning, mamma.   How are you to-day?"

The butler and second maid had withdrawn.   The countess's own maid waited, in case Mousey should express a wish.   Lipps, with a non-committal mien, stood with his shortness well drawn up behind his master's sofa, prepared for offensive or defensive possibilities as circumstances should demand.

"Oh, I am sadly fatigued," sighed the countess, "and my neuralgia scarcely allowed me to sleep an hour.   My breathing is troublesome again, too.   Isn't it, Mousey, *mon bijou?*   Come to your own mamma. Did it want to play a little, the dear little sportive lambkin?   Well, it should."   What the sportive lambkin chiefly wanted was to snarl and snort and snap at the head of the white bear skin flung over Hugo's low, broad sofa, and it gave full vent to its inclinations.

"Do you still take a few glasses of curaçoa and some sweet biscuit before going to bed?" the count inquired coolly.

"But I feel so faint, Hugo, I require it."

"It would make the boniest lieutenant begin to get puffy."

"Bony!   Puffy!   What expressions, my son!   You know very well I cannot fast.   I am too sensitive."

"I know simply this: you eat too many sweets and take too little exercise. Any doctor would tell you that. Walk regularly every day and your breathing will be all right."

"Any doctor!" exclaimed the old lady, mounting a hobby. "No doctor here understands my constitution. In fact I never met but one physician who suited me. That dear Pressigny in Paris! What a man! What a manner! What a voice! And what broad shoulders! What insight and intuition! 'My dear, dear madame,' he used to say, 'you, with your sensibilities, can never be treated according to ordinary rules!' Is your doctor capable of that, Hugo?"

"Emphatically not."

"I prefer then to be my own doctor, so far as possible following his footsteps. Poor dear man! So tender, so discriminating! We wept when he died, did we not, Mousey, my angel?"

The angel was up on the window-seat, barking angrily at a dog he perceived at a safe distance. For reasons which did credit to his intelligence if not to his valor, he was never known, unless protected, as in this instance, by the window pane, to insult an animal of his own size, but greatly enjoyed snarling at the heels of some great good-natured mastiff who would regard his petulant ebullitions with dignified surprise.

"Do you feed Mousey with curaçoa and sweet biscuit, too?"

"A wee crumb of biscuit now and then, for he loved it. Did n't you love it, pet?"

"Because he is asthmatic too. Hear how stuffed and strangled his bark sounds."

"Hugo! How cruel you are! Do you want to frighten me?"

"Not in the least. I merely say the dog is over-fed."

"His poor little stomach was rather distended last night. I rubbed it with sweet oil and gave him three globules of nux-vomica. But I know it is not his food. It is a little fever. He is so sensitive. He is going out with his mamma to take a little airing after lunch, and then he will feel better. Won't he? Yes, he will, poor little suffering, sweet thing! Babette," she called, with a sudden change of tone, "when you see that Mousey wishes to play ball, why are you not more attentive? Roll it for him nicely, Babette."

"Give him nothing but water and a bone for two or three days and his sensitiveness will be all right," the count said carelessly.

"Since I find you in this unsympathetic mood, my dear Hugo," she began rapidly in French, "I can of course leave you. I came in with the kindest intentions. For I think it is in every respect proper that a mother should sit a while every day with her invalid son. But of course if you desire, I can go in now to my lonely lunch. Come, Mousey, my comfort, my only friend! Lipps," she said sternly, "when Mousey's ball rolls under the book-case near you, can't you get it for him?"

Lipps stood as if riveted to the floor, his eyes fixed upon his master's face.

Hugo nodded, and the man took a ruler from the writing table and pushed the ball towards Mousey, who received it with engaging growls and gnashings.

"I had no intention of being unsympathetic," Hugo said, without looking at his mother.

"I know — in your state" — she began.

" Kindly leave my state out of the question," he interrupted with a quick flush.

" I know," she persisted, " that one must make allowance for your condition. But Hugo, if you would only cultivate resignation ! "

He closed his eyes and did not reply. Lipps watched him uneasily.

" Because," she continued, always in French, " after all, what God does is well done."

" I presume so," he returned with a sneer.

" Hugo," she began, rising with dignity, " one thing which I will not permit in my presence is irreverence. You know my principles."

" Yes, yes, I think I know them. Suppose we don't discuss them just now. What did you wish to say to me ? And won't you send off your woman, and Mousey ? His bell is rather distracting when one is dead tired. Lipps can go too. I can listen better, and we are a more harmonious family party without so many spectators."

" Of course, if you insist, although it is a mystery to me how you can be so hard hearted to Mousey. He wears his little bell because he was out for a frolic with Röschen, and is going out with his Mumsey directly after lunch. Blessed little sweetheart, come to your Mumsey ! " making a dive after him with some difficulty, as her velvet gown was tight in the waist and sleeves.

The gifted Mousey's human contemporaries unanimously attributed to him comprehension of every word in all languages spoken in his presence, as well as a proficiency in mind-reading which would put most popular psychic experts to shame. With an undeniable snap at the countess's persuasive hand, he dodged it easily, and retreated beneath Hugo's sofa, snarling *sotto voce*, and promenading himself tantalizingly beyond her reach. Kneeling, breathing loud, she coaxed and pleaded in vain.

" Come here, you fiend ! " said Hugo in a low voice.

Mousey with a bound came up over the back of the sofa and stood upon Hugo's breast with a sardonic grin on his countenance and a plain intimation that if he had had a tail he would have wagged it.

" How he jumped ! " exclaimed the countess, panting as she reseated herself ; " and the roguish little love always makes me lift him."

" You demon ! " said Hugo in the same low tone, parting the silky hair falling over the dog's eyes and looking at him attentively.

" Singular, that he lets you touch his head," she said jealously ; " why he scarcely bears my hand on it. But don't call him names. It hurts his feelings. Do you know he would have come when I called him, only he is a little vexed with me, are n't you, sweet pet ? because I would n't give him another lump of sugar ; but it was for your good, you darling dog-gums."

" Here, Lipps, take him out," and Hugo put the shrinking animal into the man's arms.

Again a striking metamorphosis took place in Mousey's eloquent personality. Small as he was, he seemed to diminish bodily and become the most harmless of inanimate flaxen balls as soon as Lipps touched him. His expression was meek if not pious, and he subtly conveyed the impression that he was drooping the tail he had not.

" Be attentive to Mousey, Babette, and entertaining. Ask him if he would like a run in the garden.

Adieu, my precious," throwing kisses to him as Lipps with unwonted rapidity left the room.

" I am convinced that Lipps is a bad man," the countess began when they were alone. " I frequently urged your father to discharge him."

" But my father did n't," observed Hugo dryly.

" No, — your father was peculiar in some things," she said with a sigh. " But I wish you would send the man off. Mousey's behavior is so singular. He positively shrinks before him. And when he hears Lipps's step, he often runs and hides. His more delicate perceptions teach him what is hidden to our duller senses."

Hugo privately suspected that Mousey's delicate perceptions had more than once come in contact with Lipps's indelicate boot. For when the dog's nervous patter and the incessant tinkling of his bell were heard too near the invalid's quarters, Lipps would steal out and after a somewhat excited though hushed colloquy, in which Mousey tenaciously defended his position, certain unequivocal sounds were heard, which resulted in the sudden diminuendo of the tinkling, while Mousey, as fast as his too long legs could carry his too fat body, pattered down the corridor and up the stairway, to the flesh-pots of Egypt which always awaited him in his own apartments. It was under these circumstances that the countess hearing him imperiously demand admittance, was apt to cry in rapture : —

" He wants his own Mumsey, yes he did, the dear faithful heart ! He loved his Mumsey, and his Mumsey loved her Mousey ! Yes, so she did ! " whereupon she would rain showers of kisses upon him, even upon his rather warm nose.

" I think I will keep Lipps for the present," Hugo replied with a slight smile ; " Mousey is welcome to his estimate of the man's character, but you know he happens to be in my personal service, and as Mousey did not engage him, it strikes me that it is little less than a liberty for Mousey to interfere."

" How absurd you are, Hugo ! I do not quite see how you can care to joke so much. One would think you would feel sad and dignified."

He tugged at one of his cushions and finally pushed it violently until it fell.

" I was never good in private theatricals, you remember. I always refused to play the rôle assigned to me. And you see that I am inordinately merry and full of jest."

She sighed. It was hard to reconcile so much levity with a recumbent position.

" If I had found you in a different mood, I should have talked with you about Gabrielle."

" What, again ? " he returned in unfeigned surprise.

" I have been reconsidering " —

" Then I am sorry," he said quickly. " I thought we had settled all that."

" But, Hugo " —

" Mamma," he said, raising himself upon one elbow, and speaking impetuously, " why discuss the matter ? Have we not exhausted every detail ? You know my opinion. I know yours. You shared mine at one time. You decided not to have her come. That you begin again is conclusive evidence that somebody has influenced you. Doubtless, the Frau Major," and he looked at her sharply.

" She was considerate enough to think that a bright,

sunny young girl would cheer me when I was low-spirited," the countess admitted uneasily.

" And who will cheer your bright, sunny young girl when she is low-spirited ? " he demanded hotly. " And have you intimated to the Frau Major what *dot* you intend to settle upon your sunny young girl, in case she suits your whims and Mousey's ? "

" Hugo, you forget yourself " —

" I beg your pardon," he said, falling back wearily. " Do me the justice to remember that I tried to avoid the conversation."

" It seems to me very proper to discuss a step of so much importance with one's only son."

" But if one's only son has already declared himself unalterably opposed to the step ? "

" So unreasonable," she murmured, " so obstinate ! "

" It is possible. I admit the question does not concern me materially. Your sunny young person will not disturb me. But still I protest. Why must you do it, mamma ? Why add a new name to the sad old list. You never were satisfied with one of them. You suspected them of a thousand meannesses. No, I don't intend to be rude. But remember, there was always, sooner or later, an open scene after a long smouldering quarrel ; then complaints, tears, recriminations, and the rapid exit of the companion. We have tried relatives, strangers, German, French, and English girls. There was Cousin Marie, a widow — a pleasing, gentle little woman — musical, —cheerful, — practical " —

" Don't talk to me of her, Hugo ! Deceitful little cat ! "

" Precisely. Let us for the sake of argument admit that they were all deceitful cats. In that case I don't see what is going to prevent this Gabrielle from also being a cat, and deceitful. You will adore her and caress her and call her ' Moonbeam ' if she is fair, and ' Twilight ' if she is dark, and there will be peace for fourteen days — for three weeks provided she is a miracle of patience ; then her fall from favor will be more rapid than her ascent."

" One would think, Hugo, that I was a " —

" I am not analyzing the reasons of things, but merely sketching their outward sequence. You have made fifteen trials of companions, have you not? Or is it sixteen ? "

" I have been singularly unfortunate, I admit. I am too trusting. Then Gabrielle will not be like a companion. A girl of good family — a baroness — a distant relative of ours, — she will be like a daughter of the house."

" It sounds well," Hugo returns skeptically. " But she is poor, and young, and will be in your power. Our servants have at least their Sunday out, and can ridicule us and abuse us royally down in the basement. But what vent to her feelings has the companion of a fashionable woman ? Particularly if she is a poor relative. Her dignity forbids her to complain, until she grows desperate and throws up the situation. She could not, for instance, even confide to me that she found bésique a bore and hated Mousey."

" You are complimentary — as usual, Hugo," she retorted displeased, " and yet you know well that my ideal is the companionship of a true friend," she continued in a curiously sentimental manner. " All my life I have longed for sympathy, and in vain. Why should my son wish to deny me the possibility of finding it ? "

When the countess was sentimental she always had him at a disadvantage. For thin, empty, and transitory, as her feeling was, he believed it to be not wholly insincere. He dreaded the little conscious smile so foreign to her hard features, and the schoolgirlish talk of the ideal woman-friend. Whether her own fault or not, it represented her sense of dissatisfaction with her life, her longing for something she had never had; it meant a note of unhappiness, which seemed real and human to him, and when he heard it, he was sorry for her.

"I wish I need not offend you," he said gently. "What I mean is that your personality is so — so — so dominant, so engrossing, I do not think you adapted to the intimacy which you always seem to desire with another woman. Friendship necessitates some kind of equality. You are used to the constant society of servants, whose smiles and lip-service you buy; and you are accustomed to superficial intercourse with women of the world, whose smiles and lip-service you also buy in a certain sense, at least you exchange yours for theirs; but in both cases thoughts are free and well-disguised, and I do not believe any other relationship would satisfy you. Above all, this child from the country. For the last time, I say let the girl stay where she is."

"But I intend to make her happy. I have always wanted a daughter. A daughter would have understood me." On the cold face was still the thin mask of sentimentality.

"I have heard you frequently say so. But the fact remains, this girl is not your daughter. She will have no freedom, she will have no rights. If she is animated, you will call her pert. If she is quiet and deliberate, you will find her not *prévoyante*. Whether pretty or ugly, she will be in your opinion coquette. Whether she will or not, she must drive with you, pay visits, go shopping, as if under military orders."

" And is that a hardship for a young girl from the country, I should like to inquire ? To go where I go and do what I do ? "

" I don't know," he replied curtly. " It depends upon the girl. If she is a toady, she will enjoy it vastly for a time, because she will be playing her own game. But if she has an atom of honesty in her composition, she would rather go out on the road and break stones."

He moved his hands restlessly, his cheeks were hot.

" You have a singularly unamiable way of presenting your views " — she complained, hesitated a moment, then with increasing coldness, " For my part I anticipate only agreeable experiences with Gabrielle. I have had the rose-room prepared for her."

Hugo threw back his head, rolled up his eyes toward his frescoed ceiling, and stared at a flying swallow under a cloudy sky.

The countess was never calm under disapproval.

" Well ? " she said, in peevish interrogation.

He stared persistently at the bird and did not open his lips.

" I meant it as a pleasant surprise for you. She arrives to-day."

Still no response from Hugo.

" Have you nothing to say, Hugo ? Why do you do that ? " she demanded with great irritation.

" I congratulate the Frau Major," he said at length.

" Nonsense ! You do her injustice. I sometimes think she is the only faithful friend I have."

"There is safety in your 'sometimes.' Should you always think so — *vœ victis !* — And mamma, when she has decided upon your course another time, pray dispense with my superfluous reflections. I have not over-abundant vitality. Why should I waste it attack-ing your foregone conclusions? I suppose she means Lorenz and Egon to run? I bet you five to one on Lorenz. Just give me a hint from time to time which leads. And otherwise, mamma, leave me out of your calculations. Don't ask me to burn incense when the girl comes, or fling brickbats when she goes. Once for all, I wash my hands in innocence."

"Hugo," said the countess rising, "I consider some of your remarks coarse."

"It is the nature of man," he returned uncompro-misingly.

She was angry he saw by her increased paleness. The black lace of her coquettish French cap with its crimson rose trembled wrathfully, and so did the smooth white hands. She was a handsome woman still, he thought, with her regular features, her deli-cate, wonderfully preserved skin, and her gray hair of exquisite quality, and beautiful enough to frame the pure and serene countenance of a typical, aged saint. He watched her with his flashing, unpleasant smile. Whatever self-command she had she was apt to use in his presence.

"I really ought to go," she said, "I have worlds to do, and it must be nearly two o'clock."

"I will call Lipps," and he raised his whistle.

Her cold eyes looked uneasy and wandering. She stood by her son resenting his disapproval. Lipps came in and held the door open for her. "Oh, I saw you on the lawn, this morning. You bore it well, I hope."

" Well enough, thanks."

" I am glad to hear that," she remarked formally.
" And you are sleeping well ? "

" Well enough, thanks," he said again, still with
the smile that made her uncomfortable, and reminded
her of the late count.

" That is more than I can say. My neuralgia " —
she murmured, " and Mousey is so restless — and those
horrid workmen begin now before seven. You are fortunate that they are not on your side of the house."

" Very fortunate."

" Well, a pleasant day to you, Hugo. I am glad to
be able to give so good an account of you to your
friends. As you are determined not to approve of Gabrielle, I presume I need not hasten to present her."

" No, that ceremony can be indefinitely postponed."
She extended her hand, which he again raised mechanically to his lips.

" The gracious countess is served," announced the
fat and solemn butler at the door. Presently Mousey's
bell and her voluble endearments were heard in the
hall.

" I wish to be alone," said the count to his man.
" Leave me."

An hour later Lipps stole softly in, and found the
invalid asleep. Two bright spots glowed on his cheeks,
and from time to time his hands twitched nervously.
In a distant corner the little black book lay spread out
on its face, as if flung by an impatient hand. Lipps
solicitously smoothed its crumpled leaves.

CHAPTER III.

" WON'T Mousey say good-by to his poor Mumsey?"
pleaded the countess.

Mousey emphatically declared that he would not.

" But I cannot take you to the chu-chu-train, love,
for you know that the chu-chu-train frightens my
little pet, and the noises and the crowd are so loud,
and the bad, bad men are so unkind to my innocent
lamb. I know I promised you should go out with
me, but I have been detained, and there is no time
now, dearest. Don't be cruel, Mousey; say good-by
and smile at Mumsey before she goes, and amuse
yourself well, sweetheart, until I come with a pretty
new lady to play with you."

But Mousey was deaf to her blandishments. He
would not give his paw and say good-by, a ceremony
which he always performed when she drove out and
he elected to remain at home. He had expressed his
intention to go to meet Gabrielle, and had argued the
point when the countess deprecatingly explained to
him her reasons for depriving herself of his companionship. Now, as she sought to coax a parting smile
upon his gloomy countenance, he shook his small
person resentfully, and with unspeakable disdain
turned his unæsthetic back, and went pattering off
toward the second maid's room. His wisdom recognized the inexorable necessity of occasional outward
submission to human will, since inscrutable nature
had given to his indomitable spirit so minute physical

adjuncts, that a struggle with the countess, the butler,
the coachman, and two maids for a place in the carriage would result in his inglorious defeat. But he
knew that the final victory would be his, and went off
grinning like a fiend to plan a long and sweet revenge
consisting in a delectable perspective of slights to the
countess.

She, meanwhile, a softly attractive Paris bonnet
perched upon her silvery hair, her face set, cold, and
composed, drove to the Frau Major's. She felt more
than ever in need of the balm of the Frau Major's
presence, after Hugo's opposition. In the complex
mechanism of the Countess of Kronfels' soul one need
was paramount, the oil of adulation upon the axles
of her capriciously revolving deeds. Yet, since in
spite of being held in bondage by Mousey she was by
no means a stupid woman, the lubricator of her fickle
wheels of action required unusual versatility of intellect, a nice touch on the pulse of society, as well as
many other special gifts. All of these the Frau Major
von Funnel possessed to an eminent degree. For example, the countess changed her opinions with the
wind; the Frau Major, without surprise or argument,
blandly changed with her. The countess contradicted
to-day what she had solemnly affirmed yesterday; the
Frau Major with gentle aplomb did likewise. The
countess was often irritable, uneasy, uncertain, vacillating; the Frau Major, with her unique command of
language, would soothe her friend's most impossible
mood, and tell her she was a "loving, sensitive soul,"
when others were flying to bathe their wounds.

The Frau Major did not heap on flattery with a
trowel, after the manner of a coarser artisan. She
knew that when one is surrounded by sycophants,

one's taste is cloyed with sweets, and while one's appetite is insatiable, it is only the novel and pungent flavor that one relishes. Yet the charm of her low, peculiar, penetrating voice that one heard at a dinner-party, though a dozen ordinary mortals were speaking, endowed her lightest word with profound significance.

Not only to the countess, but to every person, young or old, rich or poor, with whom she associated, she offered the tribute of peculiar interest and personal devotion. Her way of saying the simple word "you" had enthralled legions of hearts. Her noble head with its handsomely marked features, strong nose and chin, deep-set cold eyes and heavy mouth might have belonged to the wiliest statesman in an album of "Portraits of Eminent Men." But her charming smile, the softness of her curling gray hair which lay in babylike rings round her forehead, and her low magnetic voice suggested to the ordinary observer only her ultra-feminine attributes. Her manner was simple, sincere, and possessed the rare charm of perfect repose. In a crowded theatre or concert room, the noble profile and self-contained expression of the Frau Major afforded a positive delight to the weary eye, seeking beauty or character in rows of commonplace beings. Walking, she was less imposing, having a short, plump figure, and a curious waddling gait.

Few society women had done more good in the world than she. And whatever were the recording angel's private convictions, he had in his books a long list of helpful if conventional charities to her credit. She figured largely in philanthropic societies and clubs, and was prominent in benevolent bazars. In soliciting funds for her asylums she was incompara-

ble, and the man who could say her nay was almost
unknown, so persuasive was her gentle voice, so calm
and reasonable her argument, so inexpressibly significant her trusting appeal to "you."

She carried her fifty years with marvellous grace,
and made her home attractive to scores of gay young
men and pretty girls, all of whom sung her praises
with warmth. There was not one of them that did
not cherish the ingenuous conviction that he or she
was the special pet of the Frau Major; not a mid-
dle-aged woman in the circle but deemed herself the
Frau Major's most intimate friend; while clever men
never left her benign presence without the reflection
that here, at least, was a woman of rare insight, who
knew how to revere a godlike intellect. She won
affection, respect, influence, power, and her indomitable will, working with ceaseless activity and wisest
tact, kept what she gained. "She deserves her troops
of friends," people often remarked, "for she is so
kind. When does she ever say an uncharitable
word?" In truth, she never blamed, never criticised,
never did anything that could displease or wound.
She knew that all walls have ears, and that a bird in
the air sooner or later chirps to the world most spoken
words. Therefore, if some quick tongue pronounced
a woman ugly and untidy, the Frau Major would
smile lovingly on the speaker, and add, "But a dear
motherly soul." She might never have seen the person
in question with a child, might not know she had one,
and ugliness and untidiness do not necessarily suggest
motherliness to the ordinary mind. It was simply
the Frau Major's habit to praise, to praise largely,
to praise at morn, at noon, at night, in public, in
private, everywhere and always. It would almost

seem that to her human nature had no frailties, and that crime was a mere invention of romance and the courts. Her universal approval, in contrast to the habit of censorious gossip common to many women, was original and refreshing, and only an occasional grumbler, like Hugo von Kronfels, took exception to it. "Is it possible," he had asked himself many years before, "that so clever a woman is color-blind? Is black white to her? Is night day? Does she perceive no difference between noble and ignoble, good and bad? Is that rich old profligate Zwetchgen, in reality, as she says, so 'marvellously tender and noble in the recesses of his nature, so like a rich pomegranate?' Are those vapid, conscious, envious, senseless Mayer sisters 'such dear happy little sweethearts?' Her mellifluous cant would make one lose all sense of proportion;" and Hugo watched her gravely, and never enrolled himself among her knights.

But the Frau Major went her appointed way, — a broad and flower-grown path it was, — and old Zwetchgen, having heard from afar how profoundly she admired him, would succumb in her presence to the charm of her gentle and deep glances, dedicated, it seemed, exclusively to him; and his purse, closed in general to all things except his selfish pleasures, would open as if by witchery and pour its gold into her tender palm. While the dear happy little sweethearts hung about her and caressed her, and basked in her unqualified approval, and knew that in spite of her engrossing occupations, and important friends, she felt for them a "peculiar and close affection," and it is needless to add that their pin-cushions and baby-blankets were always ready for her fancy fairs. So her charities flourished, and all was loving-kindness.

" Dear Adelheid," she said, as she took her place beside the countess, and gave her hand a long and gentle pressure, "your punctuality is admirable. It is really a comfort, as well as an example to us all," continued the earnest, sympathetic voice. "You are feeling tolerably well to-day?" she asked with solicitude.

"No, I am far from well. My neuralgia is very trying, and I am fatigued and distressed," the countess replied in a nervous, complaining tone.

" You are so sensitive," murmured the other.

" Yes, I am sensitive, but Hugo never considers that in the least. Of course I make allowances for his condition," she said, irritably, " but he is often very difficult, very unreasonable."

"Men do not know how to bear pain as well as we," suggested the soothing voice. " Poor, dear Hugo! What would he do without his mother!"

" He has been unpleasant about Gabrielle. I hope it is a wise step. I hope I shall not regret it. What if I do not like her? What if she should be ugly and ordinary? I wish I had not engaged myself positively. I wish I had taken more time to consider."

These flurried doubts and fears were speedily allayed by the comforting views of her friend.

"Naturally your judgment is wiser than poor Hugo's, — although one can easily comprehend and sympathize with him; but your prompt and hearty decision has greatly pleased me, and that you steadfastly adhere to your purpose is, of course, only what one could expect of — *you*."

Praised for steadfastness, the countess looked a trifle less nervous and harassed.

" Still it is very uncertain," she urged.

"I should call it tolerably certain," thought the Frau Major, "with the express that is actually bringing the girl almost here."

"It is a little romantic," she replied encouragingly. "I have always found the loving, youthful element in you so rare and so attractive, and it is this that induces you to take this unknown young girl to your heart and home and make her happy."

"I have always wished that I had a daughter."

"She will seem like your daughter, dear friend."

"I have believed from the first that it was a good plan," said the countess with the decision of a field-marshal.

"You need some one near you to comprehend you and sympathize with you."

"I shall be so devoted to her!"

"The Dohnas are a handsome race. She will no doubt look well in your carriage."

"After the dullness of Dohna, how she will enjoy city life!"

"Always so thoughtful of others!"

"Of course I shall have to open the house again. Hugo could hardly expect me to shut out the world forever."

"No," said the Frau Major very sweetly. "You have faithful Leible on the box, I see."

"Yes, he finds people better than the footman. And I shall remain in the carriage. It makes me fairly ill to be jostled and pushed by a coarse crowd."

"If the dear girl should prove to be all that we hope, instead of a year she may remain altogether," the Frau Major suggested innocently.

"I do hope there are no flagrant irregularities in her education. Her father is a perfect cavalier, or was when I last saw him. Perhaps country living has dulled him. But he writes me Gabrielle has never had a governess. I was rather startled when I read that. I pictured her a savage."

"Whatever there may be amiss, the privilege of living with you will be a liberal education to her. With your tact and knowledge of the world you can mould her as you desire. And after all she is a Dohna; and your cousin, however far removed, cannot be uncouth or unpresentable."

Now the irregularities of Gabrielle von Dohna's education would have made any enlightened principal of an institute for the higher culture of young ladies shudder and shrink. Measured by conventional standards, Gabrielle knew those things which she ought not to have known, and did not know those things which she ought to have known. Her free life on her father's estate, her supreme importance in the adjacent village, her constant association with him, had made her his good comrade and friend, and a veritable if an unconscious autocrat.

When Ernst von Dohna lost his beloved wife, his only child was but five years old, and he scarcely thirty. To his simple and direct nature his duties lay plainly defined before him : to clear the estate of the encumbrances with which he had inherited it, and to devote himself to his little motherless daughter. The first task, he knew, would be long and laborious, perhaps beyond his strength. The second he ingenuously regarded as natural and easy. He had no theories whatever in regard to rearing girls. Gabrielle was his own and looked at him with her mother's limpid, honest eyes. He remembered that one of the first things that his father had taught him was the somewhat antiquated sentiment that he was a gentleman, and a gentleman must hate a lie. Without more ado, he impressed upon his five-year-old Gabrielle that she was a lady, and a lady must hate a lie. He remembered, too, that he had been happy as a child in his love for his horse. Accordingly little Gabrielle learned to hate a lie and love a horse. She rode beside him on her pony every day, and heard his orders to his farm-laborers; knew a field of wheat from a field of barley; had an intimate knowledge of bird-notes, trees, and animals; loved every living thing she saw, down to caterpillars, lizards, and snails ; was an eager and omnivorous reader for her age ; and these accomplishments composed the entire education of the little Baroness von Dohna, up to her eleventh year.

Then it suddenly occurred to her father that perhaps she ought to study something. He remembered that a tutor used to give him Latin and mathematics when he was even younger than Gabrielle. There were no aunts and cousins to tell him that she ought to have a governess or be sent to school, and that it was ridiculous to treat her like a boy. He had no desire to see strangers in his house, and no money to pay for their services. He therefore, with great tranquillity of spirit, began to work with the child evenings. It was, of course, the wrong time of day, but he and Gabrielle enjoyed themselves and were quite unaware that there was anything curious in their conduct. Thrown constantly upon his companionship, she absorbed much from him, and his thoughts and language descended upon her. The hearty, unrestrained child reached up with all the tendrils of her loving nature toward him, while he leaned down toward her, needed her, and depended upon her, since young as she was, she was his sympathetic and blithe little comrade, both in his work and in his hours of rest.

His means did not allow large hospitality, but when friends announced themselves, or a dinner party was inevitable, the small person who did the honors of his table was no disgrace to his name. At least, no one criticised her to him. One hardly chooses the moment of eating a man's meats, and drinking his wines, to find fault with his daughter, and his women guests were naturally lenient to the amiable widower, and all that was his.

Long winter evenings, when no mortal approached the snow-bound Schloss, father and daughter sat together in the library. It may be he forgot how young she was; it may be nobody had ever told him how gradually one ought to appeal to a child's intelligence, but the truth is, the misguided man would often look up from his book to discuss a knotty point with the long-haired, short-skirted philosopher in her low chair by the fire.

"My dear, just listen to this," he would say, reading with convincing emphasis: "Professor R. declares so and so, which is simply preposterous; whereas Professor S., by far the greater authority, distinctly states the contrary. Now if R.'s position were tenable, don't you see that," etc. Gabrielle, listening, as if her life depended upon her attention, and gravely nodding, would unhesitatingly support the theory of Professor S. If a poem delighted him, he would read it to her. Travels, inventions, politics, earnest questions of the day, he laid before her as if thinking aloud, and more for his own satisfaction than with any

defined purpose of improving her mind. When she
ceased to nod invariable assent, like a little pagoda,
when she began to understand things for their own
sake and hers, to advance fresh opinions, to question,
and now and then to differ, he no more knew than
the exact moment when dawn becomes day.

They were all and all to each other, and awaited no
change. One day was like another, and the years
went softly by. He smilingly called himself an
old man and Gabrielle at twenty-one seemed still a
child to him, when something happened which transformed all his comfortable convictions. He discovered that a man is still young at forty-six, in spite of
gray theories and gray hairs, — most ardently and
longingly young. He discovered also, in this moment
of illumination, that a spirited girl past twenty, who
has never seen the world, would be incalculably ben-
efited by the society of a lovely and experienced
woman. He pictured by his fireside in the future, not
alone his faithful comrade, but another with suave
smiling ways, learned in a so-called larger world than
Gabrielle had known.

It all happened so easily. For many years he had
as far as possible declined, because he could not suit-
ably return, the proffered hospitality of the land-own-
ers of the region. As his patient effort began to tell,
and the disreputable mountain of debt and mortgages
which he had inherited from his illustrious forefathers
had gradually contracted into a modest hillock, he
met an old acquaintance, one day, and rode with him
through the woods. The result was an invitation
to dine, which von Dohna cheerfully accepted for
himself and his daughter.

Happily Lucie von Rahden was a very good woman.

A rich and childless widow who had made the best of a bad matrimonial bargain, she was determined never to repeat her experiment, but to enjoy life in her independent, sunny fashion the rest of her days. Her uncompromising views in regard to a second marriage she was wont to expound in a pleasingly satirical manner, for the entertainment of friends. Nevertheless she with her prejudices, and he with his, fell in love at a dinner party in good old orthodox fashion.

Gabrielle came home and wept bitterly. It was her first sleepless night, except when she had watched by an ill child in the village; and she found that pity and anxiety and fatigue were after all more restful companions for a long night than these newly roused spirits of wounded pride and jealousy, these rebellious passionate feelings to which indeed she gave no name.

The next morning her papa rode away with a flower in his button-hole. Every day she wandered alone in the old familiar paths, and he rode off gayly in the other direction. She grew unhappy, unjust, and very lonely. She did not know that she was jealous. How should she? One does not lightly admit the presence of that quality. Jealousy to Gabrielle meant Othello, Eleanor, the Princess Eboli, Medea, and such people; while she was merely hurt, neglected, suspicious, and sorrowful.

Von Dohna and Frau von Rahden advanced rapidly toward a perfect understanding. One day he expressed his surprise at the new born unreasonableness of his daughter. She had been the dearest girl all her life, loving, appreciative, sympathetic, and so clear in her judgment. Now she seemed quite changed. She avoided him and his confidences, with reserve and obstinacy. She had shared his joys and

sorrows to a most unusual degree. Now she said
coldly: "I don't understand you, papa," and the
more he explained the situation, the more uncomfortable it grew.

"There is but one remedy," said Lucie von Rahden.

"And what may that be?"

"Send her away for a while."

"Lucie, she has never been separated from me a
day in her life. She would be miserable. It would
seem cruel to her."

"It would be the wisest and kindest thing you
could do."

"But why should I? Why should Gabrielle not
rejoice in my happiness? Would I not rejoice in
hers?"

"But yours has come first," returned Lucie with a
charming smile, "so you can afford to be generous."

"She cannot live with you without yielding to
your charm. The daily intercourse will win her completely. She does not know you yet. The idea of
change has startled her."

"My dear Ernst, what you are good enough to
call my 'charm' will madden the poor child, and
the 'daily intercourse' will irritate her beyond endurance."

"I was so sure that she would love you," he said
helplessly.

"It is because I am determined that she shall love
me that I advise sending her away from me at once.
See, Ernst, if we three live at Dohna together, the
situation will be frightfully strained. Gabrielle will
regard me as her enemy, nothing more or less. Do
what I will, I cannot please her. If you finally decide that this is best," remarked the wise little woman,

" of course I shall agree, and then I should not despair of gaining her affection in time, but it will take — ages ! "

" I do not think you realize how reasonable Gabrielle is," he urged.

" Ah, what has this to do with reason — when a girl sets her lips as Gabrielle does, and grows icy at the mere sight of me. And I do not blame her in the least. It is altogether natural. What she says is true. She does not understand. She does not know what love is," she added softly.

" See, dear," she went on candidly, " I will tell you all I have thought, and if you know anything better, I will yield; but this is not a light question, since Gabrielle is not a child, but a very spirited, decided girl. I even believe that she herself will approve my plan. If she does not, we will stay here, if you prefer. But all my life I have longed to travel — to travel far and with one person, who never came, — and now he is come! And you, during all your years of seclusion with your little daughter, have longed not for the world, the gay world which you used to know, but also for travel, for strange lands and new people. You confessed all that to me at. that blessed dinner.

" Why should we not, dearest?" she murmured caressingly. " You have had your sorrows and your heavy cares. I have had mine. But happiness has come to us. If we have a right to it, let us seize it like young lovers. Let us be glad and at peace. Let us go to — Japan, and — everywhere," she pleaded. " Give Gabrielle the choice of going with us. She will refuse. And it is not cruel to leave her, — it is not selfish, except so far as it is selfish to love you

and be happy; it will be the best thing in the end
for us all."

"But where — how? What could I do with the
dear girl? If we should go off on this marvellous
trip," he said smiling doubtfully, " I should have to
close the house. Perhaps Gabrielle would like to stay
at the rectory."

"At Dohna? At a country parson's? Never!"
laughed Lucie. " No, no ; send her into the world,
where, however happy the auspices, she must meet
with some insincerity, some deceptions and disappointments, and where her own sweet will cannot rule
all things as at Dohna. And then, don't you see, you
stupid man — if you were a woman you would have
understood without a word ; but then if you were a
woman I should n't love you so much ! — don't you
see, when she comes back there will be a chance
for me? And believe me, Ernst, then we shall really
be friends, good loving friends, — your child and your
wife."

" Is it not a rather roundabout course ? "

" It only seems so," she replied cheerfully. " I
shall reach her heart sooner via Japan than via
Dohna."

"Hm! And you propose giving her a course of
disappointments."

"That is a man's way of expressing it. I propose
to help you find the very nicest people socially who
would most naturally receive her, that is, relatives
of your own, city-people of course. Do you know,
it is a very good thing for Gabrielle that I appeared.
What were you going to do with her? Did it never
occur to you that a girl like Gabrielle usually marries? Indeed, you have kept her here quite long
enough."

" Is there anything the matter with her ? " he asked, conscience-stricken.

Lucie laughed.

" She is the most charming little despot I ever saw. No, Ernst, seriously she is a girl in a thousand. You have done wonderfully well with her. But she is a Sleeping Beauty in the Wood, and not a prince in sight."

" You would hardly expect me to send her hunting for one ? " he said gravely.

" By no means. Only I would let her see a few. And nowadays princes prefer city-life."

The next time, which was soon, that von Dohna and Lucie discussed this subject, it was he who proposed some of these already suggested details, and she who listened and smilingly approved.

After various tentative correspondences, the cordial response of the Countess of Kronfels allayed all his doubts, difficulties, and embarrassment, for his desire to make suitable arrangements for Gabrielle was only equalled by the countess's ardent wish to take the young girl to her heart and home. Their needs dovetailed with comforting precision. The countess alluded delicately and tenderly to her son's condition and to her grief and loneliness.

Another distant relative declared herself willing to receive Gabrielle, and promised her a gay season with her own daughters.

" You might be happier with girls, Gabrielle," her father suggested anxiously.

But Gabrielle, who had fulfilled Lucie's prophecy by emphatically declining the voyage, and by expressing a deep desire to go among strangers, now remarked quietly, —

" No, papa, I would prefer to go to the Countess Kronfels."

" She is past sixty, and it may be dull for you, dear child."

" No, I shall like it," she persisted. " I like old ladies."

" She is not a chimney-corner old lady, I believe," Lucie said demurely.

" She was a handsome woman of the world when I last saw her. What she is now we can better judge when we go on to Wynburg. And then if you don't think you are going to be happy, we 'll change our minds, little girl. We 'll run away."

" But, papa, is it not decided ? How could we run away ? And indeed, I wish to go to Wynburg. Only I would rather go alone. That is, not with you, papa. Please let me go alone, or send one of the ser-vants ; if you like I would rather begin quite fresh — not see your face there, and then miss it," she added low and pleadingly.

" But, my darling child " — he began.

" It is the only thing you can do for me — now," she murmured wistfully.

" Why not let her have her will ? " Lucie's cheery voice broke in. " She is not going among dragons. The worldly auspices could not be better. She will see life and have great social advantages."

Gabriélle looked at her gravely.

" I like old ladies, and I would like to 'know Count Hugo, and help his mother take care of him. That is why I should like to go to Wynburg."

CHAPTER IV.

GABRIELLE and her father stood in the library, and all the tranquil years and their dear memories seemed to pass in review before her.

"Be happy, child," he said folding her in his arms, "and if you are not going to be happy, come with us. If you waver — if you fear, your place is with me. You are my own precious child. If you should be unhappy I should never forgive myself," and the warm tone of his voice comforted and strengthened her.

She clung to him silently.

"I will telegraph that you will not come," he said, moved by the soft clinging arms. "You and Lucie and I will go off together."

She raised her head and smiled, though her eyes were wet.

"Think what little girls go to boarding-school, papa. One would imagine I was an infant in arms! Be happy yourself, papa, and come back safe to Dohna. If you love me, I am not afraid."

"I love you with all my heart."

"Not all, for you love Lucie," she insisted.

"I love her with all my heart, too," he said, smiling.

"Then you have two hearts, papa!"

"It may be. But nothing on earth can make my beloved child less dear to me. Remember that, whatever may grieve you during our separation. Remember that I love you always, and trust you perfectly."

" Then I shall be content," she said bravely.

It was shortly after the wedding in the village church. Gabrielle had chosen this day for her departure.

" Let us go to her," she said. " We are leaving her so long."

" She understands."

" And she will have you a whole year," Gabrielle added quickly.

" I fear I am very selfish," she said to Lucie, looking earnestly in her eyes.

" My dear Gabrielle, liking step-mothers is a cultivated taste," replied Lucie with a smile and a sigh.

" I did not know you at all," the young girl murmured, watching her intently.

" Some time you will know me," the older woman returned very kindly. " Some time I hope that you will find me worth loving."

" If papa loves you, you are worth loving," Gabrielle answered gravely, " and I hope " — she hesitated — " I will try to be fair," she said simply.

" That is quite enough," Lucie assured her cordially. " And some day, that happy far-off some day, you will understand that I am in reality taking nothing from you."

Gabrielle shook her head sadly and turned away.

She did not wish to be tragic, and make scenes, but it seemed to her that Lucie had taken from her all that she held dear, — her father, her home, her peace of mind ; and as she passed down the steps and through the great gates, where the servants were gathered weeping and wailing, — no doubt with sincere affection for their young mistress, yet also impelled by their sense of conventional appropriateness, to

accentuate the sadness of parting and the luxury of
woe, — and when the huge Leonberger followed her
to the carriage with a bitterly reproachful air, and
threw back his head and howled forth his sentiments,
she felt like little less than a dethroned queen.

The old housekeeper, who served as escort, wept
comfortably from time to time, partly with pleasure at
the thought of visiting her son whom she had not seen
in years, and partly with excitement caused by the
prospect of a journey of twenty-four hours to South
Germany. Gabrielle soothed her kindly, and felt that
she herself was very wretched. But perfect health,
youth, and a good conscience were surprisingly rapid
consolers for her grade of misery. The long journey
through the night was like a strange dream. A thousand new things interested her, and she was full of
eagerness as to her coming experiences, and confident
of her devotion to the countess, whom she pictured
quite clearly, and to Count Hugo, to whom she would
read hour after hour, and bring flowers. " I must tell
him papa says I play a very decent game of chess,"
she thought, suddenly waking from a queer vision of
old familiar things and imagined scenes with Hugo
and his mother, as the train glided into a brilliantly
lighted station at three o'clock in the morning. But
this was not her destination, and she slept the broken
half sleep of the night traveller again.

When she stepped from the coupé arriving at Wynburg, and Leible with unerring instinct accosted her,
she realized that she was launched on an unknown
sea. He seized her travelling bag and piloted her
through the crowd.

She came on with the easy step of a good walker.
Her clear young eyes, trained to long distances, saw

vividly, before she reached the carriage, the faces of
the two ladies in the open landau, both turned toward her, the correct coachman's profile, the sober
livery, the over-fed handsome bays, the people passing, a clock on a public building opposite, and a vane
by which she instinctively noted the points of the
compass and the way of the wind, remembering the
old weather-cock at Dohna, and how she watched it
at harvest time.

"Thank Heaven she is not countrified!" was the
countess's pious exclamation.

"She looks so clever and decided," murmured the
Frau Major admiringly. "Too clever, too decided, I
fear," she privately commented. "Moulding her will
be no easy task, still with patience " —

The countess kissed Gabrielle airily on each cheek
and welcomed her with incoherent effusion. The Frau
Major held both of the young girl's hands in a significant pressure, and bending her handsome, earnest
face toward Gabrielle, said in a low magnetic voice: —

"I knew your dear father, years ago. You remind
me of him. I feel a very tender and special interest
in you."

Gabrielle was charmed with the voice, which seemed
to take possession of her with its tenacious, caressing
cadence. "Is he well?" continued the Frau Major,
with her peculiar emphasis, conveying, beneath the
three words of commonplace inquiry, an impressive
undertone of interest, remembrance, and regard.

Gabrielle gave her a bright, grateful glance.

"Papa is well, thanks," she said. "I think I never
heard him mention you," she added, with frank surprise at the omission. It seemed to her very remarkable that her papa, who had described to her all his

old friends, had not mentioned this lovely person who seemed to know him so well and retained so much affection for him.

"It was so long ago," returned the Frau Major vaguely, and with her air of unfathomable calm, — regarding the fascinated young eyes opposite her gently and solemnly, and she might have added: "And no wonder he has forgotten me, since the whole acquaintance consisted in a stiff bow on his part and a smile on mine when somebody presented the shy eighteen - year - old boy to me, more than twenty-five years ago in a crowded drawing-room. But why mention the unedifying episode? Why ever recall anything that does not give positive pleasure? The one thing of which the human heart never wearies is the honeyed voice of approval."

"You must be tired," began the countess. "Nothing fatigues me like the railway. My neuralgia is always worse, travelling, and my asthma gives me no peace. Does travelling give you neuralgia?"

"It seems to give me nothing but dust and dirt. But this is my first long journey, and I know nothing of neuralgia or any illness — at least from my own experience." She spoke half-laughingly, half-apologetically, but with a very direct manner, and not a trace of shyness.

"I think one ought to know pain," rejoined the countess with her sentimental air, "at least, to be truly sympathetic. I am a great sufferer."

"That is a pity," Gabrielle said kindly, but with inward wonder. She was accustomed to listen patiently to the complaints of bed-ridden old women in the village whose loquacity in regard to their symptoms, and huge enjoyment in dilating upon their diseased organs, she had ascribed to want of breeding and paucity of ideas. An invalid of sixty odd years with skin, hair, and teeth in an enviable condition, sitting erect in an elegant landau, and wearing a juvenile love of a bonnet was an enigma to her.

The countess drew her velvet mantle closer, and remarked with a frown, as if resenting a personal annoyance : "It is so raw to-day. I am so sensitive," she explained to Gabrielle. "I am obliged to spend many winters on the Riviera. But the transition is the difficult thing in that case. One feels it so keenly, it really undoes all the benefit one has received from the warmer climate."

The Frau Major murmured a gentle acquiescence.

"I bask in sunshine," the countess explained, falling into French. "I am a sun-worshipper — a poor foolish Parsee." She smiled with pleasure at the aptness of her language, and her face wore its most agreeable expression. Her small pretty teeth revealed themselves amiably, and her fluent French ran on in airy flights.

They were driving up one of the principal business streets of the city. Gabrielle's keen eyes, accustomed to watch the flight of birds, caught clear glimpses of palms, and anemones, and pictures, and jewels, and silver-ware, and stuffs, and spring-gowns in the shopwindows, and all the time heard with a certain surprise the dominant voice of the countess, and met the reassuring, comprehensive gaze of the Frau Major.

The day was beautifu¹ to her in its breezy freshness. Last spring on just such a day she and her papa had gone trouting. How pleasant the library had been at night after their tramp in the wet woods ! How they had enjoyed their cozy supper and how

they had laughed! Could anything ever be as pleasant again? Would Lucie know his ways; when to
speak and when to be silent? How could her papa
feel familiar and easy with Lucie, when she, Gabrielle,
did not? That was the strange thing. One evening
had overbalanced years and years of sweet companionship. No, that was untrue, for her father's last em-
brace was infinitely loving, his voice was warm and
moved, his eyes wished her unspeakable blessings.
Still he would be happy with his Lucie, and the old
life was gone. This was the new life beginning, and
suddenly all seemed unreal to her, — the shops, the
busy street, the two smiling women, even she herself.
She roused herself. "But it is real," she thought.
"It has begun."

How handsome the countess was, with her silvery
hair and fine skin. How curiously, for her age and
size, her phrases darted about. Those butterfly flights
and poises seemed odd for so large a woman. She
was not in the least like an old lady, and her mind
rested nowhere.

They drove by a crowded entrance to a gallery
where a celebrated picture was on exhibition.

Gabrielle read the announcement, and said eagerly,
" Ah, I shall be glad to see that."

Upon which the countess attacked the painting and
its admirers. She did not criticise. She massacred.
She seemed to wrathfully cut the canvas with sharp
shears and trample on the fragments. Her easy
mockery, and massive disparagement, and the techni-
cal phrases which she flung one after another at the
offending landscape, greatly astonished Gabrielle.

" But he is a great artist," she said innocently.

The countess stared.

"And he has worked a year on this picture. A whole year of his life, — an artist's life. That means something."

"It means money, my dear, money," the countess returned with a little derisive laugh. "As for the praise, the critics are paid, too. Greedy, grasping set, all of them!"

Gabrielle looked at her wonderingly.

"Papa and I read the critiques. Could I have made a mistake? Could there be two artists of that name? But now I must not fail to go to see the picture at once," she announced cheerfully.

An ominous cloud was gathering on the countess's face.

"There is a charming little picture," began the Frau Major, "which we are about to raffle off at our next bazaar. The countess bought it out of pure charity; she is always doing kind things," the sincere voice explained, "and perhaps you would undertake it. A stranger always succeeds so well, and you," with her slight impressive lingering accent, "would succeed in anything. She may sell the tickets, may she not? Would it not be a good introduction? The picture, presented by the Countess of Kronfels' benevolence, and sold by the Countess of Kronfels' — cousin, — or what shall we call our dear young friend?" she asked gently.

"Well, — niece," returned the countess, after a pause, in which she measured Gabrielle from head to foot.

"We are eleventh cousins," Gabrielle said, with a quick laugh, "at least papa and I decided that we could scarcely reckon the relationship closer than that."

"A woman of my age," remarked the countess, with

a coquettish smile, which invited protest, "might be anybody's aunt."

"Why yes, — of course," assented Gabrielle, seriously, "but "—

A sweet and satisfied "Then it is all arranged," evinced the Frau Major's illimitable content. "The countess's niece will sell the countess's picture. It is a gem, of course, as it is her own selection. A girl is waiting on the shore for her sailor lover. There is a breadth, — an atmosphere "—

. "Gabrielle should wear white, — thick white," interrupted the countess.

"Thick white, by all means," assented the Frau Major, placidly.

Gabrielle saw herself summarily arrayed in a gown not of her own choice, raffling off a Sailor's Bride at a fashionable bazaar and surrounded by a crowd of strangers. Her personality seemed to have no importance except as it fitted in the mosaic of other people's plans. She was about to say flatly that she had no thick white gown, no experience in raffling, and would rather not assume the responsibility of the Sailor's Bride, when the Frau Major looked at her earnestly.

"You are going to do our poor dear countess a world of good. Youth is so comforting — and when one has griefs, and disappointments," — she murmured vaguely. Turning to the countess, "She will be indeed like a daughter to you."

Her tone of profound conviction carried weight. Her gentle solemnity was fascinating and subjugating in the extreme to the young girl. She forgot her momentary impatience, as she listened to the low, persuasive voice.

" What does it matter, after all, what I do or where
I go ? " she reflected. " Or, at least, why should I be
unamiable ? Of course there must be new things and
ways here. Of course I am not so important as I —
used to be at Dohna. The Frau Major means that
the countess suffers on account of her son. How selfish I have been not to speak of him."

With a compassionate glance, she ventured to say
timidly : —

" I hope poor Count Hugo is a little better. We
heard about it last winter. We were so sorry," she faltered. It was not easy to approach so pitiful a grief.

" It has been a terrible affliction, and wearing —
very wearing," sighed the countess. " I shall never
forget how I felt the evening they brought him home.
I went from one fit of hysterics into another. Her
majesty sent at once to inquire. We had every mark
of sympathy and attention." The young girl's honest
eyes stared at her with unmistakable, indignant reproach.

" He was so brave, so distinguished, so admired,"
the Frau Major began. " I have always been so
peculiarly fond of Hugo, for his own sake as well as
his mother's. He has a very remarkable character."

" But no resignation. If I could induce him to
cultivate resignation. I spoke with him about it to-
day. I urged him to consider it," the countess said
in an aggrieved tone.

" He is so noble ; so clever. He will surely be all
that you desire, in time," the Frau Major assured her,
soothingly, with a private suspicion that the flash in
Gabrielle's eyes boded no good.

" Hugo has much to learn," the countess returned,
loftily.

" Who could be resigned ! " began Gabrielle, before the safe conductor could avert the youthful lightnings. " And a man like Count Kronfels — papa said he was so spirited. If one were born a cripple I could understand, though it seems more natural for a cripple to be wicked and rebellious. There is one in the village. He is hump-backed. He is an angel of goodness, but I always thought if he were a thief and a murderer, a straight-backed jury ought to have the decency to acquit him. Oh ! " she exclaimed, with an overpowering remembrance of the joy of gallops over the breezy moors, of breathing the freshness of the woods, of the sense of freedom on the mountain, with only skies above one, and space and silence around, and with an intense consciousness of her own . love of action, motion, living, " how can he be resigned — how can he ? "

Even the Frau Major could not invariably predict how her uncertain friend would meet unwelcome turns in a conversation. The wise woman now preserved her inscrutable repose of manner, meanwhile anxiously watching the countess, and reflecting : " Is the girl a fool, to quarrel with her bread and butter ? If she were prudent she could command a brilliant future. That poor, ill-natured Hugo has more than enough for himself, and who knows, indeed, how long he will last ? It would certainly be a mercy to him if his sufferings should not be prolonged." For in her self-communings, the most astute of her sex did not hesitate to call a spade a spade.

But the mercurial countess, with her airiest shrug and a quizzical smile, replied : —

" How you will entertain me with your village experiences, my dear Gabrielle ! They will be quite idyllic and refreshing. As for Hugo, he would not be even grateful for your plenary indulgence. He does not — you will have to know sooner or later — extend his welcome to you, I regret to say. He does not sympathize with my delight in having you with me — the boorish boy!"

Gabrielle flushed, and was singularly ill at ease. She did not understand why Count Hugo should feel unfriendly to her, still less the smiling malice on the countess's face.

"I am sorry" — she began, "I did not know" — Then her characteristic bright look of good sense and good humor dispelling all uncertainty and regret, — "After all," she said smiling, "it is his matter. I don't blame him. If I were he, I should hate everybody. Particularly strangers."

"What principles!" exclaimed the countess lightly, adding, with a didactic air, "but remember, my dear child, every back is fitted to its burden. He doeth all things well. It is a heaven-sent trial, and the inconvenience it causes in the house no one knows except his poor mother. Will you hear that ugly pug bark? How Mousey would despise him! Mousey is a gentleman."

Gabrielle's condition of mind was bewilderment rather than antagonism or censure. "Everything is so new," she thought. "I was excited and wrong at home. I am excited and wrong here. I must be making mistakes. Nobody can be quite what the countess seems to be."

"There is the Countess Fanny," the Frau Major said cordially. "Pretty woman, and so clever — so like her papa."

"She was pretty, you mean; and as to her father,

he is clever in a certain sense. That is, he has clever intervals. But you can't deny he has just stultified himself completely in our affairs with Russia." She briefly sketched the foreign situation, and depicted the minister's errors with masterly clearness.

" In these things you are incomparable," her friend remarked. " Women are usually so stupid and vague when they speak of political matters, and no man makes a complicated question so clear to me as you."

" Oh, I always liked chess and politics," replied the countess simply, " and then one does not marry a diplomate for nothing."

Gabrielle was now more than ever convinced of her own injustice. The countess's manner was sensible and sincere, her smile young and kind, her little white teeth gleamed engagingly, and the western sunshine fell on her silvery hair. Gabrielle's spirits rose.

" How lovely it is here ! " she said. They were approaching the villa, and the largeness of the view surprised her. " It is so high and free ! "

" It is, indeed, a beautiful situation," agreed the Frau Major's low lingering tones. " We all envy the countess her ideal view."

" View ! " repeated the countess, with an exasperated air. " What is a view when those people straggle up the hill every day and intrude themselves upon it — stout fathers, and dowdy mothers, and knock-kneed babies ? And they all stand before my gates and stare ! "

The Frau Major's glance conveyed true sympathy, as she said, with a low laugh, " Poor things, how can they help it ? It is so pretty."

" The place was always too far from town to suit me," continued the countess, irritably. " And now that it has become Tom, Dick, and Harry's chosen promenade, and this incessant noise of building is going on directly under my ears, it is too near, I assure you. Pound, pound pound — click, click, click. So it goes all day long. And the clank of the chains when they lift those great stone blocks! — they seem to be pulling at my nerves. And if you have ever had my kind of neuralgia — not the ordinary kind, you know, but something quite different — seated in the finer nerves; Doctor Pressigny explained it to me, but the doctors here don't know anything about it; there is one nerve, in particular, that goes from your brain to your heels, and " —

"Oh!" exclaimed Gabrielle. The carriage was turning slowly into the Kronfels gates. In an instant she had flung open the door, and was hurrying towards a scene of dire confusion, from which infantile wails were vigorously ascending, while from the scaffolding above, the workmen looked down and laughed unfeelingly at the catastrophe. If Gabrielle had performed some dangerous feat on the high trapeze, the countess would have been scarcely more astonished, but there seemed to be nothing to do but to let the carriage wait, and to watch the young girl's eccentricities.

For some moments Gabrielle, coming up the hill in the perfectly appointed equipage, had been watching a less perfectly appointed one coming down. There was a fat baby-boy in the shaky little cart, while tied inextricably to it was another child scarcely bigger than her charge and officiating as nursery-maid, as is the imperative fashion in families where a baby a year is no novelty, and mamma takes in washing.

What could be more fascinating than the building

of a house? What more natural than to approach what one likes? With serene disregard of loose bricks, stones, bits of wood, and inequalities of the way, the shaky little cart crossed the street, dumped down into the gutter, jerked cheerfully up again, and established itself as nearly as possible beneath a great quivering stone block, going slowly up and accompanied by the sailor-like cries of men and the creaking, clanking chain. Gabrielle had been speculating afar-off upon this pigmy cavalcade, and as the countess discoursed volubly upon her peculiar high-born ailment, the young girl was heartily wishing that poor people were not obliged to send one baby out into the world to take care of another, and reflecting that if the ugly great stone should fall, which of course it would not, those two atoms would be crushed out of existence, when she saw Fate in the shape of a little yellow dog attack them from another direction.

Open-mouthed with delight, they clapped their hands at the beautiful, clanking chain; with heads thrown back, they watched the ponderous thing suspended in mid-air above them. Through a hole in the hedge, inclosing the villa garden, a tiny flaxen dog, with a paroxysm of angry yelps, appalling to infants unacquainted with the condition of his teeth, rushed straight at the sturdy but insecure legs of the leader of the expedition. She screamed and jumped. This the dog found attractive, and darted in and out between her feet, intent upon evil. The harnessed child could not escape without her train. In a frantic effort at self-preservation she sprang to the right, the left wheel struck a stone, and over went cart and children, in a helpless struggling heap, amid all the sharp-edged chaotic fragments.

It was at this crisis that Gabrielle flew to the rescue. She extricated the tangled babies, set the roly-poly protector and guide on her feet, straightened out the queer little mass of humanity in the cart, quickly ascertained that there was no harm done beyond some insignificant bruises, pulled the wagon out of all entanglements, turned the children homewards on a straight road, told the baby-girl she must not tip the baby-boy over again because it might hurt his back, and it would be better not to be harnessed like a pony, but if she must fall, to fall alone; recognized the absurdity of this sage advice to the poor little mite, and found time in the midst of her ministrations to seize and soundly cuff the dog, that, stimulated by his conspicuous success, was obviously bent on frightening his victims into convulsions.

The astonished dog, with a howl of remonstrance, started indignantly down the street, as Gabrielle, with heightened color, hastened smilingly back to the carriage.

"Why, there is Mousey! And the angel is without his collar! Mousey, Mousey, love, come to your Mumsey!" But the black, satanic eyes gave her a glance of scorn, and the small, yellow object trotted determinedly past the carriage.

"Follow him! Follow him instantly, Leible," commanded the excited countess. The portly servant descended from the box, gloom on his features and wrath in his heart. He was so large, Mousey was so small! And to follow the dog, pattering along just beyond reach, down through busy, crowded streets, to endure the ignominy of having Mousey turn and grin derisively at him, then frisk on, snapping at his betters and barely escaping horse's heels and carriage-

wheels, was odious to him.   His sense of dignity suffered; he lost his patience with his breath; moreover,
he knew well that if the idol were not restored safe
and sound to his devotee, Johann Leible's services
would no longer be required at the villa.   To-day
Mousey felt unusually insulted, his wind seemed in
fair condition, and vindictiveness lent him speed.
Leible foresaw that the chase would be long and har-
rowing.   He tried to look unconscious of the scampering little fiend in front, and assumed his best air
of respectable-family-servant out on some appropriate
errand, but his anxious eyes never lost sight of the
elusive quadruped.

"I could stand it," he thought, stopping to take
breath, remove his hat, and wipe his forehead, —
"I could stand it better if the little devil would n't
look round and laugh!"

Gabrielle watched the little girl tugging bravely
at her heavy load, but looking back with wistful eyes
at the place of delight and peril.   With heightened
color and the amused smile she had given the children
still lingering, she glanced up at the house as she
returned to the carriage.   Some of the men were
looking down.   A carver had turned from a massive
head and met her gaze.   He wore a whitish-gray flat
paper cap, and had a long, curling beard like the pictures of Jove, she noticed.

"Old putty-face seems to have got some common-
sense to go out driving with her to-day," commented
one of the beings at whom Adelheid, Countess of
Kronfels, never looked except with unseeing eyes, and
a conviction that their plebeian lime and bricks, and
wood and stone, and hammers and saws and chisels
existed purely for her discomfort.

"Oh, what an excitement! Oh, my poor nerves!" groaned the countess.

"They are not hurt," Gabrielle returned, innocently. "Poor little dumplings, they haven't any equilibrium. Of course they tip over. It is such a pity that there is nobody to take care of poor children."

"Dirty little wretches! What business had they to frighten him?"

"Him! Whom? That dog? Why, he frightened them! Did you not see? But I took care to "—

"Dear friend," and the potent sweetness of the Frau Major's voice fell like a heavy curtain over indiscreet revelations, "do take some sal volatile at once. Do try to be calm. Dear little Mousey will come to no harm. Faithful Leible is with him."

"Is that little scrub her Mousey?" Gabrielle was about to ask, but again the suave voice interposed.

"Without his collar or his bell!" the countess exclaimed. "At the mercy of everybody! Sweet little unprotected lamb! Babette shall answer for this."

A couple of frightened maids stood at the house-door.

"Babette," demanded the countess in what the servants called her "awful voice," "what does this mean?"

"Indeed, it was not my fault," pleaded the girl, "Mousey wouldn't look at his collar, and he took off his bell himself. He was in such a terrible temper! I mean he was missing the gracious countess so hard," she added adroitly, "and he slipped out sly, when he heard the carriage coming a long way off."

"The dear thing!" exclaimed the countess. "You should see his welcome, when I have been driving and he has preferred to remain at home. Such joy!

Such rapture! All the way down the stairs he leaps and cries in a kind of ecstasy! It is really pathetic."

The first maid dropped her eyes that she might not meet the glance of the second maid, for it was an open secret in the servants' quarters that Babette pinched and squeezed and shook Mousey to excite him to the desired degree of rapture, as she hurried down stairs with him in her arms.

"I do not understand how it could have happened. I am so distressed. She gave me palpitation when she jumped from the carriage, and I shall not have a moment's peace until my sweet pet is safe. That stupid Leible has no attraction for him whatever. He will go far beyond his strength. She did not startle him, did she? He is so sensitive! What did she do? I did not see what happened," she said irritably.

"Let us talk of it when you feel stronger, dear. Let me come in with you now," cooed the Frau Major. "You are so weary and unnerved! And our dear young friend here — could I give any order," she murmured, "after the long journey" —

Gabrielle, scarcely beyond the threshold of the strange house, stood as silent and unnoticed as the marble pillar behind her. Her lips were compressed, her face was a little haughty, and the want of welcome made her heart ache.

"Oh dear, yes," returned the countess absently. "Röschen can show her her room, and bring her some tea or something. I must go and lie down, or I shall faint."

"Dear child," said the Frau Major, coming forward as the countess retired and pressing Gabrielle's hands warmly and looking pleadingly into her eyes, "the countess took such pleasure in preparing your room — as if for a dear daughter. Röschen will make you quite comfortable, and I know you will soon feel at home. It is unfortunate, this excitement; it makes her so ill — she has so much heart — and the little dog is like a child to her, and " —

"Oh thanks, I shall do very well," Gabrielle answered gratefully. " Please do not be troubled about me. You are very good ; of course I understand."

"I must go to her. She is so very nervous. She is ill with anxiety. I am sure you will be very happy in your new home, though the beginning is a little agitated," and she smiled lovingly and held the young girl's hands again in her warm, comforting pressure.

The countess had disappeared without another glance at her young guest. The longed-for ideal, over which she had wept but a few hours previous, was forgotten, and her whole being was concentrated upon that little yellow animal pattering onward, ever onward, down toward the wicked city, with the luckless Leible swearing and perspiring in pursuit.

CHAPTER V.

GABRIELLE, having been treated as thin air, was relieved to find herself beyond the reach of the dog agitation, in an attractive corner-room with long windows opening upon small, semicircular balconies, which commanded the garden, the city in the valley, and hills far and near. She stood motionless after the maid closed the door, scarcely knew whether to yield to tears or laughter, compromised with a long sigh, threw open a casement, and stepped out on a balcony. The shadows of early twilight were stealing fast over the valley. She looked thoughtfully on the new landscape which for an indefinite time was to be a part of her life, and saw simultaneously the home-scenes — grove, field, and stream ; the poplar-marked white country road ; and the flat village with its overhanging, irregular red roofs. The lawlessness of thought led her to dwell more upon the absurdity of her entrance, than to reflect seriously upon her future, or even to yield herself to tender reminiscences of the father from whom she had but yesterday parted. The soft-skinned, hard-featured old lady with the coquettish Paris bonnet, jumping from German to French and back again with apparent unconsciousness, smiling winningly one instant, glancing about with shifting, uneasy eyes the next, uttering sense and nonsense in one breath, who had not thus far had a good word to say for a fellow-mortal, and who was madly infatuated with an extremely ugly and plebeian dog, seemed to the young girl an astounding and incomprehensible figure.

"She is old," she reflected, drawing off her gloves.
" I must not judge. I always jump at conclusions.
I have lost my bearings. To-morrow, perhaps, it will
all seem quite different." Yet, endeavor as she would
to be charitable, she felt guiltily confident that the
remembrance of Mousey's irate expression, as he trotted off, and of the countess's tragic and wrathful fore-
bodings would always have power to rouse her irrever-
ent mirth.

The maid presently returned with some sandwiches
and wine proffered by the Frau Major's hospitality.

As Gabrielle came from the balcony, the girl hastened to close the casement.

" The draught," she said.

" I like it," Gabrielle answered carelessly.

" The countess thinks it is sure death," Röschen
announced, with a giggle.

Gabrielle had been reared in blessed ignorance of
the fatal animosity lurking in draughts and neighbor's
opinions ; those two powerful factors in the education
of girls.

" The countess is neither young nor strong," she
said gravely and reopened the casement.

" If you please," began the maid, " the Frau Major
thinks it might be pleasanter for the gracious fräulein
to have a cosy little dinner up here instead of dining
alone down-stairs. The countess is in such a state of
nerves, that dinner's no object to her. She's going
to have her hysterics if Mousey does n't come back
soon, and the Frau Major thought the gracious fräulein would feel lonely in the dining-room."

" She is very kind," Gabrielle returned thoughtfully. She had had a glimpse, as she passed through
the hall, of a room dark with much carved oak, of a

row of tall painted chair-backs, stained glass, and a
general aspect of dusky solemnity, like a Gothic choir.
" It would be rather dreadful down there all alone,"
she thought.

" And any way there is n't going to be any dinner,"
Röschen communicated further, "for the butler is chas-
ing the dog, and they 've countermanded the cook's
orders, and the countess vows she never will eat again
until Mousey comes back, and Babette has put her into
her wrapper, and the Frau Major is giving her sal volatile and trying to cheer her, and I am to bring up
the gracious fräulein's dinner at seven."

" Then I simply have no choice.   It 's a species of
genteel solitary confinement," Gabrielle perceived, not
without indignation.   Where was the loving welcome
promised ? , Apparently only in the countess's fluent
and affectionate letters.   Gabrielle considered the wisdom of instant flight.   What if she should steal out
in the twilight and order somebody to take her and
her trunk to the station?   But no!   That would be
an ignominious step, simply because a poor old lady
was unhappy about her dog.

" And I am to wish the gracious fräulein good-night
and pleasant dreams in her new home."

" From the countess ? " Gabrielle asked, cheerily
confident that this message must have come from her
hostess.

" No, the Frau Major," Röschen answered, with her
giggle.

" Then thank the Frau Major for me," Gabrielle
said gravely, " and wish both ladies good-night."

" Oh, I rather think I 'd better not.   Because,"
continued the maid, in response to Gabrielle's look of
inquiry, " because I 'm not to go in there again, unless

I 'm rung for. Sometimes I laugh," and again the vapid involuntary giggle escaped.

" Oh," rejoined Gabrielle, endeavoring not to look amused, " that is another thing."

" Babette told me to keep out. And I 'm to help the gracious fräulein unpack. And I 'm to wait on the gracious fräulein when I 'm not needed elsewhere. But sometimes the countess needs us all. And then forty would n't be enough."

" I don't require much service, thanks. But you may help me this evening, when they send up my trunks."

" They would have come up at once if Leible was n't off with the dog. When Mousey has a tantrum, the whole house is in a muddle."

Gabrielle sat before her plate of sandwiches, her hat not yet removed. She thought this was a rather bold and loquacious young woman, but did not wonder at the mischief in her eyes when she alluded to Mousey.

The maid stood near the table, watching her intently.

" What shall I call you ? " Gabrielle asked pleasantly.

" Röschen. I am the baker's Röschen from Leslach," the girl said with a conscious sir.

" Indeed," returned the young baroness civilly.

Röschen's bold curious stare greedily followed every movement of the stranger. Gabrielle glanced at her from time to time, somewhat surprised at the pertinacity of the inspection.

" What does she see in me ? " She observed Röschen's well-grown form, her fresh color, her heavy braids neither blonde nor brown, her clear brown eyes, and suddenly, with an odd feeling of amazement, comprehended the cause of the unblushing scrutiny.

" She is really not unlike me, and she perceives it. We have about the same height, the same coloring, and I should say the same age."

The maid did perceive the resemblance, and was making minute comparisons, all in her own favor. " I 'm a good deal more of a girl," she told herself proudly. " I 've got more hair, and it 's curlier. I 've got more figure and redder cheeks, and a more taking way with me. But she 's pretty, — oh, yes, she 's pretty," Röschen admitted magnanimously. " My hand would make two of hers," she thought with a pang of envy. " And the color of mine is n't right. If I could get some of that salve, or cream, or whatever it is the countess uses " — and her meditations ran ambitiously on in pleasing visions of a beautified Röschen, her one fault — coarse hands — magically corrected ; envied by the girls, observed of all men, smiled at approvingly by the beautiful young officers who rode past the garden, and came now and then to pay their respects to the countess and inquire after Count Hugo, when she — oh, bliss ! — sometimes succeeded in opening the door instead of old Leible, who happily was slow in his motions as well as addicted to napping whenever he felt that the countess's frantic bell was not imminent.

Indulging in such ecstatic reveries, her large rough hands folded across her white apron, her gaze pursued Gabrielle as she rose, went to the window, took off her jacket and hat, opened her travelling-bag, and found her portfolio and ink-stand.

" This grows irksome," the baroness admitted.

" And since the power of the human eye belongs to
the occult sciences, I don't know what will happen to
me if she continues. I suppose a fool could make a
wise man uneasy if he looked at him long enough.
Not that I am wise."

" You may go, Röschen," she said kindly. " I will
rest and write a little."

The maid longed to continue her complacent study
of resemblances, contrasts, and possibilities. She had
always known that she was a beauty and not like the
other girls, but she had not suspected that she was
like a baroness. What would Bernhard, with his dull
notions, say to that? Well, it was the simple truth.
He could see for himself. Seamstress and second
maid in the villa — well, she did not say it was not a
good position, and easy, — but there was no doubt
about it she could look higher; and as for Bernhard
— well, he was good-natured, but things were n't settled for ever and ever yet, and nobody could tell
what might happen.

Röschen was honestly glad, too, to have another
young thing in the dull house. One could scarcely
open one's lips in the presence of the countess, she
was that crushing. And as for Count Hugo, he was
like a man buried alive. Nobody could catch sight of
him, except now and then a pair of big eyes, — like
a wild animal under a bush, or something. Herr
Lipps would not let the king so much as bid his master good-morning, if he wanted to be let alone, which
he mostly did.

Therefore Röschen lit the gas, adjusted the shades,
and reluctantly withdrew, resolving to beg the cook to
hurry with the dinner, that she might return legiti-
mately to the rose-room, and see what kind of a ward-

robe the new young lady had. For who knew when the coast would be so clear again, with the countess conveniently having her "nerves," and a body free from reprimands from superior officers, like Babette and Leible?

Gabrielle began to write rapidly. Her affection, her talk of home, her journey, her impressions of the city, all this wrote itself eagerly. But when she found herself saying: "The countess is a very handsome old lady. I am not dining with her this evening, because she is distressed about her little dog that has run away," although the facts seemed to be indisputable, she tore off the half-sheet with a doubtful smile, thinking: "Why, it sounds positively malicious," and began again: —

"The countess is very handsome, and a little uncertain in her ways, perhaps. She is not quite well this evening, having lost her little dog. My room is very pretty, with rose-colored walls and hangings, and a lovely view of the city and over the hills. The Frau Major is a most winning person, with a fascinating voice. She seems to have great influence in this house."

Again she hesitated. Her habit of unreserved expression of her ideas and feelings to her father was already restrained by one day's new influences.

"Why do I write trifling things like a village gossip?" she asked herself reproachfully. "Why do I harp upon that absurd dog? How do I know how much or how little influence the Frau Major has in this house?"

She shook her head and destroyed the page. Once more she wrote, and with a certain desperation: —

"Do not expect me to give you my impressions,

dearest papa, for they are too confused and worthless. I am in a completely new world, and must learn its ways. All that I do, all that I think, you shall know sometime. But this first evening I feel so inexperienced and ignorant, that I suspect if I find things queer, it is the fault of my own spectacles. Be happy about me, for I am safe and cheerful, except when I think too long of you! And I am interested in my coming experiences. I suppose one must have something which may be called experiences, even if one lives in a cave, which I emphatically do not, as you would agree if you could see my rose-walls and my balconies, from which I can see so far — so far — almost to you I thought just now, and then suddenly realized that I was gazing longingly due south, where you are not. You know, dearest, I am not trying to be prudent or guarded. I could not think of such a thing! I really do not know what to tell you, because everything is quite different from what we expected. The countess is not like her letter — no, not in the least. She is handsome, — her eyes are uneasy, — she kissed me on both cheeks, — and she speaks beautiful French. Her friend, the Frau Major von Funnel, who remembers you so pleasantly, has won my heart. She is a distinguished looking woman, with a wonderful voice that holds one in bondage. I cannot escape from it. You must not think I am lonely if I speak of the strangeness here, and tell you that I am alone this evening. For since my arrival, the countess has been very nervous and excited on account of her little dog that she idolizes. There, papa, I have tried to keep that little beast out of this letter, but he will pop up unexpectedly, so I might as well introduce him to you. Frankly, you would not look at him. So

far as I can judge from an extremely brief acquaintance, he is an unmitigated cur! But the poor countess adores him, and is wild with grief because he has
run away.

" Count Hugo, it seems, is very unhappy and lives
a most secluded life. His rooms are just below mine,
the maid told me. As I write, I am so sorry for him,
and picture him in his great loneliness. You and
I were not much of a family, papa, but what there
was of us was always together. Here, the countess
is at one end of the house, I am at the other, and the
poor count is in his corner below. Of course it is
merely an accident that I am to dine alone to-night,
and my constant inclination to talk about it — as if it
mattered — is a proof that I am puffed up with an idea
of my own importance. Never mind! You will forgive me, because I am your child, and it was you that
spoiled me. When you come home from Japan — oh,
papa, it sounds so long! it sounds so far! — I shall
have learned humility, and other graces — perhaps!

" By the way, the young woman detailed for my service looks astonishingly like me, except she 's handsome and imposing. You will say it is my nonsense,
but indeed, papa, it is quite true. It may be a blow
to your pride, for you have always thought too well
of me, but I am calm and reconciled. There is a veritable resemblance, not perhaps in expression, and I
venture to trust not in manner, but we are somewhat
the same kind of girl. I was startled, she looked
so familiar. 'Where have I seen you?' I vaguely
wondered. Then suddenly I perceived that she reminded me of Gabrielle Dohna. We stared at each
other like the snake at the Zoölogical Gardens and
his predestined fattened rabbit. That is, I inwardly

blamed the girl for staring; but I must have been staring too, or I would not have known that she stared. I sent her away, for which my conscience reproaches me. She did so enjoy gloating over me, it was cruel to disturb her. But I hear her now, coming with a tray and glasses that rattle. She has knocked. Papa, she cannot keep her eyes off me! While she sets my little table for dinner she is eying me, and longs to speak, but does not dare. She is a very communicative maiden. Papa, if I were the baker's Röschen, and she were your Gabrielle, I ask you, would I be like that? For instance, would I be so inquisitive? Would I giggle so easily? Suppose we'd been changed in our cradles. Imagine the two of us unpacking and arranging my possessions this evening. Imagine me philosophizing in boundless fields. It is really an extraordinary experience. It is very curious to meet your other self. Of course it makes one think. Is it true that one never sees one's real self in the glass?

" Röschen's hair curls tight, where mine only tries to wave. My color is rustic enough, but hers is carnation. She is the freshest, heartiest, most wholesome-looking girl, full of life and strength and bloom, and smiling at one like a great simple child. She is a thousand times better-looking than I, yet the resemblance is there. My anatomy may be a trifle finer. How vanity will assert itself! Yet I am compelled to admit that her flesh is handsomer than mine, and in revenge I take refuge in my bones. Which means that my '*attaches*' are smaller. Am I chattering too long about her? Forgive me. She is such a surprise.

" She has told me the news which she was longing

to announce ten minutes ago. The prodigal dog has returned and the countess is weeping over him. The Frau Major has gone home. Nobody expects anything of me whatever. Nobody shall be disappointed. I will stay here and eat my sequestered dinner.

"A knock. Babette brings me a card on a salver.

"'God bless you, my sweet child! Rest well in your new nest. Pardon my seclusion this evening. My agitation was inexpressible. You will rejoice with me that my Precious has returned. Good-night, and sweetest dreams.'

"There, papa! What more can the heart desire? Is n't it all that is kind? Is it not like the letters she wrote to Dohna? Only don't show it to Lucie, for she will laugh. And I — I am trying not to! Give my love to Lucie — no, not my love — give her my thoughts; tell her I think of her. And she must make you happy, very, very happy; yet not so happy that you will forget the old days, and your child who loves you."

CHAPTER VI.

HUGO heard the carriage drive up to the door, bringing Gabrielle. He imagined her entering the house amid kisses and embraces and voluble gushes of sentimentality. His face grew a trifle more unamiable, and he mechanically read and re-read the same sentence repeatedly. Lipps, evidently bursting with information, wished to communicate something when he brought in the count's dinner; but Hugo's forbidding expression nipped his revelations in the bud.

Lipps had discreetly chosen the moment of the stranger's arrival to store away a package of Hugo's superfluous effects in the tower-room, which lofty post of observation commanded the garden, the drive, the houses building, and a good portion of the street.

Lipps had been seriously opposed to Gabrielle's advent. To the best of his ability, he had worn upon his pink, full-moon countenance the cold and distant expression which he had observed upon his master's pale features. Not a word in regard to the young stranger had passed the count's lips in his servant's presence, therefore he too was sternly silent in the servants' dining-room.

Why the count looked so gloomy about her, Lipps was at a loss to imagine. It was enough for him that proud reserve was indicated as the attitude of " our wing," as Lipps called Count Hugo's rooms, and the man's efforts to be impressive wherever he moved that day were at least admirably conscientious.

Having deposited his convenient package in the
store-room, he took his place at the window and
watched the carriage approach, preparing to extend
to the new-comer the same unflinching antagonism
which he cherished for the countess. His hatred may
not have been sufficiently intense for a tragic villain,
— happily great hate is even rarer than great love, —
but it was the strongest emotion of the kind that his
honest soul could produce, and such as it was he gave
it lavishly. But when he saw the new young lady
spring out of the carriage as quick as a flash, pick
up and straighten down those unfortunate convoluted
babies, and cuff Mousey vigorously, not once, nor
twice, but three times, he gave his simple allegiance
then and forever to Gabrielle von Dohna, and in the
security of his lofty ambush, relieved his feelings in a
series of hearty slaps of his person, and lively gyra-
tions, sufficient to compensate for a month's aristocratic repression, downstairs. To be sure, he reasoned, those bricks and timbers may have concealed
the deed from the countess, for the young lady was
kneeling — *kneeling* quite unconcerned in all that
rubbish; still to cuff Mousey by daylight, in the
face and eyes of the countess and the universe, was
a mighty plucky performance. It seemed to him
indeed nothing less than heroism. Unpoetically and
with queer grins of reminiscence he told himself, in
substance: "*Mon âme a son secret, ma vie a son
mystère,*" and all the more he honored the daring
young spirit that dispensed with secrets and mysteries, and cuffed openly with splendid promptness. "I
must tell Count Hugo just how she did it. I must
show him how the pretty lady set up those young
things on their legs and hit out at the little beast."

But in the presence of the pale, silent, outstretched man, Lipps found no chance to speak.

The countess had many theories with regard to servants and the best methods of treating them.

" I am never familiar with them," she would often say. " Familiarity is the greatest mistake. They have not our education, they have not our souls. Kindness and indulgence, so far as possible, but no familiarity."

Meanwhile Babette knew every weakness of her heart as every secret of her toilette, and in certain relaxed, hair-brushing moments not only listened to peppered stories of noble friends, family jars, and scandals, but proffered in return her own equally spicy narratives of more humble, yet not less human circles.

Hugo, on the contrary, was sadly destitute of dignified theories as to his demeanor toward social inferiors, and had he been asked if he were familiar with Lipps would have said that it was very good of Lipps to be willing to be familiar with him, since the man was not compelled to submit to the caprices of a cross-grained invalid, but could keep a beer-shop, or be a street-car conductor, or seek independence and peace of mind in some other congenial vocation. Yet all the same, when Count Hugo wore a certain expression, Lipps dared not speak.

To-night he stepped softly to and fro, lighting lamps, adjusting shades, always casting furtive troubled glances at the invalid. Hugo shivered slightly. The man instantly laid another rug over the count's feet, and lighted the fire on the hearth, again examining the windows and drawing the heavy curtains closer. It seemed to him that the hollow circles under the count's eyes were deeper than usual, but perhaps it was owing to the fall of the light, which also gave a transparent effect to the thin hands holding a Revue des Deux Mondes. When the servant brought the dinner-tray, he saw that the magazine was open at page 255. He stole noiselessly out. Returning in half an hour, he removed the tray, which had scarcely been touched, and as he passed behind his master he slyly glanced at the Revue. Still p. 255. The man's mouth drooped sorrowfully. He came back and stationed himself out of sight and hearing in the dressing-room, where he sat on a stool in the dark, now and then stifling a sigh; motionless, watchful, his eyes fixed on the count's face, stern, white, and strongly lighted in the third room beyond. Lipps listened for the turning of the leaf, but knew too well that p. 255 still urged its right to be read, while the count stared at his ceiling.

Three hours passed. The count summoned his servant.

"Lipps," he said irritably, "I wish you would go out nights and enjoy yourself. What business have you sulking away there in the dark?"

Lipps smiled like an ugly seraph, so content was he to hear his master's voice, and without a word went softly about, making ready for the night. He put the count to bed with the tenderness of a mother to a suffering child, and with marvellous dexterity.

"Let the lamp burn," Hugo said. "And bring me those books. I am not sleepy to-night."

"Nor I either," Lipps returned with a deprecating grin. "It's something in the weather I suppose; I shan't sleep three winks all night, and so if the count would just let me sit there comfortably in the dressing-room " —

" It would be a kind of heavenly enjoyment, I don't doubt," the count broke in hastily. " Lipps, why do you insult me? Have I not passed beyond the need of watchers? And if I should happen to want you in the night, would n't my bell ring in your ears like the last trump? Don't be an idiot."

The man silently brought the lamp, books, a vial and a spoon, then took a final survey of the room.

" Good-night, Lipps," and the count suddenly put out his left hand toward the man. Lipps took it as if he did not know what to do with it, and held it a moment in his limp, loose, awkward grasp, his own fingers straight and unresponsive.

" Thanks for everything," Hugo added, with a smile which illumined his drawn face — old and haggard before its time — with the light of youth and rare sweetness, " and Lipps, you may tell me all about it another day."

Hugo was alone. The house was still. From the rooms above he had during the evening occasionally heard the muffled sound of voices, the opening and closing of casements, and footsteps on the uncarpeted floors. The wood-fire, safely screened, crackled with subdued cheerfulness in his front room. Now and then an old oak armoire gave a portentous creak, and added its tale to the other voices of the night. He looked at his watch. It was nearly twelve. His mother's last pet, Mousey's rival, after her rapturous reception was no doubt sleeping the sleep of health and virtue. " Virtue," he sneered. So far as he knew, lies could sleep as well as truth. Lies could eat and smile and prosper, and live in peace and enjoy the respect of all mankind. What was that? Footsteps? Regular, slow, soft footsteps, from one end to the other of the two rooms above him; the footsteps of a person lost in thought. What then had the chief favorite at his mother's court to consider, in the still watches of the night? After a month he could well imagine her involved in complications that might rob her repose. After three months, be she a wise or a foolish virgin, Heaven help her! But the night of her triumphant début, with kisses and joy-bells and incense still lingering in the air, why should she wander up and down like a restless spirit? He tried to read. Involuntarily he followed that soft, measured tread. He noted when she paused. He knew where she turned. The mirror in her dressing-room defined the northern limit of her course. The window toward the garden bounded it on the south. "If mamma had given her the third room," he thought impatiently as if personally curbed, "she would have longer range."

"Now what is the trouble?" he asked himself. "A happy girl does not walk her cage all night. A happy girl goes to bed and to sleep. So does a sycophant. Is she laying Machiavelian plans? Surely not. It is too soon. And if she is sly she trusts her slyness for inspiration. Is she thinking of home? Why did she leave it, if she loved it? What plans but unworthy ones — at least purely selfish and worldly — could lead her here?"

He pictured her vaguely, — her head drooping, her hands clasped, walking slowly up and down in the stranger's house. Her eyes — well what were they to him? What mattered it whether they were black or blue, since he did not intend to see them?

But would she walk and walk, and think and think, all night? A happy girl would not, and a stupid girl could not. In spite of himself, his heart softened toward her. Perhaps, after all, she had not come to take her part in the man-hunt. She might already have a lover, and the thought of him was banishing sleep from her young eyelids. Lovers indeed! When would a man learn wisdom, according to the gospel of Epictetus! What had a cripple for life to do with girls and lovers? Was he not in enough pain to-night, and weary and sad enough, without any devil-sent speculations on this lost good, to crowd his brain with mocking images and reminiscences? Did Mercedes ever pace her room like this girl overhead? No, her foot would not be so measured, so regular. She would dash up and down wildly, and wear herself out, and weep hot passionate tears, of which she would scrupulously remove every trace before seeing the French embassador. Still the footsteps, — without haste, without rest. It was impossible to resist the magnetic influences descending from the thoughtful brain and overcharged heart of the stranger. Did she call herself unhappy? If she but knew how blessed she was, being able to walk up and down on her own good feet. What is any grief, he thought, if you have the use of your legs?

She had stopped now. She had opened the casement. She was looking out into the night. He saw, with her, the star-lit heavens, the dusky valley, the broad hillside, rearing itself directly opposite her windows. With her he followed the mysterious, vanishing distances. He knew that she was wondering why here and there a light was burning. He knew that she was questioning whether it was for illness,

for birth, for death, for patient study, for revelry, for
sorrow.   Earlier in the evening, hundreds of homes
on the hillslope sent forth across the valley the radi-
ance of their cheerful windows in such a multitude of
lights that one could scarce tell where they ceased to
twinkle along the crown of the hill and where the
stars began.   But it was midnight now, and the sober
folk were mostly asleep, except for the scattered
problematic fires burning on good or evil altars far
away.

She stood long on the balcony, and the night was
cool.   A queer girl, indeed!   Now she was closing
the casement, softly, slowly.   Were his senses less
alert, and all not so still, he would not have heard her.
Would she go to rest now?   No, she was resuming
her gentle, slow walk.   His whole power of attention
concentrated itself upon that lonely figure pacing
the floor above him.   He saw her too, quite clearly,
except she seemed to have no face.   The shadowy
features eluded him.   But that did not trouble him;
it was like the hilltops veiled in mist.   The main
thing was to count her footsteps, and watch her turn
to the right by the window, to the left before the mirror.   His nerves grew tranquil, his thoughts were no
longer bitter.   Listening to the soft monotonous
tread, he ceased to ask himself why the young girl
walked, but only followed her mechanical movement.

It seemed to him of vast importance to count
busily, to know where she turned and make no error
in his computations.   Listening, counting, presently
he ceased to listen and to count, and fell asleep without his drops.

CHAPTER VII.

In the villa-garden were sheltered corners and narrow winding paths, barely wide enough for two abreast, and completely beyond range of the windows, "unless somebody was mean enough to be spying from the tower," Röschen admitted on her first reconnoitring expedition, "and neither the countess nor Count Hugo will ever climb as high as that until they go to heaven, which is one comfort," she concluded cheerfully.

The countess was apt to complain that the box-borders, cedar hedges, and close shrubbery of the old-fashioned labyrinth made it "stuffy," and she frequently threatened to transform it into a plain lawn.

"When I have time, I shall design something myself," she would often say, but as she was always nervously hurried, doing nothing at all, her time for designing lawns never came, and the objectionable mazes remained in all their overgrown and neglected luxuriance, the beckoning suggestive alleys became with every season wilder and more tangled, and the air, laden with the indefinable mixed odors of many sweet and pungent shrubs, more heavily aromatic.

For Röschen's purposes the paths were wide enough. Bernhard Dietz also found their construction faultless. At a tolerably early morning hour, there was a brief but eloquent pause in the work on the houses, and a long line of thirsty masons and joiners, in enforced single file, — their path down the side of the hill being

steep, rude steps between the vineyards, — descended
to a beer-shop for the customary first tankard. Dietz,
waiving this solace, instead of following the blouses
walked off in the opposite direction, and sheltered by
the disorder of his surroundings waited by a certain
thin place in the hedge which separated the sanctity
of the villa-garden from the profane world without.

Within the great house a supernatural stillness prevailed. Doors and windows were stealthily opened,
furniture was coaxingly moved, brooms and dusters
were employed *sotto voce*, big felt shoes bearing anxious mortals slid about on the polished floors, and no
one dared to so much as sneeze with freedom until
the countess's imperious bell announced that she had
deigned to open her eyes once more upon an unworthy
world.

Röschen, seizing her opportunity, would slip out
unobserved, hurry through the court, take a clever cir-
cuitous route round the conventionally handsome garden, and disappear in the unconventional region which
Hugo in his childhood had called "The End of the
World." Here, across the straggling cedar twigs,
Bernhard looked in her eyes, and found there all his
happiness and all his hope; while Röschen looked at
him, and at every other man she could see. The
hedge episode took place every morning. To Dietz
it was like a benediction on his day, and Röschen met
it with more punctuality than she employed toward
her other engagements. She liked the gaze of Bernhard's kind eyes well enough, and then — there were
the other men, and they too had eyes. All men had
eyes, she observed, wherever she passed.

Again, toward evening, when the countess sat en-
throned in the ecclesiastical dining-room, Mousey

reposing on her knee, or snapping sportively at the solemn butler's heels; when she was occupied with the chief event of her day, and the only thing in life, beside Mousey, of perennial interest to her, Röschen knew that no one would think of her for an hour and a half at least. For Babette and the upstairs people had only this respite the whole day long, and were making the most of it, while the cook and the butler and all the lower vassals were at the high-water mark of trepidation and active service. So, in the gloaming, the lovers returned to the trysting-place, and this time Bernhard did not remain upon the cold world's side of the hedge.

The singer was the first to begin, and the last to leave his work. Amid the innumerable sounds from the growing building, his beautiful voice was always carolling like a bird of good omen from his high perch. It was a rare moment when he was silent. Sometimes, indeed, he stopped singing to whistle, and then again, he would stop whistling to sing, and it was hard to say which was busiest all the day, his smile, his chisel, or his song.

An obstinate man was Bernhard Dietz when once he had made up his slow and gentle mind, and there were three questions which he had decided to his own satisfaction for all time.

Strangers driving past him at his work had often stopped to listen to his high pure voice, spoken together with animation, listened again, then requested an interview; and the tall, brown-bearded man, in his grayish-white blouse and whitish-gray paper cap, would answer smilingly, "Well, why not?" make a civil attempt to brush away with his handkerchief some of the stone-dust that liberally powdered his face and hands and hair, and coming down in his deliberate fashion, humming as he came, would join the strangers and tranquilly let them talk. What they had to say he had heard, indeed, scores of times, and he merely smiled at their marvellous tales, and shrugged his shoulders good-humoredly at the mention of fabulous sums which he could earn upon the stage.

" I have learned my trade," he would at length reply in his exasperatingly beautiful tenor and with the simplicity of a child, " and years and trouble enough it has cost me, and now I am going to stick to it. A voice? Every man 's got a voice, if he will open his mouth and let it out. Me strutting before the footlights in velvet breeches? I 'm obliged to you, sir. I could never learn those tricks, if I died. No, sir ; I 'll carve for pay, and I 'll sing for nothing. That is the way I 'm built." They left him as they found him, gentle, imperturbable, and deaf to their eloquence. Since money did not tempt his contented soul, they pronounced him stupid, and lamented nature's inscrutable irony in endowing so dull and grovelling a spirit with a voice of rare power and sweetness, and with the stature of a Siegfried.

Meanwhile Dietz was first tenor in a men's chorus, that shouted lustily and quaffed gallons of beer every Saturday night in the inn known as the "Ox," in Leslach. Often, too, Sunday evening Bernhard paid his forty pfennings for a seat in the fifth gallery at the opera. As he was born to whistle and sing everything he had ever heard, and as he had heard almost everything worth hearing, his carving grew to the sound of choice and classic melodies, his mammoth goddesses wore a contented air, and his fruits looked big and healthy like himself.

Another of his obstinate convictions was that life is worth living. His friend Peter lost no opportunity to advance the contrary opinion. Peter was a beetle-browed stone-mason with a long, pointed nose. He sang bass in the chorus at the Ox. The two had known each other as boys, lived in the same street, often returned from the day's work together, and preserved that species of intimacy, so hard to define, which never was and never could be friendship, yet kindly in the main, and through force of habit a distinct part of their lives.

While those handsome stone houses were building, Peter proved incontrovertibly and many times, that no man alive had any right to be rich enough to build them. He preached equality and abolition of power, and division of property, and poured forth various advanced theories upon Bernhard, who, for the most part silent and with smiling eyes, would neither lose his temper nor be enlightened.

But one rainy noon, when Röschen had declined the rendezvous, and Peter had come up to stare wrathfully at the last goddess's ringlets, and to declare in her very presence that she had no right to exist, Bernhard, after appeasing her for the *spretæ injuria formæ* by singing a charming low love-song to her as he chipped at her Olympian ear, turned, put down his chisel, listened a moment to the rain-drops falling hard upon the canvas stretched above him, and then, to the grumbler's secret surprise, replied to his last tirade.

" Why not? " he began placidly. " Why should he not build it? Why should n't he have carving on it if he likes? Where would you and I be to-day, if no one was rich enough to build houses, Peter? "

"That is n't the question."

"It 's my question, and my question is as good as another man's," Dietz said with his slow, gentle intonation.

"It 's the general question of freedom and justice," Peter returned grandly.

Bernhard looked at him smilingly and whistled between his teeth.

"In America it 's different. All men are equal there. America is the land of liberty."

"Oh, I suppose there are n't any rich men there who build houses and hire stone-masons."

"It 's the principles," Peter said vaguely, "the principles are different."

"Why not? But they 're human over there? They can't fly yet? Why, man, it 's all one thing. If there had n't been any Europe, there would n't be any America. There 's good and bad there as here. It 's a pretty sensible country, so far as I know, — but I 've no wish to emigrate. England is a pretty sensible country too," he added, "but it suits me here."

"Well, it does n't suit me, and when I get the chance I 'm going to America."

"I don't think you will like it much better."

"Perhaps I shall not. But I want to breathe free air once in my life," Peter replied irascibly. "If there is any liberty, I want some."

"Liberty!" repeated Bernhard, softly. "No man anywhere has more than the liberty of doing his duty."

"I deny the rights of kings," Peter exclaimed fiercely. "I deny the privileges of birth and inheritance. I deny" —

" Deny — for all of me. As far as I see, somebody has got to rule, and I 'd rather be ruled over by a decent kind of king who 's tried to learn his trade than by a mob of hot-headed fellows like you."

"The voice of the people " — began Peter.

"Yes, yes, I hear a great deal of talk about that voice. I don't think much of it myself," Bernhard rejoined thoughtfully. " Sometimes it shouts right and sometimes wrong. Once it shouted ' Crucify him ! ' And though I don't pretend to know much history, it seems to me it has been mostly cruel ever since ; as cruel as — kings."

"You talk so old-fashioned, Dietz," Peter said contemptuously. "You ought to come with me and hear some speeches."

" I don't think I 'd find anything new in them either. Envy and murder are as old as Cain and Abel."

" You can't smile away the oppression and injustice and suffering," Peter cried angrily, "and hard work and poor pay and no chance ! "

" I 'm not denying there is great wrong in the world, and great unevenness — some too high and some too low. But the ones that are down and trampled upon, why do they want to turn things topsy-turvy and get on top ? To help ? To show the right way of doing things because they have suffered from the wrong ? Not a bit of it ! To trample in their turn. And that 's why I say sneaking about with dynamite bombs in your pocket and blowing up kings and churches and bridges and women and little children is mighty mean business in the first place, and in the second, it is n't going to change things. The heart of things is always the same." Turning his calm, ruminating gaze from Peter toward the city and the encircling heights, " There will always be differences," he said, with a slow, sweeping gesture, " there will always be hills and valleys. That 's nature."

"Nature be hanged," said Peter, turning his back on the wet, gray landscape, and relighting his pipe. " A man 's well, that 's nature ; a man 's sick, that 's nature ; he 's dead, that 's nature too. You call in a doctor to cure him — is that nature ? "

Bernhard nodded.

" Yes, that 's nature," he admitted.

"You see, nature is anything you like. Well," Peter went on with a grim smile, " there is something we mean to cure. There is a bad kind of disease that needs doctoring. We are going to doctor it. That 's all."

Dietz folded his arms, leaned against the window-frame, and continued to stare far down the valley, with the peculiar mildness of expression which Peter found more irritating than the most quarrelsome retort of another man.

After a moment, he began again, abruptly glaring at the offending goddess above Dietz's head, —

"Look at the man that 's building these houses. He 's piling up his millions. He does n't know what to do with his money. He builds houses because he can't think of anything else to do. He is a hard man, a close man, — hard as flint. Why should he hoard, and we work and pinch? Answer me that."

" See here, Peter, I earn more money than you, don't I? — because carving pays better than masonry. Is that any reason why you should hate me, and come in the night and smash my goddess here, and steal my wallet? Well, the man that 's building this house

earns more money than either of us. I don't care
how. He's got it, and it's his."

Peter interrupted impatiently, but Bernhard went
on : "No, Peter, you have been talking at me for
months. Now it's my turn. I 'll tell you once for
all how I look at these things, and then — we 'll have
a rest. I say the man has a right to his own. But
suppose you kill him, and take his money? And suppose there is n't any law to punish you — you fellows
want to abolish the law, too, with the other things;
well, you would have the money instead of his having
it. That is all the difference I see. For there is one
thing sure. If you had a fortune, you would not talk
so loud about division of property. Perhaps there is
a poor man," Dietz added, meditatively, "who, if he
should inherit a fortune this minute, would distribute
it before sundown. When I see him do it, I 'll believe in him."

"It 's no use beating about the bush. No man has
a right to pile up money and crush down other people.
No man has a right to live in luxury, and let people
starve around him."

"It does seem as if it would help along if they 'd
use in good ways what they can't eat or enjoy or use
sensibly for themselves; but it is a hard question,
Peter, and better men than you and I are working at
it. All I have to say is, cursing and killing will never
do any good; but perhaps sometime the clever heads
will think out a way to help. If each man would do
his own work, and mind his own business, and have a
friendly thought for his neighbor, that would be all
the revolution the world needs, and I take it we 'd be
vastly astonished at the change," Bernhard added,
with a pleasant laugh.

"There's another kind of change coming," Peter muttered. "Put your ear to the ground and you can hear it gathering."

"Well, it won't change the heart of things," Bernhard rejoined tranquilly. "And it won't succeed, because it will find too many men ready to fight for peace."

"There are times when a man with any spirit in him must rebel. Let cows chew their cuds and be content."

"Thank you, Peter, thank you kindly," Dietz said, with aggravating good-humor, "but let me tell you it isn't always the spirit in a man that makes him want to fight, instead of chewing his cud like an honest cow, — sometimes it's liver. When a man's liver's wrong, he always wants to meddle. Look at yourself, Peter. Look at your long, bilious, yellow, discontented nose; you'd better take care, or you'll follow it to a bad end. Sometimes I think if the Lord's made any mistake, it's in creating too much liver."

"That's foolish talk," Peter replied, with a reluctant smile.

"But there's something in it," Bernhard persisted. "Look at Russia. There's a deal of liver in Russia."

"You needn't look so far," retorted the other doggedly. "Look at home. Look everywhere. Look and listen. It's rising. It's coming. And then the brothers of the poor and the crushed will stand shoulder to shoulder."

"Peter," Bernhard began gravely, "I believe you are better than your talk. You don't mean all that you say. I would do as much for a man in need as any of your 'brothers,' and you know it. But I have no faith in your leagues and devil's fermenting-pots.

And you 'brothers' don't hang together, either. When Johann had his fever, and couldn't pay his rent, or his life insurance, and there were the four young ones, and a baby a few days old, what did I hear you say, but that it served him right for his tippling? And when he had knocked at the doors of all his relatives and friends, and at last the Lord above put it into the heart of a stranger, — a rich stranger, mind you! — to lend him the money, were you glad? No, Peter, you were not. You said that the stranger was a fool and would never see a kreutzer of it again, but since he had it to give, he would never miss it; so the giving was no virtue, and trusting Johann no kindness; and Johann was a fool to be married and have such a family at his age, — and everybody got blame and curses all round."

" Oh, come now, Dietz, a man's hasty words have nothing to do with his convictions."

" Well, I think they have, and more than all the hashed-up talk he gets out of bloodthirsty pamphlets."

" It's being down-trodden that hardens a man " —

" You're not starving," Bernhard said dryly. " I notice that all you fellows that are smouldering and ready to break out have your beer pretty regular. I'd forgive a starving man for anything. But I can't abide you others, raving about Labor and Capital as if the poor were all saints and the rich all devils, and plotting to destroy, and all the time hating one another, and envious and grudging and quarrelsome, every man's hand against his brother. Is that the way to help along? Is that the way to make things happier? Do you call that reason? Do you call that progress? I'm obliged to you, Peter," the slow, soft

voice concluded. " I don't want any liberty thrust at
me on the point of a bayonet, or flung at me in dynamite.   A king may be old-fashioned, but I think I 'll
stick to him a little longer."

And Bernhard's socialistic notions progressed not a
whit.   And if he could not be persuaded to grasp his
own advantage and climb a musical ladder toward
fame, or join the underground brotherhood, he was a
thousand times more tranquilly stubborn, more smilingly blind in his attachment to Röschen.

His parents had never liked the girl, his friends wondered — as friends are apt to wonder — what he saw
in her, and everybody knew that he could look higher.
But since his boyhood, when he used to watch the
girls and children filling their pitchers at the old fountain in the middle of the square at Leslach, where the
closely packed, irregular houses, with tumble-down
roofs and steep gables, seemed to lean forward in the
twilight and listen with him to the gossip and laughter of the women, Röschen had been his idol.   She
had a peachy look, and a fresh smile, and a way with
her which he could not resist.   Indeed, he had never
made the faintest effort to resist Röschen, and when
he once took the loving thought of any man or woman
into the stronghold of his kind and loyal heart, he
never again let it go.

" She 's light-minded and spoiled," his old mother
did not hesitate to tell him with many a doleful sigh.
" She has her eye on the men."   To which Bernhard
would respond with a smile of security and infinite
indulgence.

He considered himself rather a travelled man, for
a patron strongly interested in him had once induced
him to go to London, where in spite of an excellent

position and high pay he grew silent and pale, neither
whistled nor sang, and one day announced to his em-
ployer, " I must hurry back."

To entreaties, arguments, and substantial promises,
he listened with an absent look in his eyes, a queer,
shy smile, and the one soft, obstinate answer, " I must
hurry back."

For a deadly home-sickness was consuming him, and
London was but a poor, wretched place without Röschen. If he stayed he could earn more money than at
home, and repay his father for the extra time and
training he had allowed him, as well as certain family debts which he had assumed, and consequently
be sooner free to marry. This consideration tortured
him a whole day, presenting itself in the light of a
possible duty. But before sundown his doubts were
fled. " Money 's not the best thing in the world,
thank God," he reflected cheerfully, " and Röschen
and I are young yet."

And he did " hurry back " to earn less, sing more,
and be happy in his own way. They were to be married in a year now, he hoped, and when, instead of a
gloomy London Sunday with no sweetheart and no
music, he could walk out arm-in-arm with Röschen,
hear music, and see cheerful faces on every side, —
and when in addition to so much bliss, some houses
requiring much carved ornamentation engaged him
weeks in the Heine Strasse, and close to the villa
where Röschen was employed, and he could catch frequent passing glimpses of her, beside having a blessed
little chat over the hedge now and then, — his sunny
spirit was less than ever inclined to remodel a world
so full of gladness and hope.

As for Röschen, she liked to walk out with him

when he wore his Sunday suit, in which he looked rather awkward and ill at ease; but she secretly disliked the long white blouse and paper-cap of weekdays, because they reminded her of the paternal bakery. That a man shaped stone instead of dough was but a small advance in gentility, provided he must still wear that ugly garment. If he were only well-dressed and smiling behind a counter! That would be finer than chipping all day at stones like a common mason. But most of all her mind was always wandering from him and his happy plans to lay its crude admiration at the booted and spurred feet of every military man that strode by.

" Bernhard, I look like a baroness," she announced triumphantly, the evening after Gabrielle's arrival. " I do, really! I look like the new young lady." Her thoughts made wild, confused flights into a realm of unknown splendor. One of the factory girls had told her of a ballet-dancer who married a prince. Well! After that, anything might happen.

" Child, you don't know how you look," the man's tender voice answered in the dusk. " You can't know. But I know, and there is something I am going to do before I die. I am going to make a figure of you. I never did such a thing, but I can—of you! I feel that I can. I see it before me night and day. And I could model you if I were blind, for you 're carved in my heart, Röschen, — carved in my heart." His voice faltered for love of her and for the daring of his thought; but her color did not deepen, her bold gaze never drooped, and her bright, satisfied young smile had nought for him that the whole world might not claim.

CHAPTER VIII.

" I DID N'T even ask him to come down. In fact, I told him he 'd better stay upstairs. There 's an east wind and he 's feeling low."

" Oh," returned Gabrielle surprised and uncertain, " I beg your pardon, but I understood that Count Hugo's rooms were on this floor, under mine. I am sorry he feels so ill."

" Hugo ? " said the mother, with a stare. After a pause, she resumed : " I happen to be speaking of my poor little Mousey. The darling is so sensitive, and I do not feel quite sure whether it is his liver or his lungs. I gave him some nux in the night, some hyoscyamus early this morning, and just now a good dose of aconite. I have great faith in aconite. He looked disgusted when I offered him beef-tea, but I finally prevailed upon him to sip a little barley-water."

It was Gabrielle's first lunch in the cathedral-like dining-room, where the countess had just appeared looking anxious and hurried. Gabrielle had been all the morning at a loss to know what was expected of her. She first awaited a summons from the countess and none came. " Perhaps she expects me to come and bid her good-morning," she thought, and wandered along the corridor toward the countess's rooms, but was intercepted by Babette, who in a civil but energetic whisper warned her off those precincts. Sympathetically imitating the air of stealthy misdemeanor worn by every one in the house at this hour, she crept down the great stairway and met the butler, who was astonished but not ill-pleased at her phenomenal appearance at nine o'clock in the morning. Bewildered as he felt, his genius rose to the occasion. Striding before her in his big felt shoes, with the conspicuous effort of a stage villain, turning now and then and beckoning encouragingly, he opened several doors for her with a practiced manipulation of knobs and a masterly avoidance of creaks, and finally ushered her into a small octagonal library with a blue dome-ceiling, where he panted as if they had just scaled a steep and perilous path, and with an eloquent pantomime — respectful, deprecating, yet insistent — gave her to understand that it would conduce to the general weal if she would remain there.

"Am I in an asylum of deaf-mutes?" thought the young girl, as she was left alone, amused, yet not without a certain sense of wounded dignity. "Last night a prisoner in the southeast upper corner, this morning in the southwest lower corner. Never mind. This is but the beginning. It simply can't go on in this manner. The little library is charming, and perhaps I'd better wait quietly here until somebody sends for me, since wherever I appear I seem to produce as much consternation as an epidemic."

Taking a book from the shelves, she seated herself at a window and read hour after hour, occasionally watching the builders and listening always to Bernhard Dietz, who was interpreting Wagner this morning — now low, now loud; now pausing to scrutinize his work; now whistling with extraordinary perfection of detail, now breaking forth in a great gush of song, tossing the melody back and forth from his whistling-voice to his singing-voice, and as unconscious of effect as a free glad bird.

" A man does good who sings like that," thought Gabrielle, and read patiently until the butler summoned her to lunch.

The countess, with a preoccupied air, kissed her lightly on either cheek. " I hope you rested well, my dear," she said, and without waiting for Gabrielle's reply, added : " We have had a wretched night. Leible, the cook is inexcusably careless. Tell her if she serves this coarse ragoût again, I shall discharge her. I need something to tempt my appetite this morning. Bring me some *paté de foie gras.*"

The anxious butler moved noiselessly to and fro. The countess ate hurriedly, finding fault with, yet devoting herself assiduously to each dish. Gabrielle had never seen any one take lunch so seriously. The atmosphere was so heavy, the countess so dominant and self-engrossed, that the young girl, though quite untrained to timidity, experienced a certain embarrassment and doubt. She ventured a harmless remark, which the countess chose to ignore. Gabrielle colored, and determined to be silent and dignified. But her stiffness produced no more perceptible impression than had her modest attempt at entertainment. It seemed to her that she had lived a century or two at the villa, and was of somewhat less consequence than the sideboard.

At length the countess deigned to look at her as if she were a visible object, and suddenly communicated the fact that she had not asked " him " to come down stairs, and alluded to "his " lowness of mind on account of the east wind.

When the identity of the sufferer had been fully established in Gabrielle's mind, she succeeded in expressing a carelessly benevolent wish for the dog's speedy convalescence, but was unable, in spite of her courteous effort, to concentrate her attention upon his various organs, which the countess with animation and unflinching realism now laid bare for her inspection.

" And Count Hugo ? " she inquired, seizing a fortuitous moment, when the countess discontinued her exposition, in order to extract a delectable bit of truffle from her *paté.* " How is he this morning ? "

" Oh," said the countess, " Hugo is as usual, I presume. There is no especial change from day to day. That could hardly be expected. I have not seen him yet. I make it a rule to go to him always before lunch," she added with a fine air of conscientiousness, " but I was detained this morning, as I have told you." After a moment she added, " There is something so pathetic in his sufferings."

" Ah, yes," murmured Gabrielle with warmth.

" A little, suffering, dumb thing," continued the countess. Gabrielle gave a slight start, and leaned back in her chair. " So innocent, so appealing," — a pretty, meditative smile played over the countess's face. " Nothing touches me like the thought that he cannot tell me where his pain is, and whether it is lungs or liver."

She excavated another truffle.

" I am sure that it is either the one or the other," she remarked with conviction.

Gabrielle had lost her appetite. She watched the countess's large, pale hands moving softly and busily with a splendid flashing of diamonds and sapphires, and began to fancy the hands themselves, independent of the woman behind them, were greedy and insatiable. The long silences and the gloom of the room oppressed her. Rallying, she asked brightly : —

" And when am I to see Count Hugo ? "

The countess put down her knife and fork.

" This is the third time," she said with a mistrustful, jealous expression incomprehensible to Gabrielle, " that you have demanded Hugo. Pray did you come here to be my son's companion or mine ? "

Not the words so much as the positive brutality of accompanying voice and look made Gabrielle feel as if she had received a blow in the face. No one had ever spoken to her in so aggressive and rude a tone. She fixed her eyes upon her hostess with unequivocal hostility.

The countess gave a short nervous laugh.

" Well, you need n't get into a pet about it, need you ? You need not stare so."

Gabrielle lowered her resentful gaze to her own plate, and said nothing.

After a long uncomfortable pause, the older woman laughed uneasily again, and asked : —

" Why are you so anxious to see Hugo ? "

" I am so very sorry for him," returned the young girl, her voice at first low and uncertain. Then looking squarely at the countess, " And I did hope to be more or less a companion to him," she added. " It was my strongest reason for coming here. I longed to do everything in my power for him. And it seems to me a very natural wish on my part," she concluded with composure and a covert challenge.

" He was a great lady-killer, before this happened," the countess informed her, with airy irrelevance. " Not that his estimate of woman was ever what it should have been, I grieve to say," with a sigh suggestive of lofty morality, " and his ideas at present are still worse, — distorted," — she cut a good thick slice of *paté* — " cynical — really quite shocking. And I am afraid, my dear, that you are going to be sadly disappointed," she continued with a malicious mocking air, " for you could not expect me to act against his wishes, poor boy ; and I can scarcely venture to refer to you again, at least not for some time, and you would not wonder, if you had seen how irritated he was yesterday, when I simply announced that you were coming."

" Oh, I certainly do not wish to see him against his will," returned Gabrielle very rapidly and trying to smile. " I shall not insist upon the acquaintance. But he may change his mind. And I am sorry for him all the same," she exclaimed with generous warmth. " I would do anything in the world for him."

" Well, well," said the countess, as if they had been discussing nothing more serious than syllabub, " I must not sit here all day. My little man will be wondering what has become of me, and at three I must drive to the Frau Major's. I should like you to come too, Gabrielle." Rising, she smiled pleasantly on the bewildered girl, and patted her shoulder. " I wish to present my new child to some of my friends. You must call me Aunt Adelheid. Wear a pretty street gown, my dear. Whoever ordered your wardrobe did well. Your travelling suit was perfect. I did not suspect you of so much elegance in your remote wilds."

" Frau von Rahden — that is, Frau von Dohna ordered everything for me in Berlin. I deserve no credit," Gabrielle returned coldly.

" Well, make yourself charming. You will have no difficulty, I am sure. This evening we will go to the opera. It is Carmen. I am a perfect child about Carmen. You know it?"

"No," Gabrielle said gravely, restive under the pressure of the countess's hand on her arm, as they walked through the hall, and wondering at the winning smiles and artless juvenile manner of her polymorphic companion.

"So much the more pleasure for you. As for me, — none feels music as I do. I am most exquisitely sensitive to it. I revel in it. I presume you have n't a conception of my feelings when I am listening to music."

"No," said Gabrielle absently.

The butler was on the alert to see in which direction he should fling open the doors.

The countess stopped, hesitated, sighed, and announced virtuously : —

"I will go in a few moments to my son. He will not thank me, but a mother's duty is sacred, whatever be the son's mood. Gabrielle, if you will dress and come to my rooms a little before three, I will see if Mousey feels like meeting you. He is sensitive to the approach of strangers, and ought not to be excited to-day. But I will ask him if he wishes to see you, and if he says he does I don't think you will do him any harm. On the contrary you might divert him. *Au revoir*, my dear!"

Gabrielle took refuge in her room, sat down, and stared blankly at her rose-colored wall. It was petty to feel so vexed and uncomfortable, she reflected. And if the old lady was impatient, what then? But she was not only impatient. She was startling and unexpected in the extreme. It was difficult to follow her volatile springs, while her disapproval was heavily aggressive and insultingly suspicious, and her direct blows were ponderous as a blacksmith's fist. "And the trouble is, she makes me conscious of myself, and that irritates me. I have never been accustomed to be peering in my own soul-windows all the time, and I don't like it." Yet Gabrielle was ashamed of her condemning spirit, of her flushed cheeks and quickened pulses, and felt inclined to blame herself for some involuntary misconception. "No doubt she is unhappy," she reasoned, "and nervous, and Count Hugo is a trial to her." But she grew more and more confused and uncertain of her own opinions, as were most people who attempted to study the Countess of Kronfels' mercurial idiosyncrasies. Resolving to have patience in any event and wisdom if she could attain to it, she tied her bonnet-strings with unwonted gravity, and vaguely commending herself to all good spirits, went slowly toward the countess's rooms, not precisely timid, but excited and with an unpleasant sense of having lost her ancient landmarks.

Her thoughtfulness, together with the serious effect of her best bonnet, gave her an unusually dignified expression as she joined the countess. That lady sat in an easy-chair near a table, upon which were magazines, newspapers, and a liqueur-stand. She was smoking a cigarette, skimming through her Figaro, and conversing at intervals with the indisposed Mousey, who was stretched upon her knee in a languid and loose attitude, his paws clasped dejectedly over his countenance.

He sprang down, however, and greeted the stranger's entrance with a volley of sharp barks, rushing furiously at and around her, and attacking her skirts and feet with futile snaps. She stood quite still during this paroxysm, congratulating herself that his teeth were few and blunt, and that his worst bite was but a pinch.

"There, there, my pet," said the countess, with an indulgent smile. "It will not hurt him," she explained to Gabrielle; "on the contrary, if he does not become over-excited, this animation will do him good. His lethargy has alarmed me. Come, Mousey, my angel, come and shake hands. Mumsey must go now and put on her bonnet."

But Mousey, who, like his mistress, could usually be relied upon for the unexpected, looked from one to the other with malicious scrutiny, and without more circumstance, turned his back and trotted into his velvet house.

"Mousey does not seem to like me," Gabrielle said demurely.

"He does not know you. He is always reserved with strangers. It is a fine trait, I think. Only shallow natures make friends easily. But you will soon see that he is no ordinary dog."

"No, I already think him a most extraordinary animal," Gabrielle could not resist the temptation to retort.

A long low growl from the velvet house followed her double-faced remark.

"Do you hear? He knows that we are talking of him. Sometimes he does not like it. He is so highly organized, so sensitive to every word and look and tone. You would not believe that I was entertaining him with French politics just now."

"Oh!" ejaculated Gabrielle with a merry laugh, which she tried somewhat ineffectually to repress, perceiving that the countess was quite serious.

"You do not believe it? Wait. You will soon find out whether my blessed Mousey has intellect or what stupid people call instinct. Your gown is very well, Gabrielle. A little serious, perhaps, but it errs on the right side. You must not be forbidding, my dear. Society does not admire that manner in youth. Don't look so earnestly at people. It is unusual. It makes one uncomfortable. You were so tall and still and grave as you entered the room, it was quite appalling. A girl like you ought to be sunny and expansive. Why, when I was your age I had — wings!"

"Indeed," was the frigid reply, and Gabrielle felt that her wings were being clipped closer every instant.

"Amuse yourself a few moments. My bonnet and gloves are self-adjusting. I leave vanity to youth." She rustled into her dressing-room, throwing a kiss to Mousey, whose bright eyes were visible, gleaming from his own portals.

His yellow head now thrust itself across his threshold. He surveyed Gabrielle with unremitting attention. Presently he came out of his retreat and advanced toward her, his shrewd gaze fixed upon her face. He sniffed her gray silk folds, reconnoitred the resting place afforded by her knees, and with a trust in her magnanimity which argued well for his knowledge of human nature, sprang up and took possession of her.

Amused at the comedy he had played, her hand fell naturally upon his little curled-up back. The dog growled and turned his head with a threatening movement.

"Oh, come now, Mousey," she began, looking in his false bright eyes, "if you can't bear my hand, I can't bear you on my knee. If it's a liberty on my

part, it is a greater one on yours, and you may get
down as soon as you like, sir!"

Mousey put his head on one side, cocked his left
eye wickedly at her, and weighed her words. Meanwhile her hand was resting quietly upon his sacred
person. Concluding that she meant what she said,
and finding himself in comfortable quarters, — he had
a special predilection for reclining upon new silk of
good quality, — his weariness relaxed, he drooped his
head, and with a long sigh of satisfaction, went to
sleep.

In spite of the self-adjusting properties of the
countess's attire, Babette and Röschen were minister-
ing to her for some time, with hair-pins, hand mirrors,
powder-puffs, and perfume ; but invariably, it would
appear from the excitement attending her toilet,
they proffered the article undesired at the moment,
and never could learn to anticipate her wish.

"The little love!" she exclaimed rapturously, as
she rejoined Gabrielle. "And you a perfect stranger.
Is not that sweet-tempered? Angel-dog!"

Gabrielle smiled, and her hand, resting on the little
warm body, moved innocently up to his head.

But no sooner did the napping animal perceive the
slight pressure between his ears, than he sprang at her
face like a mad creature, with a succession of angry
snaps.

Gabrielle, startled, pushed him down, and rose.
Had Mousey been a pack of dogs he could scarcely
have attacked the enemy at more points at once, and
uttered a greater number of fiendish yelps.

"But you ought not to have touched his head!"
shrieked the countess. "You ought not! He never
allows it."

The dog was beside himself with rage.

"In old times they would have said he was possessed of a devil," Gabrielle thought, watching him with a certain fascination, as he circled round her, seizing her wherever he could, his black eyes gleaming fiercely, his voice raised in maniacal expostulation.

"Calm thyself, my angel," cried the countess in French. "He will be so fatigued after this. Oh, how could you touch his head! How could you be so unkind!"

She stooped and seized the quivering animal, held him to her cheek and fondled him, her eyes suffused with tears.

"My treasure — my dove. There! there!" and Mousey, exhausted by the violence of his outbreak, suffered her caresses. Breathing stertorously and casting an evil eye at Gabrielle, he was redeposited in his velvet house, where he consented to swallow six globules of aconite. "He is trembling like a leaf. He is most dangerously excited," the countess said testily, wiping her eyes and breathing loud. "Why everybody persists in touching his head I can't imagine."

"But I did not know," protested Gabrielle.

"You have driven him to the very verge of brain fever."

Gabrielle had not found being the object of the infuriated little animal's aggressions a pleasing occupation, and felt disinclined to fall prostrate before the dog, or for the matter of that, before the countess. The whole scene seemed ludicrous to her, and she was determined not to make a tragedy of it.

"But what should one touch, if not a dog's head?"

she replied brightly. "Surely not his tail? Then Mousey has none, to speak of."

This derogatory remark induced a glance of stern reproach from the countess, and a growl of protest from the velvet house.

"I have always believed," began the countess solemnly, "that Mousey was once badly hurt on the head, — in his infancy, perhaps, — and that he remembers the pain, and on that account dreads being touched there."

"Why, that sounds very reasonable," Gabrielle returned cheerfully, "only don't you think he could be taught to be a little less demonstrative? It would really have thrown some women into hysterics, you know ; and then, why did you not tell me ?" she persisted, laughing slightly, and looking at the countess with resolute good humor.

"Oh, I have told people till I am tired. It makes no impression. They always know more about your own dog than you do. They smile and stroke his head in spite of my warning, and Mousey invariably responds with an attack of delirium, poor dear, — poor dear! It is his temperament," she concluded with fatalistic helplessness.

It occurred to Gabrielle that the excess of temperament might have been lessened by a judicious modicum of chastisement. Still smiling she inquired, —

"Does he entertain all your visitors with this animated scene ?"

"If they are so dull as to touch his head, yes," said the countess with a frown.

"What a general favorite he must be ! " returned Gabrielle gayly.

"If you think it good manners to ridicule an old

woman and her only friend, pray continue," said the
countess, white with wrath, and in the deep and surprising bass which, striking one suddenly, had the
effect of a mental sledge-hammer.

Gabrielle felt, indeed, more or less stunned, and
already deplored her vivacity ; yet an instinct of self-
preservation induced her to rise and front the foe,
rather than be at once and forever crushed into noth-
ingness.

She came toward the countess, who stared straight
before her, without a glance at the young girl.

"She is very, very trying," thought Gabrielle,
watching the stony, unpropitious face, and the chest
laboring for breath, " but she is more than sixty years
old and she is not well; she is very uncomfortable, or
she would not lean back and breathe like that."

"Aunt Adelheid," she said for the first time, and
with a queer little cough, as if the words choked her,
" I did not ridicule you. I was laughing at Mousey,
for he is very funny. Why may not one joke about
a dog ? "

No answer. After a long pause, Gabrielle continued with less spirit : —

" I am sorry if I have annoyed you."

No response.

Gabrielle gave a little sigh.

" We were always joking about everything at
home," she said pleadingly.

The countess rose, poured a glassful of curaçoa, and
drank it hastily.

" This unpleasant scene has shaken my nerves," she
said coldly, without a glance at Gabrielle. " I dislike
scenes, and they are very injurious to me. Let us go,
since go we must."

" Why need we go, if you do not feel well enough?" Gabriélle suggested conciliatingly.

" Perhaps you will allow me to arrange my time and engagements for myself," returned the bass voice, followed by a caressing treble, which murmured, " Adieu, sweetheart. Rest well and be comforted."

Gabrielle silently accompanied the heavy rustling figure through the corridor and down the stairway. The butler and maids knew the meaning of that rigid white face.

" She 's been rowing it with the young lady," whispered Röschen, hurrying towards the outer door with wraps. " So much the better for you and me."

" Don't be too sure ! There is always enough row left for us," muttered Babette, advancing the next moment to the coupé with extreme deference, bearing the countess's card-case, visiting-book, vinaigrette, and lorgnon, and depositing them in a carriage-pocket, as tenderly as if they were precious relics.

The countess looked large and forbidding. Gabrielle in her corner tried to make herself as small as possible, and felt like a culprit. As they drove out of the gates, Peter scowled, thinking, " There they go, the idlers, who have nothing to do but enjoy themselves and spend money, curse them ! " While Dietz, who was whistling the Minuet from Don Giovanni, glanced over his shoulder and caught a glimpse of the beautiful young lady, — who was like his Röschen, only different ; and the thought which he sent after the retreating carriage was so purely kind, it resembled a blessing or a prayer.

" Shall I speak? Shall I remain silent?" Gabrielle asked herself. " It is easier to be silent, so perhaps I ought to say something."

" How cheerful and busy the workmen sound," she
began. " I watched them a long time this morning.
It was very interesting. I think I have always taken
a house quite stupidly, as a matter of course, but to-
day I began to respect the work in it, — the patience
and skill."

" I admire the refinement of your tastes," remarked
the countess.

" But don't you think it picturesque, those groups
of busy men, and all the movement and color ? "

" I think it a horror — and an insolence to build in
one's face and eyes."

" Some of them have strong, interesting heads,"
Gabrielle continued.

" I never look to see whether such people have
heads ! "

" Have you not noticed that handsome stone-carver
with the young face and a beard like a patriarch —
and the beautiful voice ? " Gabrielle went on, encouraged to find her attempt at conversation, if not
warmly approved, at least tolerated.

" Do you mean the man that bellows from morning
till night ? "

" Oh, I never heard a voice like his," Gabrielle
exclaimed with enthusiasm, " so strong, so glad and
sweet ! "

" You have never heard much, Gabrielle," returned
the countess freezingly, " but of course if you can
oppose me, you will not lose your opportunity."

The young girl colored indignantly, shrank into her
corner, looked persistently out of the window, and
maintained complete silence until they reached the
Frau Major's.

That exemplary woman sat with a group of satellites

in her pleasant drawing-rooms. Her house was a popular resort of gay young people. One was tolerably certain to meet somebody, or hear something there; and if by chance no pretty girl drifted in, or no lieutenant bent on pleasure, one could never weary of the Frau Major herself, whose gracious hospitality was so cordial, whose dainty tea-cup was présented with a smile of concentrated sweetness born for "you," whose interest in one's pursuits was an important element of her life, whose sympathy with one's tastes was closer than a brother's; who, in short, lived and breathed in one's happiness and success, and looked so distinguished and handsome withal, and spoke in that voice peculiar to her alone of all mortal women, and to certain alluring damsels who once resided upon the island of Caprea.

Several people were gathered about her and her tea-tray: an old colonel who enjoyed young chatter, some quiet maidens who had patiently appeared everywhere for years and were a little tired behind their smiles, and two women whom the Frau Major always classified as "representative people," that is, persons of easy means and conventional deportment. Lorenz von Raven stood in the middle of the room with a cup of black coffee in his hand, and another lieutenant, equally rosy and contented, was providing the Mayer twins with very thin bread and butter. Those special pets of the Frau Major were dressed elaborately, and confusingly alike, since had so much as a ribbon been different, their acquaintances might have hoped to distinguish Fräulein Emma from Fräulein Berta. They talked incessantly and said little, scanned the horizon eagerly, adored the Frau Major and the social avenues which she opened before them,

were as inseparable as love-birds, and sincerely attached to each other, — which trait the Frau Major
accentuated in her laudations, but which Hugo von
Kronfels had once ill-naturedly denominated " self-
love," since, he declared, "nature in a frugal mood
had divided one soul between two beings."

A significant lull in the conversation greeted the
entrance of the countess and the young stranger. The
Frau Major went forward rapidly and met them almost upon the threshold, somewhat after the manner of the fair Elizabeth in Tannhäuser, when beyond
the heads of ordinary courtiers she spies afar some
royal dame, and advances with a certain sweet pre-
cipitation in her graciousness.

CHAPTER IX.

THE Frau Major conveyed her dearest countess to a large arm-chair in the centre of the older group, and with a sweetly protective manner, most soothing to Gabrielle's wounded sensibilities, led her to the young people, presenting her with smiles of perfect benevolence and low subjugating tones.

Von Raven, counting himself lucky to behold a new and pretty face, hastened to offer Gabrielle the cup of tea which the Frau Major prepared for her with tender solicitude, and von Haller, not wishing to be outstripped, followed with sandwiches, cakes, and wafers. The young girls, after inquiring how she liked Wynburg, resumed their conversation, discussing in a high, rapid way topics of which she knew nothing, — the general tenor of their remarks relating to where they had been and where they were going.

" Of course you are going to the French embassador's ball ? " said Fräulein Emma Mayer, her lively black eyes examining every detail of Gabrielle's toilet. " Everybody is going. I am going."

" Of course," echoed Fräulein Berta. " I am going. Everybody is going."

" Certainly we shall go," said the countess benignly from her central throne. " My niece must not miss anything so pleasant." She nodded affectionately at Gabrielle, the pretty little teeth gleaming agreeably, the rare rose-leaf flush tinging her pale cheek. " Ah, youth, youth," she sighed ; " alas, it comes but once ! "

" But, countess," the gallant old colonel rejoined
from his corner, with a bow and a large wave of the
hand, "there are some whom it never leaves!" And
the quality of his repartee blessed him that gave and
her that took. It promoted her kindliest mood, while
he chuckled frequently over his ready tongue, and was
comforted, and reminded of old days when the world
listened to him. He regaled various pensioned comrades with his happy retort, beginning cheerfully:
" By the way, did you happen to hear what I said to
the Countess Kronfels, the other day? It was not so
bad, I assure you." Or, "Speaking of good stories,
I must tell you a little experience of mine with the
Countess Kronfels — handsome woman still, by Jove!
I managed to turn her a compliment rather neatly.
Young Raven and Haller heard me. Well, well, when
you and I were lieutenants, we would not have let an
old fellow get the start of us with a gallant speech to
any woman, young or old. But we were live men in
those days, and times have changed since then! The
countess, you see, — always a bit of a coquette, you remember, — challenged squarely, and I with a smile
responded " — etc., etc. In fact, the old gentleman
prepared a score of introductions, and with him, for
weeks, all roads, political, philosophical, agricultural,
or military, led sooner or later to his repartee.

Gabrielle sat quietly expectant of some other element in the conversation, something in which she
could join. It all seemed preliminary to her, and she
waited. But nothing else came. The young people
were evidently accustomed to converse only in this
fragmentary fashion, with a series of half-questions,
the half-answers to which they already knew. There
was not much laughter, for little was said to awaken

it. Gabrielle, mechanically replying to Lieutenant von Raven, was guilty of listening to a story which the countess was telling in her best French manner. It was a good story, she told it well, and was altogether a charming personage, as she sipped a tiny glass of curaçoa after her coffee, with a friendly smile and an apt word for each and all.

Meanwhile the Frau Major stole softly over to gaze with tender admiration in von Raven's ´eyes, to smile at von Haller like his guardian-angel, to let her hand fall with a lingering caress upon her dear little Berta's shoulder, to murmur a word of loving commendation in her sweet Emma's eager ear, and to convey to Gabrielle in one grave, soulful glance the assurance of peculiarly delicate comprehension and sympathy.

Having exhausted the list of places where they had recently been and the places where they intended to go in the immediate future, von Raven boldly leaped over a few months, inspired to this unwonted intellectual feat by the novelty and charm of Gabrielle's presence, and inquired if she were going to the May races.

" Oh, everybody will go," chirped Emma Mayer.

"Oh, yes, everybody!" repeated Berta.

"Great thing, you know, the May races," von Haller informed her.

"Oh, yes!" exclaimed Berta Mayer.

"Yes indeed!" added Emma.

"Pretty women, toilets, crowd, gold cup," von Raven announced with a staccato effect.

"Prince's cup," explained von Haller. "We ride, von Raven and I," and both men beamed with joy.

"Oh, it will be delightful!" sighed Emma Mayer.

"Heavenly!" Berta murmured.

" I do not know whether I should like races or not,"
Gabrielle said, "but I am sure that I should like to
see the horses."

"The gracious fräulein rides?" von Raven asked,
smiling with pleasing anticipations.

" I have ridden almost since I began to walk. My
father taught me." As she uttered the commonplace
words, she saw the cool wood-paths and lanes of her
childhood, and her father towering beside her on his
high bay, with indulgent amused smiles for the little
girl on her pony, and all her chatter and eager confidences. She sighed, then said brightly, "In the country one must ride. One has so much time."

The young men looked at her with frank approval,
then at each other, von Raven deciding that his Jenny
was about up to her weight, and von Haller mounting
her in imagination on his Sylphide.

Gabrielle thought that they moved their feet about
in a very lively way, and seemed to be shaking out
their knees.

Both were ruddy and beardless, except for feeble
straw-colored mustaches. Both had a regulation
manner, and a great deal of it, which often served as
compensation for a want of lingual fluency. Both
had thin dark-blonde hair, closely cut, and a certain
emptiness or lack of resonance in the voice. Von
Raven was a trifle taller than his friend, she noticed,
and had better eyes. But they moved, spoke, and
apparently thought alike. Too angular in their ways
to possess what is called ease of manner, they were
yet never embarrassed, since the security of their
social position, together with their categorical training, had endowed them with automatical propriety of
demeanor, and when the winged word failed they did

not suspect the deficiency. Every situation of life they met with the large composure of men whom no consciousness of inferiority, no morbid introspection could perturb. Their complacency, however, was of a naive and harmless variety, as was their vast enjoyment of their sphere and their amiable indifference toward all pursuits outside of the army. With entire absence of aspiration, except to be promoted in due season, they were blessed with perpetual cheerfulness, were merry and honest, punctilious in the discharge of their duties, and in the observance of their own peculiar code of honor, which, while forbidding among other things cheating at cards and lying to men, allowed under certain conditions an indefinitely broad margin for cheating and lies to the other sex.

They drew themselves up, performed a few knee-shaking evolutions, and contemplated Gabrielle with frank pleasure. She thought that they looked very boyish, but smiled to find herself comparing them with her father. At all events, they seemed friendly and honest, and she could talk with them more easily than with the young girls. The conversation, as soon as it became exclusively equine, grew brisk. One of the quiet young women whose name Gabrielle had not understood, but whom the Mayer sisters called "dear Sofie," observing von Raven's interest in the stranger, remarked with fine acerbity, —

"We ride, of course ; but mamma prefers that we should not know much about horses."

"Then how can you ride?" Gabrielle asked simply.

The lieutenants laughed, and Sofie never forgave Gabrielle their merriment.

"Oh, we ride as everybody rides," was the annoyed answer, "but we never go into the stables."

" Dear Sofie," Berta Mayer reminded her friend, " the Princess Degenhart goes into the stables."

" Dear Berta," returned the other oracularly, " the Princess Degenhart is a princess ! "

" That is perfectly true," Emma Mayer corroborated, nodding gravely.

Gabrielle looked smilingly from one to another of her critics, not suspecting that her offence lay less in her conversation than in her attractive personality.

" What I know," she began, " is really very little. In the country, where I have always lived " —

This admission produced half-conciliated murmurs of urban superiority.

" Oh yes." — " The country ! " — " That is different."

" I have ridden sometimes all day long. And my father used to tell me one never knows one's horse completely, any more than one perfectly knows a human soul, but a good rider must study his animal. He wished me to ride well, that is intelligently, and I have loved it, and my horses, and have had, I confess, the habit of visiting them in their own — apartments," turning involuntarily, as she concluded, toward the lieutenants.

" He was right. A man never knows his horse," von Raven said with a laugh.

" You think you do," von Haller added, " and then he shows you a new trick."

" To ride well is an elegant accomplishment, but one should never be horsey," persisted Sofie, incensed at what she considered Gabrielle's arrant coquetry, and looking with appealing gentleness at von Raven.

" But why does one not know people?" Emma Mayer asked, with an air of amusement.

"Why, of course one knows people," Berta said, complacently smoothing her long gloves.

"How funny!" Sofie exclaimed. "It would really be odd if we did n't know one another, would it not, Herr von Raven?" with a melting glance.

"I suppose so," he returned indifferently. He was familiar with her *répertoire* of glances, and Gabrielle's had the charm of freshness.

At the moment, she was looking at him curiously.

"I presume Count Hugo was something like him," she thought, and presently said: —

"You were a friend of Count Kronfels, I believe? I mean, you are his friend?" For why should I speak of him as if he were dead? she asked herself.

"Oh, yes! Poor Hugo! Awful thing, that! Saw him yesterday. Looks like a corpse. Hollow cheeks. Big eyes."

"Best rider among us. Awful thing, that accident." Von Haller had the grace to lower his voice and glance at the countess.

"You saw him yesterday?" Gabrielle repeated thoughtfully. It seemed strange to her that von Raven had seen the mysterious tenant of that silent east wing. In spite of their poverty of expression, the young men evinced a certain amount of regret and good feeling.

"Was riding by," von Raven replied. "He was sunning himself. Good fellow, Hugo. Clever. Plucky."

"He was perfectly splendid!" sighed one of the Mayers.

"Perfectly!" gasped the other.

"Shall be coming to see him soon," von Raven announced with unprecedented astuteness.

"I too," von Haller hastened to say with a sly smile at his friend.

"Perhaps you would kindly tell him," von Raven added.

"Yes, tell him, please," von Haller begged.

Gabrielle colored slightly, and hesitated.

"I will tell him when I see him," she returned gravely.

"Dear countess," the Frau Major was saying in her rich caressing tones, "how noble, how tender! Yet I am not surprised. I knew well that whoever failed me, I could depend upon — you!"

"But who could fail you in so distressing a case?" demanded the countess. "Hundreds of people dead — crushed — mangled; families impoverished — children weeping for their parents — parents for their children. Oh that such things need be!"

"It is a church in Ancona," the Frau Major explained to the younger group; "the floor gave way and a wall fell. I am raising funds for the Italian Consul — he is a special friend of mine — I am planning a small bazar," she murmured. "Every one is so kind, my friends are so noble — but our dear countess is grand in her giving."

The countess's eyes were moist. She was touched by those sufferers whose moans she could not hear, whose mangled bodies she need not see, whose sorrows and wrongs were too remote to incommode her.

She rose, glancing at Gabrielle, who came quickly forward. The countess's face as she made her adieux was softened and strikingly fine.

"And dear Count Hugo," murmured the Frau Major.

"Ah, yes. I will not fail to tell him. He will surely wish to give. He of all men."

"He is always noble," returned her friend, adding in her calm tone of inward conviction, "he is like his mother."

Gabrielle's heart was full of sympathy, and not free from self-reproach. Descending the stairs, she reached out with a mute and gentle gesture, and slipped her hand under the countess's arm.

"Don't touch me!" was the querulous response. "I hate to be touched going downstairs."

"I beg your pardon," the girl returned drawing back quickly, and with the positiveness of youth inferring that the previous access of benevolence — in reality quite genuine while it lasted — had been simulated.

"The Countess Waldenberg's," the countess ordered her coachman. "Drive fast. We have stayed an unconscionable time," she complained. "It is too late to make formal visits. I will take you to a couple of houses where I go often — intimate friends. You were not especially affable to those young girls. They go everywhere."

Gabrielle looked inquiringly at her.

"How you stare, child! I do not say they are important in themselves, but they are a part of public opinion. One must respect public opinion. If I take you out with me, I wish public opinion in your favor."

"You surely cannot mean those little Mayer sisters?" returned Gabrielle, opening her eyes wide, and recalling their minute personalities kindly enough, but with the conviction that their contribution to public opinion could not be very weighty.

" Why not ? " demanded the countess sharply. " They may not be profound, but society likes them all the better for that.   Society," she continued pointedly, " does not like a young person to act like an old maid, or a blue-stocking, or be instructive or superior."

" I should hope not ! " Gabrielle rejoined with perfect unconsciousness and a fresh little laugh.

" Hm ! " said the countess dryly.

After a moment, she began : " Be a little careful here, Gabrielle.   You were too formal with girls of your own age.   You can scarcely be formal enough to please the Countess Waldenberg.   She is the most influential woman at court.   The queen is strongly attached to her.   She is marrying off her daughters now — not without difficulty," she added with an unpleasant laugh, " and she is not in the most amiable mood in the world.   The truth is, she is cold as a stone except for her boundless ambition.   But she is clever, and a great reader.   Never talk about books with young people, Gabrielle.   It is pedantic.   But if the countess begins, follow her lead.   Be intelligent, but on no account original."

" A well-bred duck turns her toes *in !* " thought the girl recalling Hans Andersen's mother-duck tutoring her ducklings before launching them upon the duck-plane of desirable society.

The countess frowned at the mischievous, wilful face turned towards her, and continued : " It is no laughing matter.   I wish you to make a favorable impression.   Otherwise you reflect discredit upon me."

Gabrielle stared at her haughtily.   By what right did this woman presume to dictate to a Baroness von Dohna ?   Surely she was not an appurtenance of the Kronfels estate.   Surely what she did or left undone concerned herself chiefly. And as for discredit — the word was strong! — her father would not fancy it used in connection with his daughter.

"Well?" said the countess impatiently.

Gabrielle was silent.

"What are you thinking? Why consider your words? Young people should be ingenuous."

"I am thinking," began Gabrielle, breaking bounds impetuously, "that the Countess Waldenberg will. have to take me as she finds me, whether she likes me or not, and perhaps — indeed, it is very probable — I shall not like her. And I am thinking that you might be the freest soul on earth! You have everything. Years enough to make you wise and sure. Wealth enough to satisfy every wish and bless the lives of thousands. Position that gives you dignity and power. Why should you care for the others? Why should you listen to what they say? Why should you not walk the streets barefoot, if it were with a good purpose and it pleased you?"

The countess, watching her with increasing entertainment, now broke into a merry laugh.

"*Tiens, tiens,*" she exclaimed, "imagine me walking the streets *nu-pieds*, like little What's-Her-Name in the play!" Then with a very successful air of kindly wisdom, she continued: "But my fiery little revolutionist, the sooner you abandon those ideas, the better. Freedom to be one's self in a city where king and court reside? Nonsense! It does not exist. The king's not free. The queen's not free. Nobody is free. In fact it would be a very vulgar state of society — your freedom!" and she raised her vinaigrette as if some unpleasant odor pervaded the atmosphere.

"In our village, the people watched and feared one

another," returned Gabrielle, conscious of fighting not only for a principle but for her personal independence, "and when the baker's wife cringed to the butcher's wife, I thought it was because they were uneducated."

"Ah, our village!" The countess lifted her eyebrows ironically and prolonged her delicate attentions to her vinaigrette. "But we wander from the subject. We were speaking of society. I assure you that if I watch the Countess Waldenberg, she watches me no less. The whole court watches — and listens. Something is hinted. Every tongue wags. It has always been so. It will always be so. Why, — it is, in short, civilization!" she concluded triumphantly.

"I would rather be a hermit in a cave!" Gabrielle retorted with indignation.

"Everybody must care for his neighbor's opinion, whether he care for his neighbor or not."

"Then everybody is a coward!"

"Tut, tut! that is scarcely civil," returned the countess with great exhilaration — "and here we are. Smooth your ruffled plumage, or they will say that we have been having a tiff, which, to be sure, is not unknown in their family, Mercedes being no dove, but they don't admit the public to their private diversions. Now be wise, Gabrielle. Don't drag out your little pet guillotine and cut off our heads," and she smiled like the most affable and simple-hearted old lady in the world, as she entered the Countess Waldenberg's drawing-room, Gabrielle following helpless and indignant, with luminous eyes, a glow on her cheeks, looking tall, holding her head high, and greeting the countess with a haughtiness which that critical dame found admirable.

"Hugo being *hors de combat*, what does our friend here mean to do with this interesting girl?" she asked herself, as she chatted suavely with her guests. "No girl in Wynburg has this faultless repose. It suits my taste far better than Mercedes' manner. She has, at times, too much Southern vivacity to please me. Why my children should both lack my fastidiousness is a mystery. I don't think this girl will interfere with Elsa. The styles are too different to conflict. And Elsa is so perfectly superficial," reflected the impartial mother, "that a man who would fancy her would find Fräulein von Dohna too earnest. But Mercedes is inclined to have ideas. Mercedes thinks. She would have found a rival here possibly. It is well that she has listened to reason. It is well that her future is assured."

Inquiring solicitously after Hugo, and listening to evidences of warm maternal feeling, of sorrow, sympathy, and loving pity, — in short, all that could be desired during a brief visit, — the Countess Waldenberg, noting Gabrielle's cold and steady gaze at the lamenting mother, decided : "Yes, she certainly has very remarkable pose for her age. It might have impressed the marquis. It is well that things are settled."

"But let me not linger upon my poor boy's sufferings, dear friend. How is Mercedes? And sunny little Elsa? You are blessed in your children," with a sigh.

"I am indeed," was the suave answer. "Elsa, I am sorry to say, is not at home. She would have been so pleased to meet Fräulein von Dohna. But Mercedes" — she paused, smiled, and gave her audience time to prepare for an impressive statement.

" I know you will sympathize with my great happiness," she resumed, — "the engagement will be announced formally in a few days; in the mean time it gives me pleasure to confide it in advance to so old and dear a friend. Mercedes is engaged to marry the Marquis de Vallion."

" Dear Olga! " exclaimed the Countess Kronfels.

" Dear Adelheid! " murmured the Countess Waldenberg.

They embraced and kissed each other.

" Mercedes is so happy ! "

" She must be, indeed ! "

" Nothing else could have gratified her father and me so deeply. The little difference in years " —

" Ah, what is that? I have known the happiest marriages in spite of that unimportant disparity. Mercedes has chosen wisely."

" We think so. And I was about to say that there is after all a certain earnestness in Mercedes, a seriousness beneath her vivacity; and this she has now proved."

" Undoubtedly. And there is an element of dignity and security in marrying a person of mature years."

" Quite true, dear Adelheid, and yet the marquis's devotion is all that the fondest young heart could desire."

Gabrielle was greatly interested. Here at last was a pleasant experience. The stately mother was so unfeignedly glad in her child's happiness, that the young girl felt at home with this simple display of natural feeling, and smiled charmingly, and extending both hands with a cordial gesture, wished the countess and her daughter happiness.

" Mercedes," said the delighted mamma, slightly
raising her voice. " Mercedes ! "

Some one replied from the next room. A heavy
portière was pushed back, and a strikingly handsome
dark woman, in black velvet, followed by the most
wonderfully made old man Gabrielle had ever seen,
came in smiling and received the Countess Kronfels'
hearty congratulations.

Glancing furtively at the marquis, Gabrielle was
sick at heart. Was this the person of mature years
who could afford rest and dignity? Who could offer
the fondest devotion, fill the mother's soul with contentment, and the daughter's with joy? She scarcely
dared to look at him for fear Mercedes might imagine
she was trying to discover how he was put together.

For Mercedes' brilliant eyes were incessantly upon
her; Mercedes' hands, glittering with gems, made
rapid pretty little gestures which fascinated her; Mercedes' laughing voice ran on, and — the wonder of
it ! — never gave a quiver or a cry of disgust. She
left her marquis adroitly with the older ladies, and
devoted herself to Gabrielle, chatting gayly of many
things, some indeed which the Mayers had mentioned, but with a world-wide difference, for Countess
Mercedes had a charm and a grace and a gleam of
feeling in all that she said, however trivial the theme.

" Your cousin must be immensely glad that you
have come," she remarked suddenly, with her flashing
smile.

" My cousin? Oh, you mean Count Kronfels.
We are only cousins by courtesy. And I " — Gabrielle hesitated, — " have no reason to suppose that he
is glad. In fact " —

" The villa must be so large and lonely for an

invalid," Mercedes went on, smiling more intensely.
"The countess is, as we all know, devoted to him.
Still he must be glad of your presence, even if he
has not said so. He must indeed have changed if " —
She broke off abruptly, cast one glance at the veterans. " Let me show you this lovely photograph of
the young princess," she said very distinctly, drawing Gabrielle toward a table at a little distance.
" How does he bear it ? Tell me about him," she
said, smiling steadily.

" He has not left his rooms since I came, and I can
tell you nothing. I have been here so short a time,
and " —

" Ah, yes, yes, I had forgotten," Mercedes rejoined
hastily. She was silent a moment. " Will you tell
him that we spoke of him — that I think of him,
often ? No, don't tell him that," she exclaimed,
laughing, " that is an imbecile message. Hugo and I
used to be very good friends," she explained ; " and
how is he looking ? "

Gabrielle had not had the faintest impulse to reveal
to Lieutenant von Raven, when he sent his friendly
greeting to Hugo, that in all probability she would
have no opportunity to deliver it ; but as she stood
face to face with this beautiful woman, whom she
liked at once, and whose eyes were seeking hers with
an intentness which the smiling mouth contradicted
in vain, she replied simply : —

" I am very sorry. But I do not know how he
looks. I have not seen him. He does not wish to
see me. Why should he care to see a stranger? I
understand it very well," she said with heightened
color. " But you," she added, after a moment, — " you
were his friend. Why do you not come to see him ?

He must be very lonely. Surely it would give him pleasure to see you!" she exclaimed with innocent admiration.

Mercedes gave her a peculiar but kind glance, and said gently, "Thank you, but I doubt it."

The veterans were looking toward them.

"Here is another one with the prince," Mercedes went on in a clear voice. "I don't like photographs where the man sits and the woman stands, do you? It does n't seem civil. But the photographers insist upon it. They say a woman 'takes' better standing. What odious beings they are — photographers! Such tyrants!"

"How brilliant and well she looks," the Countess Kronfels observed.

"Yes, dear Adelheid, it is her happiness," returned the mother placidly, reflecting: "How can she drop him like an umbrella in the corner and coolly walk off? She is not married yet!" beaming upon her future son-in-law, her senior by fifteen years, who, with a juvenile frisk and a vain smile, raised her hand to his painted lips.

The older women made the lingering adieux of loving friends loth to part. Upon reaching her coupé the Countess Kronfels glanced hurriedly at her watch.

"Shall I go? Shall I not?" she said gayly. "Yes I will, for the merest little three minute visit." As they drove away she muttered: "I must see how the Baroness Fuchs takes the engagement."

"Does it matter how anybody takes it?" Gabrielle asked sadly.

"Matter? It matters immensely. How society takes a thing is more important than the thing itself, of course. Be a little gayer at the Baroness Fuchs',

Gabrielle. She likes us to seem intimate with her. She is not one of us, you know. She is an American. Her people made hats or buttons in Philadelphia. Some say hats. Some say buttons. Whichever it was, it is now enveloped in prehistoric gloom. And she is a success here. That cannot be denied. She has married four daughters to the best names in the kingdom. No one feels the pulses of society better than she. Between us, she is a bit of a *mauvaise langue*, and hates the Countess Waldenberg. You see they both had daughters," laughed the old lady. " But they have always been devoted to me. I had a son."

" Is she your intimate friend, too ? "

" I presume that is satire," returned the countess, imperturbably. " My dear, in the great world people have little time for sentimental friendships. The Baroness Fuchs and I are on excellent terms, as you will see."

Gabrielle did see, and hear, and wished that for the moment she were blind and deaf. For the small and pompous woman with fishy eyes and a cold guarded smile implied the most unpleasant things of the Countess Mercedes, who, Gabrielle was convinced, was nobly immolating herself, like girls of whom one reads, for her family — for a principle ; and — since the Waldenbergs lived in luxury, and were powerful — for something mysterious, indeed, yet cruelly inexorable, or Mercedes would never marry that ghastly old man.

The countess's brilliant spirits continued at dinner. She chatted of Paris, of the late count, of persons whom she had known in Italy, in Spain and Russia. She laughed much and made Gabrielle laugh. For

she had travelled far and wide, met eminent men and
women, and in the rare moments when her mind
dwelt upon pleasant subjects, she knew how to be
amiable and humorous, and recalling some witticism
of long ago could revivify it with rare skill.

After dinner she smoked a cigarette, drank a little
glass of curaçoa, put on a black lace cap with a bunch
of crimson roses on one side, pinned it with diamond-
headed hair-pins, and drove to Carmen with Gabrielle,
who longed to remain at home, but was not asked to
indicate her wishes.

She was weary and excited, and the passionate, wild
music moved her strangely. In the pauses many men
came to pay their respects to the countess, and the
engagement was discussed with enigmatical smiles.
When von Raven and von Haller appeared for a
few moments, and one of them remarked: "Old skeleton. Second childhood. Handsome woman." And
the other: "Can't she waltz! Famous. It's a shame.
Upon my word," Gabrielle's heart went out with
thankfulness to these honest youths, and she smiled
cordially and listened scrupulously, for she sometimes
failed to instantly catch their meaning, and it occurred
to her if, as she had read, language was originally in-
terjectional, their mode of speech must bear some
resemblance to the natural and spontaneous ejaculations of primeval man.

"Really, I did not imagine the little Methodist
could illuminate herself to this extent," was the countess's secret comment. "She evidently enjoys attention, and is opening her batteries upon von Raven
with no loss of time."

After the opera the countess insisted upon Gabrielle's presence for a "cosy quarter-of-an-hour," smoked

some cigarettes and sipped a couple of glasses of curaçoa, laughing at trifles like a merry child, and looking
pretty and gay.

"I must think of something sweet to call you," she
said suddenly with a sentimental air.

"Don't you like my name?" Gabrielle rejoined indifferently.

"Oh, yes, but when I really love any one, I like to
choose a name for her. It is a fancy of mine. I am
full of fancies, as you will discover."

Gabrielle was tired and sleepy. She suppressed a
yawn and said nothing.

"I have it!" exclaimed the countess with her most
engaging smile. "There is something soft yet clear
in you."

"Indeed," Gabrielle returned wearily.

"Yes, and I shall call you 'Moonbeam.'"

Gabrielle would not have objected at the moment
had the countess chosen to call her Heathen-Darkness.
Her one desire was to escape. But she braced herself
to suffer some kisses, and to listen to erratic sentimental flights, and finally after twelve the countess
declared that she had had a charming day, but was
somewhat weary, and Gabrielle must remember that
very sensitive nerves needed considerable sleep.

"Good-night, my sweet Moonbeam. I am sure that
you are going to be the loving heart that I have
sought and never found."

Gabrielle shook her head, and was about to depre-
cate this assumption, but it sounded sincere and puz-
zled her. She hesitated, then said gravely : —

"Do you mean that no one has ever loved you, and
that you miss affection?"

"Loved me? I have been adored — worshipped,"

returned the countess pettishly, repudiating Gabrielle's matter-of-fact translation of her rhapsodies. "But no one has ever comprehended me fully," and she sighed. It seemed like a genuine sigh from an old grief.

With the persistency of a child Gabrielle asked : —
" Not your husband ? "

" What a question ! He was devoted to me, of course. But that is not what I mean. Then the count was very peculiar."

" Not your son ? "

" Hugo least of all."

" It is very sad," murmured Gabrielle. " It is terribly sad."

" Well, well," remarked the countess, to whom this solemn catechism was growing irksome, particularly as Gabrielle was staring at her with a kind of commiseration, — and while it was one thing to allude feelingly to one's uncomprehended superiority, it was quite another to be regarded as a forlorn and pitiable object, — " let us follow Mousey's example and sleep away our sorrows. Hear the little love snore. Is it not cheerful? Good - night," kissing her, " and God bless my pretty Moonbeam. Röschen," calling the sleepy maid waiting in the corridor, " light the Baroness von Dohna to her rooms."

When Röschen lighted the gas, Gabrielle saw with amazement that shawls were pinned across her toilet-table and every mirror.

" What does this mean ? " she demanded.

" Oh, it 's what I 've learned from the countess. Babette and I have to cover up all the mirrors every night. She 's got so many, it 's a deal of work, but here it was no trouble."

" I don't understand you."

" It is bad luck to sleep with mirrors looking at you," pretty Röschen explained with a not too respectful smile. " She 's that nervous " —

" Take those things down, please, and don't tell tales."

The girl obeyed, then waited. She was stifling her yawns, yet was curious in regard to that great, beautiful, happy world of rich people, fine gowns, and dazzling lieutenants, where the young baroness had been. Surely a crumb of information might fall from her lips, when the countess brought back whole loaves to Babette.

" You may go, Röschen. Good-night."

The maid reluctantly withdrew. The door closed upon her. Gabrielle was at last alone. She leaned her elbows on the table, her chin in her hands, and drew two or three long, deep breaths. She was no longer sleepy, no longer fatigued, and she experienced a sense of relief as if a heavy physical burden had fallen from her shoulders. She threw open the windows. The night-breeze, blowing straight through her rooms, was the one familiar and friendly thing in that great house.

" I must decide — *now !* " she thought, walking slowly up and down; and Hugo, sleepless and in pain, listened to her step, and in spite of his ready sneer for his mother's toy, was forced, in reason, to admit that she must be unhappy.

" She is a conspirator — a nihilist. She 's a Roman Catholic, trotting up and down for penance. She is a Lady Macbeth, with remorse in her soul. Or she is a good sort of girl in the wrong place."

But the mocking fancies vanished, and only the final simple conclusion remained in his mind, and his thought of her was not without pity. " Well, she must fight her own battles. After all, what are they to me ? " Yet he began to wonder again how she looked — this girl, with her unknown griefs; and what his mother had said and done; and whom they had seen, to-day, of the people whom he used to know, when he was alive.

If there was a rude simplicity in teaching Gabrielle to hate a lie and love a horse, and not letting her suspect the manifold dangers lurking in draughts and neighbors' judgments, it would yet appear that there were some advantages in the Dohna system. For a good stout hatred of lying, in general, tended to preserve her from the most insidious form of the disease — flattering falsehood to one's self. While being a girl who really loved her horse, and had ridden him gallantly, and learned to bear wind and weather, heat and cold, broiling sun and drenched raiment, fatigue, lame muscles, bruises and broken bones if need be, — and loved him loyally all the same, she had gained, it may be, a suspicion of what patience and fortitude mean. And as to neighbors and draughts, she was so ignorant of their hydra-headed possibilities, that she was able to consider her course with far more single-ness of purpose and fearlessness than if she had been preyed upon by premonitions of influenza, or the haunting necessity of suiting her decision, not to the demands of her own conscience, but to the fluctuating sentiments of the world at large.

" I must decide," she told herself. " Shall I go or stay ? I do not like it. That is sure. It is detestable. And there is no good in it, for Count Hugo will not let me be useful."

Not yet two days ? It was incredible. All the

persons she had met came passing in review. The colossal egotism of the countess had surely been appropriating her, body and soul, longer than that. How it pervaded and possessed the villa! Even those great empty rooms below, seldom used, were full of it, and every soul in the house staggered under its weight.

And who and what was the countess? *Which* was she? Which of all those rapid, confusing phases?

"Oh, papa," she sighed, "you thought that it would be so pleasant and enriching for me, — and Lucie said that I ought to see a little life, and here it is! This!

"What have I been this day? Everything that I despise. A toy, a captive, a tool. Not once has she inquired what I like, what I think or feel or am. She has simply dragged me after her chariot. But I am not her slave — not yet bought and sold. If I write, my letter will reach them in Paris. I can join them at Marseilles. Or I could go to the other 'cousins' in Berlin. If it would do any one any good, I could bear it here. But why be uncomfortable for nothing? Now if it were for papa. I could yield my will and dignity and peace of mind for papa. For papa, I would be burned at the stake!"

She paused. Her expression changed.

"Oh, would I? Would I indeed? And this is how I prove it. It's quite like me. I — I — I — that is what occupies me! I am willing to be burned at the stake, oh, yes, but I wish to choose my stake, adjust it to my size, and appoint the hour for lighting the fagots!"

She pushed back her hair impatiently. "Let me look at this thing squarely, with no nonsense. Papa has placed me here. There is still time to beg him to take me away, and he will never leave me if he knows that I am unhappy, not for Lucie — not for the whole world. He would not let me try any more cousin-experiments, he would simply take me with them, as he at first intended. He would telegraph me to join them. And when they sail, there I should be — because I cried out with pain — and ran away — because I was too babyish to be left behind — because I did not hesitate to disturb everybody's arrangements — because I was selfish, and a coward ! "

Hot tears started to her eyes, and a great longing for her father's protecting arms filled her heart.

" I shall not be poisoned, or starved, or beaten. I shall be safe, and live in a beautiful house, and drive in a fine carriage, and I shall hate it all, and be very lonely and unhappy. That is all. It is not tragic." Yet it occurred to her that what we call tragedy might be, in a certain sense, easier to bear nobly, and that in all the tragedies she had read, love and pain and sorrow and danger seemed to strengthen and elevate souls, and even sin advanced with slow motions and long trailing garments, and crime was fate, and therefore had its dignity.

But where was the dignity here ? What was this but vulgarity, from Mousey's snarls to the countess's violence ? And the circle she had seen that day ? What mattered it what they called themselves ? How were they essentially different from the old women of the village — gossiping, suspicious, unloving, and envious, yet smiling indefatigably at one another on the market-place ?

And yet, — the village-folk — how brave they were and self-sacrificing when Marco's house burned — how generous to his children — how kind when the tree crushed Karl's leg, — how they mourned when little Paul died! "It is I who am unloving and arrogant. How do I know what these people here are? How can I know what good they do, and what sorrows they have? The Frau Major is kind to all the world, not hard like me. And Countess Mercedes — has she not a thousand times more to bear than I? Yet how brave and gay she is!

"And Aunt Adelheid? Ah, when I come to her, I must shut my eyes and go on blindly, for there is no comfort in seeing the path before me, — except, we are not married, — it is not forever!"

She covered her face with her hands and sat long and motionless at the table. When she looked up, her eyes were wet, but her mouth was resolute.

She went to close the casement. Along the hillside across the valley glimmered the remote scattered lights. "I shall see them for a long, long time now," she thought. "I shall learn to care for them."

The heavens were brilliant with stars. Into the Silence, into the Unknown and Infinite, her young heart sent a prayer for strength and patience, while blended inextricably with her pure aspiration was an intense desire for personal happiness, and the warm sustaining hope that the frowning and unpromising year might yet have some fair days in store for her.

"At all events, whatever comes," — and as she turned there was a faint smile on her compressed lips, "there never was a Dohna who ran away!"

CHAPTER X.

THE Countess Kronfels had the habit of writing school-girlish notes, folding them in ingenious shapes, and sending them on a silver salver to inmates of her household. Like some other imaginative works, they were composed under various animating influences, late at night, and their loving-kindness of diction left nothing to be desired.

One of these twisted missives reached Hugo early the following morning.

MY DEAREST HUGO, — My love and blessings to my dear son, before I sleep. I must tell you how you can help on a humane and Christian work. Send some money to the Frau Major for the sufferers at Ancona. Here is a newspaper slip describing the accident. It is heartbreaking. Everybody is giving. I gave a thousand marks. She depends upon you. I really think, Hugo, it would look well, if you, under the circumstances, should contribute handsomely. Good-night. God bless you. I shall come to you to-morrow morning, and earlier than usual.

Your loving and faithful   MOTHER.

Hugo twisted the note with vindictive emphasis, as if he would like to wring its neck, then read the enclosed newspaper-cutting.

" Poor devils," he muttered. " Paper, Lipps, and a pencil."

My dear Mamma — (he wrote) — I am not, as you know, philanthropic, and I have frequently expressed to you my unalterable decision never to figure in the Frau Major's charity-lists, where I, a notorious black sheep, would surely be out of place among the pure and righteous. Since you reflect sufficient glory upon our name, pray excuse

Your affectionate son,   Hugo.

"Poor devils!" he repeated, then shook his head as if to free himself from an unpleasant thought.

"Lipps," he began, after a moment, "do you think you and the others could put me out there by the little fountain, — out of sight and hearing, you know, — there behind the shrubbery, at the end of the garden, where nobody goes?"

Lipps stoutly declared his ability to transport the count illimitable distances provided he could bear the fatigue.

"Very well, then," Hugo went on. "I think I'd like to try it out there, and as soon as possible," looking at his watch, and thinking, "She said earlier than usual, and my note will certainly rouse her. She will be in a fine rage. A masterly retreat is often good strategy. She may forget Ancona before to-morrow. She will, surely, if Mousey has the colic, which may Heaven precipitate!"

"Lipps, put me out there as soon as you can, and with as little noise as possible, you understand; and after, not before, I'm established take this note up to Babette for the countess."

"Yes, sir," answered Lipps, wisely looking foolish.

The remote and neglected garden-spot proved to be a very good place for Hugo. There was almost no wind there, and the sun beat down warmly upon a dense battalion of cedars and firs and pines, with an occasional hemlock tree and a few larches. The water plashed softly from a bronze griffin's mouth into a stone basin with a broken, ivy-grown moulding, and fragments of an urn, also clothed with ivy as with a garment, lay near.

"It is what mamma would call 'appropriate,'" thought Hugo. "Decrepit, — and suggesting dead pleasures."

Lipps looked at him anxiously.

"It is vastly entertaining out here," the count said, gravely. "I shall remain here some time. I am convinced that I shall not want to leave this spot, until after the carriage drives away this afternoon. I have everything, thanks. The books, writing block, and — oh, Lipps, just stand those crutches against the foot of my chair, will you? They'd better be within reach. I might want to fling one at somebody. Not that it would hurt him much, but it might be a relief to me. You can look after me in a couple of hours, Lipps."

He lay so motionless that a blackbird hopped along the path and stared at him, and a yellow-hammer perched boldly on the white pine near his head.

"Hundreds of them," he thought, — "children too, — poor little devils!"

He idly cut the leaves of a new magazine, and glanced at an article which seemed to reveal Napoleon in a glare of electric light. He held the pamphlet loosely, and turned the pages with nervous haste. The book fell, and as he sought to recover it, his abrupt movement knocked it beyond his reach. His interest in Napoleon was instantly augmented.

He stretched his arm ineffectually after the magazine, which lay flat on its face, tantalizing and unattainable. It seemed of immense importance to him to regain it. He exerted himself until he was weary, then raised his whistle, paused, and let it drop.

"No, I won't call him. The man ought to have an instant to breathe. I should think he'd feel as if he were chained to a corpse."

Once more he stretched his arm to the utmost, but Napoleon refused to be captured. Slowly and with difficulty, the invalid secured a crutch, and tried to rake up the book with it, but his strength failed, the crutch dropped, and he sank back with a sigh.

Suddenly he heard a sound as of a substantial weight dropping on two feet, followed by steps behind his chair, and saw first a hand and workingman's sleeve, then the being to whom they belonged, a tall, large man, with a paper cap, brown smiling eyes, a long curling beard, and a whitish blouse reaching nearly to his heels.

He silently gave Hugo the magazine, and stood looking down upon him like a gentle giant.

"Thank you," began the count, regarding him curiously. "This is unexpected good luck. I hope it will not seem ungrateful, if I venture to inquire how you happened to observe my predicament."

"Why not?" returned the man placidly. "I was looking over the hedge."

"Oh," said Hugo dryly, reflecting: "As there is literally nothing to see here but a wall of green, he was looking for somebody. 'I, too, have been in Acadia.'"

The stranger stood in the strong sunshine which brought out reddish gleams in his dark beard. His large, kind gaze met Hugo's squarely, and the count found the simplicity and repose of his presence singularly attractive.

"I am glad that you were looking over the hedge," Hugo continued after a moment, adding to himself, "whatever brought you, and it's probably that rosy last one. No man would look twice at any of the others. Mamma selects frights on principle. She assumes that ugly women are more virtuous than pretty ones. Now I never observed that there was any particular difference."

"You took a handspring from the fence outside," he remarked, noting the powerful figure and repressing a sigh.

"Yes, and I am mighty sorry you can't do the same, Count Kronfels."

"He is the first person who has spoken to me as if I were still a man," Hugo realized with surprise. "To the doctors I am a 'case.' To Lipps I am a fetich. While my pious mamma thinks I ought to spiritualize myself into a holy example for ungodly lieutenants. Raven was evidently afraid of me. This fellow is refreshing."

"You know me, then?"

"Why not? Everybody knows the count, and is sorry for him," replied the giant, in his deliberate and gentle manner.

"Ah, I had not thought of that," rejoined Hugo again with surprise.

"It is good for the count to be out in the sunshine," the other said with a strikingly sweet and cordial smile, his gaze wandering slowly from the invalid to the trees and the bare but budding pushing shrubs.

"Do you think so? Then I must come often. You look as if you knew what is good for people."

The man laughed.

"I don't know much," he rejoined, his handsome brown face untroubled and vastly content.

"Would you have the kindness to move my chair a little?" Hugo asked, with a sudden desire to make use of this big man's gentle strength. "The sun will be in my eyes soon."

Chair and invalid were instantly seized, lifted, and softly replaced.

"You are very kind — and strong."

"Yes, I'm strong," returned the other cheerfully, "and I'd like to do anything I could for you, count," again unhesitatingly accentuating the contrast between them, his clear eyes shining with benevolence.

"I like the fellow," decided Hugo.

"I ought to go now."

"Oh, must you?" Hugo rejoined with regret. "Good-by, then. Perhaps you'll be looking over the hedge again some day."

The man had sauntered on a few steps. He now returned. "I ought to tell you, count," he began, ' that there's no harm in it."

"Of course not," Hugo replied dryly, adding with a touch of his careless lieutenant-manner, "it can't hurt the hedge."

"There's a girl in your house," continued the other steadily, "the best girl in the world — and I'm going to marry her."

Hugo held out his hand quickly, regretting his worldliness. "Oh, that's it, is it? Then I wish you joy."

"Why not?" was the curious response, with a shy and happy smile.

The long thin hand with prominent veins lay in the large brown palm. The strong man regarded the emaciated fingers attentively, and said with infinite gentleness : —

" It could n't do much hard work, count."

" No," Hugo returned quietly, " it is not a dangerous fist. It would n't intimidate a burglar."

" Or even handle a chisel and a mallet," added the other.

" You are a stone-carver, then. I presumed so."

" Yes, I carry my trade about with me, like a miller," brushing the fine white dust from his beard. " My name is Bernhard Dietz."

" What are you working on, now ? " asked Hugo, inclined to prolong the interview.

" I 'm to do all the windows and doors, that is, the brackets and cornices, on both houses. I 'm on the oriel-window now. You ought to see that. That 's a rich design."

" Oh, you are the singer," Hugo said quickly.

" Why not ? " Bernhard admitted with his gentle upward inflection. " No," he continued, " there 's not much carving like that window in Wynburg. The people economize too much. In London there is some good work. But the stone is harder there."

" Ah, you have been in London ? "

" Yes, — but I had to hurry back," Dietz replied, with a soft, shy look which he wore now and then. " The men have taken their beer, count."

" But you will come again ? " begged Hugo.

" Why not ? " returned the stone-carver, with his serene smile, as if visiting lame counts in wheel-chairs had been his inveterate habit from childhood.

Hugo listened for the thump of feet on the other

side of the hedge, and shortly after, when he heard
above the noisy work on wood and iron and stone,
and the clanking chains and men's calls, Bernhard's
glad voice soaring strong and free on wings of song,
the lame man's mood, if sad, was yet without the
fierce protest of the previous day.

"That fellow has common sense. I should like to
talk with him about those Ancona people. 'Why
not?' as he says. I should like to do something for
those children, if there is any way to reach them without getting into the clutches of the fashionable phi-
lanthropists, like Frau Funnel & Co. I am too un-
regenerate to work amiably with the professionals. I
don't know the ropes in the benevolent line, and my
idea is deucedly irregular, I presume, but I am tolerably clear as to what I would like to do. For instance,
an airy, sunny house for the smashed infants, good
doctors of course, and I suppose that necessitates a
kind of hospital stiffness at first; but when the poor
little souls are well, — that is to say, well like me, —
incurable cripples, then what? Well, a good big garden, hammocks and cushioned chairs, and pretty soft-
voiced women — I suppose there may be such women
— in Italy! yes, decidedly, pretty women — I won't
have an ugly one in the house," making a note of this
regulation; "and music,"— Dietz was whistling fragments of Carmen with the swing of a whole orchestra,
and catching up a refrain with his great voice, flung
Escamillo's sentiments in triumph over all the neighborhood, — "yes, certainly," noting music. "Hm," he
muttered, reading his notes with a queer smile. "I
don't suppose they would call this practical. I must
talk with the consul. I could do the thing well
enough, I should say, for less than I have always

paid for extra horses, cards, and champagne suppers.
Though to be sure no man knows less than I the cost
of a virtuous action. So far as I can recollect, I
never performed one in my life."

He jotted down a few more notes, then under the
condition of profound secrecy imparted to the Italian
consul some of his ideas and requested an interview.
The pencilled letter, written in good faith and without
circumlocution, produced a singular effect upon the
gentleman who finally received it. His face as he read
expressed violent surprise, and he had a suspicion
that somebody was playing a practical joke upon him,
after which he laughed heartily, but kindly, and at
last had no desire to laugh, but looked thoughtful,
took out his handkerchief, flourished it largely, and
furtively wiped his eyes. "He begs me to come as
early as half-past eight, that we may not be disturbed.
I presume they are doing something the whole day to
amuse the poor fellow. And no wonder, cut off from
everything, and a heart like that!"

Meanwhile the letter, unfinished, lay on Hugo's
block, and he was looking doubtful over his plan.
How a lieutenant of dragoons feels when he sees an
indefinite future of invalidism stretching on before
him, he knew but too well; but how children, little
children, the children of laborers would feel and what
would make them happiest, he could only vaguely imagine. "Dietz would know," he thought. "I wish I
had asked him to come in again to-day."

"If I do this thing," he mused, with a curiously
defiant look, "it is simply because I wish to. It is not
to pave my way into the next world, if there is any.
It is not to make my accounts look better before I go.
It is my whim, like any other, and I won't have it

credited to me like a death-bed repentance. I 'll take my chances over the border as I have lived," he muttered doggedly.

Lipps appeared with a glass of wine and water and some biscuit.

"I am very comfortable, Lipps, and I don't want anything except to stand a moment. Help me to ground — crutches ! — will you ? "

He stood a few minutes, and with great exertion and fatigue walked two or three steps.

" It is no use," he murmured, his face contracting with pain.

But Lipps, laying him back on his cushions, lifting his feet and covering him well, declared unblushingly that there was striking improvement and soon the count would be walking off as strong as anybody ; whereupon the servant stood looking very mournful, his face working as if on the verge of tears.

" If you tell so many lies you will go to a very hot place," the count said faintly.

The servant protested that he could only say what he believed, which was that the count would be on his feet in no time, walking and riding and dancing, as gay as a lark ; and here the man gave an unmistakable sob.

" I don't wonder that such a big one as that chokes you," Hugo remarked with a kind smile. " Come, Lipps ; never mind me. I am tired of that subject morning, noon, and night. I want to ask you something. Suppose you were a little fellow, and something should fall upon you, and you couldn't run about any more — could n't work or play — like me, in short — what would you want ? What could anybody do to make things more decent for you ? "

Lipps was thrown into utter confusion.

"Surely the count knows best."

"Don't be idiotic."

"Surely the count is not asking me for my thoughts?"

"Yes I am."

Lipps was red with embarrassment.

"Out with it!" Hugo urged. "I perceive there is an idea in your head, struggling to free itself."

"Well," faltered Lipps as if confessing a crime, "if I was a little chap, and lame, — and on my back, the count means?"

"Yes, yes," Hugo said impatiently.

"I think I'd like a big red balloon with a long string better than anything in the world. I always wanted one and never had it," he admitted with a childish grin, recalling years of fruitless longing.

"Good heavens, man!" began Hugo, staring; then gravely, "It is a very good idea, Lipps. Thank you. And what else?"

Lipps grew bolder.

"Does the count allow me to say anything?"

"Anything and everything. Let your imagination run riot. Fire away. Let us have something extravagant."

"Well, then, meat once in two days, and a bit of sweet custard Sundays. There!"

Hugo was silent some moments.

"Is that your idea of bliss?" he asked at length, and with peculiar gentleness.

"Poor children don't get meat and custard," Lipps explained timidly. "In service of course a man eats well; but I almost never saw meat when I was a boy, and I remember it."

" What a selfish brute I have been all my life,"
thought Hugo, scrupulously noting on his extraordinary list, " balloons, light toys, and plenty of meat
and sweets."

The servant watched him wonderingly.

" I know no such boy," the count said, answering
the question in the man's eyes, " I am only amusing
myself."

" Yes, sir," Lipps returned cheerfully. " I did n't
think there was one round here. But if there was
any such child, and he had a balloon, and meat and
custard, he ought to be happy and no mistake."

" Happy ! Why ? "

" Because it is more than such as he has any right
to expect, or ever would expect."

Again Hugo stared at him.

" Oh, it is, is it ? That will do, Lipps. You have
answered very well. Thank you — and you can go
now."

The morning advanced. The sun grew warmer,
the balsamic odors heavier. Hugo was occupied with
his scheme. Now and then he would jot down an
item with an ironical smile. The soft plash of the little fountain sounded pleasant to him. The children
should have one. " Meat once in two days and sweet
custard Sunday. And the rivers of champagne I
have drunk!" The bells and whistles and general
pandemonium announced high noon. The men
knocked off work with admirable promptness, he noticed. Presently he heard a welcome voice : —

" Shall I come over, count ? "

" Ah, do ! " Hugo called eagerly.

" I only thought that I 'd see if you were still there
— or tired, or anything," Dietz began, standing again

by the chair. " It must be lonely for you, count, since you are too weak to do anything with your hands — except write a little, or hold a book."

" I might take up knitting," retorted Hugo soberly. Dietz smiled.

" It would n't be the worst thing for you perhaps, but there might be something better."

" What would you propose ? "

" I should have to consider, — for a man like you."

" Well, then, not for a man like me. Wait. You don't look as if you would chatter."

" No, I don't believe I do."

Still Hugo hesitated. He felt curiously shy, and dreaded, above all things, being suspected of what he called " posing " for charity and benevolence, but something in Dietz's eyes gave him confidence, and at last he muttered somewhat grimly : —

" If there were children, mangled — made useless, like me — workingmen's children " —

" Is it a fancy of yours," asked Dietz, " or is it true ? "

" It is true."

" That is a pity."

" And I would like to do something for them."

" Of course."

" I am awkward and blundering about it. I don't know anything about such children."

" How should you, count ? " rejoined Bernhard, gently.

" But you do ? "

" Yes, because I was one of them. My parents were poor as crows when I was a boy."

" Will you glance at these things for me," and Hugo abruptly thrust his letter and notes toward Dietz.

Bernhard read them slowly, and his face was calm and benign as an angel's as he turned to Hugo.

" You mean to do that? All that? You are a fortunate man to have the power to do a thing like that."

Fortunate! Hugo looked up sharply, and was about to reply with bitterness, but meeting Bernhard's tranquil gaze, asked instead : —

" What would you suggest?"

Dietz answered reflectively : —

" Schooling. Some of them could bear it, and the others would like to listen. Light work, for it's a comfort to move the hands and know one is useful. That's what I was thinking when I saw your hands so white and still on that red plush. There are many children?"

" A great many, yes."

" I'd have them learn to draw. Some would have talent, and that would be a comfort. I'd have them taught a little music. Many of them would like that best. Some will be strong enough to go out into the world later. Others won't. Well, that's not your affair. But such things would keep them good in spite of pain."

" Good? I don't care a straw whether they are good or not," Hugo retorted with some heat. " I only want to make them a little happier, if possible."

" It is about the same thing, isn't it?" Bernhard said tranquilly.

" If they draw," Hugo resumed after some moments, " they ought to have good things to look at, ought they not? Pictures and busts?"

" Yes, not too many, but good. Drawing will be a comfort to them. It makes the men happier in the prisons."

"The prisons?"

"My professor has taught drawing in the prisons Sundays for ten years. He has discovered talent that the men never suspected. There was a young fellow of twenty, a murderer, who had never drawn a stroke. I wish you could see the heads he did after six months' training. They were masterly work, and full of feeling."

"A murderer? A murderer, do you say?" repeated Hugo.

"You lieutenants don't call a duel murder, do you? Yet that is planned. His sin was one hot moment. He had had too much wine and he was jealous. Murder is an ugly word. This man was quiet and gentle and drew all day long — things the master gave him, things that he remembered. The king shortened his life-sentence to ten years, and now he has gone to America to start fresh. I was glad that he got another chance. There are good hearts in the prisons," Dietz went on thoughtfully. "There are bad ones all around us that never are found out. There is something queer in that."

Hugo looked at him in astonishment.

"Do you go into the prisons?"

"I help my professor a little now and then," Dietz answered modestly. "I am mighty sorry for them," he added. "But I must go and eat my dinner now," he announced. "I'll be thinking of your plan. It is a blessed kind of plan, count. I'll ask some of the men, if you will let me, — some of the level-headed ones. I will put the case imaginary, of course. Men with children might know best, — though I hope to have some of my own, some day, please God — and a man can think beforehand."

" Will you come in to-morrow ? "

" Why not ? " Dietz said. " I 'd be pleased to come often and talk with you, count," and he smiled his smile of peace and good-will, moved Hugo's chair slightly, re-covered his feet, and walked off, humming as he went.

He was scarcely gone when Lipps, standing as formally by a lilac-bush as if it were a door to be closed behind a guest, ushered in von Raven.

" Good-morning. Surprised, eh ? "

" I am, rather."

" Riding by again. Thought I 'd find you. Ajax pulls like Lucifer. Warm noon."

" Sit down, Lorenz. There ought to be a rustic chair somewhere in the next path if you will take the trouble to find it. I have not realized my attractiveness, consequently my audience-chamber looks somewhat inhospitable."

" Oh, I 'll stand, thanks."

Hugo said nothing.

" It 's a warm noon," remarked the visitor again.

" Very, for the season," returned Hugo politely, thinking, " Now he never came in here to tell me that."

" I say, Hugo," von Raven began after considerable hesitation. " Saw your cousin yesterday."

" Ah ? "

" Did she tell you ? "

Hugo contemplated him silently before replying :

" No, I have n't heard her say anything about you."

Von Raven looked slightly crestfallen.

" Talked with her some time. Thought she might mention it. But girls are queer."

" They are," said Hugo, staring at the sky.

" Beautiful girl, eh, Hugo ? "

" I can't say that I agree with you."

" Oh, come now ! "

" Nor am I prepared to call her the reverse," Hugo added in a judicial tone.

" Don't mind telling you. I 'm struck. I 'm gone. Nothing left of me."

" Ah, but that happens so often ! "

" Not like this," von Raven protested. " Never saw anybody like her. Beats Countess Mercedes at eyes, and can give her points on figure. All of ours are talking of her."

" Indeed. That 's quick work."

" I believe you ! Sensation, I tell you. Acknowledged beauty."

Hugo knew what a sensation in Wynburg meant. He could scarcely reconcile it with those sad, slow footsteps which he had heard at midnight. Von Raven's florid, heated face was turned eagerly toward him. He could not have told what wearied and irritated him, as he involuntarily compared the baron with the stone-carver who had stood a few moments before in the same place.

" Want to take her out on Jenny. Haller means to be along to-day. Got the start of him. Jenny is a better mare than Sylphide."

" Well ? " said Hugo coldly.

" Thought of you."

" You thought what ? " demanded Hugo with a frown.

" No end of opportunity. Chatting. Reading. Sisterly attention," von Raven went on with an empty little laugh, sketching with unusual play of imagination Hugo's helplessness and harmlessness.

"Good word, now and then. Advice. Influence, you know."

He whipped his boot with his riding-stick and looked tolerably sure of his results.

Hugo scowled steadily, resenting Raven's confidences, his appeal, for the moment even his careless and satisfied existence.

"The governor wants me to marry. Mamma is always at me. A man must, sooner or later. She pleases me," he concluded, with the lordly simplicity of a three-tailed pasha.

"Thought you would help a fellow," he added, surprised at Hugo's silence.

"Well, I won't."

"Oh, come now!" von Raven returned good-humoredly. "Old comrade. Yes, you will. Why won't you?"

"I am not a match-maker," Hugo growled. "I leave that trade to women."

"Oh, you will do a friend a good turn," laughed von Raven. "Know you. But how about Jenny?"

"I do not know Fräulein von Dohna's tastes sufficiently to answer for her," Hugo rejoined very formally, "but if she wishes to ride, of course we shall provide her mount."

"Merely thought you would n't have anything in the stables just now" —

"It is deucedly obliging on your part, Lorenz, to be looking after the condition of my stables" —

"And I thought Jenny would suit."

"Jenny won't do."

"She's light on the bit, and" —

"She won't suit Fräulein von Dohna," Hugo said angrily.

It occurred to von Raven that he would do well to lead Jenny out of the conversation, also that he could ride with the young lady whether his horse or Hugo's had the honor of carrying her.

"Splendid figure," he exclaimed. "Don't you say so?"

"I have nothing whatever to say about it."

"But her eyes, Hugo! You can't remain cold to those eyes."

"I have no difficulty thus far."

"You are in no end of a mood. Never mind. No harm done. By the way, Frau von Funnel's getting up bazaar. Ancona sufferers. Wants Fräulein von Dohna. Gypsy encampment. Hair down. All that sort of thing. Decided after ladies left yesterday. Entrance fee. Raffles. Mayers, flower-girls. Dance afterwards. Your cousin will join?"

"If she wishes to exhibit her hair and waltz in pity for the Ancona cripples, — yes."

"The Frau Major thought you'd be interested. Take some shares."

"She was mistaken. I am not interested."

"The devil! You are joking. No shares? Charity? Benevolence?"

"Nothing of the sort."

Von Raven stared, wondering if free-handed Hugo had grown parsimonious, but excused him on the plea of illness.

"Well, old fellow, can't quarrel with you. Good-by. I'll come again."

"Come when I'm in a better temper," Hugo said with a smile, putting out his hand.

"Oh, that's all right," von Raven hastened to reply. "My compliments to the ladies. By Jove, there's a pretty girl! Saw us and started back. White apron."

"One of the maids," Hugo returned indifferently.

"Fresh as a peach, whatever she is, neat, like saucy little stage-maid," and the lieutenant peered through the shrubbery.

As he strode through the garden, silly Röschen took pains to cross his path. He put up his monocle, stared at her, smiled like a coxcomb, twirled his mustache, turned and watched her walk away. Her foolish heart beat fast, and she scarcely thought of anything but that splendid vision for days, finding the gentle giant in his blouse tiresome after so much blue-and-silver and high-boots.

"It must have been Röschen," thought Hugo, — "tripping to the trysting-place, which I have cruelly usurped. No doubt she's disappointed. But there are always snug corners for fond lovers. They won't suffer."

He lay still with his eyes closed. He was exceedingly weary and could no longer think quietly of his new scheme. Von Raven had put him completely out of tune, with chatter of hair and figures and eyes and Heaven knew what. "I don't know why he set me on edge. The man is not to blame for being well and enjoying himself. But I wanted to swear at him. Let Frau von Funnel, or somebody whose back does n't ache, take care of the little cripples. Let pretty girls dance and flirt and show their long hair for the little wretches. Nobody needs me."

All was quiet near him. Now and then the breeze stirred the twigs, or a bird chirped. He heard footsteps, and the rustle of bushes.

"It's that girl again. If mamma sees her haunting

this part of the garden, when not escorting Mousey, she 'll be discharged. I wish they would all leave me in peace — still — Röschen," he called, " Röschen ! "

The person behind him stepped back quickly, as if anxious to retreat, then paused, and at length replied:

" It is not Röschen."

Coming forward, she stood beside his chair, and said, looking down upon him gravely : —

" I am Gabrielle von Dohna."

CHAPTER XI.

GABRIELLE soon found that her only free time was early in the morning. After the countess appeared, the young girl came and went under stricter subjection than Babette and Röschen, whose lax consciences allowed them subterfuges and tricks to gain odd moments now and then. Every day at lunch the countess dilated upon her own ailments and Mousey's. Every day she fulminated at the butler and threatened to discharge the cook. She never by any accident consulted Gabrielle's pleasure, or asked if she had a choice of occupation. "We are going to drive at three," she would say; "wear your gray, and don't keep me waiting. I was educated to be punctual, above all to show some deference to my superiors."

At first, Gabrielle, surprised and ready to justify herself, would answer : —

"I beg your pardon, but have I ever kept you waiting?" But she speedily grasped the portentous fact that what she had done or left undone, what she was or was not, had not the remotest connection with the countess's insinuations. It was impossible to know what was wise and right to reply. The slightest attempt at self-justification would irritate her profoundly, silence made her furious, while an amiable effort to change the theme was apt to fan her wrath to a white heat.

It is easy to call a temper, colossal in its violence, a weakness. When one is exposed to its cruelties, it

has the effect of huge and brutal strength. Gabrielle
was frequently wretched, indignant, outraged. Accustomed to exceptional freedom, she felt the indignity of
her position more keenly than a less spirited girl, or
one more docile to worldly training. She made many
mistakes, had too little tact and wisdom with the surprising old lady who could open fire on all sides at once
and was capable not alone of malicious spurts but of
sustained and dangerous hostility. Whatever Gabrielle did or said, she always had reason to wish that
it had been something different. In spite of the constant overthrow of her calculations, she would ingenuously work out problems by which she hoped to attain
to reasonably pleasant intercourse with the countess;
and every evening, honestly reviewing the day and calling herself strictly to account, she would create conversations in which the suavity and sense of her own
remarks induced refreshing cordiality on the part of
Aunt Adelheid. Thus equipped, the young girl
would go forth to meet the exigencies of the morrow
with hope and courage. But the countess's response
was invariably all things else rather than what Gabrielle's imagination and buoyant hopefulness had anticipated, and she was at last forced to sorrowfully admit
that not patience, not undaunted cheerfulness, and not
vigilance, could prevent the Countess Kronfels' rages,
or ward off her missiles.

Meanwhile the handsome old lady and the charming
young girl drove in and out of the great gates, went
shopping, paid visits, and presented to the world an
attractive picture of serene age and youthful grace,
of kindly family-life and sympathetic companionship.
The people sauntering past the villa had the naive
habit of standing and gazing at anything that pleased

them.   When the Wynburg folk went out for a stroll,
it took its pleasures simply, but it took all that there
were.   It had a frugal mind and let nothing escape
it.   On Sunday, on the frequent holidays, at evening
after the day's work was done, it was always strolling
and tranquilly staring.   It was a peripatetic populace,
and the broad well-kept roads on all the hills around
the city seemed to be ever echoing the slow footsteps
of placid-faced pilgrims, — fathers and mothers with
an incredible trail of children, and little bow-legged
babies, — since almost as soon as they had made their
appearance on this planet, they had begun to soberly
measure off long distances upon it with methodical
Sunday excursions.   Very old men and women walked
regularly by the villa, guarding tenaciously their feeble
allowance of life ; while the steep flights of steps between the vineyards on the hill behind the house were
haunted by anxious beings, ascending with painful
puffs, and eager to leave behind, not their sins, like
the motley pilgrims on the Scala Santa, but a portion
of their superfluous adipose tissue — which is apt to
prove, in most instances, a heavier burden than in-
iquity.   Once, when a man climbed three hundred almost perpendicular steps at dawn of day, he was a
poet, a painter, or a lover.   Now he is a disciple of
Schweninger.

All the little world of pedestrians looked at the
countess and Gabrielle, and envied them.   "Nothing
to do but to be happy," was the usual comment, made
with a stolid stare, a weary sigh, or a ferment of envy,
according to the heart of the speaker.   Yet Gabrielle
was counting the days of her bondage, like a prisoner
in his cell, and comforting herself with visions of
home and freedom, when her father should have

returned from far-off seas. In her quieter and better
moments, when some recent affront was not rankling,
she was beginning to realize with a kind of wondering
pity, that Countess Kronfels was a most unhappy old
woman. Gabrielle often speculated upon the quality of
the intercourse between mother and son, but had no
opportunity to see them together. So far as she knew,
the countess made a more or less hasty descent upon
Hugo's quarters, every day toward noon, provided a
formal visitor in her own boudoir or an indisposition
on Mousey's part did not prevent.

April, after a prematurely warm March, was cold
and rainy. Hugo did not leave his rooms in some
weeks, and Gabrielle while regretting the invalid's enforced seclusion, could not suspect that the weather
was not its exclusive cause.

A spirited Hungarian horse found its way into the
Kronfels stables. Its name was Sphinx, which she
thought delightful. When, one morning, Lipps told
her that there was a horse for her to try in the court-
yard, she was on his back in a twinkling, and thanked
the countess warmly at lunch for the pleasure the
splendid animal had given her. The countess said
" Hm! " and for various motives kept her son's secret,
while Gabrielle for months cherished the innocent
conviction that the horse was a living proof of the
countess's inherent kindness. After being insulted,
brow - beaten, meanly suspected, and trodden under
foot, the young girl with a triumphant want of logic
would say : " How uncharitable I am ! There is
Sphinx."

She rode early every morning with Lipps in attendance. When she found that he was detailed for her
service, she was greatly distressed, and assured the

countess that she would rather not ride at all than take Count Hugo's man, and indeed she needed no groom out on the country roads.

To this the countess responded, with her inexplicable look of jealousy and mistrust, that she would thank Gabrielle not to attempt to dictate or interfere, that Gabrielle would perhaps allow one to have some control of the servants in one's own house ; that Lipps was the only one who had time to go; that it was very indelicate for a young lady to ride alone, whatever people did at Dohna ; and as to getting in a pet, and not riding at all, if Gabrielle, after a horse had been specially provided for her, imagined that she could play fast and loose in an ill-bred and capricious fashion, she was extremely mistaken. This tirade, induced by the countess's chronic objection to independent enjoyment on the part of her subjects by her deep-seated envy of youth and freshness, and by the hot remembrance of Hugo's stern injunctions which controlled her against her will, was sufficient to render Gabrielle perplexed, uncomfortable, and indignant, but could not permanently cool her ardor. How early she began her flight, how swiftly she went, and how far beyond Leslach out into the open country, — through woods and a game-park, past sloping orchards and undulating meadows and villages nestled high and low among a myriad of hills, the countess never inquired, and Gabrielle soon learned to avoid the subject. In rash enthusiasm, she ventured to expatiate upon the delights of her first ride, and told the countess that the country was as fresh as the Garden of Eden.

" Spare me your rhodomontades ! " was the reply. " One would think no one else had ever ridden. I

was an expert horsewoman, when I was " — she hesitated, then said — " strong. Dear Dr. Pressigny told
me that I was too sensitive to bear so violent exercise.
Women who ride have usually rather tough nerves,"
she added, with a disparaging scrutiny of Gabrielle's
fresh color. After that, Gabrielle spared her, reflecting that it was very remarkable for her to sweetly
provide the pleasure, and then be so inconsistent and
unamiable because one thoroughly enjoyed it; but, as
in many another instance, the young girl concluded
to hold her peace and accept the inevitable; and as
the inevitable included a horse, the countess's antagonism sank into the background.

Gabrielle would return from her ride fresh, free,
and glad, slip in the side-door, out of consideration for
the countess's nerves and Mousey's, tip-toe up the servants' stairway, and write a happy letter to her father.
Only the man whose smallest practical need — a handkerchief from his chest of drawers, a book from his
shelves — required another's ministrations knew how
long she rode in the fresh morning world. Her letters of this epoch conveyed to the Baron von Dohna
an impression of excellent spirits, but he sometimes
wished that she would say less of her horse and the
beauties of nature, and more of the people with whom
she was living.

The line of march for the afternoon was consistent
in its inconsistency. If the countess said that they
were going shopping, Gabrielle could be tolerably
sure that they would make visits; if the order was visits, they usually spent a few hours in shops, where the
countess would sometimes buy with large and luxurious caprice, and again would grow unhappy over the
price of a necessity. Gabrielle greatly dreaded the

countess's access of economy, and particularly her
soap-quest.   With an uneasy look on her pale face,
she would drive to small out-of-the-way shops and haggle long with strange anxiety.   Mousey, who usually
accompanied them on these expeditions, seemed to
growl at dogs and men with even a darker misan-
thropy than that which ordinarily filled his fierce
breast.   While the countess was suspiciously glaring
at the humble soap-boiler and frightening his sickly
wife and the children clinging to her skirts, Gabrielle,
left in the coupé to entertain the lovey-dovey-dog-
gums, could with difficulty prevent him from springing through the glass in insensate fury at the poor
and needy whom he hated, and who in these unfash-
ionable streets, where the countess for inscrutable reasons sought to save a penny, were continually passing
with their irritating bundles and insulting baskets,
exciting him to the verge of delirium.

In large shops, where the countess would order the
last expensive thing in bric-à-brac, she was welcome,
for a skilful salesman knew how to play upon her
capricious vanity and reach her eminently respectable
purse; but she was a terrible scourge whenever her
large, stern, yet uneasy countenance appeared in a
poor man's precincts; and it often occurred to Gabrielle, as she sat struggling with the dog and watching the scene in the little shop, that if the patient and
long-suffering Wynburg populace should ever rise and
slay in revolutionary madness, the Countess Kronfels
would surely be among the first victims.

The drives, the visits and dinners grew more and
more tedious to Gabrielle, and her manner became
more indifferent every day.   If she happened to
like a face, or be attracted by some stranger, she

straightway heard a defamatory tale from the countess's mocking lips. Gabrielle might refuse to believe it, but it would haunt her memory, perplex her, and restrain the cordial greeting and outstretched hand she would have proffered if left free to follow her inclination. Perhaps her hardest trial was the necessity of listening to belittling recitals of the world in which she now found herself. No one escaped but Frau von Funnel. Toward this exemplary person Gabrielle still felt the innocent and impassioned homage which a young girl sometimes offers an older and fascinating woman. Gabrielle's desire to serve, to yield her will to that serene guiding power, to become as wax in those deft hands, had not as yet found verbal expression, because she never had seen the Frau Major except in the presence of the countess; still, without words, Gabrielle knew from the Frau Major's subtle sympathy that the mute allegiance was comprehended and accepted. Another person whom Gabrielle greatly liked was Mercedes von Waldenberg. She was beautiful, brilliant, and uniformly attentive and friendly. They became friends, so far as an affectionate and free intercourse skimming along cheerily on the surface of things means friendship. They called each other by their first names, enjoyed each other's society, and each kept her own secrets. This easy and amiable relationship bade fair to continue as it had begun, and doubtless would never have developed any ambition toward a profounder and therefore more troublesome element, had not Gabrielle been constitutionally inclined not to let well enough alone, but to struggle to make it better, also to leap before she looked, and in short to disregard all old saws in which caution figures as the highest virtue.

One night, returning home unusually late, she noticed far down the drive that Hugo's rooms were lighted. She had enjoyed the evening. After the opera, there had been a gay little supper with the Waldenberg party, at a restaurant. Mercedes was charming and in brilliant spirits. Beside her marquis she had several officers in her train, among them a man with steady, sensible eyes, whom she presented to Gabrielle as " a very, very old friend, — Baron von Paalzow, returned, at last, from Berlin."

Leaning back comfortably in her corner of the carriage, Gabrielle recalled the evening with unwonted satisfaction. She had been skilfully seated by Mercedes, in the centre of her gay young court, and invigoratingly far from Aunt Adelheid. With the removal of the crushing and benumbing influence, Gabrielle's natural cheerfulness rebounded and asserted itself blithely. Silent, smiling, lost in indolent retrospection, she was now approaching the house, when the sudden gleam of Hugo's windows between gaunt, black tree-trunks revealed his forlorn figure to her consciousness as vividly as if she were beholding his actual presence, and involuntarily she reproached herself for her light-heartedness. How hopelessly long and lonely his days were, and how different it might be at the villa, — how sunny and kindly and sympathetic ! Why could she not run in and bring him some of the laughter and brightness and careless gayety of the evening ?

" Are not Count Hugo's rooms lighted very late ? " she remarked.

" Oh dear, yes, — he reads late. Do you know, if I were the Marquis de Vallion, I would nip Mercedes and Paalzow's reminiscences in the bud ? They seemed to date from cradle-days, and they promise to multiply with amazing rapidity."

" But it is not his reading-lamp, Aunt Adelheid," Gabrielle persisted; " the whole wing is brilliantly lighted, as if Lipps had forgotten, or had been too busy to think of lights and windows. Could Count Hugo be suffering? Could he be suddenly ill?"

" Why do you deliberately go out of your way to choose annoying subjects that try my nerves? Do you wish to keep me awake till morning? And why always harp upon Hugo? Has he not the right to burn his gas as long as he pleases, without consulting you? He would not thank you for your interference and inquisitiveness, — so much I can assure you; and I don't thank you for your croaking."

Gabrielle sighed.

" I was only sorry," she answered.

" Sorry? What of that? Is that anything extraordinary? Who is not sorry? It seems to me nothing less than impertinence to tell his own mother in that tone of voice that you are sorry! Sorry, indeed! Hm!"

Gabrielle said nothing, and presently the countess went on with abated heat, but still irritably : —

"Suppose I should go to him. Is that what you mean to insinuate? I should simply meet with a very unpleasant and mocking reception for my pains. There is nothing sudden to be apprehended in Hugo's case. It is a dispensation of Providence, and ought to be borne with resignation. As for rushing in and making a scene every time he has a light more or less, — really, Gabrielle — you have positively — no tact!"

Under other circumstances the singular climax to

this oration might have made Gabrielle smile. In her present state of mind she perceived nothing amusing in the situation.

"You are right," she said with grave acquiescence, "I have none. No one in the world could have less."

The countess being in an evening mood, and her "French" mood, and a pleasingly stimulated after-supper mood, did not dwell long upon the disturbing topic of her son's infirmities. Once in her room, and having had some of her stiff worldly harness replaced by a wrapper, she sat in her favorite chair, sipping a last glass of curaçoa, — a "wee nightcap," she called it, — and, graciously ignoring Gabrielle's want of tact, reinstated her in favor as "Moonbeam" and "sweet pet," and commented with sprightliest malice upon the friends of whose salt they had just partaken.

When at last Gabrielle was released and safe in her own room, she was eager to satisfy herself that those lower windows no longer sent out their unwonted message, but the lawn was still flooded with light. Listening uneasily, she heard doors close, and once she was sure that Lipps went for something in a distant part of the house. Count Hugo was undoubtedly ill. He was always ill, indeed. But he must be suffering unusual pain. She had known it instinctively, when instead of the one faint glimmer from the shaded reading-lamp in his sleeping-room she had perceived that startlingly irrelevant illumination. She had learned to watch for his window as she drove home late, to greet it afar off as a familiar and pleasant thing, and to send him, in spite of himself, a kind good-night and gentle pitying thoughts. More than once she had smiled at the interest she regularly felt in the faintly shining distant window of a man who persistently manifested, not mere indifference, but a pronounced objection to her society. But her sympathy was too sincere, her indulgence too large, for her to be capable of any petty annoyance because of his attitude toward her. Then there was so little that was homelike at the villa, so little to which she could feel attached, that she had grown to make the most of that one window, and to regard it with a species of affection, whatever inimical sentiments toward her might be cherished behind it. She had even accustomed herself to see in imagination the invalid's face on his pillow, and the pile of books and magazines on one table, while upon another, the best possible burner under the best possible shade shed its light upon his midnight vigils. Through floors and through walls, she pictured him day by day. What she, who never seemed to ask a question, learned from Lipps, who never seemed to communicate anything about his master, was also considerable, and the boundless devotion of the simple man who rode behind her nearly every morning did not tend to make her think less kindly of the count. Then she had seen him by chance that day in the garden, and could not lightly forget his pale worn face, his searching eyes, and long thin hands. To-night she recalled him with peculiar vividness, lying in his chair among red cushions, saw him make an instinctive effort to rise, then sink back wearily, as she stood by him a little startled, yet not ill-pleased to look at last upon the mystery face to face. It was not, indeed, a grewsome mystery. She had felt that, with a warm rush of pity in her heart, as the pale man fixed his eyes in silence upon her. He had extended no hand in welcome. He uttered no word of greeting. The countess had told her, indeed, and often enough, that he did not desire to know her. But as she saw pride and strength laid so pitifully low, she had no thought of self and wounded dignity.

"I did not know that you were here," she had begun, — and how the fresh sweetness of her voice sounded in Hugo's ears after his long exile from the world she had no suspicion, — "I did not know, but I am not sorry, unless it disturbs you." She held out her hand frankly. "I have greatly wished to know you," she continued after a little pause, in which she waited in vain for him to speak.

He did not appear to notice her gesture.

She colored slightly and began again, not without timidity : —

"Could I not come and chat with you, now and then ? "

"Thanks," he said at length and very coldly, "I am not a sociable person. I am not fond of chatting."

Again she hesitated.

"I could read to you," she proposed.

"Thanks. There is nothing whatever the matter with my eyes."

"That is a mercy," she said simply. "Yes, they look strong," scrutinizing them in a business-like manner, and not as women in former days had regarded Hugo Kronfels' eyes.

"And I really can do nothing for you — nothing at all?" she asked regretfully.

"If I were not a cripple she would not insist," Hugo told himself with bitterness. "A cripple is no man. Hence her fearlessness and pious benevolence."

"Nothing, thanks," he returned with extreme ceremony.

She looked distressed and was silent, while her soft clear gaze rested long and thoughtfully upon him, noting his strong spirited features, pinched and wan now, the compressed mouth, the pallor of his hands, and the books lying on his knee.

" I am very, very sorry," she said, and turned away. Then, with a quick movement, and a sudden and charming smile, " You may change your mind," she added hopefully, "and if you should ever want me and would kindly send for me, you would make me very happy."

But nearly a month had passed, and he had not sent for her. He had been invisible, buried in his rooms. Why did he see no one? Why were things so unnatural, so uncomfortable, so much worse than they need be? If everybody would only do his best, it would all be quite different. But everybody seemed determined to do his worst. For instance, at that moment, why were she and the countess not with him? A woman's presence would surely be of some comfort. Surely sympathy, affection, kindness, would be worth something to him. The countess was human, she could not be entirely destitute of natural affection; she had her amiable qualities, there was Sphinx; and had she not subscribed very liberally for various charities? If she could only be induced to forget herself and Mousey, for her son's sake. She was so pretty when she was not angry or mistrustful. There was not a prettier old lady in the world. She could not really know how forlorn Hugo's fate was. No one was wholly cold, wholly selfish.

Ah, it seemed as if they were all led by some perverse malicious imp to do the wrong, unlovely thing. Hugo himself — one could excuse him indeed —

was the most uncompromisingly ungracious being in
the world. If he had not had such great sad eyes,
she could scarcely have forgiven him for his frigidity.

She indeed was always blundering, always awkward
and unfortunate, literally without "tact," as the countess had said. How was it possible to live weeks in
this house, and with the best will in the world never
succeed in doing anything sensible and desirable and
good? She had excelled in the art of irritating the
countess, and had advanced not an inch toward Hugo.
Yet his prejudices — the whims of a sick man — could
not be invincible. Here was no robber-knight's castle
to be stormed. Here was no arduous task. The facts
were simple, commonplace indeed, yet stubborn and
immovable, crystallized in unyielding forms. If she
had but approached him wisely in the garden that
morning! How hard, how impossible it was to be
wise! Yet at Dohna, she had never troubled herself
to consider whether she was wise or unwise.

"I have been so self-confident," she thought sorrowfully, "and I have no qualities which are of any use
in this situation. It is obvious that no one could do
worse than I have done. Lucie would know how to
make things more kindly and human," she reflected,
with sudden surprise at this involuntary tribute to
Frau von Dohna's sagacity. "The Frau Major could
advise me, but it is not easy to speak of Aunt Adelheid to her intimate friend."

And Mercedes? Could she not help matters? Why
did she not come to Count Hugo? Why did not
everybody do the simple natural thing? They had
been friends. Mercedes said so, and the world with
knowing hints and sly smiles and the all-potent "if,"
never ceased to allude to them together. At the

opera, that evening, Gabrielle had thought much of Mercedes, watching her across the house, as she came in beautiful and radiant, followed by her smirking old marquis. Afterwards, at supper, Gabrielle forgot her earnest thoughts, and enjoyed herself without restraint, for Mercedes could be as droll as she was winning, and to-night her mood was irresistible.

But now Gabrielle's problems confronted her again. Until the lights were out below, she did not sleep. She was excited, troubled, and sad. It seemed to her that it would be a crime for Mercedes to marry that old man. And as she thought of Mercedes, it seemed to her that strange magnetic currents were bringing her messages from the sufferer, telling her of his pain, his loneliness, and his defiance, — were revealing his pale haughty face, pathetic in its gloom and reserve. Was this life? Was this the world they had wanted her to see? Only a little circle, yet all wrong, where it might easily — yes, easily — be right. A touch here, a change there, and all would be transformed. Yet how powerless one was! Had one always one's self to thank for one's misfortunes? Was each soul always its own worst enemy?

The hill-lights burned across the valley. It was very still, except for a dog barking at intervals in a lower street, and somewhere — near or far she could not judge — some one was splitting wood with surprising distinctness. She wondered why, at that hour. Perhaps there were illness and suffering there too. Perhaps the man's wife or child was ill. How much sorrow there was in the world! Yet though disease and pain and death must come, if tenderness and truth need not fail — this thought seemed wonderful and new to the young girl, and took possession of her with the strength of a great revelation — might there not still be peace mightier than fate's most cruel blows — a peace that passeth understanding ?

The lawn was gradually growing dusky.   Lipps was putting out the lights.   It was after two o'clock. " Dear old faithful, patient, loving Lipps ! " she murmured.   " If we all knew our duty and did it as simply as you, and with your untiring heart !

" But I will not give up.   I will talk with Mercedes. I will see her at once — to-morrow.   She can do what I cannot.   She can do anything she will.   At all events I must speak with her — of herself — of Count Hugo — of all these thoughts that haunt me."

CHAPTER XII.

Toward nine the following morning, Mercedes sat in her room, drinking her coffee and reading a French novel in a desultory fashion, when Gabrielle was announced. As she entered, Mercedes cried : —

"This is perfect! Come and sit here by me, and tell me all about it."

"Tell you about what?"

"Why, whatever sent you down to me so early, — Heaven bless it! I hope it is an affair of the heart, if that is not too indiscreet on my part."

"You do yourself injustice," Gabrielle replied; "I have come simply to see you, — to see you freely and alone, without all the world watching and listening."

"Ah, the world!" yawned Mercedes, throwing up her slight round arms in their loose sleeves, and leaning her head back comfortably. "Poor old world! How they did abuse it! Surely you are not going to attack it, Gabrielle? It is amazingly kind to you."

"I suppose it would seem very stupid of me to find fault with what I understand so little; yet I don't always like it — that is not so much of it — and all the time. In the country, I used to meet fewer people, and meet them differently."

"Your affectation of rusticity is always a delight to me. You know very well that you crush us all with your grand air. Mamma praises you unconditionally. I can hardly expect you to appreciate the awful significance of this information," — Mercedes laughed a little, — "but I assure you it has never happened in the case of any other mortal. Some one asked me last night, Do you suppose it is possible for anybody to be as quiet as the Baroness von Dohna looks?"

"What nonsense! I am far from quiet. I am unquiet, and restless. That is why I am here."

"Ah, a heart-history, after all!" Mercedes had ordered some hot coffee, and now poured a cup for her guest. "Drink and confess!" she said with a flashing smile. She looked less fresh and young than in evening dress; her face in repose showed some hard deep lines about the eyes and mouth, and the skin was "fatigued," as the French say. But Gabrielle was a generous critic, and found the graceful dark woman, in her fantastic *négligé* of rose-colored crepe, marvellously lovely and winning.

"Come, child, which one is it?"

Gabrielle smiled. "Shall you not be interested unless I talk of lovers? I really have none."

"I am interested in you, and everything that concerns you," Mercedes replied cordially. "Still, it is a pity that you can't, or rather won't, entertain me with lovers. Lovers may not amount to much, but they are more interesting than most things women talk about. It is so good of you to help me dawdle away my morning. My book is as stupid as it is immoral, and my thoughts are far from merry." She sighed, then added brightly: "What a mistake late suppers are! They are ruinous to the spirits and death to the complexion. Particularly game-patties, don't you think so?"

"Mercedes," began Gabrielle abruptly, "do you know any happy people?"

"Oh," returned the other, smiling and lifting her eyebrows, "the inquisitor-general! Let me see that

there are no spies." She walked across the room,
opened a door, and glanced into the adjoining chamber. "My sprightly sister has gone down," she explained. "She is younger than I, she is not engaged
to be married, and her days are not too long. I am
my own mistress only in the morning, like you —
you poor dear," she added laughing lightly. "After
that, we are the slaves of age. That is not a nice
speech, I admit. You look so serious and honest, you
tempt me to speak the truth, but it's not a frequent
fault of mine, and I repent already."

"Mercedes!" expostulated Gabrielle laughing.

"Now for your catechism. Do I know any happy
people? Except children and fools, no. Do you?"

"Not here; not in Wynburg. That is, not in your
world."

"My dear Gabrielle, I must insist upon respect for
my world, in my presence. I am a worldling to the tips
of my toes. The world snaps at me, as that little vile
Mousey snaps at the Countess Kronfels, and abuses me
and tyrannizes over me, but I am faithful to it as she
is to her ugly little cur. By the way, is he not a nui-
sance? If I were you, I should be tempted to give him
a dose of cyankali. But her devotion and mine are
pathetic all the same. We cannot live without our
heart's desire."

Gabrielle smiled with candid admiration. She liked
Mercedes' rapid way of talking nonsense.

"I have seen but one happy person since I came to
Wynburg," said the young girl meditatively. "He is
a stone-carver, who works on a house near us. He
sings like a glad angel all day long. The other day,
in a violent thunder-storm, between the peals, I heard
that man's high sweet voice singing Robin Adair."

" Mark my words, he is doomed.   He will fall from his scaffolding and break his neck, or even now some curse is on him which he does not suspect.   He belongs to the children-and-fools category."

Gabrielle shook her head.   " He is not a fool.   He has a lovely face, and he looks calm and wise."

" After all, his singing proves nothing.   We all sing, do we not?   I sing."

" Not like him," Gabrielle said gently.

" But we can't all take to stone-carving and tenor solos for our peace of mind ? "

" No, but I wish we might learn his secret.   He comes in now and then to see Count Hugo."

"Ah," said Mercedes quickly, the mockery fading from her face.

" Lipps — he rides with me now, you know — tells me the count likes the man greatly."

" Lipps?   Not Count Hugo himself ? "

" I never see Count Hugo.   I have seen him but once, and that quite by accident."

" Indeed," rejoined Mercedes.

Neither spoke for a moment.

There was not a sound in the room except the gentle ticking of a crystal clock.   Mercedes, usually given to fluttering, rapid gestures, sat motionless, her head drooping, her eyes fixed upon her rosy folds and lace. While Gabrielle, her elbow on the table, her cheek resting on her hand, regarded the lovely woman before her so thoughtfully, and with so direct and questioning a gaze, that Mercedes felt it through her downcast lids.

" Count Hugo lies hours and hours alone, every day — entirely alone," Gabrielle began, low and slowly, and with little pauses, as if she saw what she re-counted.   " He reads much, of course, but one cannot always read. There he lies, thinking the saddest of sad thoughts and staring at the ceiling with his great mournful eyes. When I saw him — it was in the garden, a month ago — his face was pale as death, and his hands were thin — like a woman's at home who died. I can see him still, just as the sunshine fell on him, — shivering under his wraps, — and I remember his eyes — his great beautiful melancholy eyes."

" Don't," Mercedes ejaculated inaudibly.

" I beg your pardon."

" No, no, it is nothing. I merely — Go on, Gabrielle. Do you know," she continued lightly, " it is really beginning to be as interesting as lovers? You were saying that you remember Count Hugo Kronfels' eyes. They are very handsome eyes, so why should you not remember them? What next? "

" They are very sad eyes. They make one's heart ache. Even pain and a crippled body need not make them so unutterably sad. But they look upon nothing happy, — nothing loving and true."

Mercedes played with the lace on her sleeve, and after a moment replied, with somewhat hard mirth : —

" No, if he won't look at you, and only sees his mamma! She is certainly not happy and loving and true. What deliciously odd words you use ! "

" I doubt if she can help him," Gabrielle said gently. " I think that you are the only one who could help him, Mercedes."

" I ? Impossible," she returned with a start.

" Were you not his friend? "

" I knew him well — yes."

" And you liked him? "

Mercedes smiled singularly. " Yes, I liked him — much."

" And what was he, in those days ? "

Mercedes stared, shrugged her shoulders, was about to give an evasive reply, hesitated, then yielding irresistibly to Gabrielle's soft persistence said impetuously : —

" Hugo von Kronfels was the handsomest, kindest, sunniest, happiest, bravest man I ever knew ! "

" Then why do you leave him to suffer alone — you who were his friend ? " asked the mild, relentless voice.

" But, Gabrielle," protested Mercedes, " one does not ask such questions ! Not that my conscience has not asked them, scores of times," she added gayly, " but I have the habit of snubbing my conscience. It has not dared to give a sign of life, since — really, I forget when it last spoke, it was so long ago."

Gabrielle waited, and at length rejoined : —

" But you don't answer me."

Mercedes frowned slightly, looked sharply at Gabrielle an instant, then smiled with an incredulous air, as if so much seriousness and honesty were beyond belief.

" What a child you are ! You forget that I have promised to marry the Marquis de Vallion."

" Oh, no, I remember that only too well."

This unequivocal statement produced in Mercedes a strong feeling of surprise. What people thought of her engagement she was fully aware ; but, as she had observed, there are questions one does not ask and things one does not say, and to the steps of the altar, and beyond, she expected to be accompanied by a loud and unbroken chorus of felicitation. It was an artistic combination of perjury and orange-blossoms, but why not ? Did it not happen every day ? She looked kindly at Gabrielle, reflecting that the thing that did not happen every day was listening to truth from the heart of a friend. Yet it being the habit of her life to jest, she did not surrender at once, but rallied again.

"I beg your pardon, Gabrielle," she said with mock seriousness, "do you feel quite well this morning? Because, do you know, you have certain symptoms that are so unusual, they alarm me."

"I think that I am in my right mind," Gabrielle returned, "but perhaps I am not, after all, for everybody seems unhappy to me, and everything is at cross purposes, and it might all be so different."

"What might be different?" demanded Mercedes abruptly. Then in her bantering tone: "One must humor you, for evidently there is no escape for the light-minded and giddy."

"But that is not what you are, Mercedes."

"You do not know me."

"I know that you are beautiful and good, — and not happy."

"Happy!" repeated Mercedes bitterly.

"I don't mean that one can draw a line of demarcation between the positively happy and the positively unhappy," Gabrielle went on trustingly, and appealing always to the real Mercedes behind the mask. "Children reason in that way, and I may have had that uncompromising idea not so very long ago," she added with a slight smile. "But lately it seems to me there must be happiness, beyond all griefs, — happiness — or something better."

"Better than happiness? You are sure it isn't a conundrum? I really can't soar in your lofty regions, and happiness is quite good enough for me."

"One hears things all one's life that are only empty words, until suddenly their meaning dawns upon one.

It was so with me last night," Gabrielle continued
thoughtfully.

" It was not in church last Sunday ? " Mercedes suggested.

" Ah, let me tell you!   There were all the people,
Mercedes, and I was watching them, and suddenly I
thought : ' Each one of us is a spirit, not only when we
die, but now.'   I perceived it, I felt it, and I cannot tell
you how strongly, — as if it were my own discovery,
and no one had ever known it before.   ' Beneath the
silk,' I thought, ' and velvet, and feathers, and lace,
and the smiles, is a soul.' "

" Are you so sure of that ? " Mercedes asked scornfully.   " Some of them — yes, — but not all.   Oh,
dear, no ! "

" And it seemed to me all the souls were seeking and
not finding, and that so many were wandering on the
wrong road."

" Please don't let it be an allegory, Gabrielle !   I
can bear a sermon, having just had my coffee.   But
allegories never agreed with me."

Gabrielle looked at her affectionately with a little
laugh.

" I don't doubt it all sounds stupid enough.   I am
only trying to show you what I was thinking at the
opera, and afterwards late in the night, at home, and
then you would understand why I came to you this
morning.   I saw how lovely you were, and it seemed
to me that you were on the wrong road, too.   I thought
that your loveliness could comfort one who is sorrowful
and forsaken, and that you might find a joy deeper
than any you now know.   And I wondered why no
one was loving enough to dare to tell you so.   I
wondered why all were silent, — your mother, your

sister, and every one. Suddenly, something within
me said : —

"'But you are silent, too. Why do you not speak?'
And here I am, Mercedes, and I have spoken."

"Like a little bishop!" retorted Mercedes, smiling
gallantly still, "like an apostle to the heathen." Suddenly she crossed her arms on the table and leaned
her head upon them.

Gabrielle rose, and stood with her hand on the bowed
head.

"Forgive me, Mercedes, if I am awkward," she said.
"I don't really care for that, if only you understand.
Listen, Mercedes. Why may I not speak the truth?
You cannot love that old man. Must I pretend that
I think you do? Why do you marry him? Why do
you not come to that lonely room and seek your friend?
If he was kind and generous and brave when he was
well, is he less so now? If he loved you when all
the world was at his feet, would he not love you infinitely more, now that the world has forgotten him?
It would be so beautiful to be needed. I know one
naturally thinks first of strength, bodily strength, and
health, and all that, but when one sees the strong ones,
and how vapid they are sometimes, how thoughtless
and selfish, and then when one looks at him, why,
Mercedes, I could take you in my arms and carry you
to him!"

Mercedes neither spoke nor moved.

"I come home late, perhaps. I hear no sound from
below. Yet I cannot forget that he is lying there,
often sleepless and in pain. He is patient with pain
and neglect and loneliness. But he has lost something precious. Something dearer than health. I
think it is you, Mercedes, — and his faith. Last

night, he seemed to be ill. I saw him before me every instant. A poor man in a hut, with one soul near to love and comprehend him, is better off. I saw you too, smiling, and bewitching, — I never saw any one as lovely as you, — and I thought, if he is wretched, so is she; if his life has no love and faith, hers too is cold, and perhaps, as the years go by, hers will be the more cruel, for one could imagine his spirit free in spite of his bonds, while her chains must grow heavier in time. But these were only my thoughts — and it is not too late, Mercedes." Her voice sounded glad and sure as if heralding good tidings. "Dear Mercedes!" she exclaimed.

At last Mercedes raised her head. Her hair was slightly roughened, her cheeks were flushed, her eyes singularly brilliant, and she began in the half affectionate, half mocking tone, which she was apt to use with Gabrielle : —

"My dear child, it all sounds beautiful, but it is too late, — just six-and-twenty years and five months too late."

"I do not see why," returned Gabrielle quickly. "You would say to the marquis: 'Marquis, forgive me; I have made a great mistake, but I should make a worse one for you and for me, if I should marry you.' You would say to the countess: 'Mamma, I simply cannot and will not marry him.' Then you would come straight to the villa, and pass through the long corridor to Count Hugo's rooms, and knock. He would call, 'Come in,' quite indifferently. And the door would open, — and it would be you — you, Mercedes, standing there — and from that moment, his life would be glad!"

Mercedes made a hasty gesture, as if she would interrupt, but let the young girl go on, and finish the picture, which seemed to her so defined in its outlines, so easy of execution, and which brought a succession of emotions to the listener's face, and finally a smile at Gabrielle's preposterous simplicity.

"Oh, you little Donna Quixote! Are you going to make the crooked straight and redress all wrongs? Do you intend to tell the little Mayers that they will kill themselves if they lace so unconscionably? Now I personally think that it is not of the slightest importance, whether they squeeze their various minute organs out of existence or not, and I should never feel called to the holy mission of expostulation."

The light of enthusiasm faded from Gabrielle's face. As she had warmed with her subject, she persuaded herself with happy confidence that all would yet be well. But Mercedes' raillery discouraged her at last, and she looked pained and doubtful, as she replied : —

"You mean that I am meddlesome."

"No, a thousand times, no!" Mercedes exclaimed warmly. "It is only that you are wasting time and feeling on me, and I am not worth it. What you say is true, or would be true, if I were like you. I am not in the least like you, and you forget that."

"Nothing that you say of yourself makes any difference," Gabrielle returned eagerly, brightening again with Mercedes' cordial tone. "I am so sorry to be intrusive. Aunt Adelheid complains that I have no tact, and she is perfectly right. But let me speak out this once."

"What, have you not spoken 'out,' yet? You surely cannot surpass this?"

"Oh, you may laugh at me as much as you wish,

Mercedes. I do not feel that I have said anything, — not anything at all yet. Or if I have, I have said it so badly that it makes no impression. But imagine it said cleverly, — with 'tact,' " she pleaded, laughing a little in spite of her earnestness, and looking wistfully at her friend. " Let me try again. I think that I see a danger threatening you. I see it and feel it. Then why should I not warn you ? One lesson I have learned for all my life. If you live with some one who loves you and comprehends you, with whom you are fearless and free, whose nature you reach and rest upon, whose sympathy you need like sunshine and air, why that is the most beautiful thing on earth, whether the some one be your father or your mother, your sister or brother, or lover or husband or friend. But if you live intimately with a person who does not love you, and whom you do not love, who misinterprets every word and look, who suspects you and makes you suspicious, who crushes you, hurts you, rouses all that is mean in you, and there is no escape from her — I mean from the person — why that is, I won't say the most miserable thing in the world, for there may be something worse, but it is the worst that I know, and it is a bad thing, Mercedes, — a very bad thing, an ugly thing ! That is why I dare to ask you what will your life with the Marquis de Vallion be ? What can he give you ? What can you give him ? What kind of companionship would that be ? Oh, Mercedes, Mercedes, it will be terrible ! "

" What ! So impassioned ? Actually, tears in your eyes ! But, Gabrielle, believe me, it is not so tragic. They are not going to burn me alive. There is no sacrifice, no compulsion. I wish to marry the marquis."

" You wish to marry the marquis? " faltered Gabrielle.

" That is, I do not ardently desire to marry any one. But since it is about time that I should marry, — in fact, my sisters accuse me, with some justice, of culpable delay, — he will answer my purpose."

" But why must you marry? "

" Why? Really, Gabrielle, your 'why' is ubiquitous. You question self-evident truths; but since you insist upon categorical answers, — after a certain age one is less comfortable and free, unmarried. One is a little absurd, you know. I could be a 'Stiftsdame' as a last refuge, of course. But I have no talent for retirement, and the intimate society of other women is, to speak mildly, obnoxious to me. No, I greatly prefer men, — even the marquis. Now it 's my turn to question. Why are you not more charitable, — like Frau von Funnel, for instance? How do you know that you are not doing the marquis injustice? How can you prove that he has not some hidden charm, some grace that only I perceive? It is evident that I do not marry him for his youth, or strength, or beauty, or intellect, but how can you be sure that he has not irresistible heart-qualities? How can you reconcile it with your conscience to jump at conclusions in this manner — and doubt the elevation of my sentiments?"

" That 's not fair," Gabrielle returned, hurt and offended. " I don't deserve that."

" No, I don't think you do," Mercedes admitted reflectively ; " I rather like a fencing match, but I see that you are in no mood for one, and then I confess, although you have said very droll things to me, — in fact, from any one else I should consider them impertinent, — I do not regard you as an enemy to be routed.

You have been honest with me, and I like you for it, particularly, as I cannot discover what, in any event, you have to gain by it."

She spoke in a light, laughing voice, with much animation of manner and gesture, and a charming and friendly smile.

"Now my honesty is not your honesty," she continued, "but it is the best I can produce, and such as it is, you shall have it. I do not deny that you have said things that move me this morning, that make me think, even regret, — softened me, don't you know? Yes, 'softened' is the word in Sunday-school books, hardened reprobates always become 'softened' — but it won't last, child! Nothing lasts with me. I am fickle as the wind, except in one respect — my ambition. I must have power, and one wants more, not less, as one grows old, and one's beauty goes. I don't care to live without it. I want balls, and dinners, and toilettes, and admiration. I adore the world. I pretend that I am weary of it. I may be now and then. But I cannot live without it. I can talk about solitude and purling brooks and self-communion, but they would be insufferable to me. So you see, you dear, queer little prophet, before you rescue me you must construct, not new circumstances alone, but a new Mercedes. Cheer up, then, and wish me joy. I shall be a gracious embassadress, hospitable and indulgent to the foibles of the world, the flesh, and the devil. My married life will be perfection, for the marquis and I shall meet too rarely to quarrel. I shall drive and dance and chat with all my old friends as to-day, except I shall be freer to amuse myself, and infinitely more important than Mercedes Waldenberg."

"And Hugo?" demanded Gabrielle abruptly.

Mercedes turned, walked down the room and back, came close to Gabrielle, put her hands on the young girl's shoulders, met her direct questioning gaze with an inscrutable smile, and said kindly : —

"You are a great child. You insist upon pressing your finger on old wounds, and you are more merciless than you know. Never mind. This is my first and last confession. You have roused me to a certain excitement. Did I not prophesy that you would be as interesting as lovers? My dear, the kindest deed that I can do Hugo von Kronfels is never to see him again. Do you think that I have not considered? Can you possibly imagine that I did not weigh everything in the balance those first days when he lay between life and death, and later when his old comrades were denied admittance, and I heard how gloomy and changed he was? Do you suppose that I did not know in my heart that he was waiting for me? Have I not longed a thousand times to steal through that corridor, as you say, and knock and go in?"

"But Mercedes, see," Gabrielle urged impetuously, "you think yourself there. That is almost being there. It is still not too late. You have the choice."

"No, no, I have no choice."

"It is cruel," murmured Gabrielle; "I would go to him, if I had to crawl!"

"Then what prevents you?" Mercedes retorted calmly, smoothing a knot of ribbon on her sleeve.

"He — he prevents me," said Gabrielle innocently.

"Ah, yes, I remember."

"I pity him with all my heart, and I feel his presence always."

"I understand; and that made you exaggerate."

"I pitied you, too."

" Envy me," returned Mercedes, airily, " for I shall
have what I wish. I simply must have brightness and
gayety and excitement. I have a horror of pain and
illness and darkened rooms and fumigation and all
that. I don't think there is a phenomenon in the universe so wonderful to me as a woman who deliberately
chooses to be a nurse, unless it is a man who elects to
be a doctor. I faint at the sight of blood. I hate and
fear physical pain. You may call it what you will,
but I could not bear to see Hugo Kronfels crippled.
I did not dare to see him. I am a mean coward, you
see, but this is why I did not go and knock, and enact
the charming little comedy on the lines which you have
indicated."

" Oh, Mercedes, Mercedes ! "

" I could not look upon him broken and helpless,
he was so full of splendid life. If I should see him
now, I should be afraid of him. I should turn away
from him in horror. I should have no comfort to
give him. As to marrying him, which you ingenuously
suggest, without even knowing that he wants me, — it
would be living death to me to spend my days in an
invalid's room. It would be a tomb. For me, Hugo
died last September. *Voila tout !* "

" Ah," sighed Gabrielle, " I have made a great
mistake ; I thought that you were his friend."

Mercedes gave her a quick, keen look, but saw that
no sting lay in the girl's words, only simple, sorrowful
conviction.

" You have been constructing a little romance, my
dear," Mercedes began in a soothing tone, after a prolonged pause. " You have put together what you
have heard and seen, and more that you have felt
and imagined, and it is no wonder that you take

refuge in your own thoughts, for you certainly can't follow the countess's ; but now you see that you have exaggerated, that you are fanciful and morbid, that everything is exactly as it should be, and that I am most contented, if not blindly infatuated with my lot. Let me give you a bit of advice, my dear girl : don't run about appealing to people's better natures. They might not all enjoy it as much as I do." She was smiling constantly, and very curiously, as she went on in her quizzical fashion : "Take us sinners as we are, that is, as we seem, and you 'll find us very good company."

Gabrielle for her only answer put both arms round Mercedes, held her close an instant, and kissed her warmly on the mouth. "I will go. I have been stupid, and I have done no good."

"I don't imagine that you have done much good," Mercedes rejoined gayly. "On the other hand, you certainly have done no harm, except, perhaps, to that pretty wing in your hat, on my shoulder just now. By the way, how becoming that hat is ! "

"Mercedes, of course I don't believe half that you say of yourself."

"That proves your perspicacity, my dear child. If you were still wiser, you would not believe a word that I say — of myself, or anybody else. I do not, on principle."

"But I believe in you."

"Still? Ah, what courage ! Now I shall imagine you walking home snipping and snapping with your dear little scissors ! "

"My scissors ? "

"Yes, your little scissors," Mercedes said caressingly, "such as they give children, with blunt points,

you know, that don't hurt. I testify that they don't
hurt. You intend to cut all the intricate knots you
see with them. You think, with fearlessness and a
snip-snap, the deed is done. But the world's meshes,
you will find, are too tangled and tough for you, and
reach down strong roots into the nether regions, and
have an evil life of their own."

"Oh, do not fear. I have nothing special to say
to any one else. It was only to you. I shall try to
cut no other knots now."

"Not even the little Mayers' corset-lacings? Then
I ought to feel flattered, indeed."

"How extremely disagreeable I must have been,
since you find it necessary to punish me with so
much derision," Gabrielle returned, drawing on her
gloves.

"High-minded people are mostly unpleasant, but
indeed you have been charming," Mercedes sweetly
assured her.

"Forgive me, and don't let it make any difference
between us. You are sure it won't make you like me
less?"

"On the contrary, I think you the most adorable
little missionary that ever" —

"Ah, don't!" exclaimed Gabrielle with impatience.
"I can't bear any more of that." After a moment
she said gravely : "I wish everybody were as honest
and good as you, Mercedes." To Mercedes' incredulous disclaimer, "Oh, of course I cannot pretend to
answer you. There is so much that is incomprehensible to me, and it all seemed so simple and clear last
night. I have been very odious and presumptuous,
and yet, — what I said is *true !*" she concluded
suddenly.

" Bravo ! A sentiment worthy of Galileo ! "

" I shall think about it " —

" Shall you ? Now why ? I would n't. I never think."

" You have been very patient with me, Mercedes, and I believe in you, thoroughly."

" You could not hang your faith upon a looser peg," laughed Mercedes. " Do come again," she urged in her most gracious, indulgent, and cordial manner. " Come some morning next week, and," with her gleaming, mischievous smile, " don't forget to bring your scissors ! "

Gabrielle was hardly gone when Mercedes locked her doors. Neither to the knocks of the servants, nor to the impatient demands of her sister Elsa, and, finally, not to the repeated and hortatory appeal of the maternal voice, did she deign the faintest response. The Countess Waldenberg, in spite of her august multiplicity of ancestors, hung about the corridor like any helpless and plebeian mortal, stood irresolute, frowned, gave the door-knob a parting, futile shake, returned to the drawing-room, and blandly announced to the marquis that " darling Mercedes was so sorry, but she had a violent headache, and really felt too ill to receive him. She sent her dearest love, and would try to come down by evening." The countess asked the marquis if he did not think it might be electric. The marquis agreed with the countess that it probably was electric. The countess remarked that so many headaches nowadays were electric ; in fact, most things were electric, more or less, were they not ?

CHAPTER XIII

As the influence of Mercedes' fascinating personality grew fainter, Gabrielle's flouted convictions reassembled and formed in stalwart line, stronger and surer than before. There had been moments during the conversation when she had half doubted if she were not, after all, interfering in her neighbor's private affairs, like any other busybody. The consciousness of meaning well was but a meagre consolation, while Mercedes' playful parting thrusts seemed to give her the victory, and Gabrielle a sense of soreness and discomfiture. "It is very confusing, this life they wanted me to see," she thought, as she walked rapidly homeward, "but all the same, I am glad that I spoke to Mercedes. It is better than to think it all and not dare to say it."

At the villa gates, she stood hesitating whether to go in, or on and down the lane. Over the hedge drooped branches of long yellow laburnum blossoms like golden rain, amid masses of rosy hawthorn and pale, feathery young willow leaves; the dense foliage, in its May freshness, completely screening every shady nook and path of the old garden from the curious passer-by.

"It is enchanting in there. It is a little wildwood. I wish I might go in, but since Count Hugo likes it, and does n't like me, and might happen to come out this very morning, it seems rather mean for me to risk meeting him. Still I might take a little run, for he was surely ill last night, and the countess is still

at her toilette. It is a pity for nobody to get a
glimpse of all the lilacs and apple-blossoms and sweet
fresh things that are perfuming half the street. But
perhaps I 'd better go in the house and try to re-
connoitre first. He has been in an age now, and if
he should by chance come out to-day, it would be very
discouraging to him to meet me at once. Dear, dear,
how unfortunate it all is ! "

But with her hand on the gate, she paused and
turned again, for Mousey, without his protective collar and bell, and wearing a blue embroidered blanket
with a count's coronet worked in silver in one corner,
capered suddenly into notice, and greeted her with significant gestures and wicked leers and winks.

" What, Mousey, alone? Who ought to be on duty?
You little yellow, four-legged, inhuman — count ! "

He ran a short distance up the street, then stood
and looked to see if she were coming.

Gabrielle glanced into the garden ; no servant was
visible.

" Evidently I must go with him. He probably only
wishes to show his contempt for the workmen."

She followed him, seated herself on a block of
sandstone, watched the builders, and listened to the
incessant, irregular fall of the mallets. Dietz was up
aloft at his post. He pulled off his paper cap as he
saw her, and went on hammering contentedly, whistling an amorous ditty to his heavy-eyed goddess.
Gabrielle spoke to some of the men. They liked her
not only because they had seen her rescue the babies,
and perform other acts of good-will and common sense
to vagabond children, but for the simple reason that
she seemed to like them. The masons in their shirts
of many colors, the rolled-up sleeves showing sun-

burned muscular arms, were stooping over the great blocks, and looked warm.

"How goes it, Peter?" she said to the scowler.

"Bad," he muttered, "bad and worse."

"Now that 's a pity," she returned cheerily.

"' That 's a pity ' is easy to say," remarked Peter sullenly, always eager to mount his hobby.

The other men grinned and looked curiously at the pretty young lady.

"I know it is easier to talk than to work," Gabrielle rejoined conciliatingly.

"I could tell you things," he began, glaring at her as if she were the embodiment of the world's tyranny, and all the wrongs inflicted by capital upon labor, "I could tell you things that would make your hair stand on end."

"I am sure that you could, and I should like to listen to you some day when we both have time. It 's warmer to-day, Peter."

"It 's hot for such as have to earn their bread in the sweat of their brows," and Peter ostentatiously wiped his forehead on his sleeve.

"Yes, so I am going to send you out something cool to drink this afternoon, some light cold punch; enough for you men here under this shed."

"I 'm obliged to you, miss," Peter began gloomily, "but my principles" —

"Oh," she said smiling, "the punch has nothing to do with principles, nothing at all, I assure you. One is thirsty, you know, whatever one's principles may be."

A laugh of assent and approval greeted this statement, and the men pulled off their caps with hearty smiles, one of them finding his tongue only when she had gone a few steps toward the villa. "Thank you kindly, miss," he called after her, "and if Peter don't want his share, he won't have any trouble in borrowing a throat for it."

"Peter is chronically cross," she reflected, "but not crosser, after all, than the countess, and in her case, at least, it is not overwork that has ruined her disposition. Mousey, will you be quiet? I know that you object to the workmen, because you are an incorrigible snob, but I shall talk with whom I please, sir, and you may remonstrate until you burst."

It was impossible to associate with Mousey and not converse with him. His moral character may have been perverted, venomous, and a bottomless pit of treachery, but his acumen commanded respect, and his humor induced companionship.

"What are you trying to tell me, Mousey? Something unpleasant of course, or you would n't grin in that fiendish manner and feel so sportive." She glanced up as she passed Dietz' balcony. He was neither singing nor working, but standing motionless, shading his eyes with his hand, and peering between the tree-tops into the villa garden.

Mousey mirthfully persisted in making his mysterious and unintelligible communications.

"There is no doubt that you are cleverer than we, Mousey. You always understand us, and we rarely understand you."

Mousey put his head on one side and cocked an eye at her, superciliously intimating that the obtuseness of the human intellect had long since ceased to surprise him.

As she reached the garden gate, it was violently flung open and Röschen in peculiar agitation gasped:

"Mousey, what a fright you have given me! I

was looking everywhere. What a mercy he was with the gracious fräulein!"

"But Röschen, it was the merest chance that I saw him outside the gates. You really should not leave him an instant. Where were you?"

The girl turned away uneasily and did not reply.

"Your orders are strict, and you know perfectly well that you would lose your place to-day, if I should choose to report."

The brown eyes of the maid shot into the brown eyes of the baroness a glance of defiance and mistrust.

"The gracious fräulein is too kind," murmured Röschen.

"I certainly shall not mention the circumstance," Gabrielle rejoined coldly, "though it's no question of kindness. Only if you are in charge of the dog, be faithful and watch him well."

As she gave this injunction, she looked intently at the girl, and noticed that her cheeks were flushed, her eyes excited.

"There's a visitor," stammered Röschen.

"Well?" said Gabrielle indifferently.

"And the countess is in a state, because the gracious fräulein is out."

"She wants me?"

"She isn't dressed. She was rubbing Mousey's lungs longer than usual. She said his bronchial tube was husky. That's why he's got his blanket on. She said," continued the girl with insensible literalness, "that it was ridiculous the gracious fräulein should be gadding about, Heaven knew where, just when for once in her life she could make herself a little useful, and " —

"Never mind that, Röschen. You need not repeat

the countess's remarks. Whatever she wishes to say
to me she will tell me herself. Who is the visitor?"

"The Baron von Raven," answered the maid with a
great rush of high color up to her curly hair, and pulling her white apron nervously with her heavy square-
tipped fingers.

Gabrielle's face fell.

"I don't feel like talking with him," she thought.

Mousey, like a spoiled precocious boy that understands his elders' annoyances, drew his lips in and out
with queer grimaces, watched her mockingly, and
danced with delight.

"Where is he?"

"In the small reception room down-stairs. Shall I
open the doors for the gracious fräulein?"

"Certainly not," the baroness answered in cold surprise. "You stay with Mousey. And you'd better
take him into the back garden," she added, with a
vague remembrance that Röschen always seemed to
be hovering conspicuously about whenever Lieutenant
von Raven came.

The girl looked obstinate. "I'm to follow Mousey,"
she retorted sullenly. "I'm allowed on the lawn and
the front drive and wherever Mousey likes."

"That is true, Röschen," Gabrielle admitted gravely,
and went toward the house.

The rosy young maid let Mousey commune with himself, and devour what he pleased, and snarl and choke,
while she stood reflecting in her dull way upon the injustice of fate that sent baronesses to talk with beautiful clanking lieutenants, and let maids keep dog-watch.
She began to pace the lawn directly in front of the
house, where neither man nor mouse could come out
without meeting her face to face, and Bernhard Dietz

caught glimpses of her bare brown head in the sunshine, and singing, blessed it, and blessing it, sang, and asked nothing more of the gods.

Gabrielle went directly in to the lieutenant.

"You have been waiting long, they tell me, baron," she said kindly.

He gallantly protested that it was a pleasure to wait for her, and added that it was a fine day.

To this she assented and remarked that she had enjoyed her walk.

"Countess well, I hope?"

"Thanks, she is as usual. She will come down soon, I think."

"And Hugo, poor fellow?"

"Thanks, there is little change, I believe."

"Asked for him. Would n't see me."

"Ah?"

"Sad case, Hugo's."

"Very," Gabrielle said coldly. She had been pleading Hugo's cause too fervently with Mercedes to discuss him again with the florid lieutenant.

Von Raven, having acquitted himself of his conventional obligations, now advanced cheerfully to the main object of his visit.

"Going to be festival," he announced with a gleam of enthusiasm. "Tournament. Sixteenth century. Maximilian. Gold brocade. Wigs. Knights. Pages. All that sort of thing."

"Yes, I have heard of it. It will be interesting, no doubt. I presume that you will ride."

"In a half dozen different costumes. No end of things. But there 's a quadrille with ladies. Choice. Gracious fräulein, could I have the honor?"

"Oh thanks, but I don't think I would care for that,"

Gabrielle began. " I should like to see it, but it would be a little like a circus, would it not? Eight ladies and thousands of spectators, and one's hair flying, as somebody told me. Thank you very much, but I would rather not ride."

" You can't mean it," exclaimed von Raven. " Ladies wild about it. All want to ride. Only eight can. Charity."

Gabrielle laughed in frank amusement.

" They do such droll things for charity here."

" Droll ? " repeated the young man somewhat bewildered, " this will be great. Whole court. Toilettes. Benevolent object."

He wondered why she laughed still. His face was eager and boyish, and not disappointed at her refusal, because he could not believe that any girl in her right mind would decline such an invitation.

" Ask some one who is wild to ride, for indeed I am quite tame and would much rather be a spectator."

" Gracious fräulein is joking ? " staring doubtfully at her.

" No, no, I am quite serious. I thank you very much, but I would prefer not to ride at the festival."

" Of course she will ride at the festival," said the countess blandly, entering the room and welcoming von Raven with marked graciousness. " A young girl's No often means Yes, baron. Frau von Funnel has just written me that it will be the event of the season. My niece will be charmed to ride, I assure you."

Her tone was indulgent and slightly sportive, as if she were opposing the whim of a three-year-old child. Von Raven beamed with pleasure and gratitude for her support. But Gabrielle, rising haughtily, turned to him with composure : —

" I have already given you my answer, Herr von Raven, and if you will allow me, I will now bid you good-morning." With a slight inclination toward the astonished countess, she left the room.

Immediately after lunch that day, in the hour usually devoted by the countess to a cigarette, a glass of curaçoa, a brief siesta, a glance at Figaro, a period of love-making to Mousey, the special torture of Babette, and a few last touches on the toilette, and by Gabrielle to books, there was a significant and ceremonious interchange of cards and messages between two persons in Villa Kronfels who ordinarily had no communication whatever, while Röschen, inquisitive and alert, and Lipps, equally curious, but mindful of the dignity of "our wing," felt that life at the moment was worth living.

Gabrielle for her part was by no means sure that it was. Lunch had been a heavily disastrous experience. She had taken refuge in her room in extreme chagrin and helplessness, when a sudden idea seemed to suggest a possible way out of her labyrinth.

She hesitated, but not long, and rang for Röschen. " I can try, at least, and if I do not succeed I shall be no worse off than I am now, at all events."

" Take this to Lipps, please," she said, giving the maid an envelope.

" To Lipps ?"

" To Lipps," Gabrielle repeated with emphasis.

A few moments later Hugo read with exceeding surprise : —

" The Baroness Gabrielle von Dohna begs the privilege of speaking a few moments with Count Hugo von Kronfels."

" Hm," he muttered, eying the visiting card suspiciously; "I bet two to one that it's piety, or benevolence or something of the sort. She has n't anything to do to-day, and being bored, remembers that one must make charity-visits, for of such is the kingdom of heaven. I will lay that scheme low."

Smiling satirically, he too wrote on a visiting card:

"Count Hugo von Kronfels presents his compliments to the Baroness von Dohna, and since he is feeling very comfortable, and is well supplied with books, fruits, and flowers, and requires nothing whatever for his comfort or entertainment, he begs to decline with many thanks the honor of her visit."

"There," he exclaimed, "I should think that would do," and gave it to Lipps.

Presently down came another sealed proposal. The former was written handsomely with ink. This, scribbled impatiently in pencil, and with no formal employment of the third person, was direct if not abrupt.

"But you quite misunderstand, really; I don't want to see you at all. I only want to ask you something."

"How we men, sick or well, flatter ourselves! This is odd, and it certainly does n't sound pious or benevolent. However, I won't be beguiled," and he wrote with scrupulous ceremony: —

"Count Kronfels' compliments, and if the Baroness von Dohna does not wish to see him, could she not save herself the trouble of the interview and communicate her commands by the present easy method?"

Down came Gabrielle's third missive with surprising promptness: —

"I could, but I prefer to see you. I will not trouble you long. Please let me come."

"The deuce! It's a row with mamma. I knew that the prayer for intercession would be heard

sooner or later. She has held out very well. I will
see her, and tell her once for all that I do not choose
to interfere. Whereupon she will weep and moan
and enumerate her grievances. As if she could tell
me anything new ! ”

“Lipps, ask Röschen to beg the Baroness von
Dohna to kindly give me the honor of a few moments' conversation.”

Sooner than it seemed to him possible for any mortal to descend that long stairway and pass the length
of the house, there was a light knock at his door, and
Gabrielle came in, the reverse of lachrymose, and un-
suggestive of grievances.

“ Count Kronfels,” she said, looking down upon
him with a spirited and an eminently dry-eyed expression, “ would you be so very kind as to give me
some wine ? ”

“ Will I give you some wine ? ” he repeated.

“ About two bottles,” she continued in a quick,
matter-of-fact way. “ I should think that ought to
be enough for eight or ten men, shouldn't you? Of
course I shall not make it very strong.”

“ You will not make it very strong ? ”

“ No, I never make it strong,” she remarked with
decision. “ Papa says that my concoctions taste
chiefly of lemon peel and chopped ice. But they
always like it, and after all the main thing is that
it is cold, and that there is enough of it, don't you
think so ? ”

It seemed to Hugo that he had never seen so fault-
lessly fresh a girl. The strong light from three windows fell broadly upon her, and she stood so close
to his sofa, that he noted the fineness of her hair, the
delicate rim of the ear turned toward him, — he had

theories about ears, — the clearness of her eyes, the
wholesome red of her lips, her good white teeth, and
her whole air of sweetness and strength. " She has
lived a great deal in the open air," he concluded,
" and she looks as if she had bathed in what the poets
would call crystal fountains or morning dew or mountain brooks — something pure and invigorating, at
all events." Her hands were lying easily one in the
other, both palms upturned. They looked soft and
pink and babyish to him. " What a charming thing
a woman's hand is ! " he reflected. " Is she so excep-
tionally pretty, or have I forgotten ? Now what kind
of a revel for ten men is she talking about ? "

Such thoughts, and many more of her and of the
past, flashed through his mind during the instant
following her remark. But without perceptible delay
or surprise he answered gravely : —

" I could hardly venture to express an opinion
whether it ought to be cold or hot, but I unhesitatingly agree with you that there should be enough
of it."

Gabrielle gave a little laugh.

" Ah, I forget that you know nothing about it."

" How should I ? " Hugo returned dryly. " But
that is not important. If I owned the great Heidelberg vat, I would place it unconditionally at your
service, full of Johannesberger Schloss. If I can do
anything else for you and your friends, pray count
upon me."

She could not see the vague tantalizing visions of
festivities and merry-makings passing before him, and
she wondered at the extreme formality of his tone.

" His profile is like St. Casimir," she decided, " but
his expression is not at all saintly."

" The Heidelberg vat full of Johannesberger would be very inappropriate magnificence," she rejoined. " But I shall be very grateful for a couple of bottles of ordinary Rhein wine, or light claret. I should not need to appeal to you at all, if it were not for Peter."

Hugo raised his eyebrows.

Gabrielle, meeting his slightly ironical gaze, colored, and said apologetically : —

" I beg your pardon, count. If I take your wine, you have a right to know what I do with it."

" Not the least," protested Hugo with a deprecating gesture ; and although the young girl's sudden entrance, her spirited personality, her request, and her extraordinary allusions to ten men and Peter all filled him with wonder, he hypocritically added : —

" Moreover, I am not curious."

" No," she said gently, her eyes full of kindness and pity, and looking frankly at the invalid's room, that seemed with its luxury and its stillness miles away from the group of warm and boisterous masons out on the sunny road ; " no, of course you are not. But it is all very simple. Peter is a stone-mason, to whom I promised to send some cool drink this afternoon. He is a cross-grained and very skeptical person. It won't tire you to listen ? "

" Not at all," Hugo replied with a perceptible increase of cordiality, and conscious of sudden friendly sentiments toward the unknown Peter, and mankind in general. " But I am allowing you to stand, baroness."

" Thanks," she said, merely leaning her arm on the back of a large easy-chair.

" Peter believes that all people who are not day-laborers have bad hearts," she continued. " Now it would not be pleasant to break one's word to any-body " —

" I never knew that girls had any ' word,' " re flected the ex-lieutenant of dragoons, searching his great book of reminiscence.

" But I think I would rather fail to keep mine to almost any one else — to a gentleman — to you, for instance " —

" Thank you," said Hugo gravely.

" Than to Peter. For Peter," she explained with a mischievous and lovely smile, " expects the worst pos-sible conduct of me, and of everybody who happens to have clean hands ; and if I should break my word to him it would only strengthen his pessimistic theo-ries, you understand, and that would be a great pity, for they make him very uncomfortable."

" I am beginning to understand. But if you will not think my question ungracious, — indeed it is a pleasure to me to serve you, and a gigantic event in my monotonous life, — why did you not simply give your orders to the butler ? "

He watched her keenly, reflecting : —

" She can't resist that. Now come the grievances and mamma."

She looked at him squarely with her fearless, sensi-ble eyes.

" This morning I told them, Peter and the others, that I would send it. No doubt I spoke rashly. It was an impulse. I see now that I ought not to have offered them anything ; I ought to have remembered that I was not at home, where in such matters, in most matters, indeed, I did what I liked ; but having promised the men the punch, I do not see how I can fail to send it out to them."

" No, neither do I," remarked Hugo.

" Do you not? I am glad of that," she exclaimed warmly, then hesitated.

" Here's her hedge," thought the young man.

" At lunch I found that the idea did not please your mamma," she continued with neither complaint nor subterfuge.

" How well she took it!" he was forced to admit.

" Did mamma refuse you point blank?" he asked in a queer tone.

" It is only fair to say," Gabrielle replied, after a moment, " that perhaps she would not have refused, if I had not done something disagreeable and rude, something that displeased her, just before."

" Would it be too indiscreet if I should inquire what your awful crime was?"

" Something was said that I did not like, and I stalked out of the room. I don't think, myself, that it was a nice thing to do. I have a very bad temper," she said seriously. " But it was all petty, count. Don't let us talk about that. If it had not been for Peter, I would have gone out and excused myself, and told the men that I would try to make the punch for them another time."

" Impossible," commented Hugo with a frown.

" Not pleasant, I admit; but by no means impossible," she amended. " At first I thought that there was nothing else to do, and it seemed to me that they would believe I was sorry. Don't you think so?"

Hugo muttered some unintelligible expletive under his breath.

" Then I determined to go down town and buy some, but that would have been so unnatural and indelicate,

and perhaps unkind, and certainly very conspicuous
and defiant. Suddenly I discovered that I could not
if I would, for I had already spent my month's allowance. Altogether I felt very foolish, and like a
school-girl in disgrace. Finally, I thought of you. It
seemed probable that you would help me. Men are
usually willing to help one," she added sagely. "It
was so trivial a thing in itself, and yet had caused
me so many conflicting thoughts, that is why I burst
in upon you so strangely. When one thinks hard
of anything, one supposes that other people know all
about it. I hope that I have not troubled you too
much."

Her voice was so fresh and confident, so utterly unsuspicious, she was so loyal, so eager to do everybody
justice, no one could have appealed more strongly to
Hugo's peculiar sympathies. His thoughts were in a
strange tumult. The chivalrous sentiments, that were
current coin in his gallant past, urged him to respond
in words as simple and frank as her own. But some
wayward instinct induced him to still intrench himself
behind the defensive wall of reserve which he had
erected during these days of hopeless invalidism.

"I have gone far on my lonely road," he thought,
"and there are many beautiful girls in the world. Because this one comes in here and looks as fresh as a
June rose, is any fact in my life altered? Am I less
a cripple? I said that I would have nothing to do
with her. Let well men assure her of their interest
and protection. What is mine worth?"

"I am surely tiring you," said Gabrielle, as his
bright watchful expression vanished, and his face grew
gloomy and haggard. "Ah, forgive me! And you
were so ill last night."

How fair she was! How sweet were the sudden transitions in her voice, the trembling light and shade, the youth and warmth and pity. She had come nearer and was looking anxiously at him, with compassion in her sincere eyes.

"Are you not very weary?" she asked again.

He longed to answer: —

"God knows I am weary, soul and body, with a deadly weariness," but he merely said in a somewhat cold tone: —

"Not especially."

"I will go," she murmured.

Again an imperious longing bade him reply: —

"No, stay with me. You are beautiful and bright and good. You have crossed my threshold like an angel of light. You cannot leave me in my unutterable loneliness. Give me your sympathy, your pity. Yours I will not reject." Her hand was so near his, one slight movement, and he could have touched it. Would there not be comfort and healing in the clasp of that loyal hand? Fool and coward, what were soft hands, and lovely pitying eyes to him! They were of the past and the past was dead. Before him was a straight and narrow way which he must tread alone, and beyond — the door was open.

"Baroness," he resumed courteously, "I thank you for the honor you have done me, and if in the future I can ever be of the slightest service, pray command me. You have only to give your orders to Lipps" —

He saw the wondering troubled look induced by this plain hint, but he went on with resolute politeness: —

"Lipps will bring whatever you want now to the dining-room, and as often as you wish wine or anything else for your protégés I beg you will tell him. My wine cellar is in a plethoric condition which it would be a kindness to relieve."

" Ah," she returned, shaking her head slightly, " I shall not want to make any more punch for people."

" It has not been a pleasant experience for you," he observed less stiffly, thinking, " Poor child, how unmercifully mamma has been nagging her ! Fancy her driven to apologize to a pack of dirty masons or buying wine with her own pocket money ! It is disgusting and would be incredible — except it is mamma ! ' "

" It was not easy to invade your castle," she began with a pleading look which he understood perfectly, " but I am glad I came. It is pleasant here, and homelike." She gave a slow wistful glance at Hugo's books and pictures. " It is a little like papa's room ; " she sighed faintly, and turned to him again with a quick flush, a warm smile, and a sudden movement of the hands toward him in frank entreaty.

" Ah," she exclaimed, " if — if you — if you knew how I wish " —

" I beg your pardon," interrupted Hugo, " but is that Mousey? Do you not hear ? "

A querulous yelp and some scratching, followed by a scampering down the corridor, announced the dog's presence and departure.

" He has been listening at the door," Hugo remarked with perfect gravity. " He has all the meanest vices of humanity. He has now gone to tell his mistress that you are here."

" But that is neither a crime nor a secret."

" It is a great kindness and an honor to me," he returned with a formality that restrained her ardent impulse to beg him to let her come every day, to let her be a friend and good comrade to him. He checked and chilled her, and she could not accentuate her desire against his will.

"Mousey is the real cause of my perplexities," she said quietly. "He was out of bounds. I went after him. If I had not followed him, I should not have passed the workmen and stopped to bid them good-morning. If I had not talked with Peter, I should not have perceived that he was in an unusually misanthropic mood, which made me wish to try to appease him with gifts and libations. And if I had not promised him the punch I should not now be here. Pardon me for troubling you, and thanks for everything."

"Don't thank me," Hugo rejoined quickly. "The indebtedness is entirely mine. It has been a great and unexpected pleasure, and makes me feel singularly benevolent toward Mousey for his mediation. Although the truth is, in this house little happens in which he is not concerned, first or last."

"Yes, I have noticed that," she returned, in the same quiet tone. With every light word he seemed to increase the distance between them. How hollow his temples were, how sallow and ill he looked. How politely he smiled, with a drawing-room manner, as if he were on his feet and in uniform, not stretched on his back. She forgot the workmen and that the hour of the afternoon drive was approaching. She wished she were Mercedes, or any one who could help him and be useful and companionable to him, and whom he would not repulse with this freezing, smiling ceremony. Yet a few moments ago he had been almost friendly.

She turned to go.

Hugo raised himself slightly, steadying himself with one elbow.

" It is awkward," he said with the smile which hurt her, "that a man is forced to be discourteous, and keep this attitude when a lady leaves his room, but you will take the will for the deed."

His manner was light, even flippant, as if the subject were, when all was said, of extremely little importance.

"How can you speak to me so?" she returned quickly, looking at him sorrowfully, and with a note of reproach, even of indignation, in her voice. "Do you think me so dull and heartless that you must talk to me like that?"

Hugo's society smile faded. He stared at her silently, as she murmured her adieux and left the room.

She looked at her watch. The minutes had flown fast. The drive was imminent. " I will run up first, put on my hat and take my gloves, so that I need not keep her waiting. I don't like the concealment, but I can't help hoping that everything will be quiet, and that I can mix my draught for those thirsty men without more excitement. Afterwards I will tell her and take the consequences."

She reached her door, which was ajar, and ran lightly in, stopping suddenly with a startled " Oh!" Hugo's jest had been founded on fact. Mousey had certainly told tales. There in the middle of the room, established firmly as if she meant to remain, was the countess, stern, angry, and pale. Near her, his yellow haunches planted on a blue chintz chair, and wearing a grin of malevolent expectation, sat Mousey.

" I did not know that you were here," Gabrielle ejaculated nervously, after which platitude all three were silent. She surveyed her judges, the big one and the little one, and knew that her portion would be neither

justice nor mercy. "And it is not made!" she realized
with anxiety. "If she should positively forbid me to
make it!"

"You have come to speak with me?" she began.

"I have," returned the countess.

"Will you pardon me," the young girl said rapidly,
and with decision. "I have something to do down-
stairs; I will come back in a very few moments."

Waiting for no reply, she closed the door and ran
down to the dining-room, where with Lipps' assistance
she flung water and wine and sugar and chopped ice
and slices of lemon into a flagon.

"She won't follow me because she has not her hat
on, and she 'll never attempt the stairs twice in succession," she reasoned.

"There," she murmured triumphantly, "I hope they
can drink it. It ought to be good. It is thrown together with the madness of genius. Lipps, take it to
Peter. You know Peter. Here, Lipps, go out this
door."

He demurred respectfully.

"The dining-room balcony door? It is not usual."

"Never mind. Only go." Opening it, she fairly
pushed him out.

"Lipps," she added breathlessly, "tell Peter it is
Count Kronfels' wine, the wine of a man who would
be thankful if he could grow weary and warm and
thirsty from hard work on stone this day."

The old servant looked distressed at this message.
It was also unusual.

"Ah, say it, Lipps! It can't hurt Count Hugo,
and it may do Peter good." And when she smiled
so sweetly on him, Lipps felt nerved to commit an
even greater social solecism.

Lipps and the tall flagon disappeared behind the hedge.

She drew a sigh of relief. How excited she felt, and how eventful the day seemed, yet nothing great had happened. She pressed her hands an instant to her flushed cheeks, brushed a little sugar from her sleeve, and thought, as she passed along the corridor : —

" And now, courage ! For I am going to my execution."

CHAPTER XIV

THE Frau Major von Funnel sat in her boudoir and thought. The room was small, still, and grave as an anchorite's cell. It was here that the serious business of her life was conducted, and no bric-a-brac, nothing light and diverting, met the eye. A simple writing-table with plain appointments stood in one corner near a hanging shelf of books, consisting chiefly of Aphorisms, Wit, and Wisdom of one great author, Memorable Words of another, Anthologies, in short, collections of miscellaneous quotations in prose and verse, under various titles. She was not a reader. She had little time and less taste for books, but she succeeded, nevertheless, in conveying a very good imitation of a literary atmosphere. When at the close of a conversation with some distinguished man, already charmed by her womanliness, her sweet gravity, and her rapt attention to his remarks, she would look up confidingly into his eyes, and softly murmur a word from Marcus Aurelius, or Pascal, or Goethe, or some other condensed immortal of the goodly fellowship on her little shelf, the effect was perfect, and nothing could ever convince that man that the Frau Major was not as modestly erudite as she was appreciative of true greatness.

If some relentless inventor — in addition to the detective camera which steals and reflects our unsuspecting countenances at midnight as at noonday, and the pitiless apparatus whose mission is to transcribe and retain to our perpetual regret and shame

all our foolish and hasty words — should construct
a still more diabolically clever machine which would
print our secret thoughts upon our walls, perhaps
some of the worst of us would hold up our heads, and
some of the holiest would blush and squirm. For the
vagabonds — and what does vagabond mean but
" floating about without a certain direction " ? —
those souls whom nature has created to be, however
sweet and pure their own harmonies, forever out of
tune with the world's formal measures — have sometimes a kindly and guileless way of looking at life,
while the most highly decorous and conventionally
respected individual may proceed upon base and sordid lines. Most assuredly the walls of that little
boudoir, if detailed by the command of genius to
reveal the Frau Major's habitual meditations, would
have displayed fine and subtle hieroglyphics, and sentiments that would have startled the best society out
of its complacency.

The Frau Major was not incommoded by that
human quality or frailty — awkward and compromising at times, yet often an amiable and cheerful guide
— which we call impulse. She must indeed have
possessed the attribute, and it must have moved, —
since, as old Heraclitus informed mankind, " Everything flows," — but with her it took its rise in profoundly remote causes, and its action was imperceptibly slow, like the movement of glaciers, or the ocean
undermining a cliff.

If, for instance, she was seen in some brilliant gathering to distinguish a shy, uninteresting, and hitherto
unnoticed youth ; if she stood long with him, gazing
up into his face with the deep womanly admiration
which she always offered the superior being, man, and

which the superior being, man, always condescended
to accept in as large measure as she would mete ; if she
hung upon his words, smiled upon him with her calm,
clever, and benign countenance, spoke with him in her
measured and enthralling accents, and left him her
captive and slave for life, — somewhat astonished too
at the good sense, wit, and fine sentiments which he
had been able to display to this sympathetic woman,
when thus far in his social career his fellow-creatures
had had the effect of disastrously damming his eloquence, and he had been miserably conscious that
his only memorable words had been interchanged
exclusively with himself, either before or after the
occasion when they were demanded, — if, then, she
singled him out, and intoxicated him with bliss, her
reasons were apt to proceed from fathomless depths
of policy and " caverns measureless to man."

It was not her broad charity, which her whole following lauded to the skies ; it was not even her shrewd
principle that in certain calculations one reckons false
if one calls any mortal unimportant. These motives
would have induced an approving smile, a tender
hand-clasp, a subtly appreciative word, but not the
long and absorbing interview ; it was a farther reaching and deeper incentive which projected the Frau
Major upon this apparently unremunerative plane.

The youth was poor, but his great-great-grand-
father's cousin's wife had been rich and had left
a fortune to the collateral branch of the family, the
senior of which was at present a gouty country gentleman, aged eighty-six, the father of five sons. The
oldest of the brothers was long since dead. The second had been detected by his comrades at an officer's
club playing with marked cards, and out of regard

for his name was hustled off to America — that vastly receptive Reform School for Europe's bad boys — as fast and as secretly as possible. The third was an African explorer, for many months missing. The fourth was consumptive and seen only at Baths. The fifth was a dashing lieutenant, fond of wine and hurdle-races.

Recently the Frau Major had overheard a certain royal personage, who always had a kind word for everybody, and remembered everybody's relations, inquire after the health of the youth's aged relative, and she had been fortunate enough to hear the reply that the old gentleman had had a slight stroke of paralysis. She was strong in genealogy, — and necrology, — and knew what most persons of her set had forgotten, — the exact connection between the youth's own family and the other branch. She computed the tottering chances for a gouty man of eighty-six who had had his first stroke of paralysis, for a long-missing African explorer, for a pronounced consumptive, and for a plethoric lieutenant addicted to duelling, wine, and breakneck races, and in her calculations did not forget that the prince had twice spoken with that stupid boy, that his Highness's adjutant was reported to be in disfavor, and that the prince allowed himself now and then the luxury of a simple and unaccountable liking. These somewhat tediously involved mental processes but approximately indicate the workings of the Frau Major's " impulse " to honor the awkward youth, to invite him to her Thursdays, to present him to her special pet, Emma Mayer, and her darling little Berta, and to explain to her friends in her candid and impressive manner : " His face is so unworldly and pure it attracts me. I admire him," she would add, contemplating him seriously. " I think he looks like a poet."

The Frau Major sat motionless in her low chair and thought. Her face looked heavy and sad without the luminous sympathetic glance which she wore in society. The small cold eyes were downcast, the large unsmiling mouth was for once off duty. She was weary. Her creed was that of Major Pendennis: " Life without money and the best society is n't worth having." The best society she had, but she was obliged to work hard to maintain in it, without money, the foothold which she regarded as desirable. She cherished no illusions with regard to her own importance, but was fully aware that if she did not constantly earn popularity and prominence, she would be simply a lonely elderly woman, about whom the world would not trouble itself. Was not General S.'s wife once popular ? Did she not give dinners and balls ? The general died. What was she now ? Respected ? Dear, yes, when any one happened to think of her.

The Frau Major knew that if she did not periodically organize a charity-bazar, philanthropic theatricals, or a benevolent masquerade, the world's restless waves would sweep on and leave her stranded. She earnestly studied a note-book in which were names, dates, and mathematical calculations. Her situation, she reflected, had changed little in years. She was the most popular woman in Wynburg, welcome in many circles, praised by the wise and the foolish, prominent in all good works, a pillar of society, and with the reputation of lofty principles and fervent religious feeling. But without money it all cost unceasing toil and tact. With money she could have given frequent and choice little dinners which would command solid and permanent respect, and render bazars superfluous. " Ah," she sighed, " if I had but had daughters ! I would have married them so well ! " It was absolutely indispensable for her to obtain fresh and strong influence in several households. She was resistlessly impelled to exert influence upon her fellow-creatures, to pull wires and make complicated plans, and she was aware that her talents would have been invaluable in agitated political circles; still she saw no reason to let them rust here where fate had placed her. Life without this species of gambling would have been stagnation to her, and social insignificance was worse than death.

She regarded her human chess-board. Each pawn, like little Emma Mayer, had its own value. She saw many parallel happy contingencies, and simultaneously advancing perils. But her chief interest was centred in the Kronfels group. The countess might be, with a few modifications, — but was not, — all that was desirable for a friend. Intimacy with her was an impressive fact before the world, but no school-girl was so fickle and uncertain in her attachments, and nothing except nitro-glycerine required more careful handling. To preserve her good-will, to propitiate or at least not to irritate that cynical, mistrustful Hugo, to win Gabrielle completely, and see her safely married to Lorenz or to Egon, to be her guide, philosopher, and friend, — and Gabrielle herself with the Kronfels fortune would be a social power later, was motherless, sisterless, and surely already convinced that she could obtain no support or sympathy from the countess, — all these seemed to the Frau Major to be clearly defined duties. Beside her instinct to govern people's lives and the social prestige which she held so dear, there were certain practical advantages in associating with rich people, which she by no means ignored. There were drives and invitations to the theatre and opera, hot-house flowers and fruits, and innumerable gifts, which she knew how to accept with no loss of dignity, and which were a great aid to a small income. "One can do without the necessities of life, but not without the luxuries," she thoroughly realized.

She had not been able to pay Gabrielle any special attention yet, she reflected; it was well to proceed slowly. If the countess's jealousy was roused, all was lost, and the girl would simply be sent home portionless and in disfavor. How providential it was that Hugo and Mercedes had not married before the accident. Mercedes was never malleable, and it would be a crime for the Kronfels wealth to be cast to the four winds of heaven by that haughty, mocking, sharp-tongued, clever woman! "The Kronfels family is interesting, but not unlike a powder-magazine," she thought. "Hugo is difficult, the countess dangerous, and Gabrielle, inexperienced as she is, has a certain natural shrewdness, and a directness that is sometimes positively appalling. She has still much to learn, but I should really like her, and I could be of infinite service to her if she but knew it."

At this point in her reflections, her maid announced : —

"The Baroness von Dohna."

The Frau Major smiled charmingly. She was adored by her servants, for she had no petty vices of impatience and unreasonableness. "In the little salon; I will come at once."

The little salon was as dainty as the boudoir was austere, and Gabrielle waited there but a few moments before she saw the Frau Major's handsome face smiling upon her, while a cordial hand extended an exquisite half-blown Niphetos rose, and the incomparable low, slow voice said : —

"Dear child, I was thinking of you," with a tender lingering on the final word.

"You are very good," Gabrielle returned gratefully.

The Frau Major sat down on the little sofa with Gabrielle, took her hands, and looked intently and gravely into her eyes.

"No one is waiting for you?"

"No one. I came quite alone, and of my own accord."

"Lorenz has proposed, or Egon, and she wants a confidante," concluded the Frau Major. The gentle, infinitely sympathetic glance rested tranquilly upon her visitor.

"That is kind, and what I have often wished you would do. You are not driving to-day?"

"Not now. We were out a short time, — a few moments." Gabrielle hesitated more than her wont, for she could scarcely inform the Frau Major that the countess's temper was at white heat, that she had given the coachman three different orders in rapid succession, and after driving ten minutes had called "Home!" in a hoarse voice, and left her without word or glance in the vestibule.

The young girl looked frankly in the wise and kind face bent tenderly toward her.

"I have come to ask a favor," she continued.

"It is granted, dear child."

"Ah, that is generous, to promise without hearing it."

"I know that whatever you would ask I would do

—for you," returned the lovely voice with its calm tone of conviction. "I have a very special interest in you; and what is more natural than that a young girl should be in doubt as to her course — should perhaps need counsel?"

"But I am not at all in doubt," Gabrielle said simply, "at least not in regard to this matter. You are very good to me, and I am very grateful; but I have come to-day to ask you if you will be so kind as not to propose anything for me to Aunt Adelheid, — any pleasures, or gayeties, or anything whatever?"

"She is actually suggesting to me to mind my own affairs," the Frau Major realized with amusement.

"Dear child," she murmured, and awaited further developments.

"I know," Gabrielle went on, "that you are only thinking of my happiness."

"And of your good," added the other solemnly.

"Yes, of everything kind and sweet and gracious and unselfish, and like yourself. There really is something preposterous in my daring to ask you not to do whatever seems good to you. Several times when I have thought of it before, I have decided it would be absurd. But to-day" —

"To-day, dear child?"

"To-day, the tournament, and your letter" —

The Frau Major patted Gabrielle's hand encouragingly and listened with her wise and tranquil air.

"And a conversation I have just had with the countess, and some other things, lead me to beg you to propose nothing at all for me; nothing!"

"Dear Gabrielle, say no more! Did I not promise you your wish, though it were the half of my kingdom? I will never again be so cruel as to suggest that my special pet among all girls shall be arrayed in gold brocade and violet plush, and ride before royalty with a stately knight in armor. Is that the extent of your grief?"

Gabrielle laughed brightly.

"It does sound small, does it not? But I thank you with all my heart. You relieve me more than you know. Of course I was sure that you would have but one answer for me."

"I am a childless woman; I love young people; it was a joy to me to be thoughtful of your interests. That was all."

"I know," returned Gabrielle regretfully, "and it seems ungrateful and selfish on my part, yet it will help me very much, as things are," she added with rising color, "if you recommend nothing to Aunt Adelheid."

"I promise," said Frau von Funnel sweetly and solemnly. "But others will if I do not."

"No one else has your influence."

"As to that, you overestimate me, dear. But I can help you in no other way?"

Gabrielle looked at her wistfully.

"Ah, you could, I am sure you could! You are so wise and good. But I have no right to discuss my little perplexities, in which others are concerned."

"Remember that I know the countess exceedingly well," was the soft and significant response.

"I wish I had your secret of never offending her," Gabrielle broke out impetuously, "and that is all I have to say upon that subject, and I fear it is already too much."

"I know her idiosyncrasies, her sorrows, and her nobility. I am devotedly attached to her."

"Yes, I know you are," returned the young girl thoughtfully. "I observed that the first day I saw you."

"If I could only tell her everything and beg her to advise me. She would show me my mistakes and guide me. But I simply cannot live under a woman's roof, eat her salt, and go and discuss her faults with her most intimate friends. No, that is impossible. Then even the Frau Major cannot make Aunt Adelheid reasonable, or me clever enough to avoid friction." She gave a little sigh.

"Now for our love affairs," thought the Frau Major.

"You are troubled, dear?" said the ineffable voice.

"I have had a rather exciting day. How good you are to let me sit here quietly with you. How restful it is," Gabrielle exclaimed impulsively. "You are like a cathedral, calm and still, and large enough to receive all sorts of sinners."

"The day has been exciting, dear?" repeated the gentle voice.

"Oh, the day in itself is like any other, only this is the fourth important conversation I have had, — important to me, that is, — and it seems a long time since morning."

The Frau Major smiled lovingly at her and waited.

"The first was with Mercedes."

"Dear Mercedes!" murmured the Frau Major.

"Yes, she is very dear and beautiful," said Gabrielle warmly.

"And so happy."

"Ah, do you think that?" asked Gabrielle wonderingly. "I wish I were sure of it."

After a moment she said : —

" I think you are the only really happy person I know here. You are sure and at rest. You have nothing to seek, nothing to gain ; and you are happy, because you are loving and large-hearted, and live for others."

The Frau Major gave a little deprecating gesture in response to this excessive praise, and with a beatific smile remarked : —

" So many of my dear friends are blessed in their natures and in their lives. Almost everybody, indeed, seems happy to me."

" I may be very ill-natured, but they don't to me. They seem always restless and seeking, going up and down like the animals at the menagerie."

" Not ill-natured, but a little out of tune, perhaps. Not quite what your papa would desire in his fresh bright-eyed girl."

" Ah, papa ! " said the girl confidently. " Nothing in me would astonish him much."

" Did your weighty conversations induce your un-flattering zoölogical comparisons ? "

" I think not," Gabrielle replied laughing. " I am often reminded of the poor beasts. They remember something better, crave something better, and hate their limitations. People are very like them."

" And you, yourself, dear child ? "

" Oh, I am one of the worst. I am a young hyena ! "

" My dear Gabrielle ! " the Frau Major gently re-monstrated.

" The crowd and the whirl oppress me. I am weary of seeing so many people, and never really knowing any one. The worst of it is, while I am sure there is good everywhere, I cannot find it. It is my own fault, but it proves that I do not belong here. Indeed, indeed, I remember but too well the old days and green woods and freedom," she exclaimed.

" Adelheid Kronfels must have applied the thumb-screw long and often to have induced this state of mind," mused the tranquil, softly - smiling dame. " Positive honesty is an awkward thing. I could bring a score of worldly girls to the altar with less difficulty."

Gabrielle was still smiling playfully, but with her last words her eyes were slightly suffused, and there was a ring of repressed emotion in her voice.

" Ah, dear Frau Major, how patient you are with my nonsense! How I should like to confess and be shriven! But I cannot make it seem quite honor-able."

" Her scruples are tedious," thought the older woman.

" What Mercedes and I said seems to belong to her. What Count Hugo and I said, I could tell you easily enough, except it concerns another person."

" Ah, Hugo! Noble, interesting sufferer!"

" What Aunt Adelheid and I discussed belongs to her. Yes, most emphatically. So, altogether, I cannot ask you to show me my path."

" Dearest girl, I feel confident that you," sweetly accenting the pronoun, " will always choose the right path. Nothing else causes you doubt and excite-ment?"

" I think not," replied Gabrielle candidly.

"You do not consider my dear young friend Lorenz important, then? Yet he was full of joy at the thought of seeing you to-day."

" But you would not expect me to call his conversation important?" Gabrielle retorted mischievously. "I confess that he is concerned in my vexations, and more than I like," she added with spirit. "I thought it best not to dilate upon the matter, but perhaps I ought to tell you that Aunt Adelheid wishes me to ride with him at the tournament, and I have refused."

"Why do you not wish to ride with him?" inquired the Frau Major placidly. "He is such a favorite of mine. So gallant — so — so manly — and — sweet-tempered."

"Is he all that?" Gabrielle asked indifferently. "I find him amiable and droll. It is not that I object to him, but I do not wish to ride at all."

"And why, dear child? Tell me. Am I not your friend?" urged the caressing voice.

"Ah, yes, I am sure that you are," Gabrielle cried warmly. "I have a score of little reasons. I feel that I should not like it."

"Feel!" repeated the Frau Major, raising her eyebrows with an indulgent smile.

"For one thing, the costume must be elegant, and I cannot afford it."

"Of course the countess arranges that; you would not deny her that pleasure?"

"I cannot bear to have her buy velvet and brocade for me," the girl rejoined in her quick way.

"Your aunt" —

"By courtesy only."

"It is useless," thought Gabrielle. "She cannot and ought not to understand that it is hard for me to accept gifts and insults from the same person."

"Then the rehearsing will take so much time."

"And whose time is all her own if not yours?

Who has a better right to freedom and gayety and laughter with young companions ? "

Again Gabrielle looked perplexed.

" How can I explain that I have only the early morning, and with the blankets I am to embroider for Mousey, perhaps not that ? "

" I am more occupied than I seem to be," she replied quietly, " but there are still other reasons."

The Frau Major rose, put her hands affectionately on Gabrielle's shoulders, and smilingly said : —

" Do not search for them. They all mean simply that the little girl has made up her mind to be wilful and disappoint her friends. Why should we discuss it longer ? Please yourself, dear Gabrielle, and you will please me."

Gabrielle looked discouraged.

" Ah, you think it is merely selfish. Do you know it is the first time that I have refused an express wish of Aunt Adelheid ? "

The Frau Major replied gravely : —

" I am sure that you are considerate toward an old lady who has had many sorrows, and who greatly desires your happiness."

Both were silent some moments. Gabrielle fixed her eyes upon the rose in her hand, as if there were wisdom to be gained from its pure white petals.

" You do not urge me. You do not blame me. But you think I ought to ride," she said suddenly. " Ah, I am so little in the mood for it, believe me ! " Her honest young eyes looked pleadingly at her friend.

" Then why ride, my dear ? You ' feel ' that you would not like it. You are not in the ' mood.' "

Gabrielle watched her thoughtfully.

Was it then all selfishness and prejudice and obstinacy and caprice?

" You evidently will not persuade me, but what do you really think?" she asked doubtfully.

The Frau Major answered in her reasonable and convincing fashion, and in a tone as inoffensive as a purling brook, that she certainly did not desire to influence Gabrielle, for a girl had a right to her little youthful fancies about things, and why should she be forced even to enjoy herself? Still, if Gabrielle really wished her to give her views of a not very important situation, did Gabrielle not take it all a little too seriously? Did she not come to Wynburg, to see life, to go into society, to meet and know people? Would not her papa like her to enlarge her experience, and was it not quite natural that the countess should expect her to take part in whatever festivities were thoroughly desirable? Then the tournament would be so choice, so distinguished, so artistic; not too much of the painter element, which would make it Bohemian, but just enough to impart a fresh and attractive flavor, and under the special patronage of royalty. Indeed, his Highness was going to ride in costume. Why should Gabrielle not participate in a splendid historical pageant? Why be a recluse at her age and with her charm?

The angry countess had made use of practically the same arguments, but flowing harmoniously from the lips of this disinterested woman, they seemed new and impressive. Indeed, at all times the Frau Major's lightest words, which if spoken by a flippant voice would have sounded commonplace or false, were freighted with meaning, and suggested unlimited reserve power. She could not so much as speak of

the weather without a certain dignity and benevolence which would enlist one's sympathies for the
rawest day.

She now glided adroitly from the riding to the
riders.

" Mercedes rides ? "

" Yes."

" And that would be delightful for you, you like
her so much. You are sure that you would not prefer
Egon to Lorenz? They are both dear to me. I knew
them as children. I remember them as pretty boys
in pinafores. You do not prefer Egon ? "

" Oh dear, no," Gabrielle returned with a little
shrug. "One is as good as the other. But I wish
that they were little boys in pinafores now. I should
like them better in pinafores than in uniforms." She
began to laugh. "Do you know they would really be
lovely in pinafores? They have such plump rosy
cheeks, and such nice little shaved flaxen heads, and
such very pale blue eyes."

" We must discuss your costume with the countess,"
the Frau Major remarked, after an indulgent smile
for her special pet's little jest.

Gabrielle did not remember that she had agreed to
ride, but she felt reluctant to begin the argument
anew, and to be obstinate and unamiable to this kind
and judicious friend who had taken so much trouble
to convince her.

" The Misses Mayer," announced the maid.

" Beg them to kindly wait a few moments in the
drawing-room."

" And Lieutenant von Raven and Lieutenant von
Haller."

Gabrielle rose.

" I may slip out unseen, may I not ? "

" Ah, will you not come in and chat ? The dear little mice would be so glad. They admire you so much."

" The Countess von Kronfels," announced another servant.

" No, no, I won't come in, thanks. You have been so kind."

" Come often to me, dearest child. Enjoy yourself. And if I may presume to preach a small sermon, do not be such a serious little philosopher. The world is very kind to sweet young things like you. If we all have our little trials, we have our compensations. Your dear brown eyes will not always be clear and strong. Your hair will some day be gray like mine. Your beauty and freshness and health, which are my delight as if you were my own dear daughter, cannot remain as they are. Then be happy now, dear girl, and do not be too wise. Surely you have no real griefs."

" You are right. I have none. I am anything but wise. I am only selfish and exacting. But you have done me good. A thousand thanks."

" The Countess von Waldenberg and the Countess Elsa."

" Ah, the whole world is coming ! Let me run away. I am detaining you."

" There is no haste. I have always time for you," returned the sweet voice with its lingering cadence. " Let me be a comfort to you. Let me aid you, for you are near and dear to me. Be happy, child. And *au revoir*, since you will not come and take a cup of tea with us, and chat about the tournament."

It was with some surprise that Gabrielle found herself pledged after all to ride, but she went off full of confidence and veneration for the Frau Major, and determined to seek her counsel as often as possible and try to learn the secret of her kindly atmosphere. The countess would probably remain in that delectable circle until dinner-time. Gabrielle decided to make the most of her freedom. She passed the villa, and her friends the masons under the shed, who took off their hats with alacrity and smiled as she went quickly by; but Peter greeted her with incorruptible and morose melancholy, insisting upon the purity of his principles after as before the flagon episode.

The great broad-backed hill, green with vineyards, met the sunny May sky. She followed the lane winding along its base, enjoyed the cool freshness of the path between stone walls, and the smell of the woods and the earth. Beyond the lane, the way led past orchards and neat little patches of market-gardens, where stooping blue figures were working. "How kind they are to make the men's shirts and the women's aprons of the blue that fades into that pretty soft dullness," she thought gayly.

In Leslach she spoke to some children, whose scanty flaxen locks were strained back and braided into shining little tails. They grinned at her North German. She began to imitate their dialect. At this they laughed outright, and followed her facetiously in single file, five or six half shy, half roguish faces. How it would shock Aunt Adelheid! She gave her guard of honor a few pennies, whereupon Mariele and Bäbele and Rickele quickly dispersed to regale themselves at a booth, where an old woman sold bretzels, acidified raspberry-shrub, and floury high-colored bonbons.

A couple of young wolf-dogs grew excited and leaped about furiously as she drew near their enclosure. But when she stood and talked soothingly to them, and assured them that she was an intimate friend of their family, and had some cousins of theirs at her own home, and that she could appreciate their prejudices, for she too sometimes felt cooped-up and irritable, the fiery gleam disappeared from their small reddish eyes, and they became friendly and expressed considerable regret when she finally wandered on.

The smallest thing gave her pleasure, her heart was so light and free. For she had responded warmly and gratefully to the Frau Major's kindness, and to the affectionate tone of which she had been so long deprived. "When one is homesick, one is simply irresponsible," she admitted. "How I have been abusing everybody, and conjuring up ghouls to haunt the best society."

Smiling, looking pretty and happy and dainty, she stopped in surprise, as a great bell sounded suddenly near her, and out of a court came running, chattering, springing, thirty or forty factory girls, each holding a beer-glass, and hurrying across the pavement and the street to a garden over the way. They reminded her of the cigar-factory girls in Carmen, except here was no coquetry, no theatrical effect. Ugly and pretty, young and old, they came trooping out rudely and roughly, intent upon quenching their thirst and getting back in time. Gabrielle could not go on without pressing through the turbulent little army. She drew back and watched them. Some were stolid and weary; some comely young faces returned her gaze with not unfriendly curiosity. Others stopped with a half-finished jest upon their lips to

nudge one another and call attention to her hat or
gown. There were bold, unpleasant leers among them
too, and in the rear two women loitered and walked
so close to her that she instinctively retreated a step,
to avoid the touch of their threatening elbows and
shoulders, when one stood and devoured her with
ugly, insolent eyes in which Gabrielle, to her surprise
and discomfort, perceived something intentionally sinister and brutal.

"Why does she hate me?" she asked herself, troubled, and walked on quickly. The woman gazed after
her, neglecting her beer to follow with aggressive
glances the well-clothed, well-fed, well-cared-for girl,
who could saunter about smiling, with gloves on her
idle hands.

"That dark woman has the evil eye," Gabrielle
thought, waiting at a safe distance until the wild
troop, with emptied glasses, streamed out of the beer-
garden, recrossed the court, and returned to their
looms and shuttles. The street seemed suddenly dark
and still, after the passing of those loud colors, noisy
feet, and boisterous voices.

She turned thoughtfully toward home. On a cross
street she saw straw strewn thick before a house with
closed shutters, and from the door came a Sister of
Mercy with noiseless step and downcast eyes, and
under the white cap of her order the serene face
which such as she know how to bring from weary
midnight vigils and the chamber of death.

They were all every-day sights and sounds, but Gabrielle's spirit, startled by the hatred in the coarse
woman's eyes, had lost its brief lightness, and as she
returned through the village and the quiet lane, her
mind dwelt upon the old, old questions which sooner

or later torment every heart large enough to care for
joy and sorrow beyond its own. The toil of the factory girls, the vast ease of the countess who yet each
day manufactured wrongs and grievances for herself;
lovely Mercedes deliberately choosing that unlovely,
unloving fate, the little black-robed sweet-faced Sister;
the pain and tears of the silent house, the laughter of
the children; Peter's scowl at the world's injustice
and the malignant resentment of the strange woman;
Bernhard Dietz's healthful, joyous presence, the lame
count's dark mournful eyes and pale drawn face looking up at her from his red cushions; the people working in the fields and at the forge as she passed, — and
this time she did not think of the color of the blouse,
but of the aching back beneath it, — the gay, selfish
circle working only to amuse itself; the mean little
houses on the outskirts of the village where small children and old women were splitting wood and drawing
water, the great luxurious empty villa where fifteen
human beings seemed to be necessary for the comfort
of three, all these sharp and cruel contrasts loomed
up before her as distinctly as if they were rocks along
the path. Poverty for one, infamy for another, distinction for a third, and why — why? And why
build our ease upon the pain and misery of other
hearts?

" I wish I could go back and speak to that woman
with the hate in her eyes," she thought. " I would
tell her that I am sorry for many things. I should
like to say to her that I would rather work in that
factory all day and every day, and be with my papa
evenings, than live the life I am leading now without
him. Perhaps she would not hate me if she knew
that." Pondering upon these sorrowful problems

which met her face to face, yet innocently blind to
the vast and mournful ones of disease and crime beyond her knowledge, and reasoning in a circle after
the fashion of many a wiser head, she entered the
villa and met Lipps in the lower corridor.

He stood and stared at her in a dejected, helpless
way.

"What is it, Lipps?" she asked kindly.

" I don't know what it is; and if I don't," he began
dully, "nobody does!" he broke out with a kind of
desperation. " But I am taking a liberty. I beg the
gracious fräulein's pardon."

"Oh, never mind the liberty. Besides, it is n't a
liberty."

" I was so glad when the gracious fräulein came in
to-day," the poor fellow, thus encouraged, began to
say hurriedly, with a watchful eye on the staircase.
"Thinks I to myself, there 's one straight, right
thing happened in this crooked house. That 's what
ought to be. The young lady in our wing. And I
felt as light as air. It 's no use. He 's worse than
ever. He 's in his dumb starings."

"In what, Lipps? I do not understand."

" After the gracious fräulein went, was he cheerful,
was he happy, as I like a fool expected? No, he was
awful," groaned the servant. "Something settled
down on his face like a fog — like midnight. Oh,
I know it. It was there always at first, but it got
better. He does not move or speak; he scarcely
breathes; he only stares straight before him with his
big eyes."

" Was it directly after I went ? "

" Begging the gracious fräulein's pardon, it was. I
kind of hung round softly ; I could n't bear to leave

him like that. Says he, 'Lipps, you may go; and let no one in, no one, do you understand?' Says I, kind of venturing, 'Not even Herr Dietz?' For he is uncommon cheery, and Count Hugo watches him, and smiles in the old careless way. 'No one,' says he, and shut his mouth like a nut-cracker. I know what it means now. Dumbness for days, and a look in his eyes that makes me ache." The man gave a gulp which he discreetly transformed into a cough behind his hand.

"I am so sorry, Lipps,—so sorry!" Gabrielle stammered.

On the landing, half-way up the great stairway, appeared Mousey, freshly combed and wearing a white cravat. He regarded the two with his worldly air of intelligent scrutiny, turned himself about, and promenaded up-stairs. Gabrielle started as if he were a human messenger admonishing her that dinner was imminent, and that she should hastily prepare for that portentous rite. Shortly after, the butler, the countess, smiling and debonair in stiff satin, with a pink rose blooming in her cap and speaking French volubly to the snapping idol on her arm, demure Babette with a scarf, and Röschen with Mousey's rug, came in the usual slow and superb procession down the marble stairway.

CHAPTER XV

"How is he to-day, Lipps?" inquired Gabrielle, coming down for the afternoon drive before the countess, and meeting the man in the hall.

"Nothing but a corpse and Count Hugo can be as still as that," he answered drearily.

Each day she heard a similar response, and turned away with a pang of self-reproach.

"What did I do to him?" she asked herself. "How could I have hurt him? Ah, if I had not gone in!"

After some days, Lipps announced with nascent hopefulness, and in a mysterious whisper, for the butler was passing: —

"He's got as far as the little black book."

"I don't know what that means, but I hope with all my heart that it is something pleasant."

"It might n't be very pleasant for anybody else," Lipps admitted, "for we are gloomy still, and not so much appetite as a canary. But the book is better than the stare, and when he takes it up again, I know that he is kind of working along out of the fog."

She wondered what he meant, and thoughtfully regarded his ugly, unselfish, faithful countenance, softened now with feeling, and brightened by a slight ray of hope. "I am glad that he has you, Lipps," she said sweetly.

Lipps's affection was not rhetorical. He hesitated, gulped, stammered, coughed, flushed, and rejoined in uncouth agitation : —

" If being chopped in pieces would do any good, all
I 'd have to say is ' Chop ! ' "

But Gabrielle understood him as well as if he had
uttered the eloquent heart-cry of a poet, and replied
softly : —

" Only let me know when I can do anything for
him, or for you."

At the close of this interview, the countess, passing
down to the carriage, cast upon them the peculiar
glance of vague distrust which she habitually bestowed upon any two persons talking together in her
house with an appearance of good understanding, and
demanded testily, as they drove away : —

" Why do you talk to that man, Gabrielle ? "

" I was inquiring after Count Hugo."

" Of course. I did not imagine that you were talking astronomy. But I always send Babette, that is,
when I do not go myself ; and as His Royal Highness
is having a fit of the sulks and ostracizing me for
some days, I cannot now present myself in person.
But I never encourage Lipps to talk ; I distrust him.
Mousey's instinct is unerring, is it not, dear pet?
Yes, so it was ! Then Hugo spoils the man. You
could send Röschen, I suppose ? "

" I could ; yes."

" For my part, I neither go nor send too often to
inquire just now. I found his doors locked several
times ; but I can overlook the incivility. It is best
to wait till he recovers his equanimity. One must
have patience with an invalid's moods," she added
sententiously. " Hugo has his ups and downs. One
must have tact and consideration. Yes, one must, my
bright-eyed little man ! How clear his precious little
bark sounds. So jovial ! Gabrielle, really you have

an amazing stare. I am not aware that there is anything preposterous in my remarks or personal appearance. My bonnet, I trust, is not awry, nor my hair
in maniacal disorder."

" I beg your pardon," returned the young girl with
a slight choking sensation. "There is nothing the
matter with your bonnet, or your hair."

"You look positively incredulous," declared the old
lady, angrily insistent. "Perhaps you know best.
Perhaps you wish to contradict."

Away flew Gabrielle's restive resolutions. " I did
not know how I was looking," she began with spirit.
"I certainly never wish to be rude to you, Aunt Adelheid ; but I was thinking that if I were Count Hugo's
mother, I would not leave him night or day, and
nothing would give me any joy, — not friends, not
toilettes, or gayety, or books, or the king himself, —
nothing, nothing in the whole wide world outside
of those four walls, — nothing but the thought of caring for him, and comforting him, if with only a word
— a look — a clasp of the hand."

She stopped, her cheeks glowing, her voice broken,
and she anticipated for her crime the severest punishment known to her tyrant, — something resembling
the bastinado, followed by decapitation. But the marvellously versatile countess broke into a laugh so light
and girlish and merry that it startled Gabrielle, and
suggested, under the circumstances, the vagaries of an
unsound mind.

" *Tiens, tiens,* I must tell Hugo that. She says she
would like to sit and hold Hugo's hands. Do you hear
her, Mousey, my treasure? Oh, what a droll idea !
Bless my little angel-love ! Yes, he was an angel !
And when he died, he should go straight to heaven,

like Martin Luther's little dog, and have a little golden
tail, like his! So he should! For he was a thousand
times sweeter" (kiss) "and cleverer" (kiss) "and
handsomer and more angelic" (kiss) "than Martin
Luther's little dog, yes, so he was!"

Gabrielle shrank into her corner to retreat from the
extraordinary plunges and dives of the breathless old
lady, devouring the snarling, struggling animal with
kisses. The young girl, with a curious mingling of
emotions, a ferment of generous indignation, compassion, wonder, and disgust, found herself involuntarily
picturing Mousey in a purer world, wagging the proposed decorative adjunct; and she reflected that if, as
some claim, both man and beast will receive in another
sphere exact compensation for the deprivations of this
life, then surely a golden tail on Mousey would be but
a logical sequence.

The following morning she sat in the garden em-
broidering a yellow dog-blanket in gold. It was the
special design of the countess, who said that her idol
" with his fair hair would be a splendid bit of color,
a sunbeam, a little golden glory, a Phœbus-Apollo
doggums!"

Gabrielle looked up smiling, as Lipps came hurrying toward her.

" If the gracious fräulein pleases, the count is better."

" Ah, I am very glad," she returned warmly.

" And I am to go for Herr Dietz."

" He will be good for him, I am sure."

" But he couldn't take care of him?" Lipps stammered uneasily.

"As you do? Never! Nobody could," she declared heartily.

Lipps looked relieved, and presently said : —

" It 's an awful thing to be afraid."

" Afraid ?   You were distressed, Lipps, but not afraid ?   There surely was no danger ? "

All intelligence faded conveniently out of the man's face. " The gracious fräulein knows best," he muttered in his humblest and stupidest manner, and stole off on cautious tip-toe.

Presently he repassed, followed by Dietz.   Gabrielle had never seen him walking on earth like other men.   To her he meant a voice, a note of gladness up in the higher air, and she regarded him with pleased surprise, as the tall white figure, towering head and shoulders above Lipps, and with stone-dust powdering his great beard, emerged from the shrubbery.   He snatched off his paper-cap as he perceived her, and strode on with a slow long step.   Lipps looked eager, anxious, pleased, and fussy.   The broad-shouldered giant behind him wore an air of deep and gentle repose.

Gabrielle stitched various curious reflections into the canine Apollo's golden mantle.

Lipps ushered Bernhard into the count's room, and left them.

Dietz stood looking down with his kindly smiling eyes upon Hugo, who said languidly : —

" Ah, good morning, Dietz.   It is good of you to come over at once."

" Why not ? " replied Bernhard, noting the count's excessive pallor and the weariness of his voice.

After several moments of gentle scrutiny, Bernhard continued : —

" You have been — worse ? "   He was about to say " ill," but scarcely knew what word to use to a man always on his back.

"I have been — the devil!" returned the count with a short laugh.

The men again regarded each other in silence. Suddenly Hugo turned slightly, and with his nervous hand clutched Dietz's arm and held it fast. In that one moment the lonely soul imprisoned within the crippled body surrendered its pride, confessed its pain and weakness, and reached out through the longing eyes for human sympathy.

In Bernhard's face was boundless pity, but the kind eyes were smiling as a mother smiles on her suffering child, and slowly lifting his left arm, he covered with his broad, brown palm the emaciated fingers grasping his wrist.

At this, Hugo broke into an ungovernable paroxysm of weeping. Shaken by deep sobs, he buried his face in the cushions, and lay helpless and broken in a tempest of emotion.

Dietz turned away, bowed his head, and waited.

At length the count recovered himself. For some moments he lay motionless, except for an occasional long, shuddering sigh that shook his whole frame.

"Damn my woman's nerves!" he muttered.

Dietz approached the sofa.

"Count," he began in his calm, mellow voice, "will you let me take you out into the garden? It is a wonderful morning for freshness and birds and sweet smells. There is a little white birch out there. You can see it from your corner by the fountain. It's as pretty as a girl. So straight and slender, — and modest yet kind of beckoning. And the air — you never breathed such air — the air is the best doctor on earth, and you have been in the house too long, count. That's what's the matter."

" I wish you could stay here," said Hugo wearily.

" Well, I can't. May I take you out ? "

Hugo stared straight at the swallow on the ceiling. After a while he asked, —

" Is any one out there ? "

" That beautiful young lady — your cousin — is sitting on a bench near the house, sewing on something yellow."

" I don't feel well enough to be moved this morning," Hugo rejoined quickly after another pause.

Dietz reflected. His mind was not rapid in seizing conclusions, but he thought, " Every sick man is a child. One must act for him."

" Wait," he said placidly, and left the room.

Presently Gabrielle saw him coming across the grass toward her.

She looked up inquiringly.

He pulled off his paper-cap, and said in his tranquil way : —

" The count is coming out here."

Gabrielle sprang up, gathered together her silks and gold thread and scissors and little basket, and stood ready to take instant flight.

Dietz was surprised at this extremely rapid response to his mission, and explained : —

" He did not tell me that he wished you to go away. But he is ill and nervous. I think he dreads seeing anybody. He ought to be out here."

" Of course he ought," Gabrielle agreed heartily. " I will go at once. I am glad to go. I thank you for telling me."

She started toward the house. He followed more slowly. At the door, she turned and waited.

" You do him good, Herr Dietz," she said. " You

seem to be the only one who can," she added a little sadly.

"The fresh growing things will do him good," Bernhard rejoined. He liked her way of holding up her pretty head, and looking straight into his eyes, thoughtfully yet very cordially, and with something soft yet courageous in her manner. She was about as old as his Röschen, he decided.

"There is nobody out there," Bernhard announced to Hugo, who glanced up sharply.

"The lady who was there has gone in," Dietz added, "and I'm going to take you out now." Hugo, weary, spent, and passive, let the strong man and Lipps do with him what they would.

Dietz turned the invalid's chair toward the point in the tangled shrubbery where the maidenly birch gleamed white among the hawthorns and acacias and willows. The water plashed softly from the dragon's head. There was a warm balsamic odor from the rank neglected pines and cedars and firs and larches. The lilac bushes waved their violet and white plumes, and exhaled their strong breath to mingle with the delicate fragrance of fruit blossoms and the fine odors of innumerable shrubs. Nearer the house, a row of huge horse-chestnut trees raised their massive leafy domes, crowned with rich tropical spikes, from which with every breeze fell a snow-storm of white petals. There was a mysterious murmur in the poplar leaves, a hum of bees and insects, a flutter and a twitter and a warbling of birds.

"I am the one ugly spot in Nature's May pageant," thought Hugo. Dietz stood with his hands on his hips, looking about and smiling as contentedly as if he had made it all. "It's healing," he remarked.

"It's a disgrace to a civilized household," Hugo retorted querulously. "There's enough raw material here to stock ten respectable gardens."

Dietz gave him the sweetest glance that ever a big man in a blouse bestowed upon one of his own sex, and without speaking continued to investigate the secrets of the surrounding tanglewood.

"I'm going, count," he said at length.

"I have taken a great deal of your time," rejoined Hugo.

"Why not?"

Hugo looked at him affectionately, and with a faint flash of amusement.

"I think it would be more sensible to ask 'Why?' rather than always 'Why not?'" he remarked. But Dietz took his meaning, whatever it might have been, as another incomprehensible and unimportant whim of a sick man, and wasted no thought on it.

"Do you think you can come over again to-day?"

"I'll come as often as you want me. Don't hesitate to send, for I work by the job, you know," Bernhard added practically, "not by the day. I'm well enough along to spare a little time for you," he went on cordially, "for I begin before the other men, and work longer, and often through the nooning. That's because my work is pleasanter than theirs," he explained modestly. "If they had my work they'd like to begin earlier, when the morning is fresh. Mine is the pleasantest work in the world. Sometimes I hope," he went on with a genial laugh, "that if I'm lucky enough to get into the New Jerusalem they talk about, there'll still be a little building going on, for I shouldn't feel at home without a block of stone to chip at."

"Have you never longed to carry it farther, Dietz?" and Hugo fixed his eyes curiously on the placid face. "Have you never desired to create, to be an artist, not an artisan — a real sculptor?"

"Oh, when a man's young, he has his fancies," Bernhard admitted. "Yes, I went through all that. You ought to see the queer things I modelled. It cost me some tears and sleepless nights before I gave it up. But it's a good thing for a man to find his level. Anybody can see there's no artist in me. Still I'm the artist's very good tool. I'm a part of him and his work. That's the way I look at it, count. But there's one thing I am going to do before I die," he said with sudden shyness. "I am thinking of it all the time; I have almost got it, only it changes; it comes and goes." He put his hand over his eyes an instant, then threw back his head and smiled. "It will come yet; it will come and stay, and then I shall envy none of the great ones. But there! I am wandering off again," he said apologetically. "There are things that make a fool of a man."

Hugo watched him languidly, wondering at the softness of his voice. "Have you no troubles, Dietz?"

Bernhard hesitated.

"Yes, count, but no more than are healthy for a man. But I must go. There's something you do like a girl," he added with his indulgent smile.

"I don't doubt it," Hugo said curtly. "That is my impression of a good deal of my conduct."

"You only begin to talk when I really can't stay."

"Oh, is that all? That is my feminine slyness, Dietz. I like to keep you with me," and Hugo held out his hand. "It's no use trying to thank you," he said with much feeling.

" I wish you good rest and good thoughts, count,"
returned Bernhard simply, and went.

But he would not have considered Hugo's thoughts
good.

" The truth is," he reflected, occupying himself, as
soon as he was alone, with his ever-haunting theme,
taking it up where he had left it, as one opens a
familiar, well-loved book, and reads on wherever the
glance falls, "every man to whom the question presents itself has the right to decide it. The pious
souls who think the Bible forbids it with ' Thou shalt
not kill ' seem to feel no virtuous repugnance toward
the existence of capital punishment or war. What
twaddle conventional morality is ! Obermann is about
right. When I am able-bodied and happy and love
life, I am taught that it is sweet and glorious to die
for the fatherland. Wretched, useless, longing for
death, I am warned that I have no right over my own
existence, and that it is a crime to shorten it. Logical,
that ! If it is dear and beautiful, it is my duty and
privilege to sacrifice it. If it is hideous, I must cling
to it. It is honorable for me to march out and kill a
man who never harmed me, and who desires to live.
To seek death when I fear and hate it is noble. To
seek it when I long for it is sin. If my life does not
belong to me, what right have I to consent to risk it
in war ? Can I give what I do not possess ? If I as
an individual have no such right, whence then the
right of society, or a government, or any corporation
or union of individuals to demand my life for their
purposes ? I claim no angelic purity of motive. I
admit that my views are low and selfish. But they
relate only to one worthless existence; and are n't
they, all in all, as lofty and rational as the bickerings

of nations about boundaries and South Sea colonies and fishing-smacks and the claimants of penny-thrones — for which, in the sacred name of patriotism, governments are ready to slaughter millions of men? So far as consistency is concerned, neither saints nor sinners are in a position to throw stones. No, death comes sooner or later to us all. It is not like a wrong, a crime, or suffering that could be avoided. What harm in anticipating the inevitable end? Who dares pronounce it unpardonable? Who can prove it is not desirable? If a man has duties, responsibilities, — a wife, a child, a single soul to whom he owes protection or allegiance, the question assumes other proportions. But who on this earth is so alone as I? Not a dog would be worse off for my death! Sometimes it does seem to me like a certain form of desertion, but that, no doubt, is early prejudice, instilled into me by my elders and betters; and it may be vanity, too. One regards one's existence as too important, even in a maimed, miserable hulk like mine."

The air was sleepy and still and growing warmer. There was a ceaseless soothing murmur of living things and fluttering foliage. Hugo stared wearily into the cloudless sky. "Suppose, above that blue, there were, after all, the heaven and the great white throne in which the church teaches we must believe or be damned. Suppose I, having this day the choice to stay or go, should go, and should stand before the throne. Why, then, so far as I see, I would have the right to say : —

" Lord, it was Thy will, since Thy will is omnipotent. If Thy will is not omnipotent, then let my soul travel farther, and like St. Christopher, seek the Mightiest. Him only will I serve."

He took out his little black book.   During the few
previous weeks he had added to his notes and quotations and pasted in newspaper cuttings.   He regarded
his collection with a certain complacency.   There was
a great deal of carefully sifted information in it.

With morbid exactness he considered the great
suicides of antiquity, their motives, and their details.
"There is a vast difference between the calm and
classic manner, and the modern sensational style.
There is a rational and an irrational kind.   When,
for instance, a boy and girl lash themselves together
and jump into a lake, because their cruel parents won't
let them marry, that is eminently irrational, for the
chances are ten to one that if they do nothing rash,
they may live to thank their parents; and again, if
they were permitted to marry, perhaps they would
jump into the lake separately.   Then the 'woman
scorned' who shoots her faithless lover and herself, —
that's very yellow-covered ; and in my humble opinion, she never loved him; she loved herself.   Now
here is an account of two young girls, promenading
in the moonlight before a certain castle, and taking
poison beneath a young man's windows.   It is vulgar
and stagey.   The newspapers are full of such things.
The doctors say it is a malady, and increasing.   Looking at it fairly, it seems that in most cases in my list
it is caused by drugs, or drink, or insanity.   Poor
desperate souls !   They act too rashly ; they should
have patience ; they should wait a year, and then
perhaps some of them would be glad and gay, and
have no wish to go.

"But if after waiting a year," his eyes rested upon
the fluttering crown of fresh birch leaves, "the wish
is still there, deep and unchangeable, then not in pas-

sion, but gently and calmly — world, farewell! One ought to be willing to prove the sincerity of one's vocation for the shades, as when a worldly man wishes to become a monk. All the old fellows, Plato at the head, say that incurable bodily disease is reason enough ; and if not only the body is worthless, but the life helpless, useless, loveless, while the heart rages and struggles, and never yields, never learns what they call resignation, why, then — then — ah, father, even you will smile and say it is .well done ! "

The sunshine and the faint breeze played with the pale green leaves of the young birch.

" To look down the years, and see but this! Deathly loneliness and no control of myself, — no more than an hysterical woman, — and horror of a beautiful face, for the agony of remembrance and cowardice it awakens. Ah, father, father, I will wait, but thank God the door is open. How quietly, how thankfully I shall pass out into the great darkness, into the great calm."

The birds were busy in the shrubbery, the water plashed its lullaby, the warm, soft, sunny life in the old garden breathed upon him in countless subtle odors, spoke to him with innumerable voices.

He turned from his friends the stoics, to statements of the modern French medical school. Sometimes he forgot himself in his subject, and out of his rambling thoughts, his curious statistics, his medley of reflections, grew a singular restfulness.

" I could write a pamphlet for them ; I have studied this thing ; I not only know how it looks from without ; I know how it feels within, and whatever remains I shall know soon. If I only could wait better ! It is folly to be tragic ; but let them who teach that the spirit sits up aloft in the cranium explain, if they can, why a man loses his courage with the strength of his back. Was my soul in my spine?"

From beneath half-closed lids, he stared idly into the greenness. The breeze blew the scolloped edge of his awning to and fro.

"How it all goes on every year, — year after year. How all the color and freshness come and go in the bushes — all the leaves and blossoms, and the pink and the yellow, and the fragrance. Where does it come from? Where does it go? Where shall I go? Shall I come up again somewhere, or not? At all events, I shall not fear to take my chances. The vast Unknowable God, in whom I believe and who is everywhere, will be more pitiful than the jealous Hebrew God on his throne."

Straight before him amid the caressing foliage was the gleaming stem of the birch. Dietz was singing somewhere overhead, and the pounding on the houses was cheerfully monotonous.

"I wish Dietz would come in and stay. I don't know what it is that I like in him, but I like him all through. How the water plashes! With my eyes closed, I could think I was in Rome again, in the old Corsini garden, where the water falls under the cypresses. There was Mercedes, seven years younger, laughing and enchanting. And I a boy off for a holiday. Much I cared then for cypresses and fountains and views. But now I see it all clearly, and I am the same man — except these bonds — and Mercedes has grown wise, and will marry the French Embassador. May she have seven daughters as wise and beautiful as she, and may they all marry embassadors and make glad the heart of their mother!

" Dietz said that birch was like a girl — modest yet beckoning. The big fellow has a tender heart. How straight she stood the other day, how honest and innocent she was, and how like a tomb the room seemed afterwards. She must not come again. I am too weak, too weary. Let me be quiet, and await the end. Why suffer? Why excite myself? Surely I have suffered enough. I suppose if my senses were fine, I should see all those acacia leaves growing and hear undreamed-of sounds. We are coarse brutes, after all. Dietz said the birch was beckoning."

He vaguely saw something lovely and young in the thicket, something fair and virginal, a gracious figure with luminous hazel eyes, noticeably far apart, and a look in them of truth and fearlessness. The vision did not torture him now. He was too weary. He could only fix his languid gaze on the slender, beckoning white birch. " She had an adorable smile," he thought.

At noon Bernhard stood by him, and Lipps came cautiously from the other direction, making grimaces expressive of satisfaction. There was no movement from the lame man's chair.

Dietz once more embraced tree and bush and plant with his look of large approval, and gazed long at the sharp profile under the awning.

" I don't know why I like him," he thought, " but when he turns those big hollow eyes on me, I could take him and carry him in my arms all over the world. I never liked anybody so well — except Röschen, — bless her ! — and that's different, quite different."

He smiled to think how very different loving Röschen was from anything that ever had been or ever could be, and strolled back to his work.

CHAPTER XVI

" What was it like?" asked the countess.

"Oh, it was wonderful! Sixteen horses pawing and snorting, the thud of their hoofs in the soft tan, the gleam of their eyes, the breath of their nostrils, their plunges and bounds, and quivering " —

"Who was in the gallery?" interrupted the countess, while a vague uneasiness and jealousy of so much youth and life and spirit crept into her cold eyes and her voice. "The Countess Waldenberg, of course, since she offered to chaperon you with Mercedes. She'd better keep her eyes on her erratic daughter. Mercedes is flirting disgracefully with Paalzow, I hear."

"She was lovely this morning," returned Gabrielle heartily. "She is bewitching on a horse."

"Contradict, by all means. If I say she is disgraceful, of course you find her bewitching. When I ask a simple and natural question, instead of informing me sensibly who was there, beside the riders, and what was going on in general, you go off into a — *rhapsodie hippique!* No, my precious little sweetums, no more sugar, not a crumb. Sugar is bad for Mumsey's angel! Well?" sharply to Gabrielle.

"I did not notice the gallery much, Aunt Adelheid," Gabrielle began in a soberer tone. "The royal *manège* is so large, and the spectators were so far off and in shadow, and I was so extremely absorbed by Sphinx. He was the most excited creature," laughing and speaking brightly and rapidly again, "so full of nonsense and antics. He knew nothing whatever of quadrille figures, nor I either for that matter, and we found turning sharp corners and wheeling on our own axes very different from free riding on country-roads. Then while I tried to learn the evolutions, Sphinx was determined to learn nothing, and that created a certain confusion in our manœuvres. But Herr von Raven was patient and Mercedes helpful, and finally Sphinx and I became of one mind, as horse and rider should be."

The countess frowned.

"I have no patience with horsey talk, and the way you allude to Sphinx jars upon me. How can you identify yourself with a horse, and say 'we' did this and that? Sweetheart! Bébé! Did he want a crumb of sugar? Did he put up his angel-paws and beg? Well, he should have it, because he loved his Mumsey and his Mumsey loved her Mousey!"

The girl's eyes danced with merriment as the countess made love to the dog on her knee, whose greedy gaze was fixed on her lips, from which she conveyed to him fragments of a lump of sugar bitten small for his refection.

"I fear that my affection for horses is incorrigible," Gabrielle replied, not without mischief. "I have grown up with 'our colleague the horse,' as Professor Huxley says; I admire him and believe in him. I used to wish that I could find Gulliver's unpronounceable horse-kingdom, and live there. When I was first reading mythology, I used to imagine a centaur galloping over the plain and running away with me."

The countess replied with a mocking smile: —

" I know centaurs enough who would run away
with you — upon conditions."

" Oh," returned Gabrielle innocently, " a real centaur never stops to make any. He snatches his prey
and is gone! "

" Ours are more circumspect," sneered the old lady.
" They make minute inquiries as to the prey's *dot.* "
She stopped rubbing Mousey's stomach, and gave
Gabrielle a long, suspicious glance.

" Then, happily, they will not want me," laughed
the girl. . " But Aunt Adelheid, Herr von Raven is
really very amiable as a centaur. I like him much
better so, than in his abnormal, dismounted state. By
the way, I have discovered why he and his set speak
so curiously. They are almost always riding, and
they ride German trot when on duty, and it jolts
more of course than when one rides in the stirrups.
Consequently their conversation is broken — staccato. They have the habit of talking between jolts.
' Famous ' (jolt) ' proud of my pupil ' (jolt) ' upon
my word ' (jolt) ' to the left, please ' (jolt, jolt) ' like
chain in Lancers ' (jolt, jolt, jolt) ' quite simple '
(jolt) ' bravo ' (jolt) ' light, firm hand ' (jolt) ' perfect! ' (jolt) ! In a drawing-room one should always
imagine the motion of a horse."

" Don't mimic, Gabrielle. It is bad taste, and
silly. Should-ums did-ums want his crumb of sugar ?
There ! "

" Some of the officers' wives ride very well, but
Mercedes is most charming. She leads with Herr von
Paalzow."

" While her old marquis is constructing himself
for the day ! Was the Frau Major there ? "

" I merely caught a glimpse of her at the door."

" With the Countess Waldenberg ? "

" I really did not notice."

" But Gabrielle, you are too tedious ! "

" I will observe the whole row of chaperons to-morrow," the young girl rejoined conciliatingly. " I was so occupied with Sphinx, Aunt Adelheid. He did not know whether he wished to stand on his ear or his tail ! "

" A very refined description ! "

" I mean that he was nervous, and could not understand what was required of him."

" Horses are stupid animals — are they not, Mousey? Great blundering stupids ! Look at Mousey's frontal development," and she parted his yellow locks as one pushes back the curls from the forehead of a loved child. " Look at that ! Did you ever see anything like it? Did a horse ever have that intellect ? " She gazed fondly into the diabolical eyes.

" No, — never ! " Gabrielle rejoined emphatically. " Mousey is the cleverest thing in this world. I shall always concede that."

Either the dog found something objectionable in her remark, or resented having his forehead exposed and discussed, for he snapped at the countess's hands, and barked viciously at Gabrielle.

" Wonderful animal," exclaimed the countess. " His sensitiveness is a perpetual surprise." Mousey's rage was subsiding in a series of sniffs and grunts. " Poor little sorrowing heart ! He never allows a stranger to touch his head, and it grieved him to have us even allude to it so pointedly. It was inconsiderate on my part. His reserve is so fastidious. He is so aristocratic."

The lauded object gave a long and comfortable

snore. He was not asleep, but merely taking his ease and expressing his feelings with characteristic disregard for his inferiors.

" What do you think of Herr von Paalzow ? " began the countess abruptly.

" Oh, he is charming."

" That is unequivocal, at least ! "

" But you asked me."

" Don't be captious, Gabrielle. A well-bred girl when asked her opinion of a man usually expresses herself with some reserve. She may say he seems agreeable, or has distinction of manner. She does not start and open her eyes and smile and pronounce him ' charming ' with that amount of emphasis.''

Gabrielle colored vividly. She was apt to lose patience quickly when her conduct toward men became the subject of the countess's criticism.

" Herr von Paalzow seems to me agreeable and distinguished, since you prefer those expressions, and — if I am allowed to observe his personal appearance — I think him handsome. He is very brave, they tell me, which is more important."

" He seems to have made an impression on you, my dear."

" Why, yes, a very good one. There is something happy and sunny in his face, and he seems kind. I noticed his manner to his groom."

" It strikes me that you have noticed him closely."

" I have. When I saw him with Mercedes, I wished with all my heart that she was going to marry him instead of the marquis."

"Tut, tut ! " exclaimed the countess in her bantering tone, Gabrielle's somewhat irritated manner moving her pleasurably ; " the Waldenbergs would not thank

you for your match-making schemes. Von Paalzow
has no fortune. They would be eager enough to catch
him for Elsa, and with old Valois secured, they could
not do better, for Paalzow is a rising man. But it is
a pity that Mercedes will not let him alone. If she is
not less reckless, she will not only ruin silly Elsa's
hopes, but her own with the marquis. His old eyes
are, I admit, weak and watery; still some things are
plain enough for even a man in his dotage to see."

Such remarks always made Gabrielle restive.
"Catching Paalzow" — "securing Valois," — Mercedes deceiving an old man who trusted her, — laughing,
careless Elsa scheming meanly for a husband, — it was
all untrue, she knew that, but it was hard always to
breathe mephitic air ! She had been happy that morning, — her natural, unrepressed self, fearless and free,
prone to laughter, to sympathy. When those sixteen
splendid animals came tearing down the length of
the *manège*, neck to neck, shoulder to shoulder, then
halted as still as the bronze horses at Venice, while the
bugles blew a long shrill blast, she no longer called
the tournament a circus, she forgot her prejudices, and
was thrilled with joyous excitement. It was a taste of
her old innocent freedom ; it was like her native atmosphere, she drew it in with full glad breaths, and was
radiant when she rejoined the countess in the villa.
Now she sat silent and ill at ease.

"How is Herr von Paalzow with you ? "

"I have talked with him very little," she returned
listlessly. "He is easy to talk with. He likes many
things that I like. ·He cares for books. I never like
to talk with any one very long who does not like
books."

"Nonsense ! How pedantic ! "

"Oh, I do not mean a person who talks of books exclusively. He need not say a word of them. But one knows a book-lover intuitively. Books are such a comfort and refuge!"

"Thank you for your information. I believe I learned all that at the age of ten, in one of Lafontaine's fables. Really, how can you air such platitudes?"

"Because," persisted Gabrielle, "when I talk long with Herr von Raven, for instance, I have a sensation that he lives in one world and I in another, and there is no connection between the two, except a suspension-bridge, which we can cross only on horses."

"Hm!" said the countess.

"I think he reads nothing but the sporting news. He is so good-naturedly condescending to authors. They are not in the army, poor things!" She laughed a little.

The old lady, who bestowed her fluttering, uneasy kind of attention upon her Figaro, while adoring Mousey on her knee, and who had not read an entire book in years, replied sharply:—

"There isn't a girl in town who would not be glad to marry him. He is a soldier and a gentleman. Would you have him a book-worm to boot?"

"I don't mean that one couldn't like him, or that he may not be clever — in ways that don't appear."

The countess laughed in spite of herself.

"He would thank you for that speech."

"I do seem to make it worse instead of better," Gabrielle returned smiling. "But I meant nothing unkind. When we talk of horses, our conversation goes galloping along cheerfully, and it may be my own fault that we stumble and halt when we try other themes."

" You frighten him, no doubt, with your superior airs."

" Oh, he is not at all shy, and certainly does not suspect his limitations. We are friendly enough in a superficial way."

" Good heavens, Gabrielle, you set my nerves on edge with your phrases! Superficial. What more do you expect? Must one swear eternal friendship with everybody one meets in society? And your limitations? What kind of a word is that for a girl to use? Limitations — limitations? Really, it is an exasperating word. An odious word. Limitations, indeed!"

She rose with an offended air and walked slowly and heavily from the room. Gabrielle followed, resolving for the thousandth time never to permit herself to make a natural remark, since it was sure to displease. On the landing the countess stopped, panting audibly. She looked singularly pale, whether from fatigue or anger Gabrielle did not presume to judge, but there was an unhealthy whiteness in the large face, and the thin lips were parted, drawing short and painful breaths.

" Let me give you my arm, Aunt Adelheid. At least let me take Mousey. Why should you carry the lazy fellow up-stairs?"

But the dog, objecting to be called a lazy fellow, refused to come to her, slipped down, made an evil face, and walked up the stairs on his own indignant paws.

" Give me some Chartreuse," gasped the countess, pointing to the liqueur-stand when they reached her room.

" It is so sweet and heavy! Will it not make you worse?" Gabrielle asked kindly.

But the countess frowned and insisted. She sipped

it, nibbling a sweet biscuit, and giving crumbs to Mousey stationed on the table near the refreshments, leaned her white cheek against the chair-back, breathing with much exertion. Gabrielle watched her, silent and sorry.

The countess lighted a cigarette, and after some whiffs, murmured with bitterness : —

" It will take me off some time ! "

" Can nothing be done ? " the young girl asked compassionately.

The countess waited a few moments until her respiration was more natural, before replying : —

" Oh, I have tried one doctor after another. They all tell the same story. Exercise is their war-cry nowadays. No one has ever understood me except Pressigny."

" But if they all agree ? " suggested Gabrielle gently.

" Pressigny never allowed me to exercise. He never allowed me to fast. Once I consulted Hugo's doctor. I felt weak. I wanted a tonic. He felt my pulse, he listened to my breathing, knocked about my chest with a business-like rapidity that was positively brutal, — I might have been a beer-cask for all the deference he showed ! — and then he had the impertinence to say : ' My dear madam, I congratulate you upon your strength and constitution. You need no tonic, only less food and more exercise. I will prescribe your diet. If you follow it closely, you will soon be in enviable health. There is some fat about the heart, and if you continue to live unwisely, it may make trouble for you.' What kind of a tirade was that ! "

" But was it not true ? "

" Don't ask silly questions, and don't interrupt," returned the countess, her breathing still laborious.

" ' Doctor,' said I, ' I cannot diet.' He shrugged his shoulders. 'That is as you please,' he answered. ' I will send you my instructions. I shall not starve you or train you for athletic sports. I shall merely indicate a rational mode of life for a woman of your years and habit. Good-morning, madam,' and he whisked out of my room. He has no more delicacy, no more tact, no more sympathy, no more feeling than that poker ! ' "

" Perhaps you 'd better not talk, Aunt Adelheid."

" I prefer to talk ! " said the old lady sternly. " He sent his instructions. When I saw that he expected me to rise at eight and walk fifteen minutes up the Heine Strasse, I threw his precious rules into the fire. ' No liqueurs,' I saw too. Now I positively require liqueur. Dr. Pressigny told me that my over-sensitiveness demanded certain aromatic stimulants. Imagine the blunderer telling me to walk out at eight like a market-woman ! Is that the way to prescribe for a lady? The coarseness of the idea is revolting. I cannot walk. I never could. I am not accustomed to it. At my age one should never change one 's mode of life. Fill my glass, Gabrielle."

" I cannot bear to give you any more," Gabrielle exclaimed. " I am sure that it is bad for you. I will walk with you gladly every morning."

" Thank you ; but I shall never promenade myself at milk-maid's hours. I am not bucolic in my tendencies. Dr. Pressigny assured me that long repose was indispensable to my sensitive organization."

" Then perhaps later in the day ? "

" Don't be obstinate, Gabrielle. No one now has any comprehension of my case. The Frau Major is not without insight, but Hugo is terribly unsympathetic. I had hoped," she said with one of her surprising changes of tone, " to find sympathy and affection in you."

Gabrielle felt uncomfortable and was silent.

Suddenly the countess rose, came toward her, embraced and kissed her effusively.

" There, I will trust you! I admit I have been suspicious."

Gabrielle retained a stiff and unresponsive attitude. If for inscrutable reasons the countess chose to throw her arms about her in an eccentric manner, Gabrielle felt no impulse to fall weeping upon the old lady's shoulder.

" Let us be friends," cried the incomprehensible old woman. " Let us be all in all to each other. I have longed all my life for a friend. It is my ideal!" There were tears in her eyes and voice.

Mousey sat on the table and regarded the scene with a knowing grin. " I have seen this sort of thing before," he reflected, munching a crumb of biscuit. " There is nothing new under the sun."

" I am sorry," stammered Gabrielle, embarrassed, " but " —

" I have every element necessary to an ideal friendship," and a sentimental smile played over the hard old face ; " I have hesitated. I have doubted you, I confess. I have feared that you were insincere."

" If not always saying everything that one thinks is insincerity," Gabrielle broke out desperately, " then I am insincere."

" See, you admit it yourself! " exclaimed the countess triumphantly. " Never mind. I can be generous."

" I can only be what I have been, thus far," began the young girl, " and " —

"Now listen to me, Gabrielle. I have a great secret to tell you. I have put your name down in my will."

Mousey buried his nose in his paws and shook with silent laughter.

"But Aunt Adelheid," protested Gabrielle with a start, "you — you really make me feel very uncomfortable!"

"You are surprised? My dear, your books are all very well. Who prizes them more than I? My husband's library consisted of six thousand volumes. He had read simply everything. Hugo is a great reader. But books will not feed and clothe you and give you a place in society. Gabrielle, be guided by me. As my adopted child, you will have them all at your feet. Mark my words, you have simply to choose. Von Raven, von Haller, von Paalzow, whom you will. With me behind you, you command the situation."

Gabrielle stared at her in haughty astonishment.

"I am not adoptable," she said curtly. "I happen to belong to my father."

The countess persisted in her good humor.

"Never mind what we call it," she replied with a little chuckle.

"Do I understand you to propose to me to buy a husband with your money?"

"My dear, with the Kronfels fortune, I could buy you a prince. Who knows? Perhaps a king," laughed the countess. "There are several impecunious small majesties making themselves conspicuous in Europe just now."

Gabrielle rose.

"I decline everything," she began rapidly, with an

abrupt gesture, — palms outward as if pushing away some obnoxious thing. "I do not wish to be rude or unkind. But I decline. I cannot promise to be different to you from what I am this moment. I will be as companionable as you will let me be. I will try to please you, but I cannot be your ideal friend, and I will not have my name in your will." Her voice rang out scornfully as she concluded : "It is a poor compliment to any man, or to me, to imply that the Kronfels fortune could influence either of us."

Mousey watched her with closest attention. "This is new," he admitted gravely.

Again the countess laughed, well-pleased.

"I shall soon call you Tornado instead of Moonbeam. Seriously, Gabrielle, you surely do not expect me to believe that you, a poor girl, have never privately speculated upon the possibility of inheriting something from me? Nonsense. There never was a companion or relative in this house who had not that thought first and last. Some conceal it better than others, that is all the difference. Sly cats they were, most of them!"

"You insult me," the young girl said coldly.

"Tut, tut! don't be tragic."

Gabrielle looked steadily at her, and replied : —

"There have been wild and reckless and hot-blooded men in my race, but there never was a Dohna, man or woman, so despicable as to think the thoughts you have attributed to me."

The countess moved about uneasily.

"You are so extreme, Gabrielle, so theatrical."

"I do not bear things meekly that reflect upon my honor."

"There you go again!" retorted the countess with

a shrug. "No one has reflected upon your honor, as
you call it. Silly child! Consider. I shall die some
day. It is not an agreeable thought; I entertain it as
little as possible. I don't intend to go very soon, I
promise you. Give me a glass of Chartreuse. You
have agitated me. Very good, if you do not wish to
pour it, I will pour it myself. It is evident that I
must leave my fortune to somebody. Hugo does not
need it. I shall probably outlive him, too," she added
with a certain eagerness. "I have been obliged to
alter my will frequently. I have been deceived in
people. There is something wanting in everybody,"
she muttered with a singular expression of suspicion
and reluctance, as if she were tempted to suddenly
withdraw her proposal; "but no, I have decided!
You are a handsome girl, Gabrielle, and a social success. You be guided by me. I did not like to say
this. One does not enjoy regarding one's shroud.
Still, it is best to have the matter settled. After all,
as the Frau Major says, I may live twenty years."

"If you have the habit of inserting names in your
will and then removing them, I need not distress myself, for you will surely remove mine."

"We shall see," returned the countess affably. "But
I trust you will give me no occasion. Now Gabrielle,
which shall it be? The Frau Major is in favor of
von Raven or von Haller, she knows the families so
well" —

"The Frau Major?"

"Yes; she is going to get up some theatricals to
give you an opportunity to study Herr von Paalzow,
nevertheless."

"The Frau Major? Frau von Funnel?"

"Yes, of course," the countess answered with some

impatience. " Why you make that horror-struck face is beyond my comprehension."

" You have discussed this matrimonial plan with her? She approves? She is planning theatricals and counting upon me? " demanded Gabrielle.

" I confess I was not to tell you. It was to be a surprise. The Frau Major swore me to secrecy. But it slipped out unawares. After all, it is no crime. Oh, yes, we planned several pleasant things. She is ingenious. She has time to be."

" When was it? "

" That we spoke of the theatricals? Oh, her last reception-day — last Thursday. She said that she had been having a chat with you."

" It was immediately after the chat with me that she planned all these pleasant things for me, — the Frau Major herself? "

" Why, yes," the countess said pettishly. " Surely there is nothing extraordinary in that? She is devoted to me. She is naturally interested in you for my sake. After the theatricals comes a picnic. After the picnic, I forget what. All for charity, too. She is untiring. I should like to be as active as she," she added with a trace of jealousy, " if I had her strength and leisure."

Gabrielle sat down and shaded her eyes with her hand. Mousey employed himself in licking her wrist, upon which he detected traces of Eau de Cologne.

" She gave me her promise," thought the young girl. " She looked me in the eye, and spoke deliberately and gently. She went from my presence and broke her word. There was no temptation. There is no excuse. I will never trust her again. It does

not matter whether the promise related to kingdoms
or human lives or trifles. A lie to the friend who
trusts you is treachery. Ah, whom shall I believe
if she is false?" Suddenly she gave the countess a
searching look. "Aunt Adelheid never tells a straight
story. She does not see anything as anybody else
does. Perhaps the Frau Major knows nothing of all
this. Could that wise, calm, good woman stoop so
low? It is impossible."

But the doubt had taken root.

"I do not wonder that you are excited, Gabrielle,"
observed the countess complacently. "Any girl would
be. We shall have a fine comedy playing on our
private stage. It will amuse me. I give you your
choice, my dear. No one can call me exacting. Herr
von Raven would be easiest to manage. Herr von
Haller has a bit of a temper sometimes. This I
can assure you, von Paalzow will be apt to be master
in his own house. But all that is your affair. As to
money, one may have a trifle more than another, but
in our circumstances we can happily ignore that consideration."

Amused by her projected puppet-show, possessed
by her caprice of the moment, she chatted on smilingly, and failed to interpret the uncompromising language of the young indignant eyes opposite her.

"Take von Paalzow, my dear!" she said genially.
"He is better suited to you. I admit that the others
are more boyish. But von Paalzow is a cavalier, a
man of distinction. Then Mercedes" — she gave a
hard little laugh — "would be so astonished. She is
accustomed to reign supreme. It would be amusing
to see her routed by some one belonging to me."

"Don't, Mousey!" said Gabrielle, impatiently pushing the lapping, sniffing dog away. "I cannot bear it!"

"How can you be so harsh to my angel? Come here, lovey!" Mousey did not budge, but continued to sniff about Gabrielle's hands, until she put them behind her for safe-keeping. He had either inherited or acquired a pronounced taste for alcoholic stimulants. On one occasion, after partaking of whipped cream strongly flavored with arac, he had even been known to temporarily lose that quality of intellectual clearness which was his distinction, to ignore the laws of gravitation, and to evince but a blurred consciousness of the position of table-legs and other familiar objects. Over this frailty the countess drew a veil of tender reserve.

"In any event," continued the countess oracularly, "it would be well to be a little distant to Mercedes just now. She is compromising herself seriously. She is not yet *madame la marquise.* I have heard it even hinted that her conduct is not approved by Her Majesty. Mercedes can permit herself considerable liberty, but she goes beyond all bounds. She flings prudence to the winds."

"What has poor Mercedes done now?"

"Oh, my dear! Don't expect me to relate all the extravagances of her coquetry. She came riding gayly home the other night at twelve o'clock with von Paalzow. They had lost the path. They had lost their groom. They had lost their heads. Heaven alone knows what else they had lost."

"I have no doubt whatever that they lost the path," Gabrielle said hotly.

"Oh, dear, yes, of course!"

"Who told you it?"

"The Frau Major was deploring it. She loves and admires Mercedes. She has always endeavored to help her. But Mercedes is imperious and wilful. The Frau Major is grieved and anxious about her. If the marquis is willing to marry her still, why that alters the matter. Then of course no one has anything to say."

" Ah! I who like Mercedes must not go to see her because people who like neither her nor me prefer that I should not? Is that it?"

"Society charges her with many imprudences, my child," the countess replied with a pious air.

"I must not associate with Mercedes von Waldenberg because she and Lieutenant von Paalzow lost their way in the woods," persisted Gabrielle, "but if that old dandy marquis marries her, then she is not wicked, and I may go to see her again?"

" Why," said the old lady, with smiling conviction, " one cannot very well turn the cold shoulder upon the wife of the French Embassador, can one?"

Gabrielle broke into a nervous laugh.

"It is of no use," she said in her rapid way. "I know that before I begin. But one must say something —one must!" She paused, struggling for control. The countess's confession of faith, her social tactics, were so repugnant, so horrible to Gabrielle that she felt outraged and helpless. "About Mercedes. You know that I like her. I do not think any one understands her. I am very sure that I do not. I only wish that I had known her longer and better, for then I could be of some use to her now. I do not believe one word they say against her! I do not know what it is all about. It is ridiculous, what they say! I do not believe that she has done wrong in the slightest.

But if she has, it is because she is unhappy and desperate, and then more than ever she needs her friends.
What is friendship?" demanded the scornful young
voice. "Is it something that simpers and flatters
when all is well, and sneaks away when all is ill? Is
it a coward, a poltroon?"

"I should say," chuckled the old lady with a world-
ly-wise smile, and highly entertained by Gabrielle's excitement, "I should say that it was usually about that.
Precious little sweetheart, he was the stanchest little
friend! He could teach them all, yes, so he could!"
Mousey blinked at her ironically, and accepted a crumb
of sweet biscuit, then desiring to watch Gabrielle,
snapped at the hand that fed him.

"If you love any one," Gabrielle went on impetuously, "you love him still, though he should become a
thief or a murderer. You go to him and suffer with
him. If you hold up your skirts for fear of contam-
ination, your cowardice is stronger than your affection. If it is true in great things, it is true in small.
Mercedes is lovely and good. I am attached to her.
She has done nothing wrong. But if she had, a mistake is not a contagious disease, so far as I know. I
shall make mistakes enough in my own life, no doubt.
But it is not probable that I should catch Mercedes'
particular kind of mistake, simply from putting my
arms around her when she is unhappy."

The countess regarded her with a prolonged and
quizzical smile.

"Mousey, my seraph, listen to her! Really, Gabrielle, if these are your sentiments, we have removed you
not an instant too soon from your Dohna."

"My Dohna!" repeated the young girl with a sigh.
"I never considered such things there. Perhaps that

is why I lose my bearings here. I frequently change my mind, I know. But I never shall in this. At Dohna, or anywhere else, I hope I may never become a coward and slink away from a friend in misfortune."

" But misfortune which she has prepared for herself and deserves ? "

" Is it not misfortune all the same, however it came ? What if it were sin, disgrace? Is it not all the bitterer if one must blame one's self? Then, exactly then, one needs a friend's love. Aunt Adelheid, I cannot take your advice. I must act freely toward Mercedes. I answer unhesitatingly for my father's approval."

" Hear her, my treasure ! " exclaimed the countess in French. " Art thou not content to witness this little theatre under thy own adorable nose ? Well, well, as you like, Gabrielle. After all, I am your background. Then Mercedes is Countess of Waldenberg. One can't send her to Coventry as if she were a nobody. Besides, if you go there you will certainly meet von Paalzow. But perhaps you had thought of that yourself ? " she added slyly.

" Oh," groaned Gabrielle desperately, " it is of no use. I said it was of no use."

" He is with her constantly. Our lady mamma is anxious, but smiles and pretends that he comes to see Elsa. How long the marquis will believe her, we are all asking ourselves. For let the marquis retire, and down falls our fine castle, since it is evident that von Paalzow is only flirting."

" How do they know that ? " the girl demanded fiercely. " Has society an All Seeing Eye ? Can it penetrate the heart and read motives ? "

" Be careful, Gabrielle. I never permit in my presence anything that borders upon irreverence."

" Aunt Adelheid, if I should talk a year " —

" Pray do not, my love," returned the old lady laughing.

" I could not tell you how I feel."

" I will tell you how you feel," said the countess with her new air of extreme indulgence. " You feel romantic. Now I presume you will admit that I have seen somewhat more of the world than a young person of your years reared at Dohna. Perhaps you will believe me, when I say that I have observed the most frantic love-matches with nothing a year usually end in bickerings, misery, divorce, or worse, and that most men are not mad enough to treat a woman badly if she happens to have a large fortune settled upon herself. What young people call love, my dear, is all very well in poetry and on the stage ; though for my taste it occupies too much space there and everywhere. But it is not nutritious for one's daily food. There are a great many important things in life entirely unconnected with it. That is what you must learn as soon as possible."

" I believe that it is all of life, — the beginning and the end and the soul of it. I do not mean anything romantic, as you may think. I don't even mean marriage. That is only a part. But we do not love enough — you do not, I do not ; and there is nothing really wrong in the world, except too little love."

" Except again," remarked the old lady wickedly, and quite unmoved by the strong feeling in the young voice, " when there is too much."

" There cannot be too much. Then it is something else."

" Come, come, what does a girl like you know of such things ? " returned the countess airily.

" One cannot read, without knowing that there is sin in the world, and shame and misery."

" But well-bred girls do not discuss such things."

" I do, when I must, Aunt Adelheid. And there is one thing I wish to say, that you may make no mistake about my attitude, whatever comes. It has been in my mind ever since you have been speaking. If I should do what you propose, — trade with your money for a husband, — if I should sell myself to you, and to one of those officers, I think that I should be worse than those poor creatures we call bad " —

" Good heavens, Gabrielle ! "

" Far worse, because I should be a hypocrite, pretending to lead a virtuous life, which they do not."

" But I call this coarse. I call it revolting. I blush for you, Gabrielle."

" To me, the unspeakably coarse thing is to marry a man for his money, or induce him to marry me for mine, if I had any."

" But have I expressed the faintest objection to your falling in love with one of those young men ? "

" You tell me to pick one of them as I would pick a cherry. But I think better of all of them. Lorenz Raven and Egon Haller may not be great philosophers, but I believe that they are gentlemen at heart. As to Herr von Paalzow, there is nothing mercenary in that man — nothing ! "

" Oho ! have they so spirited a champion ? I will wager this ruby that every one of your blameless knights will declare himself before a month is gone, and with all respect, my little pepper-box, not exclusively for your *beaux yeux*. Indeed, poor Lorenz has been sighing audibly for some time. He has spoken to me. I have encouraged him. I shall encourage them all," she declared maliciously.

"I presume," said Gabrielle slowly, "that it would not be impossible for him to like me for myself."

"There! Now you are recovering your common-sense. Of course they will all like you immensely. May I inquire if it is a crime for a man to prefer a handsome, clever girl with a fortune, you, for instance, to Sofie Gobert, who has neither beauty nor wealth?"

"It is a crime for a human soul to sell itself."

"Good heavens, child, one would think I had suggested something monstrous instead of an every-day occurrence. Your ideas are dangerous. They would undermine society."

"I wish that they could, if society means trading with men and women."

"What was your lovely Mercedes intending to do, before von Paalzow appeared upon the scene? In fact, what is she still intending? For she has no idea of relinquishing the marquis as long as she can throw dust in his eyes."

"I have said that I do not pretend to understand Mercedes. Perhaps her home is not loving enough."

"A very logical reason for marrying the Marquis de Vallion," sneered the countess. "Really, Gabrielle, it is too droll, but Lucie von Rahden had a very snug little fortune!"

Gabrielle stared as if she had not heard aright.

"My papa?" she stammered, the quick blood mounting to her temples. "My papa?" Moments passed, in which she did not speak, or turn her intense gaze from the countess. But gradually as she looked at the white-faced, cold-eyed old woman, who with a cynical smile on her thin lips sat rubbing her little mongrel dog's back, he responding with small grunts of enjoyment, the young girl's anger and heat passed away, and a radiant smile illumined her features, a smile of love and faith.

" You do not know him," she said softly; and still looking at the loveless, faithless old woman, friendless, homeless, and poor in spite of her millions, Gabrielle pitied her.

A servant entered with a salver, upon which was Herr von Paalzow's card.

" Quick, Babette, my last cap. Or no, my bonnet, Röschen. Gabrielle, the ball opens. Will you come down as you are? "

" I will not go down to-day. Pray excuse me."

" But wait, let me consider. Yes, it is as well upon the whole. I will drive Herr von Paalzow to the Frau Major's. Stupid, the last bonnet, with the blush roses. *Au revoir* then, my pretty Moonbeam." She embraced Gabrielle vivaciously, to the huge edification of Mousey and the maids. " I do not mind your little excitement. We understand each other. We start fresh to-day. Everything is changed."

" Pardon me, but nothing is different," Gabrielle returned hastily. " As to your plan I am not afraid, for you will change your mind. I decline, you remember. I decline everything."

She could not make her repudiation more explicit, before the two curious maids.

" Babette, another fichu," called the old lady sharply, seated at her toilette-table, with its array of ivory and silver and crystal. " Röschen, devote yourself to Mousey, when I am gone. Sometimes after walking in the garden with you, the poor dear comes in looking quite bored. Devote yourself to him and not to your silly thoughts. Say good-by, Mousey." Mousey deigned to trot to the chair, extend his paw languidly, nod and give two short barks. The countess caught him up and kissed him until he growled.

"There, take him. Let the angel eat a little grass. I cannot imagine what makes his breath feverish. How shocking the light is. Glass is so poor nowadays. Babette, draw the shades with some reference to me!" Carefully adjusting the diaphanous bonnet whose blush roses lay tenderly on the pretty gray hair, she smiled at the handsome old lady in the mirror. "The keys, Babette!" counting them suspiciously.

Gabrielle accompanied her to the stairway.

"Do you know," the countess began with her mocking air, "you are cleverer than I thought? You almost deceived me. *Sancta simplicitas* is also a paying rôle, and you do it very well. Reject, by all means, my dear. Continue to reject!"

Gabrielle said nothing, but watched her slowly descend the stairs, heavy and uncertain of foot, and smiling back maliciously, as she paused on the landing to rest.

CHAPTER XVII

"DIETZ," said Hugo abruptly, as Bernhard sat with him one noon in the garden, "have you any religion?"

Dietz, being a slow man, — except with his music and his smile, — crossed one leg over the other, put his paper cap on the bench beside him, ran his hand through his hair, watched a blackcap on a hawthorn tree, picked up a fallen poplar-leaf, and twirled the stem in his teeth, regarded Hugo some moments with a ruminating expression, and finally replied : —

"Why not?"

"What is it like?" demanded Hugo.

"There are a great many kinds," Bernhard said after another pause.

"Why yes, I suppose there are as many kinds as there are men and women on this earth and other planets; more perhaps, but it's your kind I am asking about."

"I mean that I've got a good many kinds," Dietz admitted seriously. "Any one of them does very well for me, and I am a little apt to mix them. I suppose a clever man like you, count, would need something different."

Hugo looked at him questioningly.

Bernhard rose, parted the shrubbery with widely outstretched arms, and putting himself conveniently at one side, looked over his shoulder at Hugo.

"Can you see St. Mary's spire? Well, it is my

religion they blow with their wind-instruments from that belfry every Sunday morning."

"Roman Catholic? I should scarcely have supposed that."

"Not at all," returned Bernhard, with a low, happy laugh. "The church is good Roman Catholic. But my religion is up in the belfry at sunrise, every Sunday morning."

"I don't know what you mean, but it is lofty, at all events."

"You have never heard the music? you are asleep at sunrise, I suppose. Well, you see there's a Protestant banker down on that street. He is a rich man, and good as gold. He is working all the time for little children. He's got hundreds of them off in the country for the summer. He has babies taken care of while the mothers are working, and he's educating and helping along and cheering up, and there is no end to the good he does. Well, he thought he would like some chorals on the belfry-tower. And no wonder, they sound so sweet and solemn in the morning when everything is fresh and still and the tones seem to float over the city. Now the Roman Catholic belfry happens to be the only one in this neighborhood. So what does the banker do but go to see the priest. He is a poor man and good as gold, working in the prisons, working in the worst holes, picking people up and standing them on their feet, helping along and comforting them, and doing no end of good. So the banker says, 'Your Reverence, may I have some music played every Sunday morning on your belfry tower?' His Reverence thinks a while and says, 'Your music, of course?' 'Why yes,' says the banker. Then his Reverence thinks a while again, and says, ' I should like the music. If you will let your musicians play some of our hymns too, I shall be grateful to you, and I think there will be no objection.' They shook hands on it, and the banker pays the musicians. Now what happens every Sunday? First comes a Roman Catholic bit, for the banker is very polite and begins and ends with the priest's own music; then comes some good tough Protestant choral, then a prayer to the Virgin; but all the same, there is Martin Luther sandwiched in between the Bleeding Hearts and the Hail Maries. That is my religion, count."

"And all that goes on while we are asleep? Is nobody's conscience outraged? Why there have been wars for less."

" Oh, the ones that listen early in the morning like it too well to fight about it."

" But do you go down there to church? "

" Sometimes — to hear the organ," he added with simplicity.

Hugo smiled.

" Sometimes I stroll into the synagogue, if I have a spare hour on their Sabbath, and sometimes I go to church in the woods, and lie under a tree, and listen."

" But Dietz, that is all very well, only what do you believe? "

" I told you it would not be clever enough for a man like you," Bernhard replied gently, unconscious that the exposition of his views left anything to be desired in the way of clearness.

" But do you know, they would call you a pagan? " rejoined Hugo amused.

" Why not? "

Hugo probed no farther that day. Indeed, Dietz shortly after returned to his work, leaving the invalid smiling over the stone-carver's ideas or personality. Hugo sometimes questioned if Dietz was in himself interesting or only seemed so to him in contrast to Lipps' meagre powers of entertainment, and the tread-mill of petty complaint, censorious gossip, and sordid sentiments which the countess provided for him every morning. But the more he saw Dietz the better he liked him. The man amused him, won his respect and confidence, and soothed his irritable nerves. Although Hugo occupied himself hour after hour with more or less morbid and sophistical speculations upon subjects which Dietz had never consciously considered, the count usually found when he would propound one of his knotty queries that in the utter simplicity of Bern-hard's reply lay a wholesome truth which would return when Hugo was alone and confront him with some of Bernhard's own cheerfulness.

"Your conundrums, count, are very good to sharpen a man's wits," he told Hugo admiringly one day, smil-ing down upon him as if he were a precocious child, and as if the problems and dogmas on account of which men have been hating and slaying and burning and boiling and racking and excommunicating and crucifying one another for centuries, and the mysteries over which philosophers have spent their yearning lives, were all products of Hugo's fertile brain. It must be confessed that the count took a certain ma-licious pleasure in dragging out of their corners the world's hoariest old dry-bones of contention, and fling-ing them down before this fresh and unapprehensive mental appetite. Bernhard would dispose of them with one slow gulp, and smilingly await more.

Every day when he came over the hedge with his good thump, the stone-dust in his beard and nails, and his breath smelling of beer, which he swallowed fast that he might have more time with the invalid, he used to put Hugo on his crutches, and make him walk across the little grass-plot in front of the fountain. Hugo objected and protested at first.

" It is useless trouble and pain," he said. " I shall never walk again. I can totter across there, of course, if you enjoy the spectacle, but I assure you it is absolutely useless."

" It is more natural to walk a little," Bernhard would reply, his strong right arm supporting the count; and as Dietz was big and sweet-tempered and persistent, Hugo found himself yielding, at first reluctantly, later as a matter of course.

" You cannot make me any better, I suppose you are aware," he said one day, frowning and not stirring as Dietz stood waiting with the crutches, smoothing one with his large hand.

" I don't know anything about that," Dietz returned placidly. " Nobody knows. But it is n't natural to make yourself worse. You might as well use what you 've got left," and the calm directness of his allusions to Hugo's infirmity never gave offence, while the slightest word on this subject from the countess was apt to rouse his ire. Day after day he lay out in his sheltered corner of the garden, where he could only see the trees and shrubbery closing around him like a bower, and the sky above, and if his chair was turned in that direction, the steep slope of the broad vine-clad hill. His companions were chiefly books, but oftener and oftener as the long sunny spring wore on, he would drop his book to watch a lizard or a beetle.

The birds grew so tame that they ceased to fear the long motionless figure. He began to take an intimate pleasure in butterflies and bees. He slept more, the warmth and the odors and the interminable droning and buzzing tranquillized him, and the sound of building no longer seemed to him a cruel and noisy noise, nerve-wrenching and soul-exasperating, but something too sustained, large, and powerful to annoy him.

The countess complained that the morning visit which she conscientiously paid her son must now take place in precisely the part of the garden which she disliked, and which she declared inimical to her health and Mousey's. As she was always complaining of something, Hugo was unfilial enough to reason that it was upon the whole of small consequence what roused her lamentations.

"It seems as if it were arranged especially to annoy me," she remarked, the first time she was obliged to penetrate to his retreat. "Now, why could you not be brought out a little later, Hugo, when I go to lunch? If you knew how that odious box oppresses me, and the stuffy cedar!"

"I don't think myself that it is of much importance where I am put, — whether here or anywhere else," Hugo replied in not the most amiable tone in the world. "But they happen to like to keep me out here all day."

"They? Who are they? Whose wish should outweigh your mother's, my son?"

"On conventional principles, nobody's," Hugo retorted with scarcely a pleasant laugh. "But the doctor, for one, seems to entertain the idea that the longer I lie here every day, the better it is for me. I know you don't prize his opinion, but as I never had the honor of meeting Dr. Pressigny, my doctor happens to be the best of his species that I know."

"Don't eat that box, dearest! It will poison you," cried the countess.

"I had the impression," Hugo remarked politely, "that animals were endowed with the knowledge of good and evil herbs, and needed no warning from our smaller discrimination. That is, animals in a state of nature; I admit that Mousey's sedentary mode of life may influence" —

"Never mind Mousey," she said curtly. "You were telling me who induced you to come out to this unhealthy spot."

"Beside the doctor, who does n't count with you in the least, two others who count less, — Lipps, and my very good friend Bernhard Dietz."

"Oh, that man!" she exclaimed with hard contempt.

"Precisely. That man."

She sat silent a moment, a nervous perturbed look on her face.

"Hugo, I hope that you fumigate thoroughly. I cannot interfere with your whims, however strongly I may disapprove them. But I think that I am justified in insisting upon fumigation. When one thinks of the bad drainage and fever and Heaven knows what, that such people carry about in their clothes" —

"I'll ask Dietz if he has anything of the kind in his pockets."

"It is a poor jest, as we all may find, when he has introduced some vulgar disease into the house. I simply shuddered and held my breath, when I first saw that man passing through my corridor, and I fumigated at once. I wonder at you, Hugo, I do indeed."

He merely regarded her from beneath half-closed lids, and with an odd smile that reminded her unpleasantly of the late count.

At length, he said coldly : —

" I have already told you how I regard him. When I say that he is my friend, and that I never liked any man as well, it is sufficient, I think."

She sighed behind her handkerchief and vinaigrette held closely to her face. Her anxious, mistrustful glance wandered from tree to bush, from Mousey to her son, falling from time to time upon the box-border, whose poisonous exhalations filled her with dismay.

" Don't be nervous, mamma," Hugo said kindly enough, " there is no deadly upas-tree here."

" What does that man do ? " she asked as if the odious box and the malarial possibilities and Dietz belonged in one category. " What is it that attracts you ? It is incomprehensible."

Hugo raised his eyebrows, stared at her an instant, then said quietly : —

" He is singularly kind to me."

" Kind to you ! Kind to a Count Kronfels ! I dare say he knows on which side his bread is buttered," exclaimed the old lady with a laugh.

There was silence in the sunny garden, except for the softly plashing fountain, Mousey snapping at a toad and vituperating it for escaping, and the short, loud breathing of the countess.

" Mamma," said Hugo slowly and with his father's smile, which made her uncomfortable, " if you were a man, and if I had not the honor of being your son, and if I were not a cripple, and if it were worth while, and if, in short, a variety of circumstances were otherwise, I might feel inclined to resent that remark."

" Pshaw, Hugo," returned the countess, " I have not the remotest idea what you mean." Presently she resumed, " I had something important to tell you this morning, but this place is so trying to my nerves! Hugo, if you had one atom of my sensitiveness, you could not endure this atmosphere."

He drew a sigh of profound weariness.

" Why do you give yourself the trouble of coming to me ? Why don't you send your love or something by Babette ? "

"You know well, Hugo, that nothing would make me neglect you. It is the rarest thing that I omit my visit, only when something unavoidable detains me."

" Mousey's colic," muttered Hugo.

" It is a matter of principle with me, and I shall do a mother's duty, even " —

" Even if you have to face the perils of box and breathe the rank poison of the cedar of Lebanon."

" Laugh, by all means, Hugo. You have not my nerves."

" What was it you wished to tell me ? " he asked, moving restlessly.

" I have put Gabrielle down in my will."

After a pause she continued, " Well, have you nothing to say to that ? "

" Nothing."

" Why do you smile ? I told you that von Paalzow had come back. I think she will take von Paalzow. Have you nothing to say to that either ? "

" Nothing."

" Gabrielle is very trying at times. She is not loving. She is not what I have longed for. Ah, if I had had a daughter, she would have comprehended me! It is a sad fate to feel that strangers are scheming for your money."

Hugo made no response.

"She is ungrateful. When one thinks of all the pleasures that I provide for her! She does what I tell her, but she has no initiative. She is not *prévoyante.* There is always something wanting in our intercourse. Then when I remember how she tried to make trouble between you and me, how she actually went to your room and complained, I am uncertain of her."

"I can only repeat what I have already told you, that nothing of the kind occurred. The Baroness von Dohna, on the one occasion when I had the honor of any prolonged conversation with her, conducted herself more like a gallant man than like the enraged governess or abused companion I expected to see. She made no complaint whatever of you. As you are perfectly aware that I am not in the habit of telling lies, why can you not dismiss that doubt of her, at least?"

"A man always defends a pair of pretty eyes," muttered the old lady, wavering.

He frowned.

"Is that the only time you have seen her?" she inquired with a resentful air. "She never comes down and talks with you? Never comes out here?"

"Except that time," he began with scrupulous repose of manner, "and once here by accident, and glimpses of her in the distance, coming and going in the carriage, I have never seen her. But if I had," he broke out with a fierce, unaccountable impulse, "what then? If she had talked with me, and smiled on me, and brought some freshness and beauty and goodness into my life, what then?"

"How can you be so violent? Did you not refuse to know her? Have you not declined to take any interest in her, and scarcely had the patience to listen when I have spoken her name? You are very inconsistent. There would of course be no impropriety in her talking with you. The thing itself is irreproachable, since you are completely — uncompromising. But, as you vowed that you would not see her, and are prejudiced against her, it is evident, if you meet, that she seeks you; and you must confess, Hugo, that clandestine tête-à-têtes between my son and a girl upon whom I lavish every luxury, and for whose future I am most generously providing, are not very agreeable to contemplate. Ah," she sighed, recalling the long perspective of women, tall and short, plump and thin, dark and fair, whom before her marriage and after she had elected to the nondescript office of companion, confidante, recipient of her bounties, and kisser of the hand that smote hard and often, "they have been mostly sly cats. I am a lonely old woman, Hugo!" and tears started to her eyes.

But he scarcely heard her concluding sighs, for one phrase of her tirade had awakened in him unreasoning and vehement contradiction, and an impulse of self-assertion so strong and imperious that he would fain have cried: —

"Wait! Don't be so sure of me! How dare you pronounce me harmless? I am not dead yet. I am a living man. What if I and my crutches should hobble into the lists, and compete with your padded old sires and your brainless young ones?" A great throb of life, of painful, hungry, masterful life shook

him cruelly. It was incomprehensible. Had he not
laid these spectres low? These ghosts of joy and
desire? These visions of fair women? What then
was this insensate thought, leading him to defy, to
assert, to claim what he would for his own?

St. Mary's clock, followed by all the clocks far and
near, struck twelve, and the whistles and school-boys
began their riot.

A step was approaching the hedge.

Hugo's eyes were luminous, two bright spots glowed
on his cheeks. " Here comes Dietz, mamma," he
said. " You 'd better ask him if he has any of those
things in his pockets."

She rose with every appearance of consternation,
but before she could draw her light shawl over her
shoulders, gather up her vinaigrette and handkerchief and parasol and fan, Dietz was over the hedge
and advancing toward them. Seeing her he hesitated,
then came on with his deliberate step, smiling kindly
on mother and son.

" Dietz," said Hugo, his hand closing affectionately
over Bernhard's, " it is a great pleasure to me to present you to my mother." He experienced, in fact,
a delectably malicious satisfaction in watching his
mother's august countenance. " Mamma, this is my
friend, Herr Bernhard Dietz," he continued in the
suave accents of perfect ceremony.

Adelheid, Countess of Kronfels, actually confronted
by this representative of bad drainage, contagious
disease, and unconscionable plebeian vices, no longer
fled to her vinaigrette, but resorted gallantly to
that weapon of offence, her eye-glass, mounted on a
hammered-by-hand gold stick nearly a foot long.
Through this intimidating observatory she surveyed

handsome Bernhard's six feet two and a half inches of height, the large features of his peaceful and sunny countenance, his beard, and his blouse. In her eyes, about her thin lips and pinched nostrils, was an expression so coldly aggressive that in a lady of less degree it might have been called brutal.

She turned to the invalid.

"Good-morning, Hugo," she said, extending her hand. For the first time in his life he did not perform the parting ceremony of raising it to his lips.

"Mousey, my angel," she called, "come away." She did not say "Come" simply, but "Come away!" meaning, "Away from this infection, this pestilence that walketh in my garden."

Mousey turned, and delivered a volley of sharp short barks at Dietz. The dog's pedigree being at best miscellaneous, he felt the greater need of publicly asserting his contempt of the lowly-born. So he yelped his social prejudice at the man in the blouse, and followed the countess.

Bernhard attentively watched the black satin folds and French cap disappear behind the shrubbery, after which he sat down on the bench that the lady had just occupied, whistled softly through his teeth, glanced at Hugo, then at the tree-tops and the sky, and finally looked long at the count's excited eyes and unnatural color.

"You are tired," said Dietz after a while. "Perhaps you are too tired to walk to-day."

"On the contrary, I am eager to be off. Give me my wings."

He hobbled painfully to the fountain and back.

"Do you find me graceful, Dietz? Do you think me winning?"

Bernhard said nothing, but merely watched him with his steady, sensible, gentle gaze, glanced up at the noon-sun, moved the chair slightly, and turned the cushions.

Hugo found his wings clumsy and leaden, while his eager spirit leaped on uncontrollably.

" A crippled body on two sticks, and a rebel of a soul," he thought. "I trample on him, he gets up and defies me. Still a man does n't want to be called uncompromising, — not while he lives."

His smile was flashing and cynical, his eyes singularly brilliant above his flushed cheeks. " That 's too serious a blow. She might have let me think I was dangerous. I was already so elated, so complacent, why did she disturb me ? "

" Is n't that enough ? " Dietz suggested.

" No," Hugo replied, turning and going a second time to the fountain. He came back exhausted. Dietz took the crutches, put him in his chair, still without speaking, and sat down again, the minuet rhythm from Don Giovanni lingering almost imperceptibly in his breath, with a sound too faint to be called whistling, and in an occasional nod of his head, to mark the end of a phrase. He let Hugo rest some minutes before he said : —

" Count, why don't you see more people ? "

Hugo responded with a supercilious grimace, designed for himself or the people or both.

" Because it 's more natural."

" You forget that I am an unnatural object."

" Suppose I should lie on my back, and think of myself all day ? " remarked Bernhard meditatively.

" How do you know what I think of all day, you great — innocent ? "

" I should be foolish and fanciful," said Bernhard, calmly pursuing his own line of thought. " I should see things crooked."

" Prescribe for me, Dr. Bernhard Dietz," returned the count with a certain eagerness, in spite of his light tone. "I don't promise to take your pills and nostrums, mind you!"

"Why don't you have a big dog?" Bernhard went on, gentle, massive, and imperturbable, and replying only with his kind eyes to the invalid's interruptions. "A big dog is a deal of company and comfort. Suppose you had one to lie down there and snap at flies, and come and put his nose in your hand, and look at you with his trusty eyes?"

"Prescribe something else, my dear fellow. That ugly little bastard that barked at you suffers no rival. I have never been able to keep my dogs near me. I had a couple of Gordon setters not very long ago. I introduced them surreptitiously into my quarters via my balcony window. Mousey was sleeping the sleep of the glutton in his padded velvet box, at the extreme end of the house up-stairs. Yet I assure you that in less than a half-minute he was writhing in convulsions of jealousy before my door, and howling enough to wake the dead. Talk of magnetic currents and the psychic force! What roused the little over-fed brute? What told him that my high-bred glossy long beauties were stretching themselves on my hearth-rug? No, no, Dietz, I 'm a dog-lover, but indeed I humbly bow to Mousey's will. There are things to which it is wisest to submit. If you lived in our house, you would cringe before Mousey, with the rest of us."

Dietz obstinately regarded the point in the foli-

age where he had watched those stout black satin
shoulders and the fluttering ends of the French cap
disappear.   He still saw the hard face and soft hair
of the count's mother, and the gaunt craving look in
Hugo's weary face did not escape him.

" It is n't natural," he muttered, so low that the
words lost themselves in the half-breathed melody
from Don Giovanni.

" Why don't you see some of your old friends ? "

" Would you ? "

" Why not ?   And why don't you talk with that
beautiful young lady ?   She would like it."

He spoke slowly with long pauses, nor was Hugo
in a loquacious mood.

" Dr. Dietz, I 'm afraid that you are a quack," he
returned after some time.

" A dog, some children " —

" Children ! " repeated Hugo derisively.

" A dog, some children, some old friends, a woman's voice and hand and smile, some music, and
some laughter," Bernhard enumerated deliberately,
looking about as if he were peopling the garden according to his own scheme.

" I hated all that, you know," Hugo muttered, with
not unswerving purpose.

" Of course.   You were ill," said the sweet and indulgent voice.

" You are an awfully good fellow, Dietz," and Hugo
abruptly put out his hand.

" It does n't sound generous for a strong man
to say it to a weak one," Dietz went on, " it does n't
seem fair play, but it 's true all the same.   There
are harder things to bear than your troubles, though
yours are pretty hard, count, — yours are hard," he

repeated, nodding his conviction, and looking down with his large soft gaze on the lonely cripple.

"At least my ambition does not soar beyond my own," returned Hugo, with a flash of irritation and some astonishment.

"There's a woman down our way who's been bed-ridden fifteen years. That is a long time."

Hugo listened with at first a curious sense of personal wrong. He did not want to hear about the woman, he felt reluctant to expend sympathy or pity upon her. He was vexed with her for appearing upon his horizon.. But, perhaps because Dietz was silent for some moments, the count could not escape the thought of her, and began to wonder about her and picture her vividly.

At last he said coldly : —

"If she had n't been a fool, she would have gotten rid of herself long ago."

"I don't think she's a fool," Bernhard rejoined with much gentleness.

"Then why does she bear it?"

"I suppose she thinks it is best. She sees a good many people. They get a good deal of comfort and advice from her. It is a queer thing, there is a kind of mischief in her still, and it takes her about three minutes to get most people telling her of their head-aches and backaches. She never speaks of her condition."

"Why do you talk to me about her?" demanded Hugo with some vehemence.

"I thought you might like to have me."

"Well, I don't."

"She has children that have grown up around her," Dietz continued tranquilly. "When they were little,

she could n't work for them and care for them. That 's
the hardest thing for a woman. They are poor, and
she is an expense. That 's hard for her. She is alone
a good deal, as you are, and she has no little whistle
that will call somebody with shawls and cushions and
wine and fruit and new books."

"Dietz," began Hugo, more moved than he cared to
confess, "I 'm obliged to you for your penny-lecture.
It sounds like Sunday Chats for Little Ones at Home.
But I tell you in the first place, I can't bear your
virtuous cripple. She is distasteful to me. A well-
regulated cripple ought to swear and throw things
about." With a sudden boyish, affectionate smile,
which he often had for Dietz, he added: "But perhaps she did n't have at the start a brute of a
temper, like mine?"

"No, she did n't," Bernhard admitted, "she was
always patient."

"Confound the woman!" exclaimed Hugo after a
while. "I wish you had n't introduced her to me."

"She does more good than many who can go about
and work. I know others too. There is a good deal
to bear in the world."

"Thank you. This dose is sufficient for me to-
day."

"You 'd better see more people, count," returned
Bernhard with gentle persistence and seeming irrelevance.

"Fifteen years!" muttered Hugo. "She 'd better
get rid of herself."

"How do you know that she can?" asked Dietz.

"Why, man, it 's easy enough."

"It is easy for her to get rid of her body, I know,"
Bernhard remarked thoughtfully.

" What do you mean ? "

" I 'm not sure that she can get rid of herself, that 's all. There is something that she did n't give herself, and I don't know whether she can take it away or not. I don't believe she can."

Hugo hesitated.

" Why, Dietz," he said gravely, " have you thought about — such things ? It is n't like you, is it ? "

" I had to think about it once," Bernhard replied simply, " because a friend of mine got desperate about money, and shot himself. Every man of us would have helped him, if he had asked, but he did n't. I saw him, and I had to think about him; and I made up my mind then and there, and I have never changed it. You see," he added, " you can never destroy anything, you can only seem to. The life in us, — it does n't ask us if we want to be born, it does n't ask us if we want to die ; it is beyond us, and I don't believe it can be destroyed."

" Dietz," returned Hugo, profoundly surprised, " there are wise men who believe the contrary."

" Why not ? Every man has a right to his opinion. I should never have thought about it, probably, if it had n't been for the poor fellow. I have n't much time for mysteries, and not being a clever man, they are hard for me. But that day, when I looked in his white face, these thoughts came to me, and I was sure he had only gone on somewhere."

" You think he would have done better to stay ? "

" Of course."

" And your well-behaved cripple, your example to sinners, what if she should decide to take the matter into her own hands, after all ? " .

There was a strange quick glance exchanged between the two men, a silent furtive appeal, a calm response.

"I should be sorry," Dietz answered, "for she would have to suffer horribly before she came to that," and his voice imparted tenderness and strength to his simple words, "but I should still think she would have done better to bear it. She will bear it. She has courage."

"Oh, she has courage, has she?"

"More than any man I know."

Hugo laughed.

"You hit a fellow pretty hard when he's down."

"You'd better see more people, count. There's a good many people that would like to see you. It isn't healthy to lie all day and think of yourself."

"You are an exasperatingly obstinate man, and I am not sure that you are not impudent," Hugo said with a smile.

"I never liked a man as well as I like you," the big fellow returned shyly.

Hugo looked at him long without speaking, then broke out with, "I say, Dietz, that woman, — I don't like her, do you know she's detestable, — but will you find out what she wants?"

"Why not?"

"Get her anything she wants — from you, mind you; I want to drive the thought of her out of my head; I'm only buying my peace. Has she a good chair, for instance? No? Well, get her one like this. But don't you mention me to her. She's a horror to me, I tell you. Get her some fruit and some wine. Get her books, whatever she likes. Occupy her. Set her doing something else beside lying there and being angelic, and giving cheerful advice to her neighbors, and never complaining. She tires me, I tell you. Feed her ! "

Dietz laughed, and said : —

" Will you see some people, count ? "

" Yes, if only to stop your harping."

Dietz went back and wrought a stone-rose as big as an artichoke, and breathed the Don Giovanni minuet into its petals, while Hugo communed with his somewhat novel thoughts.

" As Dietz says, ' Why not ? ' " he reflected ; " why not be a little less like a mummy ? It is only for a while. It cannot change the end. Why not appear and surprise them ? Why not make some studies of my fellow-creatures ? I may be repulsive to some, it is true, but some who walk very well on their two legs are repulsive to me. Why not watch the race, and find out what it is that women love ? One may be as harmless as an old mule, but one does n't like it thrown in one's face."

Whether it was a mere invalid's caprice, or pure perversity roused by the maternal taunt, or docile response to Bernhard's good advice, or the unconscious influence of a gain in physical strength, or a young man's sudden desire to see a pair of eyes that had pleased him, or all these forces working together, he shortly after told Lipps to wheel his chair in front of the house.

" I wish to be seen and admired," he said seriously to the astonished and delighted servant ; and when the countess's victoria went slowly down the drive, Hugo took off his hat and wished the ladies much pleasure with matter-of-fact friendliness, and resumed his book

as if he had not heard his mother's incredulous
" Why Hugo! " or caught with a certain exhilaration
the gleam of gladness in the young girl's face.

" Now what can that mean ? " asked the countess
uneasily.

" It is very pleasant, at all events," Gabrielle ventured to reply. " It makes one's heart ache to think
of him always living like a prisoner."

" Oh, but he can't mingle with the world, it would
be too exciting to his nerves. He is very difficult, too,
poor Hugo! Very fractious! But of course one has
to make allowances. I wonder what he means by
coming out there. I wonder if he intends to ask that
man to take his ease on my lawn," she went on in the
portentous basso-profundo that frightened the maids.
" You don't suppose he will let that man sit there with
him ? That man in the blouse ? That Mietz ? "

" Herr Dietz."

" Dietz or Mietz or Pietz, it is quite immaterial. I
have implored Hugo to fumigate, but he laughs in my
face. Why he does n't ask a gentleman to sit in the
garden with him is beyond my comprehension. Why
does he not ask Lorenz von Raven, or Lieutenant von
Paalzow? Why does he insist upon grouping himself with a blouse, in a kind of prince-and-peasant
tableau ? "

" But he likes Herr Dietz."

" Likes Herr Dietz! And pray why should he like
Herr Dietz unless he likes him solely and simply to
annoy me? Does n't he see the criminal reports?
Why should he desire to encourage the lower classes ?
The lower classes ought to be kept where they belong.
They commit all sorts of crimes and excesses if they
are encouraged. Why should Hugo associate with

immoral people? Well! Answer something, can't you?"

"Have you ever seen him well?"

"I saw him face to face in the garden this morning, and Hugo actually presented him to me. I went in and took some quinine, however, and inhaled camphor."

"You are surely joking," said Gabrielle laughing.

"I am very sensitive to contagion. I always take proper precautions. There is nothing whatever to laugh at."

"I thought that perhaps you had not really seen him, for except that he is too large and strong and healthy and happy, there is something Christ-like in his expression. I have never seen such ineffable mildness in the face of any man or woman."

"You know that I never countenance irreverence," said the countess sternly.

"Then I think you mistake his position, Aunt Adelheid," Gabrielle continued, pleasantly. "He is a stone-carver, almost a sculptor."

"Distinctions in blouses do not exist for me. I am willing to subscribe for their coffee-houses, and their public baths. The Frau Major's theatricals are for something of the sort, the amelioration of some of them. I am perfectly willing to have them ameliorated. But I am not willing to have them sitting conspicuously on my front lawn."

"But if it makes Count Hugo happier?" Gabrielle said gently.

"Of course if you can oppose me and argue, you will."

Gabrielle leaned back and was silent.

The countess's insensate rage increased every moment. She was jealous of Dietz because Hugo was interested in him. She was afraid of Dietz because she suffered from a cowardly, morbid dread of contagious disease which she believed lived cheek by jowl with the laboring classes. Being jealous of and afraid of Dietz, it was the most natural thing in the world, according to her logic, to turn upon Gabrielle and threaten to disinherit her.

The countess's last will and testament was a document that could boast more action and variety of incident than most modern novels. Only her attorney knew how many times she had changed the personality of her hero or heroine, and sometimes a whole orphan asylum or missionary society would triumphantly march in and displace the last "sly cat." But the orphans and missionaries were upon the whole less entertaining. She could not very well fall upon their necks and weep maudlin tears, she could not tyrannize over them, and torture them, and dangle the golden prize before them, now high, now low, and make them leap and creep for it. She therefore preferred individuals to corporations, and by all means that the object of her testamentary caprice should live under her roof and eat her salt.

Some of her companions and distant relatives had been very good women, perhaps not strikingly clever or courageous, but it is not easy for a woman to be actively courageous on nothing a year. When, however, she has a couple of boys to educate, or an invalid girl who needs more luxuries and better care, it is astonishing how much courage of endurance under insult sometimes shows itself in the most timid woman. Cousin Marie, for instance, was neither a sycophant nor a toady, but she suffered, meanly suffered, she often told herself with blushes of shame, from the countess's cruel caprice, and was glad and believed the old lady when she promised the fortune, and wept and trembled when it was withdrawn, and vibrated between hope and misery until indignant, dishevelled, desperate, and hysterical she rushed in tears to Hugo and declared that she could bear it no longer.

She left the house the next day, with swollen eyelids and the countess's anathema, while the only comfort the poor woman carried with her, after eight months' humiliation and bondage, was in her purse, and the remembrance of the handsome young lieutenant's laughing farewell: " Cheer up, Cousin Marie, it won't seem half so bad after you get away. Here's a trifle for the little chaps, if you don't mind; " and the trifle was more than her eight months' salary. Hugo was sorry for her, but he could not help laughing, for he took life in the jolliest way in those days, and he kept a private list of the exasperated and lachrymose females who, fleeing from the persecutions of his mamma, had thrown themselves upon his sympathies. " I don't like to see the poor things weep, but upon my word it is a perfect vaudeville," he used to think.

Perhaps the ease with which the average woman's smiles and tears rotate, perhaps the childlike confidence and soft patience of Cousin Marie and her kind, had not exercised a healthful influence upon the countess; and perhaps the practice of dangling her last will and testament before needy and timid companions had not served to elevate her naturally low opinion of human dignity. At all events the will manœuvre was a weapon in her hands. It was a power. It was an old habit as familiar as her gloves.

In her angry agitation, she was now about to crush Gabrielle with it, when a most unwelcome remembrance of the girl's own haughty words occurred to her. "If you have the habit of inserting names in your will and removing them, I need not distress myself, for you will surely remove mine."

Baffled and caught in her own snares, the countess glared helplessly at Gabrielle, who turned her clear eyes and unclouded brow toward her and said kindly : —

"You look distressed. You are breathing badly again. Shall I fan you? Had n't we better drive up on the hills where the breeze is stronger?"

CHAPTER XVIII.

THE great stone houses grew under the patient hands of the builders; the young vines on the hillside grew beneath the sunshine and the dews; the army of school-boys broke loose every noon and scuffled and shouted like mad; every evening in the twilight lovers walked in the lane that led between the high garden-walls to Leslach; every day little squads of soldiers marched down from the shooting grounds, singing as merrily as if war and its preparations were a pastime or a joke; men with bowed backs and faces like brown parchment worked in the market gardens, and women in faded blue gowns and bright kerchiefs walked by with a free, strong step and with baskets on their heads; Bernhard Dietz carved his cornucopiæ and huge divinities, and sang like a thrush, and did not think as much in the course of the day as some people perhaps, but whatever he thought was sunny and sweet to the core; every morning Gabrielle rode off on Sphinx to her aristocratic circus, where she assiduously practiced figures, and laughed and enjoyed herself and found life attractive, and came home to lunch and drive and dine and go somewhere in the evening with Aunt Adelheid, when after twelve hours of the countess, life seemed but a period of stern discipline and mortification of spirit; and the villa gates swung open to admit handsome carriages bringing richly dressed women and gay men, — in short a whole little world of work and pleasure and fashion and luxury and idleness, and love of all descriptions, love in the drawing-room and love in the lane, revolved before Hugo, while he, lying motionless hour after hour, was near it yet remote, the one still, lonely figure in the lively panorama.

Yet he was steadily drawing nearer to the world which he had shunned so long, and he was learning to see much in it which he had never seen before. He did not group himself picturesquely with a blouse on the front lawn for the simple reason that Dietz would not be grouped. No argument or persuasion could move his gentle obstinacy when it once showed itself; and although for the most part he evinced a manly unconsciousness of the peculiar character of the relationship between himself and his patrician friend, he refused to sit and chat with the count except in his rooms, or in the secluded corner of the garden beyond the range of the villa windows and the curious eyes of the world. Indeed, between four walls and with a ceiling above him, Bernhard seemed less free than when he could stretch himself on a garden-bench, and twirl a leaf in his mouth, and look up at the sky through the tree-tops. As a drawing-room ornament, he was overgrown and clumsy. Nothing could induce him to share Hugo's breakfast, which Lipps brought out prepared with new and skilful devices each day, to tempt the invalid's appetite. Only once did Bernhard consent to take a glass of wine, when he stood holding it high in the sunlight, and said, " Your health and happiness, count! " with so sweet and hearty a resonance, that it seemed more like a potent benison than a mere form. But after that he invariably declined all hospitality, and to Hugo's remonstrances would simply retort that it was not natural; and farther than this his reasoning, or perhaps his vocabulary, did not extend.

Hugo's habits, then, began to crystallize into a certain routine. He would spend the whole morning by the fountain at "The End of the World." Dietz appeared at noon, and the man's tranquillity and contentment were an elixir of life, exerting strong and positive good effects upon the sensitive invalid, whom, on the other hand, his mother's excessive fidgetiness seemed as perceptibly to unnerve. In whatever mood Hugo began his day, he invariably found Bernhard's repose restful. He was no more given to morbid introspection than the tree against which he would lean, or the birds that sang in its branches. After these quiet hours, Hugo appeared at what he called "dress-parade." He became visible, accessible, even encouraging and inviting to visitors, and unblushingly frequented the front lawn. It was exceptional when his chair was not prominent somewhere near the house during the first hours of the afternoon. Mousey protested belligerently against the innovation, and the countess frequently inquired: "What can he mean?" but the villa was a very different place to Gabrielle, when every day she saw Hugo's thoughtful, observant eyes watching all that passed, and his quick smile — not always the most amiable smile in the world — flashing over his dark pale face.

Whether the wheel-chair and its fluttering awning was behind the great white rose-bush, or by the weeping ash, or under the chestnuts, Gabrielle spied it instantly and with gladness. She approached him timidly at first, fearing not only a repulse on her own account, but being also haunted by the unpleasant notion that her society if forced upon him might induce him to abandon his new mode of life, and shun his fellow-creatures in the old gloomy fashion. It was a somewhat depressing sensation to feel that with the mother she was a firebrand destined to kindle at any moment a blaze of wrath, and with the son a Medusa whose passing presence might cause days of stony "dumb starings." She was therefore greatly relieved when, a few days after his mysterious reappearance, she found him stationed so near the carriage as she went down some moments before the countess, for the daily drive, that even her unsuspicious mind was forced to admit that he must in this instance "mean" something by it. Her instantaneous impression he took pains to strengthen by saying at once : —

"Baroness, I have waylaid you to ask you if you have forgiven me yet? How long must I do penance for sins like mine?"

"But I was the culprit," she returned, hesitating, and wondering at the friendliness of his tone, which was now as incomprehensible to her as his previous coldness had been.

"Forgive me," he repeated. "I don't want justice; it would crush me. I want mercy, any amount of it." He was smiling, but his manner was pleading and sincere, and he spoke as fast as possible, fearing the descent of the countess.

"The truth is, I have ill-natured moods," he went on.

"You have cause," she said gently.

"Possibly; but I assure you I make the most of it. I stretch it. And I had no cause to be anything but grateful to you. Let us not talk about it. Let us begin again — *tabula rasa.* I don't know why you should forgive me for being disagreeable, still forgive me!" he concluded abruptly.

" Ah, you make so much of it," she said cordially, " but it is a relief!" she admitted. " I have been feeling so anxious. I have feared to look at you lest you should disappear again."

" I wish that you would look at me often and long," Hugo returned gravely, "the longer and oftener the better, if it would n't be a bore to you."

" You make me very happy," she exclaimed, smiling radiantly upon him with a sudden freedom and lightness of heart. " You are very good to speak so ! You do not know how glad I am," she added with a warmth and simplicity that touched him, and led him to rejoin a little sadly and incredulously : —

" I make you happy !" But whatever else he would have said died upon his lips, for the countess at that moment came out, breathless, hurried, and wearing an expression of vast discontent, which merged into positive displeasure when she saw Gabrielle standing by Hugo's chair.

" Aunt Adelheid," the young girl began rashly as they drove away, " could n't you let me stay at home one afternoon in the week ? Or once in fourteen days ? Even Röschen has her day out."

" The comparison is worthy of you ! "

" But suppose you should let me stay once a week with Count Hugo," Gabrielle urged warmly. " Ah, please ! "

" Did he propose it ? "

" No, it is my own idea, but he looks as if he would let me stay with him. I really think that he would let me, now," she added with evident delight.

" You 'd better wait until he asks you," the countess returned with a sneer.

" Why should I be ceremonious with a chronic invalid ? Then I like him. I think he is wonderfully patient."

" Patient ! Hugo patient ! That is news." After a while she remarked : " He has every luxury. He does not really suffer much now."

" The doctor says that he does," Gabrielle returned promptly.

" How in the world should you know what the doctor says ? "

" Because I stopped him one day in the hall, and asked him."

" You do very queer things, Gabrielle ! "

" But may I have a day off? Why should I always drive in the park and pay visits and go shopping and see the same people and say the same things ? Nobody would miss me if I should stay at home, and then it seems to me there is nothing more senseless than spending hours leaving bits of pasteboard at people's houses, and being glad when they are out."

" Pray how could there be any society without cards? "

" Oh, it is not the cards alone. It is the waste of time and the fruitlessness of a great deal of it."

" When a girl of good family has plebeian tastes and prefers to go out and talk with masons " —

" But I would much rather talk with Count Hugo, and surely his family is aristocratic enough to please you," Gabrielle retorted with a laugh. " Ah, do let me stay at home once a week with him ! "

" My neuralgia is a very peculiar neuralgia," began the old lady, " a very uncommon neuralgia, Dr. Pressigny used to tell me. I presume that it gives me more acute pain in one day than Hugo feels in a month. And when you talk of patience " —

She gave Gabrielle a look of jealous reproach and suddenly broke out with : —

" Why do you never wish to entertain me? Why is it such a hardship to drive and make visits with me ? Some girls would consider themselves very lucky to have the privilege of accompanying me. Hugo looked very comfortable. Perhaps, Gabrielle, if you had a particular nerve that went from your head to your heels, I mean if yours were in a state of the most excessive sensitiveness, you might be more considerate of other people's sufferings. I have always maintained that only through our own pain do we learn sympathy with the pain of another."

"But " — Gabrielle hesitated, looked keenly at her inconsequent companion, and concluded to let the subject drop, remembering that " there are people in whose presence one can praise only the Emperor of China." 'The countess proceeded to relate with much animation and interest the details of all the illnesses and indispositions which had ever had the honor of residing for more or less time in her corporeal frame. She dilated with peculiar pleasure upon the treatment which they had received, and the remedies used to expel them, and her therapeutic memories proved so entertaining to her that she grew unusually amiable, called Gabrielle " Moonbeam," and quite forgot the original grievance.

Some days after, she expressed the intention of walking a little after lunch. " The Frau Major thinks that it would be good for me," she announced gravely, and as if the idea were quite novel. Hugo's chair was in the chestnut avenue, as the countess, leaning on Gabrielle's arm, and preceded by Mousey, who was not in sympathy with the scheme, came toward him impressively.

"Good-morning, Hugo. I was detained this morning, and could not come to you. Mousey swallowed a piece of worsted, poor little love. I was so alarmed! I am walking for my health. Slower, Gabrielle. The Frau Major says that the new method is slow and regular."

"Ah, the Frau Major is doctor now?" Hugo said blandly. "Does she prescribe for you too, baroness?"

"Gabrielle has no need of her advice, — at least in respect to health," the countess answered. "Gabrielle has no pain, consequently no sympathies. She is not sensitive."

"Indeed," remarked Hugo, watching the young girl attentively, who colored beneath his gaze, and suggested: —

"Like a clam, or a jelly-fish."

"An admirable temperament," he said seriously. "I am educating myself in that direction."

"You have no idea how I love trees!" exclaimed the countess. "Gabrielle, I suppose you cannot imagine my feelings about trees. They talk to me. I talk to them. I love them. They respond." Upon which she embraced and kissed the stout trunk of an old chestnut, with an air of infantile vivacity curiously at odds with her proportions.

"It is plucky," commented Hugo. "I don't doubt it is stirred to its roots, but it controls its emotions like a weather-beaten man of the world."

"Why are you never serious, Hugo?" she asked with a displeased air.

" Because I have a light and superficial nature, I presume."

Gabrielle had never before seen mother and son together. She looked from one to the other, turned, and walked a few steps down the path.

" She proposed coming to amuse you once a week," the countess said with a laugh. " I don't think you need any amusement. Your spirits are better than mine."

" Why did you not let her ? " he retorted coolly. " As you have taken pains to inform me, I am absolutely uncompromising."

" Oh, as to that ! " she said with a shrug. " But it was probably only a passing whim. She has not mentioned it again. Then I cannot always tell when I can spare her. She is occupied too. Do you know we think Herr von Raven may win after all ? She has been very merry with him at the riding lately. She is playing her game very adroitly. Mercedes herself is not a more skilful coquette."

" Neither the one nor the other is a coquette," he returned curtly.

She laughed mockingly.

" Oh, Hugo ! Tell that innocent tale to somebody who will believe you ! "

Gabrielle strolled back.

" I should like to ask you something, count," she began. " Suppose some women, society women, should say something in your presence about another woman — something very ugly, I mean, what would you do ? We were discussing it after the riding this morning, and we disagreed. That is, I disagreed with everybody else."

" You mean what would I have done ? "

" No," she said quickly, " I mean. what would you do to-day ? "

" But what I do or leave undone is of no importance to-day."

She came impulsively toward him.

" Ah," she exclaimed eagerly, " your personal influence, your dignity of character is as strong now as then."

The sweet conviction of her tone filled him with unreasoning gladness.

" I never had any of those lofty attributes," he returned quietly, " and you cannot deny that a man's influence is practically stronger, when he is able to enforce his arguments with deeds. When, for instance, I could shoot a man who insulted me, or knock him down, I had what I call influence."

" Did you ever shoot a man ? "

" No," he said smiling.

" And if you ever had shot one, I don't doubt it would have made you miserable all your life. I can imagine a better influence than that kind," she said very sweetly, " and you exerting it. But you observe this is no question of pistols, for one can't shoot women."

" I have often sincerely wished that one could."

" Mousey, my gold-dog, my jewel, my treasure, come and hear how dull and pedantic these young people are! " cried the countess in French. " Gabrielle, if you had chosen to consult me, I could have told you what a man ought to do. I think that my opinion upon social questions ought to have as much weight at least as Hugo's. The man should as soon as possible simply change the subject if it is not agreeable to him. If he defends the woman, in all probability he damages her. For all the ladies smile significantly, and retort; ' Ah, yes, of course you defend her!' So she gets one more rap, and very likely deserves it!" laughed the old lady.

"That is precisely what I heard this morning," Gabrielle rejoined quietly.

"What else could you hear from rational people?" demanded the countess complacently.

"But you, — what do you say?" and Gabrielle turned again to Hugo.

"I usually acted in those days on the impulse of the moment," he began, speaking, it seemed to her, as a disembodied spirit might allude to his life ages ago, "but I believe I usually had the decency to lie, if a woman's reputation was at stake. A man has to do it now and then to preserve the balance, for the woman's lie is often against the woman."

"You speak so carelessly of lies," sighed the countess.

"If I believed the woman guilty of any indiscretion, I should certainly have had no desire to throw stones at her. I should have held my peace, if possible; but if set upon by a tough brigade of old drawing-room gossips" —

"I admire your language, Hugo!"

"Thank you, mamma. If brought to bay, and forced to deliver my opinion, of course I should have expressed myself unhesitatingly in favor of the accused."

"But if you knew her, and liked her," persisted Gabrielle, "and believed in her?"

"I should have asserted my respect for her and confidence in her until I was black in the face and my hearers were exhausted."

" Of course ! " cried Gabrielle triumphantly. " I knew you would say that."

" And you could not do anything less wise, Hugo. You could not more signally blast the woman's reputation."

" Why should an honest man deign to consider the possible inferences of low minds ? "

" That is your extravagant way of expressing yourself, Gabrielle. If he is sensible, he will conform to the methods of society."

" If society is so cowardly and so cruel, it seems to me that it is still very uncivilized," retortéd the young girl.

" Possibly," said the countess, laughing, " but your views will not be apt to transform it. If the woman is young and pretty, he 'd better not defend her too valiantly ; and if she is old and ugly, she 's not attacked."

" I had a curious experience in the country once," said Hugo. " I was riding from a friend's place, and had stopped in a small town to let my horse rest a couple of hours. I saw a crowd going into the courthouse, and followed. They were trying no less a person than their bürgermeister for falsifying deeds and obtaining money fraudulently. He was a young man still, with a good face. He was terribly hard hit. I was sorry for the poor fellow."

" Was he guilty ? " Gabrielle asked.

" There would be no doubt of that. He had a childish, silly wife whom he adored. It seems he could refuse her nothing, and she had insisted upon living beyond their means. However, that is the old story. But I learned something that was new to me at least."

"Come, Mousey, my heart's delight, and listen to the words of wisdom of Hugo the preacher. And don't run after that low dog that is insulting you beyond the gate."

"Because, my heart's delight," added Hugo politely, "that low dog, if I read his eye aright, won't stand much nonsense, and for once in your life you may meet with your deserts. I listened to the arguments for and against the bürgermeister," he continued, "and was struck with the brilliancy of the prosecuting attorney for the crown and the weakness of the prisoner's counsel. Near me, among the spectators, was a distinguished attorney whom I had met at home. 'Why does n't he have a decent man to defend him?' I asked. 'If he were innocent, that man's gabble would be disastrous.' The lawyer laughed. 'Oh, he does n't need brains to plead for him,' he answered. 'The sympathies of the court are with him, the spectators wish him well, and the country jury, every man of them sitting there looking so superhumanly stolid, thinks in his heart that the poor fellow ought to get the lightest possible punishment. General sympathy is usually with a prisoner,' he went on, 'except in one instance, — when a woman is on trial. Then, singularly enough, all the women are clamorous for her condemnation.' I was surprised, but he declared that in a long experience this had invariably been the case. He said, 'If a man is accused of almost any known crime, the mass of the people usually hope that he may be acquitted, or receive the smallest punishment. If a woman is accused, the women fiercely proclaim her guilt and declare that no fate is bad enough for her.'"

"It is a libel," said the countess.

" I don't know anything about it. I merely repeat what an expert told me."

" Then what earthly difference does it make how common women who go to common trials conduct themselves ? " the countess remarked with airy disdain. " That 's right, my blessing ! Stand at a safe distance, and tell him that he is a low fellow. Tell him that he 's a snob and you are a gentleman. Hear his little bark ! "

" But there is no way of not hearing it unless a benevolent Providence should strike us with deafness," Hugo returned impatiently.

" Did the attorney say why the women are so hard ? " asked Gabrielle, who had stood near Hugo, listening earnestly.

" He said that he had never been able to decide whether it was sheer cruelty, or something quite different, — an extreme desire to guard the sacredness of their order, a jealous sense of honor repudiating the slightest stain. I ventured to say that according to the second theory, the vestal virgins must have felt a grim delight when one of their number was buried alive."

" I am afraid that they feel it still," said Gabrielle thoughtfully.

" When I was young," began the countess, " we used to talk of things somewhat more modern than vestal virgins, and more sprightly than provincial courts. We did not resurrect such mouldy subjects. Oh," she screamed violently, " he will kill him ! O Gabrielle ! O my sweet angel ! O Hugo ! O my poor love ! "

She started towards the scene of contest, while Gabrielle ran quickly past her and gathered up

Mousey, whom the low snob had seized by the nape of the neck and vigorously shaken. Mousey sobbed and spluttered and complained, but was evidently more frightened than hurt. The countess thought that she must faint, but observing Hugo's smile, concluded that she would not.

"Send for a surgeon, Gabrielle. Send Leible. No, Babette goes faster. Get the arnica. Get some bandages. No, stay here. I feel so ill. Run for the sal volatile. Can't anybody do anything for the poor little suffering dumb doggie?"

"He's not dumb. He's swearing like a dragoon," said Hugo, who had taken the animal from Gabrielle, and was examining him. "The other fellow has only chewed him a little. The teeth have made a good impression, but they have not penetrated his sacred skin. He will feel swollen and uncomfortable for a day or two, but if you diet him, mamma, I don't think you'll have to take him to Pasteur."

The tearful, trembling, white-faced old lady, the tiny yellow dog sitting on Hugo's breast, and relating with many execrations the tale of his woes, and demanding, like a human sufferer, as much sympathy as if he had not deserved them, and Hugo with his languid, ironical seriousness, were a curious group. Gabrielle endeavored to restrain her laughter, but it crept into her voice and eyes.

"How heartless you both are! Come to your Mumsey, precious!"

Mousey snapped at her and manifested a perverse preference for Hugo.

"I warned you, you fiend," said Hugo looking straight into the dog's eyes. "I saw the breadth of beam in the other fellow's jaw. And he was not

quite big enough to bear your insolence. He had not
the chivalrous sentiments upon which you usually
speculate with safety. But he was generous after all,
Mousey. He could have slain you, and he only
choked and shook you and went his way. But if that
dog should come again, beware ! Don't call him
names, and tell him that he's a street-dog and a snob !
Not if you value your life, you — concentrated es-
sence of sneak ! "

The dog, steadily returning Hugo's gaze, listened
to the low voice, and when it ceased slunk down and
crept whining to the countess.

" See how he loves me ! " she cried. " Don't speak
of that monster to him, Hugo, and don't talk to him
so cruelly. He cannot bear it, the little maltreated,
tender-hearted lambkin ! Was he abused by a great
ferocious brute-beast ? Yes, so he was ! " She held
him against her shoulder, laid her cheek on his head,
and kissed him many times. " I will give him six
globules of aconite. He will be feverish after this
excitement. I shall alternate with aconite and bella-
donna, and keep a cold compress on his poor neck.
And I will sit with him and comfort him. Come,
Gabrielle, you can help entertain him. I shall not
drive this afternoon. Gabrielle, countermand the carriage. As if I would go away, and leave my poor
little lonely, sensitive, suffering darling ! Gabrielle,
if you had been watchful, it would never have occurred," she concluded in a rasping tone.

Hugo started and was about to speak, but reconsid-
ered, and watched Gabrielle, who, stepping forward,
took the dog under her arm.

" Shall I not carry him for you, Aunt Adelheid ? "
she said calmly, and they started toward the house.

"I have n't cut the leaves of the last Revue de Deux Mondes. Here it is. Don't you want to read it to him?" Hugo called after them. "Or the Nord und Sud?" But the countess marched on unheeding.

Suddenly Gabrielle turned, went back to the wheel-chair, and extended her hand without a word ; but her eyes were luminous, and she smiled wondrously on Hugo, and shook her head slightly as if she could not or would not speak, and her soft glance lingered upon his shawls and cushions and crutches, and the gentle pressure of her hand seemed to convey to him a tender and comforting message. It was but a mo-ment, and she was gone, but the pantomime recurred to him in his solitude, and largely occupied his thoughts, while the countess and Gabrielle and Ba-bette and Röschen and Leible were one and all em-ployed in tearing linen for bandages, and running for rose-water and lead-water and beef-tea and barley-broth and oatmeal gruel, and circling about the cush-ion on the centre-table, where the little blinking black-eyed rascal with his swollen neck lay in state and was waited upon by his hand-maids. And if the countess could have had him serenaded by the king's most skilful musicians and chief singers, or could have produced a troupe of ballet-girls to dance before him, she would have been better satisfied.

"The pathetic thing is that he cannot speak, can-not tell me what he wants, if his head aches, if he still feels sad. Look at those eyes. Ah, the sweet mar-tyr!"

She sat near him and clasped his paw.

"Hugo may scoff, but I often do read to Mousey. He likes it, it is soothing. And I would read till I was hoarse, if it would calm his nerves, his poor, dear, little quivering Eolian-harp nerves! Is n't it pathetic, Gabrielle?"

And Gabrielle, looking at the old woman and her one love, shook her head with a queer little motion which she had taken up of late to express the unspeakable, and murmured : —

"Yes, it is pathetic. Indeed, indeed it is."

CHAPTER XIX

THE weather grew suddenly warm, which the countess resented as a personal affront on the part of Providence. She announced to Gabrielle — immediately after one of the Frau Major's Thursdays — that she was thinking of running over to Baden-Baden for a few days. Wynburg people were apt, in May, to talk of running over to Baden, but the process in the case of the countess was light and rapid only in name. There was indeed a vast amount of running accomplished, but it was performed by servants and shopboys, and the transportation of her accoutrements and Mousey's was nearly as arduous as the furnishing of a man-of-war, and far more agitating. The tubs elected to make the slight journey, the predestined easy-chair and foot-stool and foreordained doghouse, together with other heavy and cumbersome objects, and the row of traps and trunks which the countess deemed necessary to sustain life amid the rigors of a hotel, were finally conveyed to Baden-Baden with the countess, Gabrielle, and Mousey in a reserved coupé, Babette, Röschen, and Leible in another, and a special wagon for the Kronfels luggage.

The countess abhorred hotels. She could not control strangers' pianos, and it seemed, indeed, that the ubiquitous Maiden's Prayer — which lurks in ambush upon every route of summer travel on the earth, though sometimes dormant from exhaustion — thrilled with new life and vigor at her approach. She was obviously powerless to prevent waiters and maids from running about the corridors at all hours, and the consciousness that other people had wishes and were actually ringing bells to indicate them, filled her with incredulous rage. Her high grade of animosity amounted to disease. Mousey too was wretched. His movements were more restricted than at home. He had not a whole great house, and all that therein was, at his sovereign disposal. He had no green and shady garden. When he listened and yelped at doors, some profane foot was apt to come out and kick him. Neither he nor his mistress possessed, even in their better moments, the animus of Abou Ben Adhem — may his tribe increase! — but how promptly, how thoroughly, and with what satisfaction their fellow-men were ready to reciprocate their hostile sentiments, they realized only in travelling, in hotels, and in crowds, where they found the huge selfishness of humanity an appalling evil. Certain English boys who approached Mousey amicably and were seized by his feeble teeth cuffed him soundly, and, what was harder for him to bear, jeered at the shape of his hind-quarters. He suffered from other disillusions, and was continually rushing to the countess in what she called high fever and treated with aconite. Afterwards he would have the sulks, which she called lassitude and treated with China.

Gabrielle had reason to ponder upon some problems in the fine measurement of forces. If the thermometer indicated 90° in the shade, how much hotter did a fidgety and utterly unreasonable old lady make the atmosphere! Also, how much did the mercury fall, under the cooling influence of a persistently suave presence! For Frau von Funnel was in Baden-

Baden, as guest indeed of the Countess Kronfels, and
had brought " dear Sofie, one of her special pets, so
sweet-tempered, so dainty, so noble, so sympathetic, so
like a little field-flower."

It struck Gabrielle that no girl could be less like a
flower of the field than Sofie Gobert, and some of
these adjectives impressed her as humorous. But she
had a dawning perception that society was not apt to
painfully strain its attention listening to the praises
of any mortal, and that the Frau Major's soft and
brilliantly irrelevant eulogies were rarely subjected to
much comment, but served rather to fill gaps in a
lukewarm conversation, with their womanly and benevolent hum, which redounded to her reputation for
goodness, and at least did no harm to her protégée.
Gabrielle's attitude toward her was now one of
unceasing watchfulness, for which she occasionally
reproached herself, without, however, being able to
relax her vigilance. She belonged no more to the
Frau Major's Legion of adoring and docile girls.
Without discussion, without explanation, she had
gradually withdrawn, and stood aloof with intelligently critical eyes, of whose significant gaze the lady
was thoroughly aware. Why the Frau Major desired
her to marry Lorenz von Raven, Gabrielle could not
comprehend; still more mysterious was the new-born
enthusiasm for Sofie. Yet she was fervently thankful
for the sweet tranquillity and unfaltering tact with
which Frau von Funnel steered her ponderous and
perverse friend. And in those days of heat and toil,
of watching races under a blazing sun, and staring
at far-off bits of red and blue which meant officers,
revolving round a white road that glared and hurt
one's eyes ; of driving and dressing, and meeting the

upper half of Wynburg, from the Waldenbergs down
to the little Meyers — Gabrielle, weary of the heat-
lightning of blame continually playing about her head,
weary of Lieutenant von Raven's attentions, and of
Sofie Gobert's jealousy, thinking much and longingly
of a quiet outstretched figure, a dark and wasted face
with hollow eyes which she had last seen under the
great chestnut-trees behind the villa, gravely admitted
that although the Frau Major's methods were tortuous
and inscrutable, it was nevertheless a great virtue to
have a supple temper, and unfathomable patience.

Meanwhile Hugo was discovering that he had been
having for weeks a species of companionship, sometimes unconscious but always dangerous, with a
charming girl, and that the villa was dull and gloomy
without her. He had heard her step in the rooms
above, her voice at the casement; he had seen her
pure features as she passed in the carriage; he had
felt her presence for months in the house even when
he had wilfully barricaded his heart against her, and
recently there had been indeed various moments of
friendly intercourse, brief but memorable to him. He
missed her, and acknowledged it with profound sadness, but calmly. Once it would have created a storm
of rebellion, now it was pain to miss her, but a pain
which he would not be without. He thought of her
incessantly, picturing what he would do, if he were
a well man. He loved her. He knew he must love
her. He had known it the moment he looked up in
her face in the garden. He had fought against it.
He had denied it. Now he could fight no longer.
This too he must bear, this too would pass away.

He was more than ever alone now, for Dietz was
gone.

" I wish you would go down and take a look at those children," Hugo had said one day to Bernhard. "Everything is beautiful by letter, but it would be a satisfaction to me to send my own envoy."

" I ? " Dietz returned with a start. "I go down there ? "

" Why yes, if you would be so kind, and since I can't," rejoined Hugo, at a loss to understand the man's delighted yet timid expression.

After a while Bernhard suggested gravely, " It will cost a mint of money."

Hugo glanced up with a surprised smile, but meeting something childlike in the big man's gaze, returned soberly : —

" I can save it in shoe-leather."

Dietz ruminated again.

" I don't know the language."

" There are interpreters enough. Better still, take somebody along who speaks Italian, and who would like to go."

" But," began Bernhard with his air of frugal forethought.

" I can save his expenses in gloves and cravats," Hugo interrupted quickly, anticipating his objection with a laugh. " My dear fellow, are you determined to make me ashamed of myself, remembering how much money I used to spend on nothing, — on clothes that I never wore, on suppers that nobody ate, because there was too much expensive wine to drink ; or are you too proud to take anything from me," he went on gently, " who take so much from you, — time and care and patience and moral lectures, — in short, everything that I can get ? "

Dietz walked away a few steps, and when he returned there was the same pleased softened look in his face.

"It is because I want to go," he said simply. "It seems too much."

"Oh, you want to go."

"I have wanted to go down there for years and years."

"My dear fellow" —

"And I never thought of being proud, as you call it. I don't know what you mean. It's natural that you'd like to see those children, or send somebody to look as nearly as possible with your eyes. But I don't know whether I am the right man, and I want to go too much to judge."

"You are the only man I intend to send," Hugo retorted with decision. "I have been waiting for you to finish that last window. You have been disgracefully lazy and slow with it. You are always wasting your time on the maimed and the halt. If you won't go for me, nobody shall. It is your verdict that I want. I want you to talk with the poor little devils. You can talk with them after a fashion, if you don't know Italian. You can find out what more they want and if they like the things they have. I want to know how they look, and how they take it, and what their names are, and who is getting better. I want to kno who scowls, and takes it hardest, and makes the most trouble, — he's my boy! You'd be surprised to know how curious I feel," he admitted in a somewhat shamefaced manner. "The consul lays the business documents faithfully before me, as you saw the other day, I see the doctor's reports, and the head nurse writes to the Honored Protector; she thinks I'm a venerable old party. But I want you to report to

Hugo Kronfels, you understand. It would be awfully good of you, Dietz. They say they have got two houses with a garden between. You can sketch it. I want the dimensions and every detail. I want to know about the baths and the ventilation and the drains. I'm great on drains. It's a talent which I inherit from my mother. And look well at each little beggar, will you? Find out where his pains are, and what particular form of smash has clutched him. It is astonishing how solicitous one grows, when one suddenly finds one's self the father of a large family, all of them resembling their papa."

Bernhard stared straight before him with smiling happy eyes.

"There's a man I know who might go, count. He's a waiter. He's had to stop work. His lungs are weak. He knows Italian. Perhaps he'd be glad of the chance to go and stay down there."

"Take him along by all means. Offer him his expenses and whatever you think best besides. Offer him something cheerful. Don't haggle with a consumptive, you miser."

"I don't deserve luck like this," Bernhard protested. "No, I never expected this."

"And of course, since you are there, you will have to run down to Florence and Rome," Hugo added in an off-hand manner.

"That's what takes hold of me — the thought of seeing the things I've read about. I've got a reason for wanting to see them. But I can go myself. Being down there, you know, I could manage it. And going to Florence for my pleasure wouldn't be your errand," he explained carefully.

"I know it's not my errand, although I could easily

invent something for you to do for me, and you
are such a simpleton you'd believe me, but can't
you do that much to please me, Dietz?" Hugo said
quietly.

Bernhard looked at him long, — slowly, very slowly
it seemed to Hugo, making up his mind.

"I'll go anywhere you like, count," he finally answered.

Hugo held out his hand quickly.

"Thanks, Dietz," he said. After a moment he
resumed: "You are the most obstinate man I know,
and a tyrant to boot. I'm proud of having my way
for once with you. If you'll hunt up your travelling
companion, and make your preparations, I'll jot down
a few notes for you, and you might start to-night," he
proposed with the eagerness of an invalid to set things
in motion.

Bernhard's face fell. How could he go to Italy
without taking leave of Röschen? And she was still
in Baden-Baden.

The count smiled.

"Nobody knows when they'll come home," he said.
"They may go somewhere else. My mother hates
travelling, but once started, she's capable of going to
Jericho."

Bernhard nodded gravely. He believed her capable
of this and worse.

"Then I'll go to-night," he agreed. "She'll be
safe in your house," he added simply.

"Oh, that's all right, that's all right," Hugo returned hastily, and not perhaps with perfect sympathy.
How a noble fellow like Dietz could worship a common,
empty-headed girl like Röschen was incomprehensible
to him, and when any allusion was made to her, which

was rare, he instinctively dropped the subject without delay. But after Bernhard had held his hand in a cordial farewell grasp, and beamed his warm parting smile down upon him, Hugo was led to speculate upon the nature of the bond between these apparently incompatible temperaments. After all, he reflected, it probably made more impression upon him, because he liked Dietz. In the great world, people were as queerly matched, for the most part. The twin-soul theory was very pretty in books, but in life a man seemed usually to get somebody's else twin. If he had head and heart, his wife as often as not was a little shrew, and many a glorious woman was chained to a vulgar fool. He remembered that his comrades had frequently filled him with amazement by marrying women in whom he saw no charm, and that he had indeed been inclined to view their matrimonial ventures skeptically, suspecting a hoax, as in their other escapades. It was as difficult to realize another man's passion as his rheumatism, — unless he happened to offer his devotion to the woman one loved one's self. But Dietz adored the girl. That was evident. Each time this idea presented itself to Hugo, he was conscious of the necessity of carefully putting himself in a receptive condition, before he could imbibe it. This was not in the least, he assured himself, because Röschen occupied a menial position in his house. Bernhard's personality had been a rich revelation to him, the man's strength and sweetness impressed him profoundly, his affection for him was great, his crippled condition was in itself so thorough a leveller of petty worldly distinctions, or rather a marvellous alembic for the distillation of the purely human quality; and all in all he felt himself capable of largely indulgent views toward any woman dear to

Dietz, — provided she were not Röschen. He could imagine the woman for Dietz. But Dietz had n't asked his advice. He had chosen for himself with the imbecile *aplomb* of a lieutenant — and he had chosen Röschen with her vain inviting eyes, her love of tawdry finery, and her bold vulgarity suitable to a third rate *café chantant*. And it was no use to call his infatuation extraordinary. It was not, it happened every day to the wisest and the best; and the kindest thing a friend could wish was that his eyes would never look upon the girl with less delight and more discrimination, but it was a sad sort of business when all was said.

Hugo found that there was always a breath of air stirring in the poplars and the pines by the little fountain, those warm mornings. It was out there that he saw Gabrielle first. It was cooler under the chestnut trees, later in the day. It was there that he had seen her last. Here he would lie until the dusk came and the bats, and long after, — motionless, invisible in the deep shadows, watching the stars and breathing the cool perfumes of the night. The roses had bloomed in profusion, and the garden was full of their fragrance. That would please her when she came. Behind the villa was a narrow road along the vineyards, — a branch of the lane that farther on ran between high walls and gardens to Leslach. It seemed to him that he had never realized what a vast number of lovers there was in the world, until he heard all the sighs and vows and amorous plaints, rising and falling, ebbing and flowing in this little lane. For hours he would listen to lingering footsteps, to low laughter, to murmurs and pleadings and feigned repulses, and protests lost again in the distance as a couple walked

on. His hearing was keen, and it seemed to him he
was learning to recognize some of these regularly re-
curring simple swains. There was a girl with a fresh
young voice, and her sweetheart had a shuffling gait.
They came every evening, and after their blissful half
hour his heavy feet went in one direction, and her
light ones ran off in the other; but regularly every
night before the parting was entirely accomplished —
it always took place with relapses — the girl modestly
exclaimed: "Now how can you, Wilhelm!" But
Hugo observed, and not without a certain altruistic
satisfaction, that Wilhelm always could.

Not all were young and innocent like Wilhelm and
his demure fresh-voiced little girl, who, for whatever
reasons she met him clandestinely, always tripped
away from the trysting-place with a light and innocent heart. Hugo invented for them a combination
of cruel parents, patient waiting, hard work and poverty, and wondered if Wilhelm knew how blessed he
was to be able to wander up and down that lane in the
starlight, hand in hand with the girl he loved. There
were unhappy couples too, weeping comfortless women
— or a man's voice, urging and begging in vain, and
meeting in response only a flippant indifferent word
or stubborn silence. Hugo found himself feeling
kindly to all these shadows of the night, these invisible beings with voices, flitting past him, each with a
hope or a grief in the heart, and he wished them well,
all of them, the just and the unjust, the guilty and the
innocent. All this sort of thing had always been
going on, he reflected; yet once these wandering
couples would not have occupied his thoughts an instant unless he had chanced to meet one face to face,
when he would have passed with the careless reflection

that policemen and maidservants must have their little recreations as well as lieutenants.   But now he regarded it all differently, he was sorry for them.   They were not simply common people idly making love in the lane because not privileged to idly make love in drawing-rooms.   They were human hearts, born to suffer, to hope, and to die.   There was feeling even in the fragmentary tones reaching him, often without words and after long silences.

Night after night he remained late beneath the drooping chestnut branches, and Lipps, who feared that these vigils would recall the old dumb mood, was relieved to see that his master's face, when he brought him into his lighted rooms, was tranquil.   It seemed to Hugo that his eyes were beginning to see clearer in the darkness than in the light of the careless old days, and that the nights were bringing counsel, from whence, from whom, he did not ask.   His thoughts followed Bernhard, and pictured the big gentle fellow, with his lovely voice and kind eyes, among the cot-beds of the injured children.   But whatever Hugo thought, whether of Bernhard, or the little cripples, or the lovers in the lane, whether of the past or the future, of life or death, of immortality or annihilation, Gabrielle was the beginning and the end of his musings, and the link between the most widely disconnected themes. She was his one delight, she was unspeakable sorrow to him.

Staring up into the starlit heavens, he felt keenly, but without the old petulance of his self-centred grief, that a vast mass of hopeless misery was revolving with our insensible old planet.   Yet was there nothing else ?   The shadowy, fugitive, hushed voices in the dusk, the languorous breath of the rose-garden, the tender stir of birds in the black foliage above him, whispered to him of something in the world that was not misery, while above all his own heart solemnly warned him that there was something stronger than misery or happiness or pain or death. As he mused thus, a woman's sob broke on the stillness. "Poor atoms that we are," he thought; "and life, — a point in eternity, — why can she not take it quietly? And I? What have I been but a peevish boy? What if it should be better to bear it, as Dietz says? To endure quietly, with one's eyes wide open on one's losses, to endure with the nerves throbbing with pain — to endure to the end? It cannot all be purposeless. Unless Cruelty governs the universe, there must be some meaning in suffering." The little black book was in his breast pocket. He touched it with a kind of affection. " Who knows? " he thought wearily. "Yet what if it were better, after all, to endure, to love, to be a decent kind of friend, to use what one has left, to be patient with one's broken life? " It was only a query, a thought, but having come once, it came often. It remained with him, and gained ground.

One day he received two letters which diverted him greatly. He played with them, comparing one with the other so often that he finally began to assure himself somewhat apologetically that a man who lies, day in, day out, on his back may be pardoned for making much of trifles; that when he was in active life he had been uncommonly busy all the time riding various horses, drilling his men, looking into the eyes of pretty women, making visits on all the old dowagers, dancing hard, eating well-chosen dinners, drinking good wines, strolling with his comrades in fashionable

streets, playing baccarat, and doing other equally important and indispensable things. Now, in his species
of solitary confinement, deprived of his legitimate
lieutenant-joys, his own thoughts were his friends or
enemies, and human character the one spectacle which
never failed to exhibit itself before his peculiar pro-
scenium-loge. From over-much musing upon himself,
he was gradually working round to long meditations
upon others. His fellow mortals had become interesting to him. Even Lipps's familiar, patient countenance, with its deep wrinkles, had a new meaning, as
it bent over him solicitously. It seemed to him that
there was a large amount of human nature in the letters.

One was from Florence, and to the effect that the
little chaps in Ancona were doing well; sketches and
notes taken as per order; that there was a little fellow
with big black eyes and a bad hip who scowled as
hard as the count himself, a fine little fellow and
plucky; that the head nurse was a kind woman and
knew what she was about; that it was a pleasure
to see things so comfortable, and the count was lucky
to have heart enough and money enough to help
along; that the sky was blue and there were no end
of things to see down there; that the waiter was a
good fellow, and had got an easier situation and was
happy and would stay; that after taking a peep at
Rome, the writer would turn about and start for home,
which, after all, was the best place for a man, but it
was a great thing to see what the great ones had
thought out and made; that he hoped the count did
not forget to do his walking every day, for it was natural not to waste what one had left, and the writer
would be mighty glad to hand him his crutches again;

that there was no need of knowing a language when
everybody was so smiling and pleasant ; when he was
hungry he pointed to his mouth, and nobody failed to
understand that ; and when he lost his way, he pointed
to a name in his book, and there was always somebody to walk along with him, sometimes a man, sometimes a woman, sometimes a child, who would take his
hand and lead him, and chatter to him as pretty as
music. But when a man had home-people to think
about, besides something particular that he 'd got in
his head, he would n't have time to talk to foreigners,
even if he knew how. But kind they were, that he
should always say, a sweet-tempered, sweet-spoken,
uncommonly obliging folk. The weather was pretty
hot, but no more than might be expected anywhere
in the month of June, besides being natural and
proper to Italy, which was a warm climate. The letter closed with somewhat old-fashioned expressions of
duty and respect, and it diffused from its simple pages
an atmosphere of affection, common-sense, and invigorating good will.

The other letter was from Baden, and informed him
that they were having simply intolerable weather, and
Hugo could not imagine how she suffered. Her neuralgia was excruciating, and she had not the slightest
appetite. Neither she nor Mousey had been able to
touch a morsel for days. Her condition made as
usual no impression upon Gabrielle, who was occupied
solely in amusing herself, dressing, driving, and encouraging Lorenz von Raven most pointedly. If she
did not marry him, she ought to, and that was the
opinion of most people. For her own part, she knew
Gabrielle was cold, and she suspected her of being
designing, and only wished she could find an unselfish

and sympathetic girl who would be a true friend. She
was not at all sure but that Sofie Gobert might be a
nice person to go to the Riviera with her next winter.
Hugo knew that she had remained at home last year
entirely upon his account, and very willingly of course,
for she shrank from no sacrifice which it was a mother's duty to make for an invalid son, but he was so
comfortable now, and her chest was so troublesome!
Sofie Gobert had perhaps not read so many books as
Gabrielle, but Sofie was sweet-tempered. The Frau
Major, who knew her intimately, said her temper was
heavenly; and when a girl read great authors, that
is, unexpurgated editions, it made her strong minded
and radical, there could be no doubt of that. Sofie
had been driving with them several times, was very
gentle and attentive, and extremely devoted to Mousey.
She, the countess, had decided upon nothing, and
certainly was most unfortunate in always being deceived in people after lavishing so much affection
and every luxury on them, and in being obliged to
change so often. If she had only had a daughter, she
would have understood her.

As for Baden, it grew more common every year. It
was crowded with cockney English, and vulgar Amer-
icans. They had been in three hotels in ten days, and
each was as dirty, as noisy, and had as execrable a
cuisine as the last. What was worse, she was positive
that where they now were the drains were defective,
and she was therefore coming home immediately, and
would arrive the following day. She was so peculiarly
sensitive to poisonous and malarial influences, she
scarcely expected to escape without a fever. The Frau
Major and Sofie thoroughly agreed with her, and they
all had taken quinine twice a day regularly together.

Gabrielle laughed unfeelingly and refused to admit that she perceived the slightest taint in the atmosphere. Hugo would please tell Lipps to tell Leible to tell the housekeeper to air the rooms and her bed all day. Babette had written to announce their arrival and give the necessary orders, but they were all so negligent there was no knowing what they would do. and as she had not had a wink of sleep since she had been in Baden, she hoped that it was not too much to expect that her own home could be properly made ready for her. The cook should prepare a little supper — some salmon and mayonnaise, and some sweetbreads and artichokes, and strawberries and cream, and any little trifle in the way of pastry that might tempt her appetite. After the heat, and the discomfort, and the obnoxious food, and being in all probability threatened with typhoid fever, she needed to be *built up*, for she was simply exhausted, but remained Hugo's faithful, devoted, and most loving mother.

When they returned, late that evening, Gabrielle far down the drive watched for his light, and seeing none concluded that he was already asleep. Concealed in the blackness of darkness, under his tree, he listened to the carriages and the luggage-van drive up, and to all the commotion incident to the arrival, the hurrying steps in suddenly lighted rooms, his mother's imperious voice, and Mousey's bark and bell. The whole house grew alive and busy, then relapsed into comparative quiet, as the countess withdrew into her own apartments on the other side. Lipps came out to report the progress of events and to ask if the count wished to be brought in. But Gabrielle was there behind those walls, and Hugo felt sleepless.

" It 's too warm to go to bed," he told the servant.

" Take a nap yourself, if you wish, and leave me for a while. You always hear my whistle, asleep or awake."

The fragrant, languid summer night seemed to descend upon him and fold its soft wings more closely about him. The house was dark, except for a light in the butler's pantry, where a shutter was slightly ajar. One long ray projected itself across the lawn and the trees began to take queer shapes: a rotund thuya assumed a grotesquely nodding head, like a tipsy friar, a weeping ash extended transparent skeleton arms, and sudden glaring ghosts walked at will in the shrubbery. Idly watching these transformations, idly hearing the great frog-chorus from the Witch's Cauldron up over the hill, he presently perceived that some unghostly person was coming along the path. He heard a light step, and was instantly aware that Gabrielle was standing near him. He knew that it was impossible for her to see him, but he had caught one glimpse of her as she crossed the shaft of light. His heart leaped and sank. He grew hot and cold by turns. It was strangely sweet to feel her sudden presence in the darkness. He would not and could not speak. He held his breath and waited, too eager to be sure of himself; as she paced slowly on, he feared she would leave him, and an involuntary sigh escaped his lips.

She started and stood motionless.

" Don't be afraid, baroness," said a low voice, moved in spite of its endeavor; " it is only I."

In an instant she was leaning over him, so near that her breath touched his cheek, and how it was he did not know, but he found himself holding her hands close against his breast. Those two dear hands in his! It seemed to him he could never let them go. He held them fast, and she suffered it. Still she

did not speak, and he could not see her face, only a
gracious shape bending over him, and the gentle
breath on his cheek was fluttering and quick. Hugo
had a whole squadron of theories of conduct toward
her; they were well drilled, and he had confidence in
them, but they now basely deserted him. He kissed
her hands many times, not with the frigid frugality
of demonstration displayed when he brushed his
mother's fingers with his mustache, but with warm
lingering lips and famished eagerness.

She withdrew them, and after some moments, in
which she was trying to recover from her surprise
and the rush of glad, warm feeling in her heart, she
remarked mechanically : —

"I came out here to be alone."

"And found me!" he replied for want of a better
answer. "What a disappointment!"

"No," she returned softly.

In a moment she said in her natural voice, except
it persisted in sounding too glad for her matter-of-fact
communications: —

"We have seen a great many people. We have
been very busy. That is what I mean. Your mamma
is tired and ill. It is not a sleepy night. I thought
I would come down alone for a few minutes. The
garden is cooler, and the roses are so sweet."

"I heard your Noah's Ark disgorging itself at the
door. No wonder you are tired, travelling with such
a caravan."

She laughed a little.

"How have you borne the heat?" she said.

"Better than most people, I presume. If one is
always lazy, a little additional laziness is unimportant."

"And what have you been doing all this long
time?"

"Eavesdropping.   I have become an expert.   And
you?"

She hesitated.

"I think I will tell you to-morrow, or when I can.
I will go in now.   Good-night.   I am glad I found
you here," she added very softly.   She did not give
him her hand, and she was gone before he could reply.

Again the sweet, dense, silent night closed around
him, and shut out everything but Gabrielle, and nothing in the past, nothing in the future, nothing in the
universe was strong enough to prevent him from being
glad that she had come.   Between dreaming and waking he felt her hands on his breast, and to the impla-
cable ominous thoughts already hovering near his spirit
pleaded, "Not to-night.   Not yet.   You have pursued
me long enough.   Let me be happy this night.   Let
me forget."

From the same direction in which she had appeared,
again he heard a step.   His heart beat fast.   Was it
she?   Had she returned to say one word more?   He
was about to speak, but some instinct restrained him.
It was not like her to come back, and the step was
not hers.   It was heavier, yet stealthy and slow.
Hers had come lightly and steadily on.   This made
pauses, as if the person were listening.   If it were not
she, it was immaterial who it might be.   A servant.
A rendezvous.   The lane again.   His interest ceased.
Whoever it was would have to pass the butler's treach-
erous light.   Without curiosity, and merely because
his chair and eyes were turned toward that quarter,
he watched a woman with a scarf over her head cross
the Rubicon.   He could not see her face, and she was

wary enough to take the danger with a rapid bound, but the tall, well-grown figure suggested Röschen. His mood changed instantly. It was as if a rude hand had snatched some marvellously precious thing from him, and left dross in its place.

" What in the deuce is the girl prowling about for at this time of night? She never came down for the coolness and the roses! "

He listened with mistrustful attention. " Röschen," he called, low but distinctly. " Röschen! " he repeated louder. " I can't swear that it 's she, but I 'll risk it. Confound the girl! What is she doing? She must have heard. She 's running across the lawn where her tread is lost. She 's going slow again on the paved court. She 's out the gate. She 's up the lane."

He had risen on one elbow the better to follow her movements. Now he sank back, with an unpleasant sensation, a presentiment of evil.

" Dietz in Italy," he thought, " and I sent him off! "

He heard her footsteps, brisk now and decided, hurrying in the direction of Leslach.

But why should a man always suspect evil? Because he finds it in his own heart. Still, to look at it rationally, her parents lived there. She 'd been away. She might have reasons for wanting to see them at once. A girl of that sort did not mind going out at night. Then the lane was quiet. Lovers did n't care for other people. And the billing and cooing seemed to have ceased. His mother was so sharp she forced servants into such things. No doubt it was all right.

Still he did not believe that it was all right. He felt uneasy. He saw Bernhard's trustful eyes! What was it he 'd said? " She 'll be safe in your house, count."

Safe? Of course she was safe! What a fool he was to work himself into a fever about nothing. She had rushed home to see her mother. At this, the old skeptical, lieutenant voice in him hooted, and derisively inquired if he really thought her so tenderly desirous of the maternal presence, and if he would trust a girl with that look in her eyes, round the corner.

Up the lane from the Wynburg side now came a new step, loud but not heavy, and which Hugo could affirm that he had never heard there before, although familiar to him elsewhere. It was a long, precise, trained step, the unmistakable, consequential tread of a certain type of military-man, the tread of the foot that never forgets it belongs to the Prussian army. Hugo knew its kind well, and why should it not go by, Hugo asked himself with irritation. He was not a detective, or a guardian of public morals, or his brother-officer's keeper.

The step passed the gates, and after some moments, on the still, soft, rose-scented air came the faint odor of a cigarette, Hugo's favorite brand, and much affected by the lieutenants at the Casino.

"I am hunting mare's nests. If I were in bed, where I ought to be, I should not be constructing ill-favored romances. In the first place, it was n't Röschen, probably; and if it was, what can I do about it? In the next place, she may have nothing whatever to do with the man who has just gone by." But he listened intensely, with increasing foreboding and with the thought of Dietz weighing heavy on his heart. Against the steep hillside, sounds in the lane below seemed to strike, rebound, and travel far through the still air. He now heard voices, a conscious exclamation, a shallow laugh. "It is nothing serious, at all events," he thought. He could not judge how far off they were, — the acoustic properties of that lane had already impressed him as curiously deceptive, — but it was a rendezvous and a flippant one. He felt a sudden fierce anger with them, whoever they were. After twelve o'clock at night, people need n't meet to giggle, and toy with each other, and alarm one for the sake of an honest man, whose happiness might be trembling in the balance. Anguish, desperation, passion, in short a great love had its supreme rights, but for vapid, empty, coarse flirting, surely there were time and opportunity enough, without profaning the mystery of a night like this.

But Röschen had just returned. In a Baden hotel, there had been more chance for her ambitious arts and wiles than at home. There must have been a legion of lieutenants coming to pay their respects to the ladies, and staring hard at the pretty maid in the corridor, perhaps whispering a word in her ear. "What fools men are!" he thought with disgust. "I as much as any. But thank God, I have n't that sort of thing on my conscience. As bad perhaps — but not that."

"I must find out who they are. That is plain. If it 's Röschen, she will try to slip in as she went, and I may not see her, especially since the butler's light is out. And if I challenge, she won't answer. But the man I must see, for Dietz's sake. And if it is not she, I must know that for Dietz's sake. And if I whistle for Lipps and inquire for her, it will make a commotion, and perhaps she does n't deserve it. Dietz does n't, anyhow. So there 's no help for it."

With these thoughts he took his crutches and pulled himself up, a feat which he never attempted without aid, stood an instant to steady himself, and

started out painfully across the lawn. It was not far
to the gate, but several times farther than the length
of his daily promenade from his chair to the fountain,
which distance he could accomplish twice in what he
called his good days. This was not a good day. The
sultry air charged with electricity seemed to have
drawn his small strength from him and put pain in its
place. He more than once thought he should fall in
a helpless heap on the grass, and ingloriously summon Lipps to pick him up. He was ashamed of his
physical fear, his cowardly dread of falling. "Confound the girl!" he muttered, and staggered on. "No
doubt I am a fool for my pains. But now there is no
retreat." On he plodded doggedly, compelling his
trembling body to obey him to the utmost limit of its
meagre provision of strength. In the annals of his
family was a tale of another Hugo von Kronfels, who
in the sixteenth century added glory to the name by
attacking, single-handed, a band of caitiffs, and rescu-
ing a high-born damsel from their miscreant hands.
He slew them all, of course, and married the fair Cun-
igunde. But since slaying was the accomplishment
in which the noble youth was most proficient, and since
his valor was stimulated by the presence of helpless
beauty, it is possible that in his historical bravoure-
feat, he actually expended less force of will, less bodily effort, and less simple courage than his namesake,
who with no thought of heroic deed, feeling, in fact,
very mean, with a certain mental nausea caused by the
situation, and a positive physical nausea induced by
over-exertion, was now dragging himself with infinite
pains over thirty yards of ground, when no doctor on
earth would have pronounced him able to walk ten.

With weak, spasmodic, faltering, and slow movements, he finally reached the gate. " The girl may go to perdition, for all of me; but if anything's wrong with her, I never want to see Dietz's face." He groaned, not exclusively from physical pain.

He leaned partly on one crutch, partly with one knee on the stone moulding, and worked his right hand and wrist convulsively into the iron fence, that he might not fall, for his heart was beating violently and there was a curious feeling in his head. Crouching against a stone post, he tried to recover his breath, but had not much time, becoming aware of the close proximity of a couple sauntering down the lane. One dull gas-lamp was burning at some distance from the gates.

" She shall not escape me when she comes in, but him I must see when the light strikes him."

Hugo raised himself again on his crutches. " Hold out one moment now, and then collapse if you will!" something within him cried contemptuously to his quivering body. The couple approached. From the blackness of his shelter, Hugo peered toward them. It was Röschen, with her silly, vain, flattered giggle. He saw her distinctly, saw her spring back into the shadow, heard a sportive altercation, a man's laugh as familiar as Hugo's own. It was altogether facetious, entertaining, and mirthful, this midnight encounter.

" Be careful. We are too near the villa. Somebody spoke as I came out. Or I imagined it. I was so flustered. Do you really think me prettier than her?"

" Of course. No end. Miles."

" Oh, I know *you!* " Hugo thought savagely.

" Well, I suppose I 'll have to believe you," rejoined Röschen coquettishly, " though I must say it 's a great compliment."

What the man responded, Hugo could not hear. The two were sauntering slowly up and down beyond the light. Again he caught, —

"Must go. Friend waiting. Important. Will come sure. Which house?"

He lost the beginning of the answer, but heard, —

"Kohler's. Don't make any mistake. And it's only to talk things over, and all you've promised."

"Pretty little witch. We'll talk things over," the man retorted with a complacent laugh.

"There'll be a friend of mine there. It's her room," said Roschen, with a spasm of propriety. "And I wouldn't see you, only you do beg so awfully hard, and it isn't easy to refuse you everything, for you've certainly been very polite to me, though to be sure all the young gentlemen were polite at Baden; not that I haven't heard of barons that liked poor girls before now, though they were probably an awful sight prettier than me."

"Fool!" muttered Hugo.

"Prettier? Couldn't be," protested the man, laughing. "Nobody prettier. Whole court nowhere. Upon my word."

Hugo felt convinced that the speaker was victoriously twirling his moustache.

"Now I know that's flattery," giggled Röschen.

"Mean every word. Such a figure!" Here he seemed to be putting his arm around it. "Such cheeks!" From the little outcry Hugo concluded that he pinched them. "Such a deuced tempting mouth!" There was no doubt that he kissed it.

"Now I shall be mad with you if you do that again," said the girl, her voice excited, her resistance feeble. "We must talk everything over before you do such naughty things. Because I am a very respectable girl, you know."

"Awfully respectable," returned the young man, "and awfully sweet," holding her long in his arms, and stifling her protests with greedy kisses.

"Oh," she panted. "Don't. That is n't fair. I am going."

"And I 'm coming."

She hesitated. "No, you must n't."

"But I will. You said so."

"Well, are you really, honestly, truly fond of me? Not playing with me the way young gentlemen sometimes do?"

"Dead gone. Awfully fond of you. Little beauty. Handsome as a peach. Stony heart."

"Well, you 'd better not come," she said archly.

"Would n't let you go now. Must. Friend. Engagement. Paris train. Come straight to Leslach. Find you sure."

"Then you must be very good. We 'll talk things over."

"Oh yes, we 'll talk them over."

Hugo lost a few hurried sentences, heard some laughter, some ejaculations; then, to his dismay, perceived that Röschen, instead of coming toward the house, was running along the lane toward Leslach, while down the middle of the road, consciously smiling and stroking his moustache, Lorenz von Raven came striding beneath the light.

Hugo was about to call to him then and there, when suddenly the iron to which he was clinging retreated from him, his crutch on the other side tottered strangely, and the whole world began to sink, as he fell fainting on the grass.

When he recovered his consciousness, he lay a few moments stupidly wondering how he was ever going to get up, for his whistle was tied to his chair, and it was evident that no power of his own could help him. A step on the gravel-walk near the house and Lipps's loud ejaculation of terror at finding the empty chair happily suggested relief. He called faintly, for even his voice had deserted him, and at the third summons Lipps heard.

"Here I am under the bushes at the right of the gate," Hugo called languidly.

"O my poor count! O my poor count!"

"Don't blubber!" said Hugo sternly, venting all his outraged nerves and sensibilities upon the innocent first-comer. "Just bring along the chair."

Lipps, fairly sobbing with excitement, obeyed.

"O my poor count!" he exclaimed, returning. "On the ground! What wretch did this?" and the man knelt and slipped his arm under Hugo's shoulders.

"I did it," he said feebly. "I was communing with nature. Wait. Put me down. Do you think you can lift me? All of me? I am helpless. I'm a rag."

Lipps knelt and raised him to a sitting posture, stood and lifted him to his feet, took him in his arms, laid him on his cushions, and after these three adroit and successful movements began to wheel the chair toward Hugo's balcony.

"Stop, Lipps. Don't take me in yet. There isn't time, and I'm tired. I want Fräulein von Dohna."

"O my poor count!" groaned Lipps.

"I'm not delirious. Appearances are against me, I admit. But you go and get the young lady and you'll understand later. Knock softly, and don't wake anybody else."

"She was on her balcony not long ago."

"So late? All the better. Speak from mine. Ask her to be good enough to come to me, and to wear something on her head."

It seemed to Lipps that his master was very ill, but if he had requested the moon, the man would have taken proper steps to procure it, and therefore with a heavy heart he delivered the message to Gabrielle, who sat looking at the hillside lights, and was keenly aware that Hugo had not yet come in for the night. To her it did not seem in the least degree unnatural that he on whom her thoughts were concentrated should summon her. She stole from her room with all possible caution and down to the lawn, where Lipps met her and conducted her to Hugo.

"My poor count's very ill," he confided to her.

"Lipps, you idiot, it is all right. Go and get me a swallow of wine, and don't come back till I whistle."

"He says you are ill," said Gabrielle anxiously.

"He is mistaken."

Hugo was silent a moment.

"I am afraid I must ask you a strange question — a brutally direct question," he began.

"Ask it," returned Gabrielle astonished, and responding to the repressed excitement quivering beneath the gentleness of his voice.

"It's an impertinence. But here in the dark, and to me who am nobody" —

"Ah!" she murmured.

"Perhaps you can answer. Do you — are you — that is, have you any special interest in Lorenz von Raven? Answer bravely. Trust me."

"I will answer that to all the world and by daylight," she returned in a cool, clear tone. "None whatever."

" I knew it," he exclaimed with involuntary exulta-
tion. "Then you can help me. There is something
wrong. You are the only person in the house with any
sense. Röschen is in Leslach waiting for von Raven."

She started. "Röschen? Impossible. She went to
her room long ago with a bad toothache. Her face
has been bandaged all day. I begged Aunt Adelheid
to excuse her."

" I wish she were muzzled and chained, but she is
not. She 's roving wild and free in Leslach."

" But where ? "

" Imbecile that I am, I can't tell you. I could n't
hear. I saw them both in the lane. I did n't understand. I thought she would pass me returning to the
house. I heard them plan a meeting. I never imagined it was for to-night. I have n't managed it very
cleverly to let them both escape. At the end, I was
— awkward. She ran off. He 's gone to the station.
There 'll be a lot of men there, and it will be some
time before he gets back."

He spoke with extreme rapidity and she in the same
manner replied : —

" I will go and find her and bring her home."

" It 's an abominable business for you to be mixed
up in. But it would break Dietz's heart."

" I know " —

" They said Kohler's " —

" That 's the beer-garden."

" But she can't be there. It 's too public. Besides,
it will be closed. And she won't be at her father's.
There least of all. She said a friend's room. Nothing
could be more indefinite."

" Never mind, I will find her. Has she been gone
long ? "

"I don't know. I think not."

This answer seemed odd, but she had not time to consider it.

"Good-night," she said, and started.

"But Gabrielle"— He had never before called her by her name. With a swift movement, she was by his chair. "You are sure you are not afraid?"

"What should I fear?"

"Ah," he murmured with passionate protest, "to lie here like a log, and let a woman do such work for me!"

It was the first complaint she had ever heard from his lips.

"Hush," she said sweetly. "Don't speak so. I would do anything in the world for you, and this is not much. The lane is quiet; the village still and small. I'm not in the least afraid."

"Then go," he said with a groan. "Go for Dietz's sake. I see no other way. If any one can find her, you can. She would laugh in Lipps's face. And we can't expose her. I don't think there's any great harm — as yet," he continued with some embarrassment, "but I don't much like the probabilities."

"I understand everything only too well," she replied quietly. "I saw a great deal at Baden."

"Lipps shall follow you immediately, and wait at the fountain in the middle of the square. He can't keep up with your pace, and you can manage the girl better without him. But he will be there soon, and if you call from any house, he will hear."

"Nothing will harm me. If only I can find her! I shall knock where I see a light. There won't be many lights in a village at this time." Suddenly, in a pleading and an unconsciously caressing fashion, she added:

"Now, you will let Lipps put you to bed, won't you? For you are very tired. I hear it in your voice. And it is so late. And you have been having adventures out here. I will do everything I can for the poor girl — and for Dietz — and for you," she concluded softly, and went. Hugo blew his whistle.

Taking the wine from Lipps's salver, he drank it at one draught, then said to the bewildered servant : —

"Put me to bed as fast as you can and follow the gracious fräulein. Station yourself at the fountain in Leslach, and be ready to answer her call. Keep your eyes open and your mouth shut. There's nothing the matter except Röschen is a fool, which neither you nor I ever doubted. And I have fainted once to-night, and if you're not uncommonly quick in following Fräulein von Dohna, I intend to faint again."

With a long sigh of exhaustion, he delivered himself passive and silent to the servant's ministrations. Shortly after, he looked up from his pillow with an eager : —

"I've got him now! Lipps, you stand at the fountain and listen. You will probably hear a cavalry officer's step. You can't fail to hear it if it comes. You go straight toward it, and you'll meet Lieutenant von Raven. Give him Count Kronfels' compliments, and perhaps it would interest him to know that the Baroness von Dohna is in Leslach with Röschen. And will he be good enough to give Count Kronfels the pleasure of a brief interview to-morrow morning at eleven? Now step out well."

CHAPTER XX.

It was scarcely a half-hour's walk to Leslach, and Gabrielle in her excitement reached the heart of the village in twenty minutes, meeting no soul on the way except a stout policeman, who trudged by, humming, yawning, illuminating himself vividly with his lazily swinging lantern, and not burdening his mind with superfluous conjectures in regard to hiding-places afforded by the jutting corners of vineyard-walls, against one of which Gabrielle shrank as the guardian of public safety passed on his accustomed beat.

The village was dark and still. An inconsequent cock was crowing in a desultory, feeble, and premature manner. She stood by Kohler's garden and looked about. The place was ostensibly closed, but there was movement behind the shutters. In the garret of a house across the square a light was burning. Some men sat in the dark garden, singing solemnly, softly, — as if apprehensive of interference, — and with good voices, each pitched in a key independent of its neighbors, the after-echoes of their last chorus. Some one came round from the side of the house, and a woman's voice said, —

"Better go home, boys."

"Can't. Got to finish it," replied one of the men with thick utterance. She laughed, and they with maudlin conscientiousness continued their muffled and impotent chorus.

" I will speak to her," Gabrielle resolved, and walked
toward the advancing figure, meeting her under the
lantern which lighted the fountain and the great tank,
and recognizing the factory-girl with the ugly stare.
She was carrying in either hand a mug of foaming beer.
She gave a start as she saw Gabrielle, and stopped
short.

Gabrielle looked questioningly at the beer for two,
and at the light in the garret-window. She was sure
of nothing, but chance and her instinct indicated the
way. Here was a woman, at all events, and one could
talk to her.

" Do you know where Röschen Bauer is ? " she asked
gently.

" Is it any of your business whether I do or not ? "

" I think so."

" Well, I don't know. I suppose she's sound asleep
in your big house down there."

Gabrielle looked steadily in her defiant eyes and
said : —

" No. She is not. She is here. Please help me.
Please take me to her."

" You let me alone. What do you mean by gluing
yourself on to me ? " demanded the woman with concentrated offensiveness, turning her back and walking
on, but taking the precaution to change her course.

" I shall follow you," returned Gabrielle.

The two went several steps across the silent square
enclosed by black gables against a vague and sombre
sky, the woman with her beer-mugs in advance, Gabrielle three paces behind.

Suddenly the woman stopped with a coarse laugh.

" Come on, then ! If you want to make a circus,
make it. I 'll take a front seat."

She turned sharply, and led the way in the opposite direction toward the garret-light.

Gabrielle followed silently, ascended three steep and narrow flights of stairs in utter darkness, groped her way along a sticky wall, stumbled over brooms, wood-boxes, and various other obstructions, — at which the woman chuckled, — and entered a small room with a sloping roof, and lighted by a foul-smelling kerosene lamp.

Röschen sprang up with a cry of consternation.

"Sit down," said the woman reassuringly. "This is my place. No bows and scrapes here. Let her find a chair for herself, or stand."

Röschen, trembling, stood staring at the baroness. But her friend, putting her hands on the girl's shoulders, sat her down forcibly; then seated herself at the bare pine-table, in the only remaining chair.

"Here's your beer, Röschen. Make yourself comfortable. Don't be put upon. People that invite themselves can look out for themselves."

Gabrielle came forward.

Again Röschen, from force of habit, rose in the presence of her mistress.

"Sit down, I say!" roared the woman.

Gabrielle looked from one to the other with a certain bewilderment. Intent upon her object, she was as yet almost unmindful of the insults. The woman was rough and aggressive certainly, but what did that matter, provided Röschen would come quickly?

"But I don't care about chairs," she said gravely. "I only want Röschen. Röschen," — with a note of unconscious and quiet haughtiness in her voice, the voice that with her beauty had descended to her from an imperious race, accustomed for centuries to com-

mand and to be obeyed, — "you must come home
with me now.   Come at once, please."

The girl turned away sullenly.

" I have come down here alone in the middle of the
night for you.   Will you not come back with me ? "

The girl did not speak.

" Well," began the mocking voice from the other
side of the table, " is that anything to boast of ?   You
wanted to come, did n't you?   A good many women
have to walk about at night, whether they want to or
not.   I know a woman seventy years old who starts
at two o'clock in the morning, three times a week,
and walks five hours up hill and down, to bring
her butter and eggs to market for such as you to eat.
Drink your beer, Röschen.   Don't be upset.   Let her
jaw."

Gabrielle turned to her haughtily.

" Will you be good enough not to interfere ?   I
am speaking to Röschen.   It surely does not concern
you."

" Well, I like that," answered the other with fierce
mirth.   " She pushes her way into my room.   She
comes where she 's not wanted.   And will I be good
enough not to interfere, she asks as cool as a cucum-
ber.   And she 's speaking to Röschen," imitating Gabrielle's clear-cut accent.   " Well, I 'm going to interfere, as you call it.   And I won't stand any airs
either."

With her hands on her hips she advanced threaten-
ingly, lowering at Gabrielle, so near, so long face to
face, eye to eye, that the young girl, erect, not retreating a hair's breadth, wondered if a blow would follow
that hostile demonstration.

" There 's going to be fair play, I tell you."

"Fair play is all I wish," said Gabrielle, her voice trembling with excitement and indignation.

The woman stepped back, and looked keenly at her, as if surprised at the answer, then said: —

"Oh, afraid, are you?"

"Of you? Not the least," was the cold response.

The woman resumed her seat.

"Will you not come, Röschen? It is so very late. It is so strange here. Come now, and we will go quietly home, and we will not discuss anything to-night, not a word. To-morrow, you shall tell me everything that troubles you. I will be kind to you. I will help you. I promise it."

She went to the girl, and put her hand on her shoulder, and looked pleadingly into the sullen face which, destitute at the moment of all coquetry and consciousness, heavy with disappointment, fear of consequences, fear of the overthrow of her ambitious plans, and the old jealousy and envy, seemed to Gabrielle far handsomer than ever before, and with the frown between the large downcast eyes, the fresh sensuous lips pouting strongly in selfish distress, the rich hair growing low on the brow, the cheeks velvety and vivid as a Jacqueminot rose, was like the face of a beautiful, naughty child.

"Go with the pretty lady, Röschen, and tell her all your troubles. She'll be kind to you, don't you hear her? Trot along like a little lamb, and she will lead you with a blue ribbon."

Röschen guarded her obstinate silence.

Gabrielle withdrew her hand and sighed. She had not counted the costs of this undertaking. It had seemed to her she had but to find the girl and all would be well. She had found her and was powerless.

The woman smiled maliciously.

"You see she isn't your property. You haven't got any mortgage on her. She's a girl as much as you are. She's a right to her pleasures as much as you have. She has a right to her friends, — yours, too, if she can get them. You'd better go home."

"I shall not go home without Röschen," Gabrielle declared, her eyes steady, her voice low and resolute.

"She's going to stay all night."

"Then I shall."

"I like that! What if I put you out the door?"

"I shall wait on the stairs."

"What if I help you down stairs — fast?"

"I shall wait at the door below."

"Where you'll meet him first!" shrieked the girl, roused at last to speech by her jealousy. "You want him yourself! You know you do!"

"Röschen, you forget yourself," Gabrielle reminded her icily.

"None of that!" exclaimed the woman brutally. "There's no baronesses and no servants here this night. Any woman that comes into my room without my asking has got to put up with my terms. Go ahead, Röschen. Don't let her freeze you up. Don't be bullied."

But Röschen needed no urging now. A vision of Lorenz von Raven, or rather of his uniform, his shell, dazzled her foolish brain. Her deadly fear of losing him, her long-repressed envy, burst forth in vehement, foolish words, while her friend rocked to and fro on her chair in an ecstasy of evil glee.

"He doesn't want you. He has told me so a dozen times. He says I'm handsomer. He told me so to-night. He was only coming to talk things over. He says barons have often married poor girls. Everybody knows they have. There was a prince married a ballet-girl. And I am better than a ballet-girl. I am perfectly respectable. There is n't any harm in it, if he does like me. When he comes to see you, I let you alone. When he comes to see me, why can't you let me alone?"

"That's the talk! Give her another."

"O Röschen, Röschen," murmured Gabrielle, appalled.

The girl was sobbing violently.

"And now you 've come and spoiled everything. You 'll tell of me. You 'll do something hateful. You 'll get him away from me. But he likes me best, and he thinks I 'm handsomer. He wants me. He does n't want you. And now you 've come to get him away."

A great sickening disgust of the girl and her angry, puerile, complaining insults, of the bad leering woman, of the smoky room, of Lorenz von Raven and the whole odious situation, seized Gabrielle with overwhelming force. For a moment she was on the point of yielding, of abandoning it all, of fleeing to seek pure air to breathe, pure thoughts to think, of changing her garments contaminated by that tainted atmosphere; she longed indeed to change her whole self, steeped now in these noxious and impure fumes.

"You 've tried to get him all the time, and he likes me best. You 've come to take him away, and it 's mean, for we 've never had a chance to talk things over," whined Röschen. "You can't deny it. You know you want him, and he wants me!"

It seemed to Gabrielle that if her life depended

upon it she could not answer the girl's senseless re-iteration, could neither admit nor deny her charge, could not speak one word that even approximately assented to the loathsome supposition that Gabrielle von Dohna and Röschen Bauer were rivals in the affec-tions of this despicable man.

"You are a little fool," said the woman, but not un-kindly. "Let up on that. Strike up a new tune. Don't you know she'd die before she'd answer you fair and square? Don't you know you and she can't be mentioned in the same breath? You've both got legs and arms, and flesh and blood, and you can like and hate; you are both girls that men fool about and kiss and lie to, but there's something altogether different about her. O Lord, yes! She's a sort of little High Altar!" She threw back her head and laughed derisively.

Gabrielle turned to her with a quick revulsion of feeling. There was truth in the coarse speech. It fairly described her attitude. It surprised her vastly, but it appealed to her sense of justice. She had thought all along if it were not for this person she could prevail upon the girl to come with her. She had felt only horror and impatience toward her. Now she regarded her more attentively. There was hate and rancor, but intelligence, in her eyes. And Rös-chen was too dull to listen to reason. The woman must help. If she had that sort of divination, then perhaps she could be convinced that one meant only good to the girl.

With a strong effort toward the suppression of her natural instincts of delicacy and reserve, and wonder-ing if she were really unjust, Gabrielle said gently and somewhat vaguely to her chief antagonist: —

"I am sorry. And I will try to be fair and square with her, as you say. It is true that we are both only girls. But Röschen, will you not come? I beg you to come. There will be a worse scene if we remain. Surely this is scene enough," she exclaimed involuntarily.

"But we enjoy it," jeered the woman. "We don't have as much excitement as you others. We don't have the money to put on fine clothes and drive behind high-stepping horses down to our opera-box. We never happened to have a baroness performing for us before. Röschen is going to stay where she is."

Gabrielle hesitated, and a score of conflicting impulses struggled for supremacy, before she gravely addressed her eccentric hostess : —

"Will you kindly give me a chair? I am extremely tired. If you were staying as long in my room, I would offer you one."

The woman stared, grinned, pushed her own chair toward Gabrielle, dragged a box from under the bed, and sat down on it, her head leaning against the wall, her feet stretched out generously in an attitude unimpeded by small scruples.

"Thank you. Now Röschen, I will try to be fair. How have I ever injured you?"

"There never was one of your kind on this earth," the woman broke out impetuously, "that was fair with one of our kind! Get all the work out of us you can when we are steady, and when we are not, ' reclaim ' us, ' elevate ' us. O Lord, yes! I know all that gabble. ' There's so much good in the poor things,' she minced in scornful mimicry. "Give charity-concerts, and build a pretty little coffee-house for us, and spend more money on the clothes you wear to your committee-meetings, and the carriages you drive in, and the suppers you eat afterwards than all you gain."

" I agree with you in some respects," rejoined Gabrielle with cool courtesy. " But allow me to suggest that if you were in my room trying to talk to a third person, I would not continually interrupt you. If you demand fair play for Röschen, why will you not give it to me also ? "

A quickly suppressed flash of genuine amusement appeared in the woman 's face.

" Fire away ! " she remarked to her friend.

" You can't deny he thinks me the handsomest," Röschen began.

" I don't deny it, and you are handsomer."

" And you know he wants me."

" He does not want to marry you," Gabrielle forced herself to say.

The low reluctant words were barely uttered before Röschen retorted : —

" That 's a lie ! He does."

Gabrielle, with a flash in her clear eyes, drew back quickly, but controlling herself, appealed with punctilious civility to the tribunal on the box.

" Is that fair play ? "

" Why not ? "

" A lady does n't tell falsehoods."

" Well, I don't know anything about that," drawled the woman with ineffable insolence. " Then there ain't any ladies here. There 's two girls quarrelling about a man, and me to see that there 's a fair fight. If she thinks you lie, she 's got a right to say so. You think one thing. She thinks another. Nothing is proved either way. I rather think you 'll have to bear it."

Gabrielle reflected.

"Very well, I will bear it. Röschen, let me assure you that you are mistaken. I am telling you the truth. There is some terrible misunderstanding. But trust me. Try to believe that I am not your enemy. Indeed, indeed, I am not. It is all false and dangerous and wicked. Don't think of it. Let us come away from it. I am sure you have meant no harm. But think of your friend who is away, — the kindest, best, sweetest soul, — he will be coming home soon, and he will know how to take care of you."

At this prospect Röschen began to whimper.

"Oh, come now, don't pile on the agony. Don't worry her with your sermons. Your kind changes its mind now and then, does n't it? Flirts with one man, likes another, and marries a third for his money?"

"Yes."

"Then it ain't any worse in her than it is in a girl with a handle to her name?"

"Certainly not. But when one thinks of Bernhard Dietz, and " — she faltered, she could not speak von Raven's name, "a man not worthy to wipe the dust from his shoes " —

"Oh, well, that's all according to taste," remarked the woman impartially. "Dietz is n't a bad fellow, if he is a fool in some things. But she 's got the right to choose, to change her mind, to play fast and loose, like your kind, — to go to the devil if she pleases. That 's where I stand."

"A right, do you say? It is folly to discuss it. There is never any right in treachery."

"But I have n't done anything wrong," the girl broke in, petulant and frightened. "You talk as if I were somebody else. Everybody knows Röschen Bauer

is perfectly respectable. Bernhard himself would n't
have a right to blame me if I should change my mind.
Other girls have married barons."

"You have known Bernhard so long," pleaded Gabrielle patiently. "He has been so good to you."

"All the men are good to me."

"He loves you so."

"Other men like me too."

"You have been promised to him years and years."

"I was too young to know my own mind."

"But why, why is it?" persisted Gabrielle sorrowfully.

"Oh, what 's the use!" cried the girl irritably.
"I 'm tired of it all. I hate work. I 've had to work
all my life. I should have to work with Bernhard.
I don't say there 's anything wrong with Bernhard.
But he 's tiresome. I hate to be shut up. I want to
see the world. I want to dance, and sing, and go to
big places where there are lights and people. I want
to be gay and enjoy myself. I want to drive in a
carriage like you. I want to wear handsome clothes
like yours. He would give me such things, if you
would n't take him away from me. And Bernhard
would get over it. Why should n't I enjoy myself?
It 's my nature. Why should n't I have things that
I want?"

Gabrielle's heart sank as she listened to these sulky
sentences jerked out unwillingly one by one; but was
there not a familiar strain in them? Was not this
miserable, sordid, fickle, loveless creed practically the
same as what Mercedes von Waldenberg had laugh-
ingly professed, with variations, indeed, and softened
by her grace and her humor, but similar in its general tenor? And Mercedes was clever, with every

advantage of worldly training and education. Gabrielle was attached to her, and believed in her in spite
of her own words. Could one, then, be hard and
stern with this senseless, deluded girl ? Moved by a
great compassion, Gabrielle began : —

"This is all very sad, but it's not too late to clear
away the misunderstandings. There are things one
does n't talk about, but " —

"Of course," sneered the woman. "Did n't I tell
you so ? You 'll give bread when you have eaten all
you want, but you 'd die before you 'd give a word
from the inside of you to such as us."

"But," continued Gabrielle, ignoring the interrup-
tion and going on determinedly, "Lieutenant von
Raven deserves no consideration at this moment. He
formally proposed to me this morning at Baden."

Röschen gave a cry of rage.

"And he has frequently discussed his intentions
with the Countess Kronfels. Any man who would
seek me as he did this morning and you this evening is unworthy of either of us, or any decent woman.
Now will you come home with me ?"

"But you ? What did you say ? "

"I refused him."

"You did n't want him ? " gasped the girl incredulously.

"No."

"Oh, how do I know that it's true ? How do I
know ? "

"I have nothing better than my simple statement
to convince you. But if you will have patience till
to-morrow, Count Kronfels, who saw and heard Lieutenant von Raven in the lane with you, and who
knows his attitude toward me, will give you some

proofs, I am sure." She spoke soothingly and stood by Röschen as she had frequently during the evening, gazing at her earnestly, pleadingly, compassionately.

The girl burst into tears.

"It 's your money, then," she declared. "If I had it he would n't look at you."

"That 's the right kind of talk. That 's hitting the nail on the head," said the woman, from the dormer window where she had frequently gone to watch a mysterious man standing motionless by the fountain. Now she saw two men, and one had square military shoulders. "Hm!" she muttered.

Gabrielle went back to her place with a sense of utter defeat. Anything more exhausting and more loathsome than this struggle, she could not imagine, unless Lorenz von Raven should walk in that door. This impending calamity led her to turn to the woman with an imploring —

"Help me. Help Röschen."

"Me?"

"You. You can. She won't listen to me."

"No. She 's listening for somebody else," returned the woman with a singularly clear glance of intelligence at the baroness, and a derisive shrug at Röschen's imbecility. Then, as if repenting her momentary abandonment of her colors, she added doggedly:

"But she 's got a right to."

"Why do you always say that?" demanded Gabrielle indignantly. "You know better."

"Oh, you want to have it out with me, do you? Come on then. You 'll find me primed."

"Why do you help her do wrong? You are older. You know what you are doing. It is wicked."

"I have told her she was a little fool. But I say she has a right to be if she wants to. It is nobody's business. Least of all yours."

"Pardon me. It is mine."

"Because it makes you mad to have a maid mixed up in your affairs. You 're too mad to take him now. You 're too proud. But marry her to Dietz, and then you 'll shut your eyes, and forgive your baron. I mean she shall have her chance. You mean she shan't."

"Yes, that 's what she means," groaned Röschen.

"No, no, a thousand times no," cried Gabrielle with horror, and not glancing at the feebler accuser. "And you do believe me. I see it in your eyes. You believe me in spite of yourself. It is because she 's a girl — a girl like me in danger — that I am here to help her. Count Kronfels sent me. He wants to help her. Herr Dietz is his friend and far away. It is Count Kronfels who is protecting her this moment. I am only his messenger. He will know what to do to-morrow. And to-night I will not leave her unless safe in her room in the villa. If Count Kronfels had not cared, had not been large-hearted and loyal to his friend, do you not see " —

She faltered, her voice broke, she turned away, the words died on her lips.

"The cripple," said the woman slowly with neither malice nor apparent sympathy.

"Yes he is a cripple, but his heart is not crippled, and the man who has made all this trouble, his soul is stunted and deformed. He is nothing to me. He never was, never for one instant. You must believe me. I am speaking solemnly and sacredly. And now I will never see him again if I can help it. He is worthless."

Her low voice vibrated with icy scorn.

"Now that 's an awful pity," remarked the woman with venomous emphasis. "For I 'm sorry to say I do believe you. I 've lost the game. She " — pointing her thumb contemptuously at Röschen, "said you wanted him. She has told me so all along. She said it was a neck-and-neck race. And I was waiting to see you beaten."

"You have been deliberately trying to hurt me ? "

"That 's about it."

"Why do you hate me ? I wanted to ask you that long ago."

The woman looked at the fair, high-bred girl standing there in a gown far simpler than Röschen's, looked with lingering scrutiny at the lovely face to which this strange and trying night had lent an unusual pallor, at the limpid, wistful eyes fixed steadily upon her own, felt the nameless grace of purity and innocent daring, of the whole maidenly presence, and threw herself back against the wall.

"Why do I hate her ? " she exclaimed. "O Lord ! O Lord ! " breaking into vehement, dreary, ironical laughter.

Gabrielle waited an instant. There was something terrible to her in the weight of mysterious malevolence hoarded in this fierce heart. She forgot Röschen, the hour, the circumstances.

"Yes. Why do you hate me ? " she insisted.

"Why ? That why reaches up — up," she flung up her arms as if the low roof oppressed her, "up to heaven where a God ought to be, and is n't, and it 's as long as forever and ever."

"Tell me," said Gabrielle, drawing nearer and watching her with dilated, fascinated eyes.

" It 's no use. You won't understand."

" I will try to understand."

A gleam of dreary triumph lighted the woman's
features as she saw the baroness standing in soft entreaty before her on her box. She stretched her legs
still more recklessly. She was judge. This girl and
her kind were accused before her bar. She laughed
with hoarse, sad laughter.

" Were you ever cold ? " she demanded abruptly.

Gabrielle, wondering, replied : —

" Cold? Of course. But," catching the woman's
meaning, " never without knowing where there was a
fire that would warm me."

" That is n't being cold," rejoined the other contemptuously. " Being cold is when it settles in your
bones and your marrow, and creeps into your very
thoughts, and is deadly round your heart, and you
forget you ever were warm, and when there 's no fire
for you on this earth, and you 'd go to hell to find
one."

" No," said Gabrielle faintly, " I never was cold."

" Were you ever hungry ? I don't mean did you
ever wait an hour for your dinner. That 's not being
hungry. Hunger is never having enough, never in
your life, always the gnawing in your stomach, and
the pain, not knowing whether you 'll get to-day as
much as barely kept you alive two days ago ; hunger
is when you 'd sell your soul for a bone they throw
a dog."

" No, I never was hungry," murmured Gabrielle.

" Were you ever beaten, — flogged, for everything
you did and everything you did n't do, waked in the
morning with a blow and a curse, kicked into your
corner of the bare floor to sleep ? "

Gabrielle shook her head.

" Then what do you want here ? What have you got to do with me ? "

The woman rose and faced her, haggard, unwholesome, her eyes blazing with the light of old wrongs and griefs.

Röschen, always listening greedily for a footstep on the stairs, not caring for their dull talk, staring moodily into the lamp-flame, now lifted her swollen eyelids and wet lashes, with a trace of curiosity.

" Suppose you 'd never known anything else ? Suppose you 'd always been hungry, always been cold, always been cursed and beaten ? Suppose you 'd never known your father and mother ? Suppose you 'd lugged a baby round when you were hardly more than a baby yourself ? Suppose you 'd slaved for poor folks to get your bit of crust to eat, and your bit of garret-floor to sleep on ? Then suppose you were sixteen, and little and light, not having had much chance to grow in your life, and not bad looking, and quick with your smile and your word, and suppose you got your first chance, a place in a great country house ? And suppose you got on fast, having a bit more sense than some, and were promoted and praised, and suppose you heard the first kind words that anybody ever spoke to you, soft wheedling words, whispered to you all the time, in odd places and odd minutes, not by one of the servants, oh no, they let a girl alone, but by the young baron himself with his handsome face and gay laugh, and friends and horses and money, and his pick among twenty women of his kind. Well ? " she demanded fiercely. But Gabrielle kept her great pitiful, innocent eyes on her and did not speak.

" They drove me out. They said it was terrible so

young a girl could be so depraved. They said of
course young men would be young men. They married the baron to his cousin. She was your kind. I
was a long time in the hospital. They said the child
was my shame. The child was the only decent thing
there ever was in my life. The child was the only
thing I ever was proud of. It was white and soft, and
it smiled and knew me. It was beautiful and big
and strong. It did n't look like a poor girl's baby,
and me so little and thin. I never was so glad. I
did n't care for the neighbors' talk. I did n't care for
the misery in the hospital, or anything that ever had
been. I was happy. I went into the factory. It
was regular work, and paid well enough, and I could
keep the child near, and run to it at beer-time, both
morning and afternoon, and have it two hours at noon,
and the whole evening and all the night. I did n't
envy the queen. I felt kind to everybody. I kept
myself neat and mannerly. Then some charity-women
came nosing about. They pulled down their mouths
because I was only seventeen, and they preached at
me considerable, but I did n't mind it, for they went
wild over the child. He was a wonder, if I was an
awful sinner. They talked about their 'crib,' and
they told me something might happen to him alone in
my room while I was at work, and they would take
care of him. They were friends of the working-women,
and all that trash. They were your kind. I know
what it means now. But I was young then, and like
a fool I believed them, curse them! and one morning
I took him there well, and when I went for him at
night he was stone dead. They had killed him."

"Killed him!" stammered Gabrielle aghast.

"They talked about convulsions. They talked about

teeth.   How do I know?   He was always well with
me.   I was n't there.   I only know I left him warm
and crowing and cooing, and I found him cold and
stiff.   If I had had him he would n't have died.   Why
did n't they let me alone?   Why did they come and
take him away?   I say they killed him."

Gabrielle was grasping the chair-back rigidly with
one hand, and covering her eyes with the other.   She
shuddered visibly, and made no attempt to speak.

"Oh, it makes you ill, does it?   It shakes your
nerves?   And it 's only words — words — words," the
harsh voice shrieked.   "Live it and see how you feel.
The lives of such as us, and the misery crowding
around you on every side, you can't so much as hear.
It takes the gloss off the little High Altar.   Live it, I
say!"

"But me?   I still don't understand why you hate
me," murmured Gabrielle, almost inaudibly.

"Not yet?   I should think you 'd had enough.   But
there is another reason.   You are like her.   You don't
look like her, but you are her kind, the kind they
make happy and handsome, and keep away from everything.   When they found out they said, 'For heaven's
sake don't let dear Véra suspect.'   But I got a chance
and spoke to her.   She was so pretty and pleasant I
always liked her.   She was n't much older than me.   I
thought she would have a fair word for me and help
me, and I was frightened and half crazy.   First she
blushed.   Then she turned pale.   It was a lie to pretend she did n't know.   Girls are sly.   They always
know what 's going on.   'You must n't talk to me,' she
said.   'You are a very wicked girl.   If you don't go
away I 'll call mamma.'   'I am so miserable,' I told
her; 'I am so afraid.'   'Go off!' she said.   'I don't

want to know about improper things.' Her eyes were
as hard as flint, and she turned me off like a dog.
And her babies did n't die! She 's got them all,
grown now. She 's prospered. She 's kept her young
looks. And when she drives by a lot of us she 's sort
of pleased and surprised, like you the day I saw you
staring at us by the factory, as if we were a new kind
of monkey put there to amuse you."

" And he ? "

The woman drew up her knees to meet her elbows,
held her face in her palms, and stared at the opposite
wall.

" I 've hated him twenty years," she muttered;
there was utter silence in the room, she drew a hard
breath; " and there was n't one moment of it when I
would n't have forgiven him if he 'd come back."

" And this girl here?" demanded Gabrielle, her
tone low, clear, and solemn, her eyes still shaded, her
brain making its best effort to comprehend, and real-
izing that this woman must be met with intelligence
or all was lost. " Why were you — you of all women
— helping her toward sorrow and shame ? "

" Well now, I was n't ! " The woman's mocking
laugh was startling. " You see I should have seen
him to-night. I thought perhaps he did want to
marry her. She said so, and there 's every kind of
fool among men. I thought I 'd find out. But if he
did n't want to marry her," — she stopped, glanced at
the sullen figure, then keenly at Gabrielle, and with
scathing disdain continued, " why, she 's got a streak
of your kind in her. I 'd trust Röschen to look out
for herself with any man. She 's respectable. For
a house and a title she 'd take considerable trouble,
but bless you, she 's cool-headed. She knows where

to draw the line as well as you others. Oh dear, yes. Röschen is respectable."

" Well, I am," declared the girl. "I have always been. And I intend to be."

Gabrielle never glanced at her. It seemed to her that Röschen was of no importance whatever. It was this fierce woman whom she must answer, and she longed for a higher and more profound insight. Not pity alone, not gentleness, and soft assurances of sympathy could win this defiant spirit, it would laugh them to scorn; but sense, strong sound sense, must meet it on its own ground.

" And now you know why I hate you. Have you got enough? You 'd better go off now. She's all right, you see. And I 'm a bad lot. I never was respectable, and never wanted to be. Her father would be in an awful rage if he knew she was here to-night. He 's one of the respectables. You go home now and send me a tract, and tell me you 'll pray for me. But you 'll have to pray hard. I 'm not the only one. There are thousands like me."

" You don't hate me," began Gabrielle, her eyes resolute and shining brilliantly in her pale face. " If you had hated me you would never have told me your poor sad life. You would never have trusted me to understand. You know in your heart that you don't hate me. And you are unjust. You talk a great deal about fair play, but you don't give it."

Incredulous and amazed the woman got up slowly and came forward.

" You are hard to my kind, as you call it, hard and cruel. Isn't it enough to have had all your sorrow and pain without filling your heart with doubt of everything good? You have a terrible pride. You are prouder than we. You are no cheap, empty-headed woman, no narrow brain and thin nature. You are wise enough to see things right. You are strong. You are loving. You are loyal. And yet you make yourself cruel. You make yourself blind. Oh no, you are not fair. You wrong me and my kind. I blame you for your hard heart."

With widely opened eyes and parted lips the woman stared, as if dumb with amazement. Gabrielle was not slow to perceive her advantage.

" If your poor little baby had lived, you would have worked to keep him white and sweet and beautiful. You loved him so. You were so proud of him. You would have made his home clean. You would have tried to keep him from harm. And when he was older, you would have done everything in the world to make him good and happy. You said it yourself. You were not hard then. There was only kindness in your heart when your poor little baby was with you. And would you not have been right to love him and care for him ? And what more does my kind do than to love and care for its own? To want to keep its children from harm, and to give them bright, soft, beautiful things? Would you not have done all that if you could? And would your little baby have been to blame if he had grown up happy and contented, and unconscious of even your former misery? You cannot condemn us there. There our kind and your kind and all the world are alike."   .

The woman made a gesture as if she would reply, but Gabrielle said with soft insistence : —

"No, let me speak now. You have told me your life. Now hear mine. Where you as a child had blows and toil and curses and cold and hunger, I had tenderness and warmth and ease and careless joys and freedom. You were beaten, I was caressed. You never had a home, you were neglected, you have been grossly outraged and betrayed, you suffered miserably in a hospital, you lost your beloved child. And I have known only truth and devotion in my home, only scrupulous respect from the world. I never have had a great sorrow, at least since I was old enough to understand it, and I realize to-night that I never have had even trials, only petty annoyances that I in my selfishness chose to construe as important. I scarcely know physical pain. And yet do you think I am ashamed to stand before you? Ah, no! For I was always sorry for you — sorry for you before I understood, sorry before I ever saw you. You say there are thousands of you. There are thousands of us longing to be something better than ignorant and careless and heartless, yet not knowing how to reach you, — exactly such women as you, and if we make mistakes, if we cannot grasp it all at once, if we go to work awkwardly, it proves nothing against us, the longing is still there. If we are hard upon what we do not understand, you are harder, you are prouder, you build a great wall of envy and hate and mistrust between us, you shut us out!

"I grieve for your cruel childhood. For your sorrow — *all of it* — there is only pity in my heart. In my life there is such wealth of love and promise, I long to draw you toward it and cover you with the sunshine of my own past."

"You can't," said the woman, drearily. "No God and no devil can give me my lost chance."

"Who knows the future?"

"They killed mine long ago."

" Forgive them ! " cried Gabrielle passionately, with as gallant and generous an impulse as ever inspired any boy-knight of the old Dohnas to succor a wounded enemy. " Forgive us. Forgive me. There are wrongs on both sides, but ours against you are a thousand times the blacker. Don't you suppose we know it? Can't you see my heart is breaking over you this night? Be merciful. Don't shut me out. Forgive. Only the strong forgive. You *have* lost your chance. You lost it long ago. But you can turn your misery into gladness and blessings for many."

" Me ? "

" Yes, you! You! You can reach them when we are helpless and awkward. You understand them. To you they will have no mistrust, no reserve. Ah, don't you see that? That is the one thing needed. We do have hearts, but we don't know how to find yours. But if some of your kind and some of my kind would only stand firmly together, shoulder to shoulder, we could move the world ! "

Her voice rang out like a young prophet's, and she smiled from her brave and hopeful heart.

Neither spoke for many minutes.

" Will you not try to trust me a little? There is something in you that I trust. And there are things you say which I believe — and *I* think you would find that I should learn to understand." She held out her hand frankly. " Won't you believe at least that I mean to be fair with you ? "

The woman did not take the proffered hand. Long and searchingly, with a singular watchfulness, she studied Gabrielle's face, and finally with grim delight in her own irony, —

" I 'll give you a trial," she said dryly.

" Will you come to see me ? "

" What will you do with me ? "

" I don't know yet."

" You won't try to reclaim me, or anything ? " the woman asked with redawning mistrust.

Gabrielle shook her head, as if that were scarcely worth answering. " Would you like something to read ? "

" Something you read yourself, or something selected for my kind ? "

Gabrielle smiled, in spite of her night's work, a fresh, young, girlish smile of amusement and sympathy, and the woman liked it.

" I am reading a pamphlet, and all of the leaves are not yet cut. You can see for yourself. Would you like that ? "

" What 's it about ? "

" About prisons in France, and what people are trying to do to make them better and more humane."

" Are they doing anything particular ? " she asked negligently.

" It seemed so to me."

" Well, I don't mind looking at it. I ought to know more about prisons than you. I 've been in 'em."

" Will you come and get it ? "

" You 'd better bring it to me."

" But you will come to see me ? "

" No. I don't like old Putty-Face."

" Will you come to see Count Hugo ? " Gabrielle asked with a sudden inspiration. " He is Bernhard Dietz's best friend."

" The cripple ? " the woman said in the same expressionless tone as before. " Well, perhaps I would n't mind coming to see him."

"And now will you let me take Röschen home?"

The girl had fallen asleep with her head on the table. Her friend shook her.

"Wake up! It's three o'clock in the morning. Your circus is over. Your officer stalked off long ago."

Rubbing her eyes, rosy, dimpled, her curly hair in disorder, Röschen looked younger than ever, and stared at them like a suddenly roused baby.

Gabrielle felt ages older than she, older indeed than the Gabrielle of a few hours since.

"Poor Röschen," she said indulgently. "You are only a great child. I am sure you meant no harm. And everything will be happy again when Herr Dietz knows it all."

"When Bernhard knows!" shrieked the girl, now thoroughly awake. "You are not going to tell him? Not going to take away the baron, tell Bernhard, and leave me without anybody?"

Gabrielle looked at her in dismay.

"But you will tell him, Röschen? You surely would not marry a man without telling him? You could not."

"There's no knowing what queer things very respectable girls will do," remarked the outcast, with her bitter smile. "Hold your tongue, Röschen, and come along home. I'll come, too," she added, but looked sharp inquiry at Gabrielle, who said : —

"Yes, come. I should be glad."

The morning twilight, as the singular company marched in silence back to the villa, revealed two haggard faces. The woman's tinged with chronic sickliness, and Gabrielle's marked with dark circles of weariness and excitement beneath the eyes. The girl

for whom they had fought walked along sullenly, like
a stupid, greedy child deprived of an anticipated feast,
but handsome and fresh-colored still, refreshed by her
long nap, and not preyed upon by over-much feeling,
while Lipps in his faultless livery followed Gabrielle
at the regulation distance; on his clean-shaven face
was no intimation that he perceived the slightest ec-
centricity, or in fact that he even saw any one but the
baroness, for whom his master had sent him.

As they passed the market-gardens, there were
lights moving in some of the little houses, sounds
within and without, a wagon had been brought forward to load, and a man was gathering salad.

The woman with a brusque gesture called Gabrielle's attention, who nodded gravely.

At the villa gate the woman said surlily : —

" You 've beaten this time."

" Ah, no," returned Gabrielle warmly. " It is you
who have beaten both me — and yourself."

They stole into the house by a back entrance. Gabrielle watched Lipps lock the gate and doors, and
pocket the keys, then crept with the lightest possible
step to her balcony.

" He is asleep, of course," she thought.

" Is all well ? " asked Hugo's voice instantly.
" You 've got her ? "

" All is well," she returned in a stage whisper.

" You have been gone so long. You have had
some odious scene. I have been very anxious about
you. You must be dead tired."

She waited a moment. Then he heard her voice
low and tremulous and glad : —

" I never was so happy in my life."

CHAPTER XXI

"I DON'T mind a noise at night," the countess announced with acerbity, "if I only know what it is."

"That's precisely my case," rejoined Hugo. "For instance, when I merely suspect it to be a burglar, I am not happy, but when I positively know that it's a spook, bliss is no name for my condition."

She frowned.

"But there were noises last night. Doors, footsteps, creaks. Mousey was wild. I can't tell you how many times the poor angel started from his restless sleep and barked. He was perfectly aware that something was going on."

"My dear mamma, something is always going on," he returned pacifically. "Why agitate yourself? How many times a year do you complain to me of mysterious noises in the night? Obviously they can't be burglars, for we don't miss any spoons. Suppose we accept the spook theory and be tranquil. But if you'd walk a half-hour in the garden just before going to bed, and not touch curaçoa or Chartreuse, and would lock Mousey every night into a padded cell, a shindy of burglars and spooks together could prance all over the house without disturbing you."

He hoped by this light charge with the old and hated weapons to divert her attention from the main body of her grievance, and he also put much faith in his undignified language as a successful irritant, but she insisted querulously: —

"My nerves cannot bear it. As the Frau Major says, my nerves must be considered above everything. It was between three and four o'clock this morning, that I distinctly heard one of the house doors and some other doors."

He regarded her covertly from his pillow and resorted to another species of defence — sometimes the best mask in the world — the truth.

"It was without doubt Fräulein von Dohna returning at that hour from some midnight adventure."

"Nonsense, Hugo!" she exclaimed irritably, now convinced of the absurdity of her vague suspicions.

"Come, mamma," he said affably, "let's talk politics. You are better at politics than any woman I know."

"Aren't you rather pale, Hugo?"

"If you say so, it must be true," he responded with equivocal civility. "The weather is a trifle sultry."

"Yes, it is frightfully enervating. My pulse is scarcely perceptible, and Mousey can hardly hold up his head."

"Is he pale?"

"He is fatigued," she answered curtly. "How can you bear to stay in bed so late?"

"It's indolence. Then my duties are not onerous."

"I wish mine were not," she sighed. "And I am so troubled and uncertain of my course."

"Indeed!"

"I think there is no doubt that Gabrielle is insincere. I don't exactly know what it is my duty to do. Of course I desire to be scrupulously delicate in my consideration of the family. But after one has that peculiar feeling in regard to any one, it is irksome to always have her about. And I am confident

Gabrielle is not the best person to take with me to the Riviera next winter. I shall remain here during the summer. One is cooler after all at home. And Mousey hates being cooped up in those horrid hotels in warm weather. But I wish to go away as early as September, and I must decide. It is very trying."

Hugo held four long emaciated fingers above the sheet, and surveyed them with his father's smile.

"What are you doing? You look like Launcelot Gobbo."

"Counting months. Why should you be in doubt, mamma? It's much longer than your average."

"Do you mean that you approve?"

"Certainly."

"Of sending Gabrielle away and taking Sofie Gobert?"

"By all means. Why hesitate about such a little thing as that?"

"Do you think Sofie will suit me?"

"Better than Fräulein von Dohna? Unquestionably."

"But you always seem to think Gabrielle is perfection," she rejoined petulantly.

"Pardon me. I have not intimated that I personally should prefer Sofie Gobert to Fräulein von Dohna in any imaginable position. I am merely giving my attention — in the most scientific and objective spirit which I can command — to your interesting system of rotation of companions. Sofie Gobert has every quality which Fräulein von Dohna has not."

"Oh, Hugo, even when you pretend to take some interest, you are ironical. I am very unhappy."

"I am not ironical in saying take Sofie Gobert. You require change. Take it. You are tired of ·Fräu-

lein von Dohna. Send her away. You wish to invite
Fräulein Gobert to pass the winter with you on the
Riviera. Invite her. I shall never oppose you again
in such a matter. Man proposes. Frau von Funnel
disposes. Kismet."

"I wish you would take things more seriously. If
Gabrielle were not so disappointing — so inscrutable,"
she went on with a vacillating, distressed expression.
"I don't know what she wants. She has encouraged
Lieutenant von Raven for months, and then refused
him point blank at Baden. It is ridiculous."

"I think it is."

"And it's disgraceful. She knows what I expect
of her. Of course she does n't mean it. I told him
so. He is coming to see me to-day. If she would be
reasonable I could overlook much."

"Raven has been here."

"What!"

"He came to see me a few moments. He did n't
stay long. I think he was in a hurry."

"Did he ask you to intercede for him with Gabrielle?"

"Well — no, he did n't. I rather think he has
given that up. I fancy he is going to get leave of absence for a while. He seems to want to go to Geneva
to improve his French. I told him I thought it was a
good plan. His French ought to be improved."

"And he did n't ask for me?"

"The conversation was short, and I remember it
without difficulty," Hugo said dryly. "Your name
was not mentioned."

"I am astonished. I don't understand it." After a
while she said ponderously, "This is the last straw.
This decides me. She must go."

" You have not told her yet ? " he asked carelessly.

"No."

" You see her father is off there," he suggested mildly. " Of course you'll give her a little time to look about. One does as much as that for a cook. And I believe their house is closed."

" She has friends somewhere, I presume. And then those Berlin Dohnas."

" No doubt. No doubt."

" And I shall be most punctilious in my conduct toward her."

" Naturally."

" I 'm going to have the Waldenbergs to dine while the roses are so abundant. I shall not tell her till after that. She might be disagreeable."

" No, I would n't. Have you any other candidate in view behind Sofie Gobert ? Because I advise you to keep a row of them to windward." His tone was utterly gentle and inoffensive. She began to breathe uneasily.

" You are so unfeeling," she exclaimed. "If" —

" Ah, mamma, let us leave that unborn sister of mine out of the question ! " And earnestly, kindly, sadly, knowing the fruitlessness of any appeal, but moved, as the wisest of us may be now and then, to attempt the impossible, and wrestle with the gigantic invincible fatality of temperament, " How wretched you make yourself ! " he said. " Have faith in Gabrielle. Be content. Be at rest. Trust her. She is truth itself, and generosity and goodness."

She stood by him panting slightly, and with her sudden painful look of jealousy, her singular mingling of sternness and vacillation,

" I cannot," she whispered helplessly.

He sighed and said no more. He knew that she could not. He remained in bed several days, by his doctor's orders, and feeling, indeed, no temptation to disobey them. Lipps, dissatisfied with the count's appearance, had on his own responsibility summoned the physician, who after his examination inquired : —

"What have you been trying to do?"

"Athletic sports," returned Hugo.

"It looks like it. You'd better stay where you are for a while."

A message of cheerful import was conveyed to Gabrielle to the effect that she no longer need be anxious about her stupid sheep, for the wolf had left town. Beyond this, she had no communication with Hugo, he being invisible, and she in closest attendance upon the countess, who developed a peculiarly difficult and exacting mood, and required her constantly. She sent down wistfully from her balcony every evening a soft little "Good-night." There seemed to be a great deal unspoken between them, — all the events of that nocturnal expedition, and much, much else. It was not always easy to wait.

Dietz came home and reported to Hugo, laying notes and sketches before him, but singularly uncommunicative about the journey. He was cordial, grateful, affectionate, but not his restful self. He seemed preoccupied, and the count feared that the poor fellow had been met at once on his arrival with the tale of Röschen's performances, and when Dietz said somewhat shyly that he was rather busy, and should not be able to come again very soon, Hugo pressed his hand in mute sympathy, thinking, "A man has to fight that sort of thing out for himself. I can't speak till he speaks."

One afternoon the Frau Major was closeted long with the countess, while Gabrielle, in her room, congratulated herself that she was not summoned. Standing on her balcony, wondering when she should be allowed to see Hugo, whom Lipps said had been promoted to the sofa, she saw the two ladies in the rose-garden, and retreated.

"You are fatigued, dear friend," she heard the Frau Major say tenderly.

"I have had to arrange all the flowers in this great house. I have nobody who thinks for me, who saves me care, who is *prévoyante*. With my chest, and my nerves, I need a sustaining influence. Gabrielle is so self-engrossed, so unsympathizing."

"She is young, still. Youth is apt to be self-absorbed," returned the other indulgently. "Let us remember she is unaware of her deficiencies. Sofie is older — and the sweetest temper. But Gabrielle is very, very dear. She has been a special pet of mine. I interested myself greatly in her — on your account. With your wise guidance, she might still" —

"She has a great deal to learn. She has treated Lorenz von Raven abominably. She is very ungrateful."

"Perhaps the dear heedless child really prefers Egon. I am going to give a *fête champêtre* for the Orphans, and we could arrange some pleasant little combinations. As to sweet Sofie Gobert" —

They had passed. Gabrielle, hearing her name, had instantly withdrawn as far as possible within the room, but this choice conversational fragment floated up to her nevertheless.

She sighed and smiled. That morning after she cut the roses, she began as usual to fill the vases.

"Let me do it!" said the countess jealously. "Flowers are one of my few joys. You might at least allow me to arrange my own roses."

"It is a trifle," thought Gabrielle; "yet a few months ago it would have broken my heart. It must be growing tough with use."

Some one knocked lightly, and Mercedes von Waldenberg's handsome head looked in.

"They said you were here. I insisted upon not being announced. This is my revenge-visit. We won't reckon all the stiff ones on the countess. This is solely for you. How pretty your room is! I shall never forget the day you sat in my room and reviled me, you dearest girl!"

"I shall ask, as you did, what have you come to tell me?" Gabrielle returned, laughing. "Lovers, I know!"

"Not lovers, a lover," Mercedes corrected prettily. "The one."

"I knew it!" and Gabrielle threw her arms about her warmly.

"Oh," began Mercedes, "if you could suspect all the wickedness I've been perpetrating. It is delicious! I have come to tell you wonders."

"Mercedes," Gabrielle broke in impulsively, "if you would only come down with me and see Count Hugo. You have always refused, but now you are so near; and I think he would be glad, and you would not be sorry, and I — I wish it so much."

"I shrink from seeing him, Gabrielle. I don't deny it."

"Oh, you need n't be afraid of him," retorted Gabrielle with a little heat. "He looks very handsome and noble."

Mercedes smiled with mischief and quick intelligence.

" It is not that alone," she said. " But send down and ask him."

Hugo's civil reply to their message came up promptly, and presently he saw them — the two women who had had the strongest influence upon his life — entering his room together.

Mercedes took his hand with perceptible timidity. The elegant composure of the woman of the world fled before this gaunt vision of the friend of other days, whose last gay and gallant greeting as he passed the crowded tribune before starting on that fatal race, and turned in the saddle to seek her glance, she remembered well.

" This is very strange, Hugo," she murmured helplessly.

He looked at her and saw his youth, with its long vista of dead delights, of sunny moments gone forever, of dear lost hopes. His heart was tender to them and to her. But suffering had transformed not his body alone. It was a changed soul that greeted her through his deep and luminous eyes, and before he answered, they sought Gabrielle with a grave, lingering glance.

" Perhaps it would not seem so strange to you if you had come before," he said with quiet friendliness.

" Yes, I ought to have come," she admitted remorsefully.

" I have sometimes thought so."

" But I never was famous for doing what I ought."

" I remember that," and he smiled, adding, " I do not reproach you, Mercedes, and it is very good of you to come to-day. I am glad to see you again."

Reassured, she began brightly : —

" But I 'm better now, Hugo. I 've reformed. You have no idea. Gabrielle has plucked me from the burning."

" I never before heard the Marquis de Vallion called by that name," Gabrielle retorted coolly.

Mercedes gave her a quick smile.

" Hugo, of course you hear all the gossip about me. I want your blessing," she said, less at ease than she appeared.

" It is the heavy stage-father who blesses," he returned languidly. " I fear I am scarcely corpulent enough."

" Never mind. Give me as good a one as you can. I would rather have a little from you than a large one from most people. And I need it. It 's the reverse of blessings that have fallen on my head lately. I have something to tell you. Of course you know already. My iniquities are published far and wide. Indeed, it has not been easy for me. Some day I will tell you both the whole story. There have been scenes for painters, and diplomacy enough to run the government the remainder of its existence. But I must talk fast to-day, for mamma is walking in the rose-garden with the countess and Frau von Funnel, and may send for me any moment." She hesitated an instant. " Erich von Paalzow has always been celebrated for his courage, you remember, Hugo. He has proved it again," she continued, demurely. " He is determined to marry me."

" I don't think he will regret it," Hugo returned cordially, extending his hand.

" But the delicious part of the matter is, they — mamma and Frau von Funnel — have actually suc-

ceeded in persuading the marquis that it's Elsa he
wanted all the time, and Elsa needed no persuasion.
Oh, do let me laugh! At home it is impossible. We
are too proper and serious in this business. The Frau
Major is the cleverest woman in Europe. She origi-
nated the transfer. But mamma was not slow in
assimilating it. And the two have not only converted
the marquis to the new faith but made him supremely
happy. And there is no embarrassment. We are the
sweetest family! We are perfect. Elsa always having
been one of the Frau Major's specialest special pets,
and most responsive to her saccharine methods, it is
the Frau Major who will be in a certain sense the real
Marquise de Vallion. Benevolence will flourish here
like a green bay-tree next winter, and there'll be an
epidemic of matrimony. See what you have done,
Gabrielle! But don't molest Elsa. Don't interfere
with her future after ruining mine."

"You bring the freshest and most entertaining
news, Mercedes, one wonder after another; but might
I inquire what possible connection Fräulein von Dohna
has with this romance?"

"Ah, don't, Mercedes!" protested Gabrielle, fearing the mischief dancing in her friend's eyes, and
about the corners of her mouth.

"She? She has done it all. She is a dangerous
person and a match-maker. She came one morning to
me and objected in plain language, very plain, to my
engagement with the Marquis de Vallion. She insisted in the most peremptory manner upon my falling
in love with somebody else, more to her taste. She
urged me violently to come up here and fall in love
with you. But I was considerate," — she gave the
word a certain audacious emphasis, — "I refrained.

Still, her suggestion remained in my mind. Some of the extraordinary things she had said had an unpleasant way of occurring to me when I looked at the marquis. Then I looked at him as little as possible. Indeed, the diamonds he brought always edified me more than his personal appearance. I tried to forget her sermon, but it clung to me. Finally I acted upon it. I fell in love with Herr von Paalzow, entirely in my effort to lead a better life and please Gabrielle. It created an indescribable tumult in my family, a perfect cyclone. Mamma's consternation was simply pathetic, until the Frau Major von Funnel came gliding in, perfect mistress of the situation, and showed mamma how she could still be happy. Mamma is — mamma — and not dull, but only one mortal woman could have executed this *coup d'état.* Few would have had the genius to even design it, but only she the skill to sweetly burrow it along to completion. Sift powdered sugar and it shall be sifted unto you again, is her unerring motto, and with it she wins her tens of thousands. But now you understand, Hugo, that if Gabrielle had not induced me to like Herr von Paalzow, Elsa would not marry the French Embassador, hence Gabrielle is a match-maker."

"You of course are at liberty to believe as much of this as you like, Count Hugo," Gabrielle said, laughing heartily, "but I would merely beg to state that when I talked with Mercedes that morning, I had never seen Baron von Paalzow. I did not even know such a man existed."

"That is an unimportant anachronism. It does not injure the general character of my history in the faintest degree. Oh, I will come and tell you some tales! I will act some scenes for you. I will bring

Herr von Paalzow. What we two have suffered! Talk about the way of the transgressor being hard! The way of the transgressor is easy, easy as waltzing. It 's when the transgressor turns about, and tries to be an honest woman, that her path becomes almost impossible. Never have I had such obstacles set before me, and never, whatever I did, have I so horrified Mrs. Grundy as since I have conscientiously endeavored to act upon Gabrielle's advice."

" It was a very free translation of my advice."

" I can't help that. I hold you responsible. If Herr von Paalzow does not treat me well, does not make me happy — and I require considerable to be happy — I shall blame you. And I have told him, that if the Marquis de Vallion should disappear soon, which is highly probable, — I have thought for some time that he was in danger of shrivelling and blowing away like dry thistle-down, — and if he should leave our silly little Elsa a young widow with all that wealth and power, I should simply die of envy. I have told Erich worse than that. I think I have told him everything," she said more seriously, and with a straight glance at Hugo ; " but he has n't blenched yet. He 's a brave man."

" Ask him to come soon to see me," he rejoined. " And it 's pleasant news you bring to-day, Mercedes. I am far too good a friend to like the idea of your marrying old Vallion. But Paalzow is one of the best men I know. It seems to me that you are both doing a very sensible thing. I 'll give you my blessing or whatever you choose to call it."

" Ah, Hugo," she said gratefully, " you always were a dear ! We will come soon together. We will come often if you will let us. We shall be here next win-

ter, although we expect to be ordered off to some horrid little garrison in the spring. I shall be miserable. I despise small towns. I shall quarrel with all
the women and flirt with all the men. I have warned
Erich categorically. Fancy me rusticating, and Elsa
in a palace! Then the weddings. Hers comes first.
That's Funnel-salve for the marquis's feelings. It will
be large, superb, embassadorian! Mine, the oldest
sister's, follows, small, modest and meek like Erich and
me, — and his pay. Elsa is going to have seven
bridesmaids, — seventy if the Frau Major thinks best.
And I am going to have only one, if I can get her.
Can I, Gabrielle?"

She chattered on, and they laughed at her droll
complaints, while her eyes were shining with a soft
and happy light.

Meanwhile, she was thinking : —

"Poor old Hugo! I wish that I had come before.
I have been a selfish coward. It is n't so bad as I
feared. But I should die to be always here. It
would be like living with a ghost. I shan't mind so
much when I can come with Erich. And no doubt
one can accustom one's self to it. Gabrielle has evidently. He does look handsome, but so ghastly, and
his eyes are like flames."

And Hugo told himself that she was beautiful, she
was graceful, she was charming, she was good, but
was it she who had caused him such agony and despair but a few short months ago? Was it longing
for her that had nearly driven him mad? A great
wonder and incredulity descended upon him, and a
sense of the elusiveness and mystery of the human
heart.

His grave gaze lingered upon Gabrielle.

The two were summoned soon to have tea with the others, and Hugo realized, only when they were gone, that he and Gabrielle had scarcely exchanged a word. He would have said, without considering, that they had had a long and profoundly intimate conversation. He had still his episode to relate to her, and she her long adventure. Dietz, too, had evidently much on his mind, and even the countess had not divulged her intentions. They were like a mass of storm clouds, ready to discharge. Yet the less he saw of her the better. In September, she would probably go south after all. His mother could simply set her adrift, and might have fifty plans in the meantime. Poor little girl, so bright and brave, and not dreaming Sofie Gobert was her Damocles sword. It would be the happiest thing for Gabrielle to go anywhere away from his mother, still being dismissed would be scarcely pleasant. He must ask her about those people in Berlin. It would be well for her to go somewhere as soon as possible. Yes, she ought to go away. He could not bear the look in her eyes much longer. He would not ask her to come to him. It was better so. When she came accidentally, with others, he would see her, but he would not beg her to come, not once again.

He had gone too far the night she came home. He should not have kissed her hands, at least, not in that way. He must listen to his mother's talk of the atmosphere of sympathy which she desired in her own house, and he must see the loveliest, freshest, sweetest, truest-hearted girl on this earth turned out of it. The house happened to belong to him, and him alone, a wise provision on his father's part against the danger of sudden and capricious sale. The idea was distasteful to his mother, and she ignored it with consistency, always saying " my house," and up to this moment it had merely amused him. But now he might not shelter under his own roof the woman he loved, must even welcome any chance that might drive her away. Welcome it for her sake, he reflected with an infinitely sad smile.

Gabrielle herself interrupted his musings.

" I have not come to talk with you now," she began brightly, unconscious as a bird that pours forth its glad song when one's heart is heavy. " I have so very much to tell you, but I have escaped only an instant. I was asked to bring Mousey's blanket from my room, the gold embroidery, and I am on my way. They are going immediately and without me; and Herr Dietz is at the side-door, and says he would like to show me something and begs me to come with him. He says he will show it to you later. But it would be a great favor to him if I would look at it. Don't you think that is very strange? He seems odd, but I really cannot say whether he is glad or sorry."

" Oh, he 's sorry enough."

" But I am not sure this is about Röschen," she said doubtfully.

" It must be, or he would not come to you. It 's a letter, I presume."

" But would n't he simply bring a letter? And he has a carriage waiting. I shall go, of course, whatever it is. If it is Röschen's affairs, it is very painful, but of course I must tell him what I know."

" Must you ? " he returned in consternation.

" But ought n't he to know? She will not tell him. It would seem a cruel thing to do, but I greatly fear you or I ought to tell him, if she won't."

"I? Never!" Then thoughtfully, "A woman sees those things differently, I suppose. I could not tell him. I would rather shoot him. And I don't see why he ought to be told. She is the only one who can tell him."

She colored. "I must go. I think he ought to know," she reiterated gently.

"I'd think about it," he returned. "And will you come to me afterwards and tell me what has happened?"

Dietz scarcely spoke as they drove out to Leslach. Always the village! And she found it to-day, in her cooler mood, a more curious experience to be sitting in a droschky with Bernhard Dietz than to hurry on foot through the lane at midnight. He looked odd to her in his ill-fitting Sunday suit. She watched him furtively. Again her instinct told her that there was repressed excitement but no grief in his face.

The carriage stopped. Dietz opened a gate and led her through a narrow court, where children paused in their play to stare, and a head appeared miraculously at every window. Dietz, who could not usually pass a child without a word or a caress, looked neither to the right nor the left. Once, with a soft but mechanical movement he lifted a sprawling baby out of her way. He unlocked the door of an unfinished room in a shed, and relocked it after her. A cloth was nailed carefully across the window, and something tall and draped stood in the middle of the floor.

Dietz turned and looked at her. It seemed to her that he wished to speak, to give her some introduction, some explanation, — but could not. There was a struggle of some kind in his mind. He smiled, shook his head, and removed the damp cloths.

It was a girl's full-length figure in clay, revealing, beneath scant, short clinging skirts, an open blouse, and rolled up sleeves, free, long, lithe limbs, and the chaste breast but faintly beginning to round into the curves of dawning womanhood. With one uplifted arm steadying a water-bucket on her head, one bare foot thrown firmly forward, the other lightly poised, the charming head turned slightly, with a smile on the full, parted lips, as if, going reluctantly, she would fain listen to the gossip of the women by the fountain ; listening, smiling, looking back, seeking, longing for her pleasure, she seemed moving, so real were the vigor and grace of her pose. And more touching than her mere beauty was the flowerlike freshness, the innocence, the rare maidenliness which the loving soul of the artist had breathed into his creation.

Dietz saw the excitement in Gabrielle's face. Its cause he could not know, but it emboldened him to speak.

He drew a long, deep, happy sigh.

" Now I 've got that done," he began, and his beautiful voice was shy and unsteady, " I am willing to die. I don't want to die. I am happy. There 's no man on earth so happy, and with so much reason. But there 's a feeling that everything has come to an end. That 's what I mean. You are a woman, and you know her. You see her every day. Somehow I can talk to you, if you don't mind."

Gabrielle murmured an unintelligible assent.

" It has been so long, so long that this thought has been in my head. Since I was fourteen, and carved my first rough ivy-leaf at the night school. It has n't been a happy thought always. It has troubled me. It has been a kind of pain. I could n't do it, and I could n't forget it. I 'm a slow man, and I 'm not a clever man. A fellow who began with me was clever. He could model everything. They sent him to Rome. He was a good fellow, and quick. I did n't envy him. I did n't want to model everything. I only wanted to model her. This is the way I always saw her, but I could n't seize her. I 've dreamed of her a thousand times like this. She has waked me from my sleep standing before me so. But I was too dull to reach her. It was in me somewhere, but it was n't in my head or in my hands. It was n't where I could get at it. I never should have gotten at it if Count Hugo had not sent me to Italy. He has helped me find it. He has given me my dearest wish. And I 'd rather owe it to him than to any man on earth.''

He paused, and smiled like a seraph. She clasped her hands tighter and more painfully together, and waited for the slow, soft, tranquil voice.

" I was as frightened as a boy when I came home last week. I thought I 'd got it, but I was n't sure. I had seen so much that the great ones had done, and I saw how they went to work, — bold and fine all at once, you know, — with a strong eye and a light hand and a deep soul, and I thought I had caught something. But I had my fears, and they made me sick. You see if a thing has been coming and going before your eyes since you were a little chap, you can't be sure. But this much I knew, — if I could n't catch it and fix it now, I was lost for all eternity. Well, I 've hardly seen anybody. I have been queer even to Count Hugo, who has done it all. I suppose I 've been half crazy. I locked myself in here, and went at it. And I 've caught it at last. It can never run away from me again."

He gazed with ineffable tenderness at the pure contours.

"There she is," he murmured, whether to himself or to her, Gabrielle was not sure. "That's her pretty throat. That's her dimple in the left cheek. That's Röschen. God bless her! Why I never hollowed out the heart of a rose without longing to carve her lips instead. I never worked at any head without seeing her sweet face, and aching to chisel it. It has been a kind of hunger all these years, and often I have feared I would carry it to my grave. But there she is. I wanted you to see her. You know something about such things, and you know her."

"Yes, I know Röschen."

"I don't deserve it," he broke out. "I don't deserve such happiness. It's enough to make a man afraid. There were some debts I've had hanging on to me since I started. I shall get the last one paid next month. In October, Röschen and I are going to be married. She has promised. And this off my mind! Why, it makes a man as free as air!"

"Röschen has promised you?"

"Yes. She never would set the time before. She is young yet, and likes her freedom like any young thing. And I couldn't urge her until I got the money all paid off. But I'm going to get a lot of money for this," he said shyly. "It seems odd, but my professor says so. I showed it to him first. He always looks at all my work. He says it is good. He says he never believed it was in me, and now I must go on. That is the first mistake he ever made with me. I never shall go on. I don't want to go on. Why, I'm thirty years old and slow. This is all there is in me. This is me. This is Röschen."

" And she 's the best girl in the world. It is n't like meeting a pretty girl on a holiday and being pleased with her, no matter if you like her ever so well," he went on softly, his smiling eyes fixed on the figure. " I 've always known Röschen. She 's like my own life. Why, I carried her in my arms when she was a baby. She looked like a peach, even then. And I 've watched her going to school, and helped her carry bundles and draw water, and seen her growing up, always sweet as sunshine, always kind and good, and working with her mother, and making the house bright because she was in it, always tidy."

" Yes, she is tidy," gasped Gabrielle.

" And gay as a lark, and sweet-tempered, when another girl as beautiful would have had her head turned long ago. For far and near she 's the beauty, and ever since she was a little thing all the strangers that stopped to water their horses at the fountain have talked of her hair and her eyes and her smile; for she has a way with her, and everybody that sees her likes her, and the old folks are proud of her, and she could look higher, but she 's promised to marry me in October — that 's Röschen."

He was tranquil. He had spoken from his overfull heart to this gentle lady. He folded his arms, and regarded his work in silence.

" It is beautiful," Gabrielle began, uncertain of her voice. " I thank you with all my heart. I will tell Count Hugo everything."

" When it is in marble, he shall see it first."

" I will tell him how beautiful it is, and he will be proud of you, as I am, proud to have you for his friend. And I can 't begin to tell you what I feel — perhaps later; and I wish you 'd take me home now."

Her voice was so tremulous and abrupt that he feared she was ill. He hastened to take her back to the villa. She passed through the house, meeting no one, went straight to Hugo's room, and entered with a pale, set face. Throwing herself into the great easy-chair, —

"O Hugo!" she cried, "O Hugo!" and burst violently into tears.

He watched her with a drawn look and longing eyes. This was one of the things it was better to bear. If he were a strong man she might be weeping in his arms and on his breast instead of on that chair-back. She had come to him in her sorrow. She had called him by his name. He loved her. Therefore it behoved to him to be wise. He had not believed his mother's fickle stab would wound her so deeply. Surely, she had sounded every note in that gamut. All had come as he had foreseen, and she, — she the bright and strong and beautiful, — with her clear, brave eyes and resolute lips, was weeping now like all her predecessors, sobbing passionately, and he could not comfort her, could not protect her, could not murmur loving words in her ear, could not touch her though she was within reach of his hand. Cousin Marie had flung herself into that same chair, he remembered, but how different her tears had seemed. He had not had the remotest desire to kiss them away. He smiled a long, sad, patient smile.

Gabrielle turned her wet, flushed face toward him.

"How good you are! Any one else would have talked to me. Forgive me. Indeed it is not like me. I rarely cry."

"Why should you let her hurt you so?" he asked, with well-controlled kindness.

She looked a quick inquiry.

" Oh, it is not that. It is not she. And it is no misfortune. It is something beautiful. That night, when everything sad and dreadful was poured into my ears, I was quite calm. But your friend Bernhard Dietz has almost killed me with his loveliness. If I had listened to him a moment longer I should have broken down like a baby, there in his little shed."

Hugo, holding himself in an iron grasp, thought that her fresh, young, candid smile was harder to bear than her tears.

" And I, like a prig, was going to take things into my own hands and direct them ! I was going to tell him. I thought he ought to know. I was ready to tangle up the affairs of Providence. As if an angel did not stand at his right hand ! As if he needed me ! As if that man's boundless love had not strength to warm and purify any heart, even Röschen's ! "

" I did n't think you would hurt Dietz much," he replied with his quiet smile. " I knew him, and I knew you. Can you tell me now what happened ? Don 't hurry. I can wait."

She rose, looked at the great chair, pushed it aside, saw a low stool, drew it near his sofa, and seated herself, earnest and unconscious as when, years before, at home in the firelight, she had told important tales to her papa.

" There is so much to tell," she said, as if he had a claim upon her confidences. " But I must begin at the end."

Warmly, eagerly, her eyes still wet, her voice rich with emotion, she repeated Bernhard's words, and told Hugo how her heart had swelled with pity and pain, listening to the man's simple story of patience and tenderness and faith. How she trembled for him, seeing, instead of his pure ideal, only a cold, sordid, and grasping girl, yet how after all she ceased to pity or to fear, for such nobleness and such love were in themselves divine, and who dared say what miracles they might not work? Röschen was silly, vain, heartless, false, but she could not — no woman could — look in Bernhard Dietz's tranquil, trustful eyes, and not confess her weakness and be forgiven.

Hugo listened with utter incredulity as to any saving grace to be evolved by any means whatever from Röschen's inner consciousness. But he had not the heart to make skeptical comments and cool Gabrielle's enthusiasm.

He watched her intently. He realized what she in her eagerness did not remember, that this was the first time they two had been alone together, in free and close companionship. It might be the last. He saw deep down in her heart as she spoke, and perceived treasures of richness and sweetness. His smile grew more resolutely patient. His eyes never left her face.

She confessed, among other things, that she blamed herself in a vague way for Röschen's escapade. It was not easy to say what she had left undone, but if she had been wiser and kinder, perhaps the foolishness might not have assumed such dimensions. She thought with the best will in the world there were still a great many remains of old prejudices in her, and echoes of stupid traditions of rank and dignity and the relations of mistress and maid. She reproached herself for a certain negligence toward Röschen, a carelessness of her danger, and an indifference to her claim upon her as a woman, near and misguided.

Hugo had his private opinion of this question of conscience also, but listened without comment.

She related to him every detail of her adventure at Leslach. It filled him with profound tenderness that she fearlessly and pitifully revealed to him that whole tale of sorrow and sin, — her voice unfaltering, her clear eyes seeking his own.

Having told him her hopes and plans with regard to the woman, who she declared was a strong character, full of delicacy and feeling beneath the coating of brutality her life had given her, Gabrielle now sat silent and thoughtful, a little smile of reminiscence hovering over her lips, when Babette brought in a note with many apologies, for she thought the gracious fräulein was out, but had seen her a moment ago from the garden, where she was walking with Mousey.

"It is from your mamma. May I read it?"

"I would undertake to read that telepathetically," he replied.

She opened it and read it beneath his gaze.

"It is impossible!" she said softly, and passed it to him.

MY DEAR FRÄULEIN VON DOHNA (it began):
You are too clever not to have already perceived that our relations are too strained to be prolonged, and not to have foreseen my request that out of consideration for my nerves, which require the utmost tranquillity and sympathy, you will seek the protection of some other family. I shall be happy to facilitate your going in every way in my power, and am ready to send you with escort to your relatives in Berlin. But spare me, if you please, any discussion. I am fully decided. In my own house, I require a more restful and con-

genial atmosphere, and in my chosen companion affection and above all perfect ingenuousness.

Sincerely yours,

ADELHEID VON KRONFELS.

She sat so near him, staring incredulously into his eyes, yet an impassable chasm separated them. Not even in this moment of insult might he protect her.

"I fancy your relatives in Berlin will not be able to surpass that," he said quietly.

"My relatives in Berlin," she repeated slowly. "Why, you do not think"—

He stared at his old friend, the swallow. He could not look in her eyes and speak the words which he was resolved to say. She was too lovely, too near and too dear to him. There was a softness in her bearing, — it might be pity, it might be something else, — but whatever it was, it was dangerous, and the sooner she went the better. His mother's characteristic missile was a blessing in disguise.

"It is a disgusting letter," he began. "We don't need to waste any words on it. But it will be a happy release for you. It is a mystery to me that you have borne your life here so long. I wonder that you stayed here a week. There are three daughters in your cousin's family in Berlin, I think you said once," he remarked with considerable animation. "You will be sure to like Berlin."

She merely looked at him.

"There is everything to interest you there."

"I am interested here," she returned softly.

"This is a dull little place."

"It is not dull to me. I should be sorry to leave it."

" But — after that letter " —

" She may change her mind."

" I think not in this case."

" The letter impresses one because it is a letter," she hastened to explain. " Words seem stronger, written. Why should I take it more seriously than things she has said? It would be a pity to take it too seriously. It would be a pity to feel offended, — and go among strangers — to leave — you all."

Her voice appealed to him cruelly. He would not look at her.

" Oh no, I cannot go merely because she is displeased with me. She has been often displeased, and afterwards quite friendly. I came to stay a whole year. It would be absurd to go away because she wrote that letter in a mood that may change completely to-morrow. I cannot go. I know people well at last. I have work to do, earnest work. With that strong woman, there is no end to what one may do, — good human work. And I want to be better to Röschen. I have something to atone for to her. And perhaps I can induce her to tell Bernhard. And I must see the statue in marble. And I must be Mercedes' bridesmaid. Why, I seem to have taken root here! It would be a little like dying to go away. Do you not see? I cannot go!"

She gave a score of reasons, all indeed but the one supreme reason, but that he heard trembling sweetly in her voice.

" Why do you not look at me? Why do you not speak? Why do you not tell me I cannot go away?"

Still he was silent.

" Ah, Hugo, Hugo!" she murmured desperately.

At this he fixed his sorrowful, yearning eyes upon her.

"You must go," he said. "If you will not go for your sake, — then in pity for mine!"

With a rapid movement she was kneeling, her face close to his on his cushions.

"Now I will never leave you," she said solemnly.

He groaned.

"Listen to me," he began, and in his struggle, his voice grew stern. "I suppose this had to come. God knows I tried to avert it. But let it stop where it is. Don't say any more. There is no harm done." He went on with an attempt at lightness. "We won't be tragic." His smile was a miserable failure. "Draw that chair nearer, won't you? You will be tired kneeling there. And let us discuss it like the good friends that we are, Gabrielle. Let us be reasonable."

"I don't want to be reasonable," she murmured without moving.

He began again in a different key with a semblance of graybeard wisdom : —

"I understand it all so well. I understand it a thousand times better than is possible for you. And I shall never forget your goodness and your pity and your generosity. But to-day — I am very tired to-day, — if you would kindly leave me, — another time."

He grew paler as he spoke.

She shook her head. "No, no."

Again he pulled himself together.

"You are a little romantic," he exclaimed indulgently. "It is natural for a girl of your temperament to have her theories and fancies. But trust me. Indeed I am your friend. Some day you will thank me.

The only thing for you to do after that letter is to act upon it promptly. There is nothing else to be done!"

Suddenly she put up her arms and clung to him.

"Dearest, I love you," she murmured, and laid her head on his breast.

At her touch he forgot. He seized her in his arms, and clasped her close and kissed her hair and cheek many times with hot and hungered kisses.

Then he held her face in his hands, looked in her eyes with nameless longing, and pushed her gently from him.

" Forgive me," he said ; " let me be an honest man."

" I love you, Hugo."

" And does that make the crooked straight and the lame walk ? " he broke out bitterly, at the end of his strength. " Don't I know that you love me ? But I ought not to listen if you are mad enough to tell me so. I do not know how it has come that I am listening to such words from your lips. You ought not to say them. I ought not to hear them. We will forget them. Ah, child, child, how hard you make it for me ! "

" Hugo, look at me. Don't turn away. Look in my eyes. It is you whom I love. What is it one loves ? A man's riding or walking ? That would be a poor thing to love. I love you — you — you ! And a thousand times better for your sorrow and your loneliness, for your dignity and your patience. You are a greater hero in my eyes than if you were leading men to battle. You may send me away now if you will, but you will break my heart. For I want nothing in the world except to be near you, to be your friend, to be your love. It is not pity. It is not romantic. It is something else. Ah, Hugo ! "

He shook his head desolately.

" I shall never be well.   I am a cripple for life."

" I know," she sighed, with a tender smile.

" I lie here always in the shadow of death.   Who knows when my faint pulses may expire ?   Who knows when " — He did not finish.

" Every soul that is born lives always in the shadow of death.   Should that make one afraid ?   Is it not right to love and be glad a little while ? "

" It would be like being chained to a corpse.   All that the world holds dear would be lost.   Pleasure, gayety, distinction " —

" They are all good in their way, but did they ever make any one happy ?   Is there anything better than love ? "

" You do not know what you are doing.   You do not know me.   I am not patient.   I am rebellious and defiant.   I have many moods.   I am irritable, bad tempered, and perverse."

She lifted his frail hand and kissed it.

" Hugo, you cannot frighten me.   I would rather be wretched with you than wretched without you.   But I shall not be wretched.   I shall be so glad that you will be comforted.   And you will see how useful and helpful you are, how different it will all be, how far your spirit will reach in wise thought and control, and I shall be your proud messenger.   Out of this quiet room, out of the depths of your suffering there will come power and peace.   The woman would not come to me, but she will be glad to come to you, Hugo.   She will not feel strange with you.   It is pain that draws hearts nearer together."

He covered his eyes with his hands and breathed deeply.

" I ought not. I dare not. It is incredible. If a man were here to help me — to convince you ! "

It was long before she spoke.

" Hugo, this is all I ask. Let me be your companion next winter instead of your mamma's. You surely will consent to that ? There is nothing so terrible in that. And if you do not like me, you may send me away, but try me first." There was a glad, sweet playfulness in her tone, a ring of comfort and security.

" If I do not like you ! "

" Because," she continued, " toward spring papa will come, and then there will be a man to help you, and if you will agree to be guided by him, I will — and oh, Hugo, if he himself asks you, you will no longer be afraid ? "

" Ah, Gabrielle," he sighed, and took her head between his hands and pressed it convulsively to his breast.

" Shall we not leave it so ? " she asked. " Why should we distress ourselves about the future ? Is it not enough to be together ? And when papa and Lucie come — you will like Lucie — they shall decide. Only keep me with you now, Hugo. Don't let me be sent away. Let me be near you," she whispered. " This is my place."

" But you have not seen enough men," he said after some time, and abruptly contrasting people he had known in his old brilliant life with this poor shadow of his former self, and crowded drawing-rooms with his monotonous quiet.

" Oh, I have seen so many, so many," she returned in tender triumph, "soldiers and statesmen, and scholars and artists, but no one like you."

" Poor little girl ! "

Suddenly he thrust the little black book into her hand. "Read this, and then talk of my dignity and my patience."

She took it innocently, but as she read her face assumed a pained intensity. She glanced at him with a strange and alarmed protest, then rose quickly and went to the other side of the room, where he no longer saw her. He heard her turn the leaves. There was a long silence.

She brought it back with tears of pity and terror in her eyes.

"I cannot read it all! I cannot! I have read enough. Let me burn it, my poor Hugo. Let me burn the black thoughts that have haunted you so long."

A startled look answered her pleadings. He put out his hand and with distinct anxiety closed it upon hers that held the familiar little volume. Over it the two gazed with mute entreaty into each other's eyes, and neither would give way. But as he looked upon her loveliness, and felt it near him — and his own — and knew her pure soul was near his own soul for all time, the nervous tension in his pallid face relaxed, his trouble merged into profound calm, his eyes seemed illumined by a deep inner flame, as of the spirit, and he said with extreme gentleness: —

"Don't burn it. What I say may sound strange to you. But the book has helped me. It has been my friend. It has taught me something, and it has occupied me and comforted me when I had small comfort else. I can't talk of my infirmities, Gabrielle. But you unseal my heart. It is as if I spoke to my own soul that knows my burden is not light. You see, for months Lipps had to turn me in my bed like a log.

He turned me four times every night. And there are
cramps that a fiend would not have the heart to wish
one. But enough of that. Such things don't make
a man like me good. They don't give him either
sense or courage. They give him black thoughts, as
you say. But the book and all that went to make it
revealed the misery in other lives, taught me that I
did not suffer alone, and that such thoughts are also
human and have pursued men — not always the worst
and smallest men — pitilessly, in all ages. I have begun to believe that there is a vast and mysterious purpose in it all, that so much, so over-much grief cannot be blind chance; that it is best to submit to the
Great Law, call it by what name one will; that it is
worth while to endure without complaint; that it
would have been better to bear my curse more quietly
than I have been able to bear it; and that it is not
a man's right to shorten his time of dwelling in the
body. That time is short at best. And the Power
that put him there is eternal, whatever life or death
comes next. But I am an ill man. I am a weak
man, a man of shifting moods. Who knows what
sinister doubt may master me again? Let me keep
the little book, Gabrielle, I like it," he said, with a
faint boyish smile. " I may need it sorely. I don't
dare to let it go," he confessed with appealing eyes.
" Now you know what a mean fellow I am."

She slowly loosened her grasp. She withdrew her
hand. She comprehended. He slipped the book into
its old place. To die for him that instant would
have been rapture. She stood speechless, moved by
the strength of her pure passion and illimitable pity.
She stooped and kissed his forehead with a sense of
consecration.

Without in the corridor they heard the approach of an imperious voice, and the incessant tinkling of a little bell.

"You have been too much alone, Hugo," she said simply. But in her heart a voice cried with exaltation : —

' "I fear no evil. Love guards the door. And what is so strong as Love ? "

Works of Fiction

PUBLISHED BY

HOUGHTON, MIFFLIN AND COMPANY,

4 PARK ST., BOSTON; 11 E. 17TH ST., NEW YORK.

———◆———

Thomas Bailey Aldrich.

Story of a Bad Boy. Illustrated. 12mo $1.25
Marjorie Daw and Other People. 12mo 1.50
Marjorie Daw and Other Stories. Riverside Aldine
Series. 16mo 1.00
Prudence Palfrey. 12mo 1.50
The Queen of Sheba. 12mo 1.50
The Stillwater Tragedy. 12mo 1.50

Hans Christian Andersen.

Complete Works. In ten uniform volumes, crown 8vo.
A new and cheap Edition, in attractive binding.
The Improvisatore; or, Life in Italy 1.00
The Two Baronesses 1.00
O. T.; or, Life in Denmark 1.00
Only a Fiddler 1.00
In Spain and Portugal 1.00
A Poet's Bazaar 1.00
Pictures of Travel 1.00
The Story of my Life. With Portrait 1.00
Wonder Stories told for Children. Illustrated . . . 1.00
Stories and Tales. Illustrated 1.00
The set 10.00

B. B. B. Series.

Story of a Bad Boy. By T. B. Aldrich.
Captains of Industry. By James Parton.
Being a Boy. By C. D. Warner.
The set, 3 vols. 16mo 3.75

William Henry Bishop.

Detmold: A Romance. "Little Classic" style. 18mo 1.25
The House of a Merchant Prince. 12mo 1.50
Choy Susan, and Other Stories. 16mo 1.25
The Golden Justice. 16mo. 1.25

Björnstjerne Björnson.

Works. *American Edition*, sanctioned by the author,
and translated by Professor R. B. Anderson, of the
University of Wisconsin.
Complete Works, in three volumes. 12mo. The set 4.50

Alice Cary.

Pictures of Country Life. 12mo $1.50

John Esten Cooke.

My Lady Pokahontas. 16mo 1.25

James Fenimore Cooper.

Complete Works. New *Household Edition,* in attractive binding. With Introductions to many of the volumes by Susan Fenimore Cooper, and Illustrations. In thirty-two volumes, 16mo.

Precaution.	The Prairie.
The Spy.	Wept of Wish-ton-Wish.
The Pioneers.	The Water Witch.
The Pilot.	The Bravo.
Lionel Lincoln.	The Heidenmauer.
Last of the Mohicans.	The Headsman.
Red Rover.	The Monikins.
Homeward Bound.	Miles Wallingford.
Home as Found.	The Red Skins.
The Pathfinder.	The Chainbearer.
Mercedes of Castile.	Satanstoe.
The Deerslayer.	The Crater.
The Two Admirals.	Jack Tier.
Wing and Wing.	The Sea Lions.
Wyandotté.	Oak Openings.
Afloat and Ashore.	The Ways of the Hour.

(Each volume sold separately.)

Each volume 1.00
The set 32.00

New Fireside Edition. With forty-five original Illustrations. In sixteen volumes, 12mo. The set . . . 20.00

(Sold only in sets.)

Sea Tales. New *Household Edition*, containing Introductions by Susan Fenimore Cooper. Illustrated.
First Series. Including —

The Pilot.	The Red Rover.
The Water Witch.	The Two Admirals.
Wing and Wing.	

Second Series. Including —

The Sea Lions.	Afloat and Ashore.
Jack Tier.	Miles Wallingford.
The Crater.	

Each set, 5 vols. 16mo 5.00

Leather-Stocking Tales. New *Household Edition*, containing Introductions by Susan Fenimore Cooper. Illustrated In five volumes, 16mo.

The Deerslayer. The Pioneers.
The Pathfinder. The Prairie.
Last of the Mohicans.
  The set $5.00
Cooper Stories; being Narratives of Adventure se-
lected from his Works. With Illustrations by F. O.
C. Darley. In three volumes, 16mo, each 1.00

Charles Egbert Craddock.

In the Tennessee Mountains. 16mo 1.25
The Prophet of the Great Smoky Mountains. 16mo . 1.25
Down the Ravine. Illustrated. 16mo 1.00
In the Clouds. 16mo 1.25
The Story of Keedon Bluffs. 16mo 1.00
The Despot of Broomsedge Cove. 16mo 1.25

Thomas Frederick Crane.

Italian Popular Tales. Translated from the Italian.
With Introduction and a Bibliography. 8vo . . . 2.50

F. Marion Crawford.

To Leeward. 16mo 1.25
A Roman Singer. 16mo 1.25
An American Politician. 16mo 1.25
Paul Patoff. Crown 8vo 1.50

Maria S. Cummins.

The Lamplighter. 12mo 1.00
El Fureidîs. 12mo 1.50
Mabel Vaughan. 12mo 1.50

Parke Danforth.

Not in the Prospectus. 16mo 1.25

Daniel De Foe.

Robinson Crusoe. Illustrated. 16mo 1.00

Margaret Deland.

John Ward, Preacher. 12mo 1.50

P. Deming.

Adirondack Stories. 18mo 75
Tompkins and Other Folks. 18mo 1.00

Thomas De Quincey.

Romances and Extravaganzas. 12mo 1.50
Narrative and Miscellaneous Papers. 12mo . . . 1.50

Charles Dickens.

Complete Works. *Illustrated Library Edition.* With
Introductions by E. P. Whipple. Containing Illustrations by Cruikshank, Phiz, Seymour, Leech, Mac-

lise, and others, on steel, to which are added designs of Darley and Gilbert, in all over 550. In twenty-nine volumes, 12mo.

The Pickwick Papers, 2 vols. Dombey and Son, 2 vols.
Nicholas Nickleby, 2 vols. Pictures from Italy, and
Oliver Twist. American Notes.
Old Curiosity Shop, and Re- Bleak House, 2 vols.
printed Pieces, 2 vols. Little Dorrit, 2 vols.
Barnaby Rudge, and Hard David Copperfield, 2 vols.
Times, 2 vols. A Tale of Two Cities.
Martin Chuzzlewit, 2 vols. Great Expectations.
Our Mutual Friend, 2 vols. Edwin   Drood,   Master
Uncommercial Traveller. Humphrey's Clock, and
A Child's History of Eng- Other Pieces.
land, and Other Pieces. Sketches by Boz.
Christmas Books.

Each volume $1.50
The set. With Dickens Dictionary. 30 vols. . . 45.00
Christmas Carol. Illustrated. 8vo, full gilt 2.50
The Same. 32mo 75
Christmas Books. Illustrated. 12mo 2.00

Charlotte Dunning.
A Step Aside. 16mo 1.25

Edgar Fawcett.
A Hopeless Case. "Little Classic" style. 18mo . 1.25
A Gentleman of Leisure. "Little Classic" style. 18mo 1.00
An Ambitious Woman. 12mo 1.50

Fénelon.
Adventures of Telemachus. 12mo 2.25

Mrs. James A. Field.
High-Lights. 16mo 1.25

Harford Flemming.
A Carpet Knight. 16mo 1.25

Baron de la Motte Fouqué.
Undine, Sintram and his Companions, etc. 32mo . . .75
Undine and Other Tales. Illustrated. 16mo . . . 1.00

Johann Wolfgang von Goethe.
Wilhelm Meister. Translated by Thomas Carlyle.
Portrait of Goethe. In two volumes. 12mo . . . 3.00
The Tale and Favorite Poems. 32mo 75

Oliver Goldsmith.
Vicar of Wakefield. *Handy-Volume Edition.* 24mo.
gilt top $1.00
The Same. " Riverside Classics." Illustrated. 16mo 1.00

Jeanie T. Gould (Mrs. Lincoln).
Marjorie's Quest. Illustrated. 12mo 1.50

The Guardians.
A Novel 1.25

Thomas Chandler Haliburton.
The Clockmaker ; or, The Sayings and Doings of
Samuel Slick of Slickville. Illustrated. 16mo . 1.00

A. S. Hardy.
But Yet a Woman. 16mo 1.25
The Wind of Destiny. 16mo 1.25
Passe Rose. 16mo 1.25

Miriam Coles Harris.
Rutledge.   Richard Vandermarck.   St. Philips.
The Sutherlands.   A Perfect Adonis.   Missy.
Frank Warrington. Happy-Go-Lucky.   Phœbe.
Each volume, 16mo. 1.25
Louie's Last Term at St. Mary's. 16mo 1.00

Bret Harte.
The Luck of Roaring Camp, and Other Sketches. 16mo 1.25
The Luck of Roaring Camp, and Other Stories.
Riverside Aldine Series. 16mo 1.00
Tales of the Argonauts, and Other Stories. 16mo . 1.25
Thankful Blossom. " Little Classic " style. 18mo . 1.00
Two Men of Sandy Bar. A Play. 18mo 1.00
The Story of a Mine. 18mo 1.00
Drift from Two Shores. 18mo 1.00
Twins of Table Mountain, etc. 18mo 1.00
Flip, and Found at Blazing Star. 18mo 1.00
In the Carquinez Woods. 18mo 1.00
On the Frontier. " Little Classic " style. 18mo . . 1.00
Works. Rearranged, with an Introduction and a
Portrait. In six volumes, crown 8vo.
Poetical Works, and the drama, " Two Men of Sandy
Bar," with an Introduction and Portrait.
The Luck of Roaring Camp, and Other Stories.
Tales of the Argonauts and Eastern Sketches
Gabriel Conroy.
Stories and Condensed Novels.
Frontier Stories.
Each volume 2.00
The set 12.00

By Shore and Sedge. 18mo $1.00
Maruja. A Novel. 18mo 1 00
Snow-Bound at Eagle's. 18mo 1.00
The Queen of the Pirate Isle. A Story for Children..
    Illustrated by Kate Greenaway. Small 4to . . . 1.50
A Millionaire of Rough-and-Ready, and Devil's Ford.
    18mo 1.00
The Crusade of the Excelsior. Illustrated. 16mo . 1.25
A Phyllis of the Sierras, and A Drift from Redwood
    Camp. 18mo 1.00
The Argonauts of North Liberty. 18mo 1.00
Cressy. 16mo 1.25

Wilhelm Hauff.

Arabian Days Entertainments. Illustrated. 12mo . 1.50

Nathaniel Hawthorne.

Works. New *Riverside Edition*. With an original
    etching in each volume, and a new Portrait. With
    bibliographical notes by George P. Lathrop. Com-
    plete in twelve volumes, crown 8vo.
Twice-Told Tales.
Mosses from an Old Manse.
The House of the Seven Gables, and The Snow-Image.
The Wonder-Book, Tanglewood Tales, and Grand-
    father's Chair.
The Scarlet Letter, and The Blithedale Romance.
The Marble Faun.
Our Old Home, and English Note-Books. 2 vols.
American Note-Books.
French and Italian Note-Books.
The Dolliver Romance, Fanshawe, Septimius Felton,
    and, in an Appendix, the Ancestral Footstep.
Tales, Sketches, and Other Papers. With Biograph-
    ical Sketch by G. P. Lathrop, and Indexes.
        Each volume 2.00
        The set 24.00
New "*Little Classic*" Edition. Each volume contains
    Vignette Illustration. In twenty-five volumes, 18mo.
        Each volume 1.00
        The set 25.00
New *Wayside Edition*. With Portrait, twenty-three
    etchings, and Notes by George P. Lathrop. In
    twenty-four volumes, 12mo 36.00
New *Fireside Edition*. In six volumes, 12mo . . . 10.00
A Wonder-Book for Girls and Boys. *Holiday Edi-
    tion*. With Illustrations by F. S. Church. 4to . 2.50
The Same. 16mo, boards 40
Tanglewood Tales. With Illustrations by Geo.
    Wharton Edwards. 4to, full gilt 2.50

The Same. 16mo, boards $0.40
Twice-Told Tales. *School Edition.* 18mo 1.00
The Scarlet Letter. *Popular Edition.* 12mo . . . 1.00
True Stories from History and Biography. 12mo . 1.25
The Wonder-Book. 12mo 1.25
Tanglewood Tales. 12mo 1.25
The Snow-Image. Illustrated in colors. Small 4to . .75
Grandfather's Chair. *Popular Edition.* 16mo, paper
   covers 15
Tales of the White Hills, and Legends of New Eng-
   land. 32mo 75
Legends of Province House, and A Virtuoso's Col-
   lection. 32mo 75
True Stories from New England History. 16mo,
   boards 45
Little Daffydowndilly, etc. 16mo, paper 15

Mrs. S. J. Higginson.
A Princess of Java. 12mo 1.50

Oliver Wendell Holmes.
Elsie Venner. A Romance of Destiny. Crown 8vo . 2.00
The Guardian Angel. Crown 8vo 2.00
The Story of Iris. 32mo 75
My Hunt after the Captain. 32mo 40
A Mortal Antipathy. Crown 8vo 1.50

Augustus Hoppin.
Recollections of Auton House. Illustrated. Small
   4to 1.25
A Fashionable Sufferer. Illustrated. 12mo . . . 1.50
Two Compton Boys. Illustrated. Small 4to . . . 1.50

Blanche Willis Howard.
One Summer. A Novel. New *Popular Edition.* Illustrated by Hoppin. 12mo 1.25

William Dean Howells.
Their Wedding Journey. Illustrated. 12mo . . . 1.50
The Same. "Little Classic" style. 18mo 1.00
A Chance Acquaintance. Illustrated. 12mo . . . 1.50
The Same. "Little Classic" style. 18mo 1.00
A Foregone Conclusion. 12mo 1.50
The Lady of the Aroostook. 12mo 1.50
The Undiscovered Country. 12mo 1.50
Suburban Sketches. 12mo 1.50
A Day's Pleasure, etc. 32mo 75

Thomas Hughes.
Tom Brown's School-Days at Rugby. Illustrated. 1.00
Tom Brown at Oxford. 16mo 1.25

Henry James, Jr.

A Passionate Pilgrim, and Other Tales. 12mo . . $2.00
Roderick Hudson. 12mo . . . . : 2.00
The American. 12mo 2.00
Watch and Ward. "Little Classic" style. 18mo . 1.25
The Europeans. 12mo 1.50
Confidence. 12mo 1.50
The Portrait of a Lady. 12mo 2.00

Anna Jameson.

Studies and Stories. New Edition. 16mo, gilt top . 1.25
Diary of an Ennuyée. New Edition. 16mo, gilt top . 1.25

Douglas Jerrold.

Mrs. Caudle's Curtain Lectures. Illustrated. 16mo . 1.00

Sarah Orne Jewett.

Deephaven. 18mo 1.25
Old Friends and New. 18mo 1.25
Country By-Ways. 18mo 1.25
The Mate of the Daylight. 18mo 1.25
A Country Doctor. 16mo 1.25
A Marsh Island. 16mo 1.25
A White Heron, and Other Stories. 18mo 1.25
The King of Folly Island, and Other People. 16mo 1.25

Rossiter Johnson.

"Little Classics." Each in one volume. 18mo.

I. Exile.	X. Childhood.
II. Intellect.	XI. Heroism.
III. Tragedy.	XII. Fortune.
IV. Life.	XIII. Narrative Poems.
V. Laughter.	XIV. Lyrical Poems.
VI. Love.	XV. Minor Poems.
VII. Romance.	XVI. Nature.
VIII. Mystery.	XVII. Humanity.
IX. Comedy.	XVIII. Authors.

Each volume 1.00
The set 18.00

Joseph Kirkland.

Zury: the Meanest Man in Spring County. 12mo . 1.50
The McVeys. 16mo 1.25

Charles and Mary Lamb.

Tales from Shakespeare. 18mo 1.00
The Same. Illustrated. 16mo 1.00

Harriet and Sophia Lee.
Canterbury Tales. In three volumes. The set, 16mo $3.75

Mary Catherine Lee.
A Quaker Girl of Nantucket. 16mo 1.25

Henry Wadsworth Longfellow.
Hyperion. A Romance. 16mo 1.50
Popular Edition. 16mo 40
Popular Edition. Paper covers, 16mo 15
Outre-Mer. 16mo 1.50
Popular Edition. 16mo 40
Popular Edition. Paper covers, 16mo 15
Kavanagh. 16mo 1.50
Hyperion, Outre-Mer and Kavanagh. 2 vols. crown 8vo 3.00

Flora Haines Loughead.
The Man who was Guilty. 16mo 1.25

D. R. McAnally.
Irish Wonders. Illustrated. Small 4to 2.00

S. Weir Mitchell.
In War Time. 16mo 1.25
Roland Blake. 16mo 1.25

Lucy Gibbons Morse.
The Chezzles. Illustrated 1.50

The Notable Series.
One Summer. By Blanche Willis Howard.
The Luck of Roaring Camp. By Bret Harte.
Backlog Studies. By C. D. Warner.
The set, 3 vols. 16mo 3.75

Mrs. M. O. W. Oliphant and T. B. Aldrich.
The Second Son. Crown 8vo 1.50

Elizabeth Stuart Phelps.
The Gates Ajar. 16mo 1.50
Beyond the Gates. 16mo 1.25
The Gates Between. 16mo 1.25
Men, Women, and Ghosts. 16mo 1.50
Hedged In. 16mo 1.50
The Silent Partner. 16mo 1.50
The Story of Avis. 16mo 1.50
Sealed Orders, and Other Stories. 16mo 1.50
Friends : A Duet. 16mo 1.25
Doctor Zay. 16mo 1.25
An Old Maid's Paradise, and Burglars in Paradise . 1.25
Madonna of the Tubs Illustrated. 12mo 1.50
Jack the Fisherman. Illustrated. Square 12mo . . .50

Marian C. L. Reeves and Emily Read.

Pilot Fortune. 16mo $1.25

J. P. Quincy.

The Peckster Professorship. 16mo 1.25

Josiah Royce.

The Feud of Oakfield Creek. 16mo 1.25

Joseph Xavier Boniface Saintine.

Picciola. Illustrated. 16mo 1.00

Jacques Henri Bernardin de Saint-Pierre.

Paul and Virginia. Illustrated. 16mo 1.00
The Same, together with Undine, and Sintram. 32mo .75

Sir Walter Scott.

The Waverley Novels. *Illustrated Library Edition.*
Illustrated with 100 engravings by Darley, Dielman,
Fredericks, Low, Share, Sheppard. With glossary
and a full index of characters. In 25 volumes, 12mo.

Waverley.	The Antiquary.
Guy Mannering.	Rob Roy.
Old Mortality.	St. Ronan's Well.
Black Dwarf, and Legend	Redgauntlet.
of Montrose.	The Betrothed, and The
Heart of Mid-Lothian.	Highland Widow.
Bride of Lammermoor.	The Talisman, and Other
Ivanhoe.	Tales.
The Monastery.	Woodstock.
The Abbot.	The Fair Maid of Perth.
Kenilworth.	Anne of Geierstein.
The Pirate.	Count Robert of Paris.
The Fortunes of Nigel.	The Surgeon's Daughter,
Peveril of the Peak.	and Castle Dangerous.
Quentin Durward.	

Each volume 1.00
The set 25.00
Tales of a Grandfather. *Illustrated Library Edition.*
With six steel plates. In three volumes, 12mo . . 4.50

Horace E. Scudder.

The Dwellers in Five-Sisters' Court. 16mo 1.25
Stories and Romances. 16mo 1.25
The Children's Book. Edited by Mr. Scudder. Small
4to 2.50

Mark Sibley Severance.

Hammersmith: His Harvard Days. 12mo 1.50

J. E. Smith.
Oakridge : An Old-Time Story of Maine. 12mo . . $2.00
Mary A. Sprague.
An Earnest Trifler. 16mo 1.25
William W. Story.
Fiammetta. 16mo 1.25
Harriet Beecher Stowe.
Agnes of Sorrento. 12mo 1.50
The Pearl of Orr's Island. 12mo 1.50
Uncle Tom's Cabin. *Illustrated Edition.* 12mo . . 2.00
The Minister's Wooing. 12mo 1.50
The Mayflower, and Other Sketches. 12mo . . . 1.50
Dred. New Edition, from new plates. 12mo . . . 1.50
Oldtown Folks. 12mo 1.50
Sam Lawson's Fireside Stories. 12mo 1.50
My Wife and I. Illustrated. 12mo 1.50
We and Our Neighbors. Illustrated. 12mo . . . 1.50
Poganuc People. Illustrated. 12mo 1.50
The above eleven volumes, in box 16.00
Uncle Tom's Cabin. *Holiday Edition.* With Intro-
duction, and Bibliography by George Bullen, of the
British Museum. Over 100 Illustrations. 12mo . 3.00
The Same. *Popular Edition.* 12mo 1.00
Octave Thanet.
Knitters in the Sun. 16mo 1.25
Gen. Lew Wallace.
The Fair God ; or, The Last of the 'Tzins. 12mo . 1.50
Henry Watterson.
Oddities in Southern Life. Illustrated. 16mo . . . 1.50
Richard Grant White.
The Fate of Mansfield Humphreys, with the Episode
of Mr. Washington Adams in England. 16mo . . 1.25
Adeline D. T. Whitney.
Faith Gartney's Girlhood. Illustrated. 12mo . . . 1.50
Hitherto : A Story of Yesterdays. 12mo 1.50
Patience Strong's Outings. 12mo 1.50
The Gayworthys. 12mo 1.50
Leslie Goldthwaite. Illustrated. 12mo 1.50
We Girls : A Home Story. Illustrated. 12mo . . 1.50
Real Folks. Illustrated. 12mo 1.50

The Other Girls. Illustrated. 12mo $1.50
Sights and Insights. 2 vols. 12mo 3.00
Odd, or Even ? 12mo 1.50
Boys at Chequasset. Illustrated. 12mo 1.50
Bonnyborough. 12mo 1.50
Homespun Yarns. Short Stories. 12mo 1.50

Kate Douglas Wiggin.

The Birds' Christmas Carol. Square 12mo 50

Justin Winsor.

Was Shakespeare Shapleigh? A Correspondence in
Two Entanglements. Edited by Justin Winsor.
Parchment-paper, 16mo 75

Lillie Chace Wyman.

Poverty Grass. 16mo 1.25

www.ingramcontent.com/pod-product-compliance
Lightning Source LLC
Chambersburg PA
CBHW022028110726
47901CB00006B/1696